CRY OF MORNING

Cry of Morning

BRIAN CLEEVE

MICHAEL JOSEPH · LONDON

First published in Great Britain by
Michael Joseph Ltd.
52 Bedford Square
London, W.C.1.
November 1971
Second Impression January 1972

7181 0762 4

Reproduced and printed in Great Britain by
Redwood Press Limited, Trowbridge & London
and bound by the Dorstel Press, Harlow

for Edwin Harper
and
Mike Legat
with many thanks

1

The lights beat down on the big studio like jungle sun, thick and hot and sweating, filling it with nerves and tension and a fierce excitement, making it difficult to think. Only John Lennox in the black armchair behind the desk and the microphone looked easy, sitting quiet like a fighter before the bell, thick shoulders relaxed inside the smooth, expensive jacket, mouth smiling under the short, hooked nose, the dark brown glossy hair. Only his eyes were neither smiling nor relaxed. They were coldly watchful, weighing up the hour in front of him, the things that could go wrong, the fourteen other people in the studio who could make it go wrong.

Not the three cameramen, or the Floor Manager, or the stage-hands: they wouldn't make it go wrong. The fourteen guests, half of them there under protest, in spite of themselves, the other half burning to have a really ugly brawl. Two or three of them capable of turning it into the kind of brawl that even television can't stomach, and another two or three of the fourteen powerful enough to make somebody—anybody—pay for what they had suffered. And John Lennox sat watching them, smiling, showing nothing of what he felt, of his own nerves, of the cold tension that always built inside him before every show, before every *Friday at Ten*. The John Lennox Show, and half a million people in Ireland turning it on with the feeling somewhere in the back of their minds, almost a hope, that there would be a disaster, a tremendous, unforgettable row that would give them something to talk about for days. Like a gladiator in the arena, pampered, cheered, spoiled, famous. As long as he wins.

The Floor Manager said, 'Four minutes, everybody. If any of our guests would like to smoke? You've all got ashtrays?'

Between John Lennox and the two rows of guests in their own black armchairs, one row slightly raised behind the other so that the cameras could see their faces, the three cameras rolled and manœuvred, trailing their rubber cables, the cameramen lifting and lowering, closing in and focusing, altering shots for the director's choice and judgement, his voice whispering to them in their earpieces from the invisible control-room.

'Give me Franky O'Rourke in close up,' the voice whispered. 'Camera Three, give me Mr O'Rourke.'

One of the cameras swung round, slid in towards the left-hand group of seven guests, closed on the black-haired man with the big moustache, the small hot blue eyes that seemed already on the edge of fury, the stiff, gammy leg stuck out in front of him like a challenge. Step over it if you dare.

'Closer, Number Three. I want him to fill frame.'

He was on the edge of fury. That bastard Lennox ringing him up, trying to cod him along, with his plamas about 'You've got a very convincing argument, Mr O'Rourke, if you'll only tell it to the people. This is your chance.' And the hint behind it all that he was afraid of coming, that he was afraid of Lady Honoria and Father Tracey and all their gang of bloody yelpers. Afraid! Of that lot? He'd been coming to a slow boil of rage ever since. He took out the big blue silk handkerchief that Maura had tucked into his breast pocket a couple of hours earlier, and mopped the sweat off his forehead, leaning forward, his shoulders hunched. Shoulders as big, bigger than Lennox's, harder, tougher, built up by years of swinging a shovel, twelve hours a day, seven days a week sometimes, months on end. Could still do it if they had to.

'If we see him looking like that we'll take him any time,' the director's voice was crackling in the cameraman's earpiece. 'It doesn't matter who's talking. God, what a picture! What a bastard!'

Francis O'Rourke pushed the handkerchief back into his pocket. 'Don't lose your temper, Frank,' she had said. 'Keep calm.' Keep calm! Jesus! Every bastard telling him to keep calm. Paddy Gunn behind him poking him in the bloody back, telling him to keep calm, not to lose his temper. Jo Clancy beside him waking up every few seconds and saying, 'If there's a row I'll have a heart attack. I shouldn't've come, Franky, I'm not able for this. Please don't start them at us.'

The Floor Manager whispering orders to a cameraman, to a stage-hand, the stage-hand shuffling captions on the caption stand, dropping one, the sound like a pistol shot in the hush of the studio.

'Three minutes, everyone.'

Father Tracey leaned back again, half closing his eyes. Almost as if he was praying, his face gaunt and pale. He had refused the offer of make-up, and no one had dared insist. Not because he was an influential priest, which he was not. Anything but, poor man. Or even because he was a priest. But because he was the kind of priest he was. As if he burned inside with priest-hood, with an unhealed wound, and to put cream and powder on his face, to hide the sick pallor of his skin, would be an insult to the spirit. Of all the people in that studio his motives were the purest, the least touched by vanity, or greed, or lust for power, or lust for mischief. And of all of them he would be the most mis-understood, and the most vilified. He knew it, and that too was in his face. He was beginning a long road towards his own Calvary. But that was why he had become a priest. He prayed inside his heart, Christ let me fight well, let me fight well for those You love.

For Mrs Fehily and Mrs Larkin, sitting one behind the other at the ends of the double row of chairs. And for Con Danaher, the squatter, who in a way had started all this? Did Christ love him, with his white forehead and his fanatic's eyes? Did He love Denis Farrell, the Communist, sitting behind Con, appropri-ately behind him, the soft manipulator of the fanatic; soft and colourless and nondescript, almost invisible? My beloved Saviour, let me be wise for this hour, let me see my path. Was Lady Honoria Gandon a child whom Christ loved? Sitting beside Father Tracey, smiling softly yet dangerously like a well-fed aristocratic cat that still dreams of mice, the hatreds of five years concentrated in her sleepy, half-veiled eyes as she looked across Father Tracey's bony chest towards Francis O'Rourke, and the assembled Enemy.

'What ruffians they look!' she whispered to the priest.

Jo Clancy covered his eyes with both hands. He was going

to have a heart attack, he knew it. They were going to kill him, between them. Why hadn't he retired years ago? He thought wildly of saying that he felt ill, that he had to get home. Get someone to phone his son Victor, to fetch him home.

'One minute, everybody.'

It was too late. He hadn't the nerve. Andrew Fane patted his thick arm, moved by a spasm of humanity at the old man's suffering face. 'Cheer up, Jo,' Andrew said. 'What can they say that hasn't been said already? And at least you can answer them back.' Even in offering a scrap of comfort he had to hold something back, he had to say *you* and not *we*; to underline the fact that he was not really one of them, that he was simply the architect for the new building, and had nothing to do with the old ones, the slums that the row was about. But Jo Clancy never noticed the comfort, or the reservation. He had never liked Andrew Fane from the beginning, and contrived to ignore him at all unofficial times. A bloody pansy. Ten, twenty years ago he hadn't believed that such men existed, let alone got rich and famous. And couldn't in a thousand years of trying have believed that one day he himself would be employing a man like that, he and his partners would be employing him, relying on him, giving him thousands and thousands of pounds to design a bloody monstrosity of a building that was going to ruin them all.

'Thirty seconds to air.'

Behind Andrew Fane and Jo Clancy, Willy Doyle sat beside Johnny O'Hara and Paddy Gunn. Willy Doyle the handyman, the foreman, the jack-of-all-trades, small and neat as a pin in his clean blue serge suit, his thinning hair for once slicked down with brilliantine, his new tie in a tight and careful knot, his black shoes lovingly polished for him by his wife Jenny. 'We'll all be watching,' she had whispered, not really believing that she'd actually see her Willy on the screen. 'Oh, Will, if it was me I'd be so scared I couldn't speak, I'd die.' But her Willy wouldn't die.

The monitor screens alive, six, five, four, three, two, one— into film, music rolling, louder, louder, the *Friday at Ten* theme music, harsh and challenging and unmistakable, the screen filled with people marching, banners, faces. The march from Oxman Street, Father Tracey leading it, Con Danaher beside him, behind them a column of marchers, tenants out of Oxman Street, women with babies, men, children, all of them shouting, shouting for the cameras they had just seen, shouting for justice, for homes, for the world that politicians had been promising them for fifty years, and had never yet given. The banners cried out in shrieks of anger *Give us Homes! . . . Did Pearse Die for Office Blocks? . . . Remember 1916!*

Faces growing gigantic on the screen, filling it with anger, swaying sideways, vanishing. Out of the heart of Dublin a great well-spring of suffering, and the tall, gaunt priest at the marchers' head, coat hanging on his bones like a scarecrow, face lifted to the sky. *Give us a decent place to live.* The priest's lips moving. A woman with a child. *Remember 1916!* The woman holding up her child to the camera. *Look at his face! Look at the rat-bites!*

Her shriek fading as the soundtrack faded, letting the theme music swell up again, the programme title coming over the last few feet of film. *Friday at Ten.* John Lennox on.

He leant forward, staring into the lens of Camera One, his mouth hard, the slightest suggestion in his eyes that in a grimly sardonic way he had enjoyed those forty seconds of film and was going to enjoy what followed, in the studio.

'That was Dublin, last Monday. Our capital city in the year of grace 1964, after forty-three years of independence. Irish men and women led by a priest, shouting for Justice. As they shouted for it in the Great Strike of 1913. As they died for it in 1916, almost fifty years ago. Still shouting, still marching for it nearly fifty years after Connolly and Pearse died in Kilmainham for an Ireland that would cherish all the people of Ireland equally. All its children. Including Thomas Murphy from Oxman Street, two years old, whose face is already scarred for life by rat-bites. And who is going to be evicted, tomorrow, the day after, one day next week, with all the other tenants of Oxman Street, to make room for an office block.

'Maybe it's right he should be evicted, should be moved out of

Oxman Street. Certainly it isn't right that he should go on sharing his bed with rats. But what are we going to give him in exchange? Not only what kind of room to sleep in, but what kind of country to live in, to grow up in? What kind of Brave New Ireland? That's what that demonstration was really about. Not just one slum, a few families evicted to find somewhere else to live. If they can. It was about the new Ireland that's being born out of the economic revolution of the last few years, that's being created in front of our eyes, day by day. In the new buildings, the new industries, the new ways of thinking, in the television that you're watching now. In everything that's happening.

'And while the new is being created, the old is being destroyed. Old buildings, old traditions. Maybe, old ideals. What are we creating? And what are we losing? That's what that demonstration was really about. That's what this programme is about. The kind of Ireland we're going to hand on to Thomas Murphy, and all the other children of Oxman Street, and Dublin, and Ireland. What's it going to be like? It's going to be very different to Pearse's Ireland. And ours. But is it going to be better? Or worse? Are we already making mistakes that we'll bitterly regret? Letting things be destroyed that we'll curse ourselves for not preserving? Or hanging grimly on to other things, old ways of life, traditions, prejudices, that we'd be far better off without; far better off if we developed them into something very different, that would have a real meaning for the 1960s.

'There are as many answers to those questions as there are people watching this programme. But broadly speaking they fall into two main groups, and I've suggested what they are already. The Preservers. And the Developers. I've fourteen people with me in the studio, all of whom for different reasons have burning, harsh feelings about what you've just seen and what lies behind it. Seven of them are Developers.'

The red light on top of Number Two camera sprang into life, and the screen showed a wide shot of Francis O'Rourke and the others with him: Johnny O'Hara; Joseph Clancy, pale and fat and sweating, half collapsed inside his loose, sagging coat that seemed to have been made for him when he was two stone heavier than he was now; Andrew Fane with his elegant white streak in the carefully arranged dark hair; Jer Mullins; Paddy Gunn; Willy Doyle with the Brilliantine beginning to melt and trickle in shining rivulets down his forehead.

'They represent the interests which want to develop Oxman Street and the streets round it. Their companies have bought the houses in order to destroy them and replace them with one gigantic office-block. And while they're quite obviously and understandably doing it to make themselves rich, they say that only by people like themselves doing things like this can Ireland itself become rich. That if it doesn't become rich Thomas Murphy's son is going to be as badly off in 1990 as Thomas Murphy is today. And that for Thomas Murphy and his family and neighbours to be evicted from Oxman Street is a very small price to pay for the country's future prosperity.

'The other seven are Preservers, who think that it is too big a price to pay, and that we don't know what we're doing, what we're allowing to be done, both to people and to Ireland; what we're allowing to be destroyed.'

Camera One coming alive, giving its wide shot of Father Tracey and his ill-assorted allies: Lady Honoria and Con Danaher the squatter; Denis Farrell the Communist and Matt O'Carroll the old trade-unionist; Mrs Larkin and Mrs Fehily, the tenants, spokeswomen for a hundred others, bundled and stifled in their Sunday coats, already lost in terror at what was happening all round them, the machines, the lights, the voices from nowhere and from everywhere.

'They believe that some old buildings are better and more precious than any new ones; that some old ideals, some traditions, are irreplaceable; that although we must have change, and desperately need some changes, it will only be worth while if we preserve the best of what we already have. And above all that it is wicked to evict people from the most wretched tenement unless and until there is somewhere better for them to go.'

Camera Two on John Lennox, putting him on the screen in bland close-up, impartial as a judge.

'Let's start with the Developers, since they're under atttack. Mr O'Hara, how do you justify what's been happening in Oxman Street?'

It was one of the few concessions that Johnny O'Hara and Paddy Gunn had been able to wring out of John Lennox in exchange for agreeing to appear, that Francis O'Rourke should not be given the first question. They were afraid that he would explode before anything rational in their favour got said at all, and that the remainder of the programme would turn into a screaming-match.

'I don't accept the word *justify*,' Johnny O'Hara said, already angrier himself than he had expected to be and making so strong an effort to control his face and his voice that he looked as if he was half paralysed with camera fright. But he was a long way from being frightened. 'I don't accept that anything we've done needs justifying.'

Across the studio there was the sound of several people drawing breath, getting ready to interrupt; a kind of ground swell of indignation. John Lennox lifted a hand to stop it and it cut off short, and yet it contrived to hang suspended like a threat, like a storm-cloud.

'We've come here to state our case, on your invitation. Either let us do it, or we'll go home.'

John Lennox smiled gently. 'I've asked you to state it.'

'Christ——' Francis O'Rourke began. Paddy Gunn's finger took him between the shoulder-blades like a bone dagger and he stiffened and stopped, clenching his fists on his knees.

'Right,' Johnny O'Hara said. 'This is our case. Oxman Street and all that district was a slum from years back, long before we ever saw it, let alone bought it. We bought it not because we wanted a slum, but because we wanted a development site. We're not responsible for the rats, or the state of the plumbing——'

'What!' It was Father Tracey.

'Go on, Mr O'Hara,' John Lennox said, his hand lifting again, shushing the Preservers.

'The fact that it's a slum is not our problem. What we're going to give the city is something fifty, a hundred times more valuable *to the city* than nineteen derelict houses. We're going to create employment. Create wealth. You said it yourself. Out of that wealth the city can rehouse the families from Oxman Street ten times over, and in places where that child will be far better off.'

He had lost his tension and was beginning to feel that it had been worth coming, to get this said. He leaned forward and half stabbed a long finger towards John Lennox. He was always pale, and under the heat of the lights his face was like a mask of wax, thick, oily with sweat, his eyes narrow slits of darkness. 'I want to make one thing absolutely clear. You've tried to sound as if you were unbiased. But what you've actually said and shown on that bit of film so far is as biased as hell.'

Again there was the start of an explosion from the two rows of Preservers.

'Go on,' John Lennox said with cold good humour.

'There are two issues here, and you've confused them. One is whether people should have to live in slums. That's nothing to do with us. The second issue is development, rebuilding Dublin so it fits in with the 1960s, and the 1970s and the 1980s. In fact if you don't allow us to do it, if the people don't let us do it, you're going to have more slums, not less. What you've done so far is make it seem that Developers are slum landlords, that anyone who wants to build an office-block is a heartless monster who wants to see children bitten by rats.'

He stopped for breath, and John Lennox turned smoothly to the Preservers as if Johnny O'Hara had clearly finished.

'Father Tracey, do you accept that defence?'

Father Tracey in close-up, gaunt, absorbed; Savonarola searching for the word, for the launching-point of his sermon, waiting for it to be given to him by an inner voice.

'No,' he said, grinding the word out like sand between his teeth. 'Who is responsible for what happens in a house if it is not the man who owns the house? The man who collects the rent? And when these people are evicted, where will they go, where will they find a home? Who cares? Does Mr O'Hara care? Do his rich friends and partners care? They talk about creating wealth.

Who are they creating it for? What kind of wealth? A long time ago an Irish poet wrote of a land "where wealth accumulates and men decay". Is that the Ireland that they want?'

'For God's sake!' shouted Francis O'Rourke, unable to contain himself any longer. He hardly felt the stab of Paddy Gunn's bony finger. 'If that's your idea of economics——'

The camera closed on him, filled the screen with his face, the hot, furious eyes, the mouth open under the heavy black moustache, showing the small fierce teeth like a mask of fury. And in a quarter of a million homes in Ireland people watched, waited to see what he would do, what way he would lunge, like a vast and still torpid crowd at a bullfight as the banderillos begin to go in, to hang from the bleeding shoulders of the bull, and his rage rises, the first streaks of crimson brilliant on the glistening black skin.

'. . . if that's your idea of economics——'

'We have seen yours,' said Father Tracey. 'On that child's face. Is that better than mine?'

'And am I supposed to be looking after him?' Francis O'Rourke shouted, beside himself, incapable of thinking of the effect of what he was saying. 'What about his parents? What are any of them doing about it?' He stabbed a shaking finger, thick and stubby, on the end of his thick, stubby, powerful arm, pointed it with something close to hatred at the two poor women in their best coats and hats, worn cloth coats with moth-eaten fur trimmings, tight round their middle-aged collapsing bodies, and they stared back at him in terror, as if he was going to leap at them across the floor and tear the rent out of their gullets.

The camera nearest to them swung in fast and caught their terror, cut from Francis O'Rourke with his threatening arm and furious, shouting face to their hypnotized, stricken simplicity.

'What the hell have your husbands ever done to get somewhere better to live? What have any of you done? You sit there squalling about the rats and the lavatories and you wouldn't cross the street to help yourselves——'

'Who put the rats in the cellars?' Con Danaher shouted suddenly, leaning forward as if he had been suddenly folded in the middle, his black hair falling on his white forehead, his eyes like the eyes of a man dying of fever, like charcoals burning, all his thin, racked body shivering with hatred. In front of him was all that he hated in the world. The rich, the powerful, the tyrant in a hand-made suit and a silk shirt; Capital made sweating flesh. 'You poured cement down what you dare to call the lavatories——'

'Oh, my God . . .' whispered Jo Clancy. He put one flabby hand against his heart and shut his eyes.

'That's a damned lie!' Francis O'Rourke shouted; but Con Danaher had the running and kept it, treating the studio like a street meeting, pouring out his abuse and hatred, like acid flung on living flesh, and even Lady Honoria, who had been sitting like a purring cat, seemed momentarily shocked at what she had joined herself with.

For half a minute, for a minute, it became a screaming-match, while John Lennox watched, his eyes sliding from shouter to would-be shouter: Con Danaher to Francis O'Rourke to Johnny O'Hara to old Matt O'Carroll anxious to pour oil, to Jer Mullins itching to get in and make a political speech, a political point. He half made it. 'Do you know how many people have got employment in the last three years? How many new houses——'

Con Danaher almost came to his feet with rage and contempt and passionate hatred. 'How many jobs? How many houses? In the last thirty years your party—your Party of Reality—has been responsible for more than a million people leaving Ireland because they couldn't earn a living here, couldn't get a job, any damn kind of job at all to keep their body and their soul together. That's what your party of reality has been responsible for. Some party! Some reality!'

Jer Mullins white in the face, trying to shout him down, little and loose-jointed, like a puppet dangling from strings, twitched and jerked by unseen hands; Matt O'Carroll shouting, old, dignified shouts lost in the venomous uproar. Francis O'Rourke shouting at Father Tracey: 'Why doesn't your Order do something if you're so concerned with the housing shortage? How much land have they got lying idle in Dublin that they won't let go of? Would you like to tell us that? Would you like to tell us what your Father Provincial said to the Corporation when they asked him to sell them a bit of land for a Corporation housing scheme? "Why should I sell it," he said, "when it's better than money in the bank the way it's going up in value?" While you're down on the street corner yelling your head off about the sufferings of the poor.'

Father Tracey looked as if he had been struck across the face with a scourge. 'I'm not here to answer for my Order,' he said in his grating voice that seemed to grind against the shouting like a carborundum wheel. 'I'm here to speak as one man who believes in justice and a decent society.'

'Decency begins at home!' roared Francis O'Rourke with sweating, bull-voiced triumph. Behind him Paddy Gunn, Knight of St Brigid, already high in the councils of the Knights and widely spoken of as their future Head, shuddered as if he himself had been struck. He could imagine the Father Provincial reaching for the telephone; all the telephones that would be going; they wouldn't stop for days.

'Father Tracey,' he said, sliding his smooth persuading voice into the turmoil like a knife-blade, like a fencer effortlessly weaving his foil between the clumsy sweeps of a cudgel, 'no one is criticizing your Order's affairs. They have nothing to do with——'

'I'm criticiz——' Francis started to roar. He almost lurched forward out of his plastic armchair with the force of the stab that Paddy gave him from behind, ramming his dagger finger into the thick, hunched flesh of Francis O'Rourke's back.

'I think we're achieving more heat than light,' John Lennox said. He took control again, never really having lost it. Having simply allowed the fighting to reach the point where it threatened to cease being good television. 'Let's see where we've got to. . . .' He began to summarize, lowering the temperature, making a careful show of presenting the best of the Developers' arguments, smoothing over the attack on the Father Provincial and the Order of the Bernardines to which Father Tracey belonged.

'. . . Can we have some facts and figures?' John Lennox said.

'I don't think anyone has explained yet why these houses can't be repaired *as* houses, and why the office-block can't be put somewhere else? Andrew Fane, you're the architect. Can you tell us?'

Andrew Fane lifted his elegant, delicate, actor's profile, half shrugged as if to show that the whole disgraceful row was no real concern of his and that he found everything connected with it distasteful and indescribably unprofessional and vulgar. 'It's very simple,' he said. 'Those houses are not worth repairing. If you spent twenty thousand pounds a house you might get a few more years out of them. But bricks and mortar have a lifespan. Theirs is over. Quite apart from dry rot.'

'I don't know that everyone would accept your figures,' John said. 'But even if you're right, why has your office-block got to be there?'

'Because it's the place for it. It's ridiculous to have dwelling-houses in the centre of a city, on the most valuable land. It's the place for business.'

'How much is your building going to cost?'

Paddy Gunn tried to slide in and stop the answer. 'That has nothing——' But before he could finish, Andrew Fane was answering, lifting his hand to smooth the white streak in his waved black hair, his big carnelian ring glittering in the lights.

'A million and a quarter,' he said with the air of a man presenting an unanswerable argument.

'A million and a quarter!' Con Danaher screamed, and Father Tracey said in a lower but even more carrying voice, 'For an office-block, but not for people?'

'A million and a quarter,' Mrs Larkin whispered, stunned and awed.

All over the country people were repeating the figure, awed, critical, thoughtful, impressed, incredulous, but sharing a feeling that they had been told a secret, that they had learned a little more of how the world worked, what went on behind the façades. All of the programme told them that. They would never feel quite the same about politicians, about the rich: about priests, about authority. That was one of the things that people liked best about the *Friday at Ten* programme. It showed you things, told you things you wouldn't ever have heard before television came.

Denis Farrell the Communist leaned forward, plump, smooth, almost priestly with his small, rosebud mouth curling in a delighted, satirical smile, his eyelids drooping. 'Isn't this the heart of the matter?' he said gently, so gently and yet so force-fully that he seemed to create a silence in which his gentleness could be heard. 'We can find money for business, for profit, to make more money. But not to make life worth living for ordinary people. That land is too valuable, Mr Fane says. Too valuable for what? For people to live on. But not for an office-block for people, nice scrubbed obedient people, to work in eight hours a day. Where will they go when the eight hours are over? Somewhere valueless, so cheap and nasty that even people can be allowed to use it simply for living on? Until another Mr Fane, another Mr O'Hara, another Mr O'Rourke comes along and tells them that because of all the work they've done that land has become valuable as well, too valuable for them to waste it by living on it; and they must go quietly away and make room for another beautiful office-block.'

'You keep saying *office-blocks* as if they were dirty words!' Francis O'Rourke shouted. 'How the hell do you think the country is run?'

'Very badly,' said Denis Farrell with his sweet smile. 'And mostly for the benefit of you and your friends in the Guardians.'

Three-quarters, more than three-quarters, of the people watching had no idea what the Guardians were, had never heard of them. The Guardians of the Flame, the select and wealthy group of businessmen who provisioned the Party's war chest with large donations. 'The Guardians?' people said, looking puzzledly at each other. While the ones who knew smiled and nodded, thinking that Denis Farrell had made a great hit and by God the Party wouldn't like that one little bit. And again there was the feeling that the programme was showing them the inner heart of things, like taking the back off a watch, like lifting a stone in a field to show the maggots underneath. One more small blow like the thousand and thousand blows that television was delivering at the foundations of society, threatening to bring the whole fabric down in ruins, or, if you looked at it another way, promising to smash the barriers of forty and a hundred and forty years, and let in the sunlight and the fresh air. Denis Farrell was the first live, flesh-and-blood Communist that most of the viewers had ever seen. And he had no horns, and no tail, and was on the same side of the quarrel as the priest. It was unbelievable.

It was a long time since there had been Communists in Ireland, visibly fighting for the poor. More than forty years since the pathetic, hopeless Workers' and Peasants' Soviets of Munster had gone down under the Free Staters' guns in 1922. Most of the viewers had never heard that such an incident had ever happened. A Communist!

The commercial break. John Lennox saying with his hard smile, 'We'll leave it there for a couple of minutes. But stay with us. There's more to come.' And the screen filling with the Good Life, the washing-powder to end washday blues, the mild cigar that gives you *real* satisfaction, the nougat bar that makes you feel good deep down inside. You *deserve* a nougat bar, you've *earned* it. The Good Life as lived by Lovely People, clean and sweet, fine and virtuous, mindlessly jolly. Not much sex, because this is Ireland, and television is only two years old. It isn't time yet for that phallic fondling of the nougat bar, the houri swooning at the smoker's knee, waiting to be raped when he's finished his cigar, the cigar itself his promise of what's to come. The Irish ads still lived in a world of happy bachelorhood, where only women marry, and children come on hire-purchase.

Friday at Ten again, John Lennox smiling. 'Welcome back.' The fight restarting. Father Tracey grinding into the scandal of the slums, of the indifference of the rich to how the poor lived, the indifference of the Government, the Corporation, the gombeen men who had taken over power from the English and used it worse than the English used it.

Lady Honoria waiting, watching, her face changing with childish suddenness, at one moment arrogantly bored, as if she was wondering how she had ever become involved in this sweating, ill-bred galley, her face cool and carved and beautiful and remote; and as suddenly folding into a warm, malicious joy at something one of her allies said, like a child watching a quarrel. But even then she managed to retain a look of impudent, careless aristocracy that made Francis O'Rourke and even Paddy Gunn look like grotesque peasants. Not that Francis O'Rourke was conscious of that. He knew her by instinct, had known her character the minute that he first laid eyes on her five years before; knew her for a jumped-up slut that had come from nothing, with the mind of a guttersnipe and the morals of a cat. In the commercial break John Lennox had begged them all to keep their voices down, not to shout. 'You don't need to shout,' he had said, 'you've got a microphone.' But Francis O'Rourke couldn't keep his voice down. He roared at her:

'If you'd kept your damn nose out of this they'd have got houses years ago. What do you think you've done for them with your preserving and your public meetings and your appeals to the Minister and all the rest of the codacting? Kept them stuck in what you call a ratpit. You see how much gratitude they feel for you. Ask them. Go on, ask them.'

Lady Honoria smiled one brief, child-wicked smile and said what she had come on to the programme to say, the one sentence she had been treasuring in her mind for days. 'How much did you pay for the planning permission that we've objected to? Will you tell us that?'

The words fell into a momentary quiet, turned it into silence, spread and lengthened and widened and deepened the silence until it filled the studio, seemed for a long moment to fill the country. John Lennox let the silence hang. Two, three, four, five, seconds of silence in a television programme can seem enormous and enormously significant. The man who knows how to manipulate silence in television has learned the medium's ultimate secret, or has been born with an instinct for it. John Lennox had been born with it. He let the silence, the dismay on some faces, the anger on others, the simple astonishment on yet others again, say what he himself as chairman could not say:

that the accusation must be true, because it was not immediately and thunderously denied. In fact no answer would have mattered very much. Once a thing like that is said on television it is true because it has been said. But silence emphasized the point. The art lay in stretching that silence for as long as Francis O'Rourke and his allies stayed speechless, judging the exact fraction of a second in which one of them would recover his wits and begin to answer—and forestalling him. And over and above that, in making the forestalling look like a kindness, an act of charity.

Francis O'Rourke sat open-mouthed, the veins in his forehead, in his neck, swelling, his face mottled with fury. Even Johnny O'Hara was caught off balance; Paddy Gunn hesitated, choosing and rejecting answers, stomached by the brutality of the attack, the unfeminine directness of it coming from the one opponent he would have been certain would use, however strong her feelings, his own kind of discreet indirection.

John Lennox waited, not smiling, not frowning; but watchful, concerned, grave. Everyone in the studio who thought about his reaction at all, every viewer who caught a glimpse of him as the director got his face on to the screen in expectation that he would say something, that he would have to intervene, now, now, in another second—no? Christ, what was he at, what was he waiting for, sitting there bloody well waiting like a cat, leaving those poor bastards stewing—of course—of course—good old John, make them sweat—every viewer who saw his grave, concerned, waiting look, directed almost, but not quite, at Francis O'Rourke, thought if he thought at all, Ah, aha, it's true, and he knows it's true and he's shocked, but he doesn't want to show he's shocked, he wants to give even a villain like that a fair chance—or else he thought, What a cunning devil, he's worked this one, he's put her up to asking that question, he knew she was going to. That's what this whole programme was got up for. And felt that warm, intimate sense of knowing, guessing, being shown what really happens, what goes on behind the scenes. While in the studio they thought with even more venom or admiration, He's done this on purpose. Because he's committed. Because he's really on our side—or, in the case of the Developers, Because he's against us, the Commy bastard.

But those last feelings missed the entire point. He wasn't committed, he wasn't on anyone's side, not even Lady Honoria's, who until a year or so before had been in a sense his patroness. He was committed to nothing, he believed in nothing, except perhaps those shadows flickering on the monitor screens scattered about the huge chiaroscuro of the studio. He had no belief in Developers, in Preservers, in Socialism, or in the Party of Reality; not even in money in any important sense. Only in those shadows, and even that belief had come to him by accident, by the chance of being offered this job that had become his life, that had suddenly and astonishingly fitted his soul like a glove sliding over a hand. Apart from that tenuous, professional belief there was inside him only an echoing, bottomless emptiness, that he himself was afraid of probing. Of finding that there was no end to it, that there was nothing, nothing, nothing there. Like the boy in the fable who could not shiver, could not feel fear; he could not feel anything. Which was, perhaps, why he was so good at television, why and how he understood the use of silence.

Francis O'Rourke swelled, made an attempt to say something; Johnny O'Hara leant forward, opened his mouth; Paddy Gunn began saying a word and changed his mind to make a start on a different word. The fact that John Lennox was looking towards all three of them without looking at any of them in particular, so that each thought he must be looking at one of the others who was about to say something, made it even more difficult. And in that agonizing silence Lady Honoria raised her high, clear voice again, joyfully triumphant. 'How much did you pay?'

John Lennox turned to her, his smile at once indulgent and reproving. 'Lady Honoria! I'm afraid you're stepping beyond the limits of this kind of debate. There's no question of——'

'But there is! I'm asking it!'

Father Tracey said harshly, seemingly not looking at anyone or anything in the studio, 'If there's no question, why hasn't it been answered?'

By now Paddy Gunn, Johnny O'Hara, Francis O'Rourke, even, in a strangled, heart-clutching way old Mr Clancy, all of them together were trying to answer, and making things seem worse by shouting each other down. 'Can it not be answered?' Father Tracey called out.

John Lennox allowed himself the briefest smile, that again several thousand people read as partisan, and that was in reality simply a part of the act, hiding if it hid anything, a sense of pleasure at having done what he had set out to do; make good television, dangerous, skating-on-thin-ice television, creating a row, coiling opponents in a steel mesh and giving them a smiling *coup de grâce* while appearing to be helping them free, untying them from the net.

'We're getting away from the point,' John said blandly. 'The point is not the mechanics of how this sort of thing is done. The real question is whether it ought to be done. Are the Developers right, or are you, the Preservers right?—and you can't treat that as a foregone conclusion. For example you, Father. If all that you claim is true, and you've been claiming it for some time very publicly, then a lot more of the clergy should have been agreeing with you. And yet they haven't. I don't think any priest, let alone any bishop, has spoken about this at all, and certainly none of them has come out on your side. Are you the only one in step?'

'I'm not claiming anything,' Father Tracey said. Under counter-attack he seemed to draw into some inner, spiritual fortress. Even his eyes, his expression, seemed to be turned inwards, looking towards some bleak future, a martyrdom which he already sensed was prepared for him. Although he could not surely have sensed what that martyrdom would really be, how remote it would be from this quarrel about an Irish street. 'I'm not *claiming* there is inhumanity, that there is injustice. I simply see it. And what I see I describe. And I am not, I cannot be alone in seeing them. We have all seen that piece of film. Some of us have seen the conditions that lie behind it. No one can be in or out of step with those conditions. One can only condemn them. I do not know any priest who would not condemn them.'

'But they haven't condemned them, Father.'

Paddy Gunn came breaking in. 'John, really, I may seem to be on opposite sides of the fence from Father Tracey in this particular argument about the houses in Oxman Street, but I think you're being rather unfair to him now. We all recognize, everyone recognizes, Father Tracey's real and burning Christian interest . . .' He went on and on, smothering the issue with bland, consensus words like a great foam of detergent under which every real detail vanished, making it appear that John Lennox had really been attacking Father Tracey instead of making a veiled attack, or opening for attack, on the Church.

The argument splayed out. Matty O'Carroll came in with a rambling speech about how for thirty years he had had the cause of the poor at heart and none of them closer at heart than the good people of Oxman Street who had voted for him as their number-one choice in every election since he first stood for the Dail before some of the people on this programme had learned their three Rs. And he yielded to no one, no one. . . .

Jer Mullins, twitching and jerking inside his expensive, badly fitting suit, tried to make another party political speech. Con Danaher shouted about the rats again, about the lavatories, about slates taken off the roofs at night, about babies with green diarrhoea.

'What the hell has that got to do with us building offices, damn it?' roared Francis O'Rourke, and Johnny O'Hara brought Willy Doyle into the fight at long last, brandishing him metaphorically like the ultimate weapon, the honest working man. 'Ask him. Ask him. What were the lavatories like before we got there? What could anyone do with them without demolishing the houses first to get at the sewers? They run under the foundations.' Willy Doyle with his carefully brushed and oiled hair and his new tightly knotted tie, murmuring, whispering agreement, blushing crimson, the sweat running, Brilliantine melting, making a silver shimmer of his face. 'You couldn't do nothing, not really, they're gone beyond the beyonds.' And his wife at home clasping her hands in love, in terror, saying, 'There he is, there's Willy, ma, look, there he is talking.' Our Willy. Answering Con Danaher's shouts with whispering, half-lost answers. 'There was millions of rats before we got there. What would we want with buying rats, don't be stupid.' Saying 'don't be stupid' before he realized what he was saying, and then collapsing into his jacket with embarrassment.

Lady Honoria trying to get her question in again, calling out in her loud, piercing, aristocratic voice, 'How much did you——' Trying to catch the camera's eye, to deliver her last triumphant sword-thrust in front of the whole of Ireland. Joan of Arc at Orleans.

The seconds ticking, the Floor Manager giving his last signals to John Lennox, one minute, half a minute, the slow circle of his arm for fifteen seconds left.

'Sorry, sorry, everyone,' John said. 'Time's run out on us.'

Everyone shouting, Matty O'Carroll realizing that he had never made it clear that even if he was sitting on the same side as the Communists, Danaher and Farrell, he wasn't on their side in anything else. 'I want to make one thing clear, Mr Chairman, I want——'

'Sorry, sorry. Time's up.' Camera One closing in on John Lennox for the wind-up, on the smooth, muscle-padded face, the hooked nose, the thick mass of chestnut hair, the hard, confident smile. 'That's all from us for another Friday.'

'Mr Chairman——'

A jumble of half a dozen voices, calling out like shouts from drowning men, cancelling each other out, while John Lennox smiled, tilted his head slightly as if to say, These enthusiasts, what an uproar, but it's all over now, don't worry, television has won once more. What he actually said was, 'Next Friday, same time, ten o'clock, we'll be back again. Until then, good night.'

The camera pulling back, cross-fading to a wide shot on Camera Two of the whole studio, all the guests still trying to make themselves heard, to protest at being cut off, not allowed to make their last vital, all-important point, correct whatever lie an opponent had just shouted, as if they were still on air, were still real people, instead of diminishing shadows on the screen, turned into silhouettes gesticulating in the background, as the titles began rolling up and over them: Sound, Lighting, Camera, Research, Director, Producer, an Irish Television Production; the theme music fading, gone. The screen suddenly filled with an advertisement for menthol cigarettes, cool, cool as winter snows, a girl skiing, sweeping down a wide, pure ski-slope into close-up, skin-tight ski pants over powerful legs; laughing face, goggles pushed up on to healthy forehead, a man offering her a cigarette; strong handsome man, their faces close together over the lighter flame. Man and girl. Cigarettes and snow and health. Sanitized desire.

The people in the studio broke up into their natural groups. The technicians dismantling cables, microphones, dousing lights, stretching, yawning, stacking captions, the guests coming to themselves with a sense of wonder like people waking out of a dream, trying to remember what they had said, what they had forgotten to say, looking for an opponent to say it to even now when it was too late. John Lennox gathering his notes, smiling at Francis O'Rourke like a challenge, waiting to be attacked and ready for it. Knots of argument, the production assistant coming down to shepherd everyone to the hospitality-room, the director coming out on to the balcony to say, 'Thanks everyone, thanks, John, I'll be down in a minute.'

The arguments went on in the hospitality-room until first one and then another guest went away, tired, or angry, or fed up or even satisfied.

'I don't think we did too badly,' Johnny O'Hara said, standing in the semi-dark outside the building. He was taking old Jo Clancy home because Jo's son had said he couldn't come to collect his father that night and old Jo never drove himself since his illness.

'I wish Francis hadn't ...' Paddy Gunn began, and left it hanging.

Francis O'Rourke didn't bother to answer him, getting into his Jaguar and snarling away down the long drive, the headlights lancing in front of him like weapons. Bloody stupid waste of time. What the hell had they done it for, why had he ever damn well

e square stretched in front of them, all round them, for-
ly, dilapidatedly beautiful, tall Georgian houses gradually
ined into slum tenements, surrounding what had once been
owners' private communal garden, and that was now a
mped and battered playground for the tenement children.
For Sale notice hung at a forlorn angle in a broken window,
e corner peeled from its fastening of glue so that it was hard to
d the name of the auctioneers. It looked as if it had been there
r a very long time.

'I bet you'd buy that house for next to nothing,' Francis said.
Maura looked at the house and the square with contempt. She
ad been brought up in Dublin although her parents were Mayo,
nd even in her time it had been a slum. 'If you think I'd live in
a place like this——'

'For God's sake,' Francis said. 'You don't have to live in a
bloody house because you own it.' He couldn't have said himself
why it attracted him. Except that it was big, it was in Dublin, it
had an air of . . . he didn't even think of it as having an air of
anything. Only that something about it spoke to him. Grandeur.
But not the snob grandeur of that damn couple at the airport.
Grandeur he could buy. And bloody cheap too from the look of
it. Grandeur fallen on hard times.

Children had been playing in the dusty gutter and now they
stood in a nervous cluster by the railings, looking at the astonish-
ing car, the strange people in it. The three O'Rourke children
stared at them through the windows. Ragged children, some of
them barefoot. Francis O'Rourke got out of the car. Most of the
children prepared to run away, but the barefooted ones, who
spent their evenings begging in O'Connell Street and were
therefore used to the rich, stood their ground.

'Do any of you live in that house?'

The children stared at him as if he was talking Chinese, or had
just stepped out of a Flying Saucer.

'Come on, come on, who lives in that house? Any of you?'
For more than twenty years he had been used to London
children who always knew everything and told everything,
fighting to tell it first. He had forgotten that Irish children were

given in to them and gone along? Christ, oh Christ. His rage
smouldered all the way home to Rathfarnham, until he was
turning into his own drive, into the big garage standing open,
waiting for him. And as he switched off the engine it seemed to
die down with the engine. After all, it had given him a chance to
tell them something. And by God he'd taken it. Damn and blast
them he had.

He sat for a long minute in the dark, suddenly quiet garage,
thinking of what he had told them. Like a pack of bloody
mongrels. Yelping and snarling at something that was too bloody
big for them to understand. A tenth of it, all that they knew
about, was too big for them to understand. O'Rourke House.
Concrete. Glass. Stainless steel and aluminium. Rising out of the
dirty mess of Oxman Street and Marietta Street and Aram Court
like a palace, new and shining. He hadn't got words for what it
would be like. He could only see it. Feel the concrete under his
hands. Raw, undressed gravel-concrete inside, harsh and tough
and everlasting. The windows looking out over the scrubby
rooftops between Oxman Street and the river. And then one day
those rooftops themselves would be gone, and it would be all
new buildings, a great square of buildings surrounding an open
plaza. Grass, fountains, courtyards, paths, statues, new shops.
And above the shops the cliff walls of glass: offices for banks,
insurance, it didn't matter a curse in hell really what they were
for. Like cliffs of glass. And in the tower of O'Rourke House his
own office. Looking down on all of it. That he'd made, built,
financed, hacked and battled out of a slum.

And those snivelling bastards snarling round his ankles to try
and stop him. He'd see them scream in hell before they'd stop
him. He hadn't come this far to be stopped now. He sat thinking
of how far he'd come. From Connemara. From the small shivering
kid that his mother had dumped on the Brothers of Compassion
after his father was shot. From the emigrant ship and the road
gangs in England. From coming back to Ireland ten years ago
with fourteen thousand pounds of savings and not an idea of
what to do with it. From buying that first house in Chesterfield
Square. Ten years ago. A hell of a long way. He got out of the

Jag, letting the door thud softly shut behind him, remembering his first sight of the square and the house. Number 38. And the Buick with its chromium flower vases that made it seem like some kind of a wedding car, that he had hired because it was the biggest he could find. It was a hell of a long time ago.

2

Ten years ago. 1954. Just back from Englan

The Buick sliding into Chesterfield Squar
stunned by the size of the car, the leather
lighter, the flower vases, the engine that
couldn't tell whether it was running or not. T
what he had wanted coming back. To feel tha
round him like a wall, like a protection against a
of poverty and cold and hunger and fear.

In the back the three children were also stunn
row in the middle of the seat that was like an en
couch; their faces clean, their necks red raw from
the hotel bedroom; Joseph Anthony, already ten ai
age, in a tweed suit that looked as if it had been
Venetia, six, a tiny female pierrot, in a tulle and cl
dress, covered in frills, her small spiky face all nose a
staring solemnly out of the dress's starched chiffon co
Dermot, four, but still his mother's baby, everyone's l
white sailor suit, as if he had escaped from a family ph
of 1910.

They were too awed by the car and by this first visit to l
their Ireland, where daddy and mummy came from,
everything good came from, religion and manners and
Irish and being different to the English, too awed by all
even to quarrel about who sat where. Now and then Venetia
a cautious palm over the cold leather beside her thin, matchs
legs. 'Janey,' she breathed, reciting the only Irish swear wo
that she knew, learned in secrecy from the other Irish girl in t
school in Croydon, 'Janey.' Her eyes as round as a mouse's eye
behind the thick National Health spectacles, drinking in the
splendour. Ireland, Dublin. Driving in a car like the Queen.
'Janey Mac.'

'Look at them houses,' her da was saying. 'There's a grand solid house.'

different. That nobody but a madman or an informer answers
questions from strangers. They stared, mute. The O'Rourke
children stared at them, at their dirt, their raggedness, their dumb
hostility. Francis O'Rourke took a rolling step forward, reaching
out to catch hold of an arm. The children broke like a flock of
sparrows.

'Dirty whiskers!' one of them screamed. 'Hairy-face whiskers!'
and they ran scattering, a practised fan movement of
escape, no two children running in exactly the same direction.
No Garda had ever caught any of them, and only very young
and inexperienced Gardai had ever tried.

'If I catch one of you . . .' Francis shouted, and then, aware of
his family looking at him, turned back to the car with a threatening look that killed any idea of laughter stone dead. 'You look
after the kids,' he commanded Maura, 'and don't let any of them
set foot outside the car or I'll take the skin off them.'

He crossed the road towards Number 38, swinging his stiff
leg like a sailor, like a pirate stumping and rolling his way across
a heaving deck, the heavy sole of his built-up shoe coming down
with a thud on the road. Inside the car baby Dermot fidgeted on
his seat. 'I want to do my wee-wee,' he whispered.

'Oh, Jesus Mary and Joseph!' Maura said. 'You only just
went before we started.'

'I want to do my wee-wee.'

'You heard what ma said, you can't.'

'I've got to.' The fidgeting suddenly stopped.

'He's doing it,' Venetia said in an awed voice. 'Right on the
seat.'

'Mother of God,' cried Maura, 'stop him. Give him to me!
Dermot! Joseph, stop him!' But nothing could stop him. When
Mrs O'Rourke hoicked him over into the front seat it was like
lifting a leaking bucket. She began to smack him. Outside, the
returned flock of gutter-children inched closer, watching the
spectacle. Baby Dermot's screams filled the car, seemed to fill
the square.

But Francis O'Rourke was already beyond earshot, inside the
high, magnificent hallway behind the scuffed and kicked front

door. Paved with great slabs of Wicklow slate, under a high, stucco ceiling, the hall was still beautiful, even after fifty years of neglect. Late eighteenth century, from the brief period of Dublin's greatness, the twenty years of 'Grattan's Parliament', when Ireland, or at least Protestant Ireland, had governed itself, and houses like these, and all the finest Georgian streets and squares had been built by and for the Ascendancy, for the Irish peers, the Members of Parliament, the place-seekers and hangers-on, the lawyers and merchants, the fortune-hunters and fortune-spenders; the rake-hells living on their debts; the sober, solid country landowners come up to marry a daughter or place a son. Houses and streets and squares and great town estates built and developed by grandees who themselves had grown rich on the corpse of Gaelic Ireland; so rich that they could afford extravagance of ambition, could build not only for profit, but for prestige; great families of developers, Gardiners, Gandons, FitzWilliams, Beresfords, competing with each other for architects, for tenants of high standing, above all for a reputation for magnificence and taste.

It lasted less than a generation, given its death blow by the Act of Union that abolished the Irish Parliament and reduced Dublin once more to a provincial city, filled with more fine houses than it could supply tenants to occupy. The wealthy and the would-be wealthy moved to London, and their houses were taken over by occupiers of the third and fourth rank. Small merchants, professional men, lawyers by the hungry hundred. Number 38 Chesterfield Square was bought by a coal-merchant, a Mr Thomas Mason.

Three generations later, when Thomas Mason's great grandson married a Miss Journeaux, the Mason family itself seemed like a last remnant of aristocracy in a square by then given over to clerks and shopkeepers, and half-pay officers, and worse. Miss Journeaux, become Mrs Mason, lived on in the house as wife and then as widow, kept company by her one-time lady's maid Miss Connolly; the two old ladies growing older and poorer as the square grew older and poorer round them.

It was Miss Connolly who arranged the letting of the basement, given in to them and gone along? Christ, oh Christ. His rage smouldered all the way home to Rathfarnham, until he was turning into his own drive, into the big garage standing open, waiting for him. And as he switched off the engine it seemed to die down with the engine. After all, it had given him a chance to tell them something. And by God he'd taken it. Damn and blast them he had.

He sat for a long minute in the dark, suddenly quiet garage, thinking of what he had told them. Like a pack of bloody mongrels. Yelping and snarling at something that was too bloody big for them to understand. A tenth of it, all that they knew about, was too big for them to understand. O'Rourke House. Concrete. Glass. Stainless steel and aluminium. Rising out of the dirty mess of Oxman Street and Marietta Street and Aram Court like a palace, new and shining. He hadn't got words for what it would be like. He could only see it. Feel the concrete under his hands. Raw, undressed gravel-concrete inside, harsh and tough and everlasting. The windows looking out over the scrubby rooftops between Oxman Street and the river. And then one day those rooftops themselves would be gone, and it would be all new buildings, a great square of buildings surrounding an open plaza. Grass, fountains, courtyards, paths, statues, new shops. And above the shops the cliff walls of glass: offices for banks, insurance, it didn't matter a curse in hell really what they were for. Like cliffs of glass. And in the tower of O'Rourke House his own office. Looking down on all of it. That he'd made, built, financed, hacked and battled out of a slum.

And those snivelling bastards snarling round his ankles to try and stop him. He'd see them scream in hell before they'd stop him. He hadn't come this far to be stopped now. He sat thinking of how far he'd come. From Connemara. From the small shivering kid that his mother had dumped on the Brothers of Compassion after his father was shot. From the emigrant ship and the road gangs in England. From coming back to Ireland ten years ago with fourteen thousand pounds of savings and not an idea of what to do with it. From buying that first house in Chesterfield Square. Ten years ago. A hell of a long way. He got out of the

Jag, letting the door thud softly shut behind him, remembering his first sight of the square and the house. Number 38. And the Buick with its chromium flower vases that made it seem like some kind of a wedding car, that he had hired because it was the biggest he could find. It was a hell of a long time ago.

2

Ten years ago. 1954. Just back from England.

The Buick sliding into Chesterfield Square, Maura beside him, stunned by the size of the car, the leather seats, the cigarette-lighter, the flower vases, the engine that was so quiet you couldn't tell whether it was running or not. The richness. It was what he had wanted coming back. To feel that bulk of money round him like a wall, like a protection against all the memories, of poverty and cold and hunger and fear.

In the back the three children were also stunned, sitting in a row in the middle of the seat that was like an enormous leather couch; their faces clean, their necks red raw from flannelling in the hotel bedroom; Joseph Anthony, already ten and big for his age, in a tweed suit that looked as if it had been carpentered; Venetia, six, a tiny female pierrot, in a tulle and chiffon party dress, covered in frills, her small spiky face all nose and glasses, staring solemnly out of the dress's starched chiffon collar; baby Dermot, four, but still his mother's baby, everyone's baby, in a white sailor suit, as if he had escaped from a family photograph of 1910.

They were too awed by the car and by this first visit to Ireland, their Ireland, where daddy and mummy came from, where everything good came from, religion and manners and being Irish and being different to the English, too awed by all of it even to quarrel about who sat where. Now and then Venetia ran a cautious palm over the cold leather beside her thin, matchstick legs. 'Janey,' she breathed, reciting the only Irish swear word that she knew, learned in secrecy from the other Irish girl in the school in Croydon, 'Janey.' Her eyes as round as a mouse's eyes behind the thick National Health spectacles, drinking in the splendour. Ireland, Dublin. Driving in a car like the Queen. 'Janey Mac.'

'Look at them houses,' her da was saying. 'There's a grand solid house.'

The square stretched in front of them, all round them, for-lornly, dilapidatedly beautiful, tall Georgian houses gradually declined into slum tenements, surrounding what had once been the owners' private communal garden, and that was now a stamped and battered playground for the tenement children. A *For Sale* notice hung at a forlorn angle in a broken window, one corner peeled from its fastening of glue so that it was hard to read the name of the auctioneers. It looked as if it had been there for a very long time.

'I bet you'd buy that house for next to nothing,' Francis said.

Maura looked at the house and the square with contempt. She had been brought up in Dublin although her parents were Mayo, and even in her time it had been a slum. 'If you think I'd live in a place like this——'

'For God's sake,' Francis said. 'You don't have to live in a bloody house because you own it.' He couldn't have said himself why it attracted him. Except that it was big, it was in Dublin, it had an air of ... he didn't even think of it as having an air of anything. Only that something about it spoke to him. Grandeur. But not the snob grandeur of that damn couple at the airport. Grandeur he could buy. And bloody cheap too from the look of it. Grandeur fallen on hard times.

Children had been playing in the dusty gutter and now they stood in a nervous cluster by the railings, looking at the astonish-ing car, the strange people in it. The three O'Rourke children stared at them through the windows. Ragged children, some of them barefoot. Francis O'Rourke got out of the car. Most of the children prepared to run away, but the barefooted ones, who spent their evenings begging in O'Connell Street and were therefore used to the rich, stood their ground.

'Do any of you live in that house?'

The children stared at him as if he was talking Chinese, or had just stepped out of a Flying Saucer.

'Come on, come on, who lives in that house? Any of you?' For more than twenty years he had been used to London children who always knew everything and told everything, fighting to tell it first. He had forgotten that Irish children were

different. That nobody but a madman or an informer answers questions from strangers. They stared, mute. The O'Rourke children stared at them, at their dirt, their raggedness, their dumb hostility. Francis O'Rourke took a rolling step forward, reaching out to catch hold of an arm. The children broke like a flock of sparrows.

'Dirty whiskers!' one of them screamed. 'Hairy-face whiskers!' and they ran scattering, a practised fan movement of escape, no two children running in exactly the same direction. No Garda had ever caught any of them, and only very young and inexperienced Gardai had ever tried.

'If I catch one of you . . .' Francis shouted, and then, aware of his family looking at him, turned back to the car with a threatening look that killed any idea of laughter stone dead. 'You look after the kids,' he commanded Maura, 'and don't let any of them set foot outside the car or I'll take the skin off them.'

He crossed the road towards Number 38, swinging his stiff leg like a sailor, like a pirate stumping and rolling his way across a heaving deck, the heavy sole of his built-up shoe coming down with a thud on the road. Inside the car baby Dermot fidgeted on his seat. 'I want to do my wee-wee,' he whispered.

'Oh, Jesus Mary and Joseph!' Maura said. 'You only just went before we started.'

'I want to do my wee-wee.'

'You heard what ma said, you can't.'

'I've got to.' The fidgeting suddenly stopped.

'He's doing it,' Venetia said in an awed voice. 'Right on the seat.'

'Mother of God,' cried Maura, 'stop him. Give him to me! Dermot! Joseph, stop him!' But nothing could stop him. When Mrs O'Rourke hoicked him over into the front seat it was like lifting a leaking bucket. She began to smack him. Outside, the returned flock of gutter-children inched closer, watching the spectacle. Baby Dermot's screams filled the car, seemed to fill the square.

But Francis O'Rourke was already beyond earshot, inside the high, magnificent hallway behind the scuffed and kicked front

door. Paved with great slabs of Wicklow slate, under a high, stucco ceiling, the hall was still beautiful, even after fifty years of neglect. Late eighteenth century, from the brief period of Dublin's greatness, the twenty years of 'Grattan's Parliament', when Ireland, or at least Protestant Ireland, had governed itself, and houses like these, and all the finest Georgian streets and squares had been built by and for the Ascendancy, for the Irish peers, the Members of Parliament, the place-seekers and hangers-on, the lawyers and merchants, the fortune-hunters and fortune-spenders; the rake-hells living on their debts; the sober, solid country landowners come up to marry a daughter or place a son. Houses and streets and squares and great town estates built and developed by grandees who themselves had grown rich on the corpse of Gaelic Ireland; so rich that they could afford extravagance of ambition, could build not only for profit, but for prestige; great families of developers, Gardiners, Gandons, FitzWilliams, Beresfords, competing with each other for architects, for tenants of high standing, above all for a reputation for magnificence and taste.

It lasted less than a generation, given its death blow by the Act of Union that abolished the Irish Parliament and reduced Dublin once more to a provincial city, filled with more fine houses than it could supply tenants to occupy. The wealthy and the would-be wealthy moved to London, and their houses were taken over by occupiers of the third and fourth rank. Small merchants, professional men, lawyers by the hungry hundred. Number 38 Chesterfield Square was bought by a coal-merchant, a Mr Thomas Mason.

Three generations later, when Thomas Mason's great grandson married a Miss Journeaux, the Mason family itself seemed like a last remnant of aristocracy in a square by then given over to clerks and shopkeepers, and half-pay officers, and worse. Miss Journeaux, become Mrs Mason, lived on in the house as wife and then as widow, kept company by her one-time lady's maid Miss Connolly; the two old ladies growing older and poorer as the square grew older and poorer round them.

It was Miss Connolly who arranged the letting of the basement,

and then of the ground floor, and soon after that of the first floor as well, so that they would have enough to eat, and enough to buy coals. Old Mrs Mason never knew about the tenants. Perhaps she would not let herself know. Not even, at the end of 1940, about the new upstairs tenant, the artist, who took over the attics that had once been a nest of creaking bedrooms for scullery maids and the boots, and knocked them all into one vast sky-lighted room to work in.

When she heard the sounds of hammering Miss Connolly told her it was Micky Joyce the boot boy, breaking up packing-cases for firewood. Mickey Joyce who had died in the Kaiser's War, as a machine-gunner on the Somme.

'Of course,' Mrs Mason whispered. 'Of course. I thought—I thought someone told me Mickey had gone away. Sometimes, sometimes I don't remember things quite clearly.'

She lived on until 1951, until she was ninety-seven years old, dying in the coldest of the winter, so small and shrunk in the big bed that she was like the skeleton of a leaf. And Miss Connolly died three days after, sitting beside her mistress, holding the leaf-thin hand to warm it. Died of cold and hunger and fear and her own eighty-nine years.

And for the three years since then the For Sale notice had hung in an upstairs window, waiting to tempt some buyer to come in. But it was not a period for selling houses. Francis O'Rourke was the first person to stand in that hall with even the vaguest notion of buying.

It would be crazy to think of buying it. At any price. He could smell the dry rot from where he stood, mixed with the smells of dirt and urine, mice and rats and boiled napkins and sweat and bedbugs.

He tried to think of arguments that would convince Maura. Rent? Ten bob a room? There must be twelve, fifteen rooms in a house like this. He looked at the ceilings, the foot of the wide, handsome staircase, so perfectly proportioned that nothing that had happened to it in these last terrible years had destroyed its dignity.

The door beside him opened and a woman peered out. Thin

cheeks, swollen, dropped stomach, dirty apron, dirty baby in the crook of her arm, two small children hanging on to her torn, stained skirt. She stared at Mr O'Rourke in dull surprise. Her mouth fell open while calamities ran through her mind like rosary beads. The bailiffs? The Guards? The rent? The truant officer for one of the kids? Her husband killed at work? But he wasn't working. She tried to think of something to say.

'Mind if I have a look at the room, missus?' he said. When she didn't move or answer he reached over her shoulder and gave the door a push, leaning his body sideways a little to see in. A marble fireplace, cracked and blackened, marble angels carved in deep relief at either side of it, staring at him from their shrouds of soot and dirt. A black kettle simmering on a fire of smouldering turf sods, the harsh smell of turf smoke. A cot with a child in it, lying too quiet and still, its eyes vacant. The corner of a brass bed, an old armchair, a table, a mattress on the floor, rags covering the broken window.

He looked up at the high ceiling, over eleven feet high, out of the reach of even the most active child. Scrolls and acanthus leaves and rich rosettes of stucco work; a great central relief of a woman in floating draperies with hounds at her side and a hunting horn, enclosed in a big oval frame like a picture made all of painted plaster. From the three corners that he could see little naked boys blew horns towards the centre. The background had been a rich, sky blue and the figures startling white. Smoke and time had faded them but they were still beautiful. They gave him a kind of shiver, and he nodded to the woman who was trying to shape a question in her mind that would find out where he was from. The Vincent de Paul? The Corporation? Maybe he had come about the lavatory but he looked too grand. Some kind of an inspector he must be.

Mr O'Rourke went on down the hall and out into the back. Piles of kitchen refuse lay heaped against the walls of the yard. A rough straggle of brick and rubbish-strewn grass sloped down to the ruins of a coach-house. Beside the courtyard an extension at the back of the main house contained the outside lavatory. A broken sewer pipe oozed filth down the wall into the area that lit the back basement. An old woman with a child beside her stared up at him through the bars of the basement window. The child sucked its thumb.

Mr O'Rourke went back inside and up the staircase, his heavy foot thumping on the creaking stairs. He'd be out of his bloody mind to buy a house like this. Voices behind shut doors. A child whimpering, a woman saying, 'Stop it! Stop it, blast you!' The smack of a hand on bare flesh and the whimper changing to a screech. *'Stop it!'*

Up the next flight of stairs. Shadows where the sun from the big windows of the stairwell failed to reach. The shadow of an old woman in a long dress. Only a shadow, nothing there. The sounds of children from outside. Voices screaming. Singing a skipping song. 'Two policemen and a man, weeler, weeler, wolyer.'

He looked out of the window on the highest landing. Small girls skipping over a rope, one end of it tied to a lamp post. 'Are you the woman what killed the child, down by the River Solyer?'

A donkey pulling an old clothes cart through the square, cart piled with rags, donkey harnessed with bits and pieces of broken straps and knotted rope, led by a hunchback in a flapping overcoat, his head shaking with palsy, black with dirt.

'Yes, I'm the woman what killed the child, weeler, weeler, wolyer.'

It seemed very cold on the landing and he shivered again. Stark raving mad to buy it. Stark mad to come back at all. Better to pay the bloody income-tax and stay in England. He almost walked down the stairs again and out, but there was a door at his back and he pushed it to see if it was open, to see what kind of view there was from the back of the house. It gave on to a huge room, the whole breadth and depth of the building, it must have been fifty feet by thirty, all the attics knocked into one. And in the centre of it a broad column of sun from a skylight, slanting on to a dais and an old red armchair. A painter's easel beyond it, a black iron stove with a chimney disappearing up into the shadows of the roof beyond the skylight. A wooden table piled with rubbish, a milk bottle, a palette, half a loaf of bread, books. Clothes lying on the dusty floor, an empty whiskey bottle.

He heard heavy breathing, and saw a man lying on a bed against the far wall, on his back, mouth open and snoring, a raincoat and a grey army blanket falling away from his fat body, leaving the pink chest and shoulder, and one fat, almost woman-ish arm naked in the shadows. Mr O'Rourke went closer and smelled the fog of whiskey rising up from the bed. The man's head was huge, mottled purple with drink, the hair black and thick as horsehair, almost as if the head didn't belong to the pink, hairless body.

He must be a painter. There was a pile of canvases stacked untidily against the wall at the foot of the bed and Francis O'Rourke picked one of them up and turned it over. It looked half finished. A woman in a green shirt. A horse in the back-ground. The sort of woman that would have a horse. A right bloody arrogant bitch, staring down her nose as if she didn't like being looked at. The same kind as that damn couple at the airport, shouting good-bye to their friends as though they were the only human beings in the place and everyone else was made of wood or invisible. The girl had looked a bit like this. Red hair and a white face, and the feller like he'd just fallen off some kind of a horse. Bandy legs like a bloody jockey and one of those hats that were too small for him stuck on top of too much hair. It was the same little bastard that had taken the last taxi at Dublin airport and left him and Maura and the kids to go into Dublin on the bus.

He put the portrait back with the rest of the junk and went and looked out of a window. Below him he could see the yard and the coach-house. Beyond that a jumble of dark rooftops, black slates touched with silver under the brightness of the sun. Church spires, the cranes of the docks like leaning spires stripped down to skeletons, the Custom House. And beyond the river, beyond the smoke-blue shadows of South Dublin, the dark green shoulders of the Wicklow mountains. He was back. Not in Connemara, but at least in Ireland. What was he going to do? Fourteen thousand pounds. Fourteen thousand three hundred and eighty-one pounds five and seven. A bloody fortune. He could buy anything with it, do anything.

He stood at the window, heavy, tough, his small blue eyes that always seemed on the edge of anger staring at the roofs of Dublin, that didn't care whether he lived or died, came or went. By Christ he'd make someone care, a lot of people care. Here. In Ireland. To own something. Not just money in the bank. But something solid. That would last. Francis Xavier O'Rourke. *Francis Xavier O'Rourke, Contractor.* On a brass plate. He could see it on the door of an office. Polished. He might start the digging contracts here. They must use bloody electric cables here the same as in England. Form a company. Childishly, so childishly that he knew it was childish, he thought of that couple on the plane walking past, seeing the brass plate, reading the name. *Francis Xavier O'Rourke, Contractor. Limited.*

He left the studio without another look at the drunk in the bed, and went down the stairs and into the sunlight of the square. As he got into the car there was an unnatural silence from his family. It lasted until he had the engine started, the car beginning to move.

'Da!' Venetia said, beginning to bounce up and down on the back seat with the pressure of her secret. 'Do you know what baby——'

Her mother turned to scowl at her but it was too late.

'. . . Dermot did? He did his wee-wee right on the seat, all over it, Da, before we could stop him.'

3

The young couple that had annoyed Francis O'Rourke so much at London airport and again at Dublin had never noticed him, absorbed in themselves, their new marriage, their homecoming. The day that Francis O'Rourke went into the house in Chesterfield Square they were driving west to Mayo. Also in a hired car, although not a Buick. A small grey Hillman.

They crossed the Shannon and it was the West, the real West, the road very lonely, stretching far ahead not only into Mayo but into childhood, the past. The barren fields like pale green velvet between their grey stone walls. A cottage huddled against the brown slope of a mountain, a lake like a grey eye.

'Stop the car for a minute,' Kate Lennox said. He stopped, and she sat staring out of the window as if she wanted to absorb the landscape into her brain. 'It hasn't changed,' she said at last, her voice dreaming.

'How the hell would it change?' he said, trying not to sound impatient. He was worried about his grandfather, and didn't want to show that he was worried, and still less that he was worried about a good many other things, including Kate's feelings about Ireland and Mayo.

She put her hand on his, still holding the wheel as if he was on the point of driving on again. 'Don't you feel it?'

'Feel what?'

'Oh, John. He'll be—he may not be as bad as Agnes said. You know what she always was for alarms.'

'I know.'

'Then what is it?' Rabbits were out in a field beside them, sitting very still for the moment, alarmed by the coming of the car, by the sense that something strange was near, a big grey buck sitting on his hindquarters, staring towards them. Gold flowers on the gorse bushes that studded the pale summer turf. Far ahead of them a lorry came rumbling down the mountain road. 'What's wrong?'

'Oh.' He shrugged and held her hand, and said, 'Nothing. Of course nothing's wrong.'

'He's eighty-nine,' she said. 'We have to face it. This year or next or the year after.'

'I suppose I feel a bastard for not coming back before.'

Six years. Four years at sea. Two years in Africa. He looked at the landscape with narrowed, reflective eyes. He was surprised himself to find how little it meant to him. Coming in to Dublin on the plane, last night in the Shelbourne, he had felt almost excited, he *had* felt excited. Six years. He had been seventeen. One more year to go in school. Then Trinity. The Colonel would have found the money somewhere. And Kate. All the long summer holidays. At home. And on the island, Inis Beag, fishing, and lazing in the sun, pretending to brush up their Irish with old Mrs O'Malley. Fresh-caught lobsters and mackerel and island mutton and, very secretly, when the old lady's back was turned, a small glass of poteen from Tim Bourke the ferryman, or Sean Daly. Coming back to Castle Lennox, the horses, the dogs, autumn coming, and the shooting, and log fires. Himself and Kate. Even then he hadn't known what exactly was wrong, what had changed from the previous summer. He had spent the school year looking forward to the next summer, the island, everything, and everything had been as perfect as he had hoped and at the same time it was as though it was hollow, filled with sawdust.

Half a dozen times he had provoked quarrels with Kate, simply for the pleasure of knowing what was wrong. Of having something concrete to be unhappy about. And the two of them had gone round the house like thunder-clouds, making everyone on edge: the Colonel, Agnes the housekeeper, Kate's mother, anyone else they could annoy. When he didn't quarrel with Kate she quarrelled with him. And then they would make it up and swear they would never quarrel again and go off riding, or looking for grey crows with a shotgun, Suki and Patch making so much noise that any bird in its senses left the parish. What the hell had been wrong?

Kate's mother who was also his aunt had been in terror that

they were in love and had had long agonized confabulations with Agnes—the Colonel would never have listened to her, never had listened to her about anything in the ten years she had lived in the house. And Agnes, under the deepest oaths of secrecy, had repeated it all to Kate, or to John, whichever of them happened to be with her when the mood for a good secret took her.

'She has a holy dread on her, the poor mistress, that the pair of you are head over heels in love.'

'Agnes! For Heaven's sake! Me? With Kate?'

Or: 'What! Me? With him? I hate him!'

'And you being first cousins and brought up like brother and sister. You know what they say happens if first cousins marry?' Dropping her voice to tell horrors in the big stone kitchen, the pastry rolled out in front of her on the marble top of the kitchen table.

'You *are* an idiot, Agnes. I'd as soon marry poor old Mea Culpa. I'm not going to marry for years and years and then it's going to be someone immensely rich who'll buy the whole of Inis Beag for me. Do you know the Dalys are leaving the island? They're trying to get a farm on the mainland. If I had any money I'd buy their cottage and go and live there all by myself.'

'Go away out of that with you, Miss Kate. Who'd look after you?'

'I'd look after myself. I've got O'Malley blood. That's pirate blood.'

'I seem to remember hearing that before. Have you washed your hands?'

'On my granny's side we go right back to Grace O'Malley, the Pirate Queen.'

'Pirates indeed. You ought to be grown out of such nonsense long ago. I hope you've an appetite for your tea?'

He hadn't even kissed her. It hadn't occurred to him. Marry her? They must be mad. They told each other it was mad, out in the stables grooming Jenny, the mare, and he was so relieved that he did kiss her and it seemed to be the strangest thing that had ever happened to him. As if she was suddenly someone else. It only lasted a second but it seemed a very long second. Then they went on currycombing the mare, Kate with her head turned half away from him, her cheek slightly flushed.

'You didn't mind?' he said at last. She only shook her head. He put his hand on her shoulder and she shook it away and ran out into the stable yard. When he had finished the mare and tried to find her she was sitting with her mother in the small sitting-room, reading a book, not even looking up when he came in. And his aunt Ann looked at him sideways as if he was some kind of dangerous animal. It was that night that she announced at dinner that she had finally decided to accept her second cousin's long-standing invitation to visit him in Kenya. Kate would go with her and they would spend the winter out there. No one seemed to think it irrational to take Kate away from school in the year of her final exams. Even the Archdeacon, the Colonel's brother Henry, approved. To John, it seemed that his great-uncle was looking at him as he said, 'Splendid idea. Splendid. A magnificent climate, I have been told.'

A fortnight later, in the middle of all Aunt Ann's and Kate's preparations for the journey, he had run away, to Dublin, to London, and to sea, knowing that he was leaving behind such a confusion of wrong ideas with everyone that it was pointless even trying to write a letter from London to explain his motives. He simply wrote a brief note to his grandfather, apologizing for what he had done, and saying that he was sick of school, he would never make a lawyer as had been vaguely planned, or a diplomat, as had also been suggested, and that he wanted to see the world. He would write again from wherever he got to, and please give his fondest regards to everyone.

He had written, two or three times a year, and had occasionally got replies from the Colonel, forwarded on from the London office of the shipping company, to Venezuela, or Kuwait, or Karachi, or Durban. A bad fight in District Six in Capetown had left him in hospital with a broken arm and a twelve-inch scar from a bicycle-chain curling round his left shoulder and the back of his neck, and he stayed in South Africa, moving north to

Rhodesia with a man who said there was a fortune to be made shooting crocodiles. He already knew that Kate was still in Kenya, with her mother, who had remarried out there.

He wrote, and was invited to stay. Aunt Ann's letter, enclosing one from Kate, was enthusiastically nostalgic. She had obviously forgotten all her suspicions, or long recovered from them. Or thought that Kate was now secure. 'We've an awfully nice neighbour, Derek Waters, an English boy, from a very good family. I'd love you to meet him. He and Kate . . .'

He had loathed Derek Waters on sight. Long flapping English shorts, pink knees, a small fair moustache and a habit of calling Kate 'Kath'. 'Kath, old girl.' 'Have you seen Kath's mater, old boy?' He had obviously written John down as an uncouth South African and was overwhelmingly helpful to him about small details of Kenya etiquette, only stopping short of telling him which knife and fork to use at dinner.

'You can't possibly like a bastard like that,' John said. 'Your mother must be out of her tiny vague mind.'

'We're unofficially engaged,' Kate said. 'Derek is thinking of having the wedding next year after he's got the crop settled.'

'And what are you thinking of? Six little boys with floppy shorts?'

'I wish we'd never invited you.'

A week later John and Kate drove down to Nairobi in the farm truck, bought themselves a suitcase full of more or less respectable clothes, and flew to London. They were married by special licence, with half a dozen school friends dug out of the telephone book as witnesses and wedding guests and a long telegram from Derek Waters beseeching Kate to step back from the brink at the last moment and to take refuge with his mother in Kensington.

Four of the six friends had seen them off at London airport, making up for the awkwardness of no longer really knowing each other, or the bride and groom, with an excess of heartiness. Now they themselves were here, and he was still not sure why he had done any of it, or what they were going to do next, beyond see how ill his grandfather really was and have a kind of honeymoon in Castle Lennox. They might have a week or two on Inis Beag as well if the old lady was still alive and taking visitors. And then? He had a suspicion that Kate had already made up her mind that they were going to stay in Ireland.

'I've always thought it was the most beautiful place in the world,' Kate said. 'And it is.'

'God, you do talk rubbish. How on earth can you say a thing like that when you've been living in Kenya?'

'Kenya!' She searched in her mind for something scornful enough to dismiss Kenya, and thought of Derek and began to laugh. 'He'll be so mad. *Mother will look after you.* I'm so glad we did it.'

He put the car into gear to cover his own failure to equal her enthusiasm. Of course he was glad they'd done it. Of course. Until he started to think about it. When he was touching her, when they were holding each other, when he wasn't thinking of anything, it was all as wonderful as she thought it was. As long as he didn't think.

When they had met again a few weeks ago, in Kenya, for the first time in six years, it had been like coming home, it had been so wonderful that he had known then, on the instant, without thinking about it, that they were going to do this, that they were going to marry, he was going to get her away from her mother, from Derek Waters, whoever the hell he was, that they were going to take up from where they had left off that summer. As if the six years between had been a night, nothing, had never happened. In one way she looked as if they never had happened. Nothing about her had changed as he looked at her. The same thin, somehow leashed-in girl, as if she was being held from leaping forward, running towards him. The red hair, the pale skin, the face that seemed to be carved out of new ivory, so smooth, so beautifully shaped it caught his breath for a second seeing her; the long green eyes, the long swift hands lifting to touch him, catch hold of his hands, touch his face, as if she needed to touch him before she knew he was there, before she recognized him fully.

'You've grown, John!' The same eager, swift, tumbling voice, high-pitched and yet soft. Holding him by the shoulders, at the full length of her arms, straining her head back, crinkling her eyes. 'Darling John!' If she had kissed him then, if he had kissed her . . . It was odd how that moment in which nothing happened came back to him. He hadn't wanted, not really and reasonably wanted to kiss her then, in front of her mother, her stepfather, twenty or thirty people standing around, most of them nodding acquaintances, if nothing more, of Kate and her family. If they had kissed each other it would have had to be a cousinly, friendly, family peck. And both of them by instinct had avoided that as unsatisfactory, inadequate, not at all their true relationship. But why hadn't they had the courage to kiss as they wanted to kiss, as they never had in their lives because six years ago they had been children and had not known what kissing was, what it could mean and signify? They knew now what it meant. He knew. And he had only to look at her twice to sense that she knew. She wasn't the same Kate he had left six years ago. How could she be? She was a woman. Perhaps he was afraid of that, of realizing that?

He had looked at her again, at the skin that the sun, even the Kenya sun, had failed to darken, but had enriched, so that the ivory glowed, and hidden in its pale depths there was a sense of blood, of fire burning. And her hair had changed, grown even more alive, dark red changing to red gold, to a kind of fire, twisting and shimmering in the sun under her white hat, and her green eyes like emeralds, and yet not cold, also catching the sun with a sudden flash like green fire, like a . . . not like a cat's eyes but like a leopard's, narrowed and beautiful and dignified. Perhaps the dignity had stopped him. He hadn't expected that.

But what had stopped her? What leash had held her? Derek Waters? The trouble was it still held her. Even now. So that each of them seemed like two people. One pair just married, everything perfect, splendid, laughing, light-hearted, irresponsible, all the things that lovers should be; only the worry about the Colonel to shadow them, darken the sun for a moment. But the other pair, their real selves, standing very quiet and still in the shadows, afraid to touch each other, afraid to let go. Why? Why? They had lain in bed together, made love together, done everything that lovers do, enjoyed it, told each other they enjoyed it, whispered all the stupid things that every lover has ever whispered. But in the shadow of their minds, their inner selves had stood very stiff and reserved, and afraid, barely touching each other. Did this happen to everyone, to all couples who've just married?

He thought of other girls, other women he had been with, some that he had thought for a day or two he had loved, and others that he hadn't thought anything about at all except that he wanted to sleep with them. Had that shadow been there? He tried to stop himself asking the question, because it seemed wrong even to make a necessary comparison between those times and Kate. Was it simply that they were cousins, that they had been brought up too close together, brother and sister almost? Was that what was wrong?

Or simply the bachelor thing, that all the jokes are about? The end of freedom. You're done for now, old man. No more drinks with the boys, no more nights out. The little woman'll see to that. Of course it wasn't. Neither of them thought like that, not remotely like that. But another kind of freedom? Of feeling that the whole world lay unrolled in front of him, that he had no one to care about, no one to look after except himself, go here, go there. North, south, east, west. Back to sea. Down to the Cape. North to the Sudan, west to Angola. Anywhere. Pull the string of the duffle bag, climb into the truck, and go. A thousand miles, two thousand, five thousand. They could still do it, still go and go and go. But could they? Even when they were getting on to the plane in Nairobi, their hearts beating half with laughter, half with a kind of childish, childhood fear of being caught, brought back, scolded and separated, even in that moment he had looked round the airport, felt as if he was seeing it for the last time. As if he was being robbed, dragged away from the one freedom he had ever had. And yet he had been doing it of his free will, wanted it. And while he was thinking that his pulse had been racing for Kate, for her nearness, for the touch of her arm against his, the sudden warmth of her skin in the sleeveless dress, burning from the sun; the sun that beat up from the concrete, off the glass of the airport building, off the silver of the fuselage. And the sudden coolness inside the plane. Like a shutter falling. Half his heart full to bursting with Kate, with love for her, desire for her. And the other half breaking. For what? For what? What was to stop them coming back, living in Africa, spending their lives roving from end to end of it; and yet he knew that they wouldn't. She wouldn't. She hadn't said it, she hadn't needed to. All her talk had been about Europe. About Ireland. Home.

And he had realized as they settled into their seats, fastened their seat-belts, that his home was Africa, as Ireland had never been. Ireland had been simply childhood, a place to grow up in, a place to leave. And she was going to bring him back to it. He had wanted to run out of the Registry Office. And again outside, standing in an awkward, noisy group on the pavement, he had wanted to run. Trapped. And she was going to fasten the trap still closer round him, very kindly, not ever knowing it was a trap for him, not ever seeing it as a loss of anything. She didn't ever see anything the same way that he saw it. Neither the Kate of everyday, the one he could touch and see and quarrel with and laugh at and get angry with, nor the inner Kate that he could scarcely touch, scarcely reach in any way at all. Neither Kate saw things the way that he did. For her this was freedom probably. This narrow landscape, this white road between small green hills. The Ireland of her dreams.

A long way ahead of them there was a horse-drawn caravan, creeping up the hill. Tinkers.

'Look!' she cried, and as they overhauled it, 'Stop and ask them if they know the Connors, and where they are.'

Green canvas stretched over the hooped roof, tins banging by the tailboard, the small painted shutters at the back open and an old woman leaning on the half door with a pipe between her gums, staring at the car coming up behind her. 'It's her! It's Mrs Connor!' Kate shouted, and lowering the window shouted louder 'Mrs Connor! *Nus a dhalyon dhuilsha!*'

The old woman stared, and they were past the caravan and pulling into the roadside fifty yards ahead. It lumbered up to them, an old man and a young man driving the one skewbald mare, a chestnut foal trotting beside its dam on the end of a straw rope.

'Gretis!' Kate shouted and it was the old man's turn to stare, strangers getting out of a motor car and a young woman shouting his tinker name at him as if she herself was a tinker. What in the name of God? He felt for the heavy stick beside him on the wooden seat, not seeing what the danger could be, but also not seeing how anything so strange could not be dangerous. He brought the caravan to a prudent halt, ten yards short of the motor car, and sat where he was, his hand still on the hidden stick.

'Will I get down, da?' his son whispered to him in taral. '*Mwilsa dyonadu asirt, gater?*'

'Stay where you are, boy.' The girl was running up to them, holding out both hands. The man following. His mind raced with what it might mean. Had Grunles stolen anything, had they seen her? Or the dog? His wife was parting the canvas curtains at his back.

'What is it, Gretis?' she was whispering. 'What were they shouting at us?'

The old man's eyes were sliding this way and that to see if there were police, anyone else besides these two. But they could catch him in a breath if he tried to whip up the mare, and he couldn't leave the caravan to take to the fields.

'Don't you remember me? Satlin?' The girl reaching up and catching his hand. Was she a madwoman? 'Satlin and Gyison.' Vague memories stirred in his mind, old, old memories, but they were connected with children. It was his wife who remembered.

'The children of the big house,' she whispered. 'Is it them?'

'Don't you remember us?' Kate said. '*The bini sharog lakin?*'

'Arrach God!' the old man cried at last. 'Is it yourself? The little red-haired one?' But in the same instant he was overcome with nervous embarrassment at talking to a woman of the settled people as he had once talked to the small child, and he half bent his head and looked first at Kate and then at John under the grey tangle of his eyebrows. His face was dark brown, the wrinkles darker again, seamed and blackened by turf smoke. He had a red handkerchief knotted round his thick, corded neck and he put up a nervous hand to twist the knot away from his Adam's apple. He remembered them both, remembered them well, although not in the way that settled people remember, by month and year. Anything more than a year past was simply long ago, unless it was so long past that it was when he was young, or the time that his son Libisk was born, or his daughter Grunles; or the time one of the babies died. Although even those deaths were welded together now into one unhappiness, the kind of heartbreak that stays like a stone in a pool, not moving unless you tread on it.

But he remembered them. Two children. The wood. Across the river from the big house. They hadn't known the wood belonged to the big house or they would have been afraid to camp there. It was the time they had had the bad fight with the Bannions down by Galway. His brother had lost an eye and been put in gaol and died there, and one of the Bannions had gone to bladunk for three years for the death. Well he remembered. He had brought the family north to Mayo to avoid getting killed in revenge for the gaol term, because it was his brother who had started the fight. The memories of the fight swirled in his head, more vivid than the children.

The man talking to him. 'How have you been keeping?'

'Well enough, sir, not too bad, your honour.'

There was no real connection in his mind between those children who had come creeping down to their fire and these grown people with their motor car. The woman was talking taral to him, words and phrases, and to his wife behind him and to Libisk, paralysed with strangeness on the seat beside him. He found it harder to understand her gamman than her English except the single words. The children had come often to the fire. He hadn't known the district then and they had few camping-sites where they were sure of not being shifted on by the muskro or whoever owned the land. They had come back and back to that place because the children promised them they were safe. They had been good children.

'And where's the little girl?' Kate was saying, and could have bitten her tongue out because as likely as not she was dead. But the old woman said, 'She'll be looking for a bit of bread and maybe an egg or a potato, milady.'

Like her husband she didn't know what to make of them, of this rich woman who had once been a child. She wanted to beg from her but something held her back. It frightened her to hear their own language in this stranger's mouth.

'*Gegen the pek?*' Kate said, laughing, feeling as if she had been given an enormous gift, a piece out of her childhood put into her hands. Looking back it was as though the Connors had always camped in that wood, there had always been the red eye of their fire between the winter trees, the smell of woodsmoke, the shadow of a horse moving, the tap of a hammer on tin. In reality it had been a dozen times, three and four days together, a week, spread over three years. After that, as the Connors widened their district, found richer places to beg, and sell their tin buckets and their clothes-pegs, it had become no more than twice in the year, or only once, and Kate and John had been away in boarding-school as often as not when they came by. But those early visits were the ones she remembered. They belonged to childhood, to that magical foundation of reality which is laid down for some people when they are five or seven or ten years old, made up of trivial, irrational things, and which for ever after govern every-thing else that happens in their lives.

A dog came over the ditch, a grey lurcher, slinking as quiet as a shadow, sniffing strangers. The girl came after him, stopped on the bank with one foot raised, leaning sideways to take the weight of the bucket she was carrying. She saw the car, the two strange people, stood like a post. Police? The dead rabbit in the bucket under the potatoes the farmwife had given her weighed on her arm as if it was alive and kicking, trying to betray her. The lurcher vanished.

'Grunles!' The strange woman calling her by her name. Did the woman own the rabbit? Would she be put in gaol? She swallowed and shut her eyes. Her brother said softly not to be afraid of the strangers. '*Nides getul a gransa.*' She came down on to the road, a small woman at thirteen, her body already beginning to fill the dirty red cotton dress that trailed down round her ankles. Her hair was dark yellow like her brother's, and she had a fierce, nervous handsomeness like a young fox. The strange woman was holding out a hand to her and she thought for a moment that she was giving her something and cupped her own hand to receive it, ducking her head and knee in a kind of curtsy she had learned from her mother, to thank the house people for food or money. But the woman only took hold of her hand and shook it.

'She doesn't remember us,' Kate said, smiling, but also hurt. How could she not remember? As if the gift she had been given was being taken away again.

'We'd better get on,' John said. She saw him putting a pound into Gretis's hand, the old brown fingers folding over it like a conjuring trick, and for that second she hated her husband worse than she had ever hated him in any quarrel in all the years of their growing-up. How could he? How could he insult them like that? She wanted to turn round and hit him, apologize to Gretis, do anything. The blood came up into her face like a scarlet fever. John had her arm in his hand, was pulling her imperceptibly away, 'We'll see you in the wood,' he said.

'Let go of my arm,' she whispered savagely.

'You can give us some tea in a tin can again,' John called, pushing her into the car and shutting the door.

'I'll kill you,' she said.

'Don't be so bloody stupid. The girl had something in the bucket they didn't want us to see. And anyway I don't think they remember us from Adam.'

'How could you give him money? I thought I'd die.'

'God above! D'you think he didn't want it?'

'We were their friends.'

'We were two rich tourists in a motor car. I don't suppose they had an idea on earth who we were or what you were on about.'

'I hate you. I wish I'd never married you.'

'If you want to go back to floppy shorts I'm sure he'll send you a ticket.'

They didn't talk to each other again for more than ten miles. They came to the edge of Lough Nephin, the road following the lake shore, the water like polished steel and the islands floating, tufts of trees reflected like drowned woodlands.

'I'm sorry,' John said. He stopped the car again and they touched hands and looked. They were seven miles from home. A long time ago this had been the edge of the known world, a morning's journey in the pony cart, an adventure, to picnic on one of those half-moons of gold sand among the rocks. For the time they spent looking at the water he felt what she felt, or thought he did.

Like a door opening, and they were back in a landscape more wonderful than any countryside of adult life could ever be. Everything possible. Over every hill, round every turn of the road a wonder, every wood a forest, every traveller just back from Tir n'an og. But although he could see it he couldn't share it. Which was strange because according to common sense it was more his landscape than hers. He was born in it. And yet he had never belonged to it, never felt that it was really his. Walking on Sundays to the Protestant church, the Colonel holding his hand, the people passing them on the road lifting their hats to the Colonel, speaking pleasantly, but with a different pleasantness to other days of the week, a feeling of separateness in their voices, a more cautious respect that held a thousand, ten thousand shades of meaning and history and unknown sufferings. The small knot of Protestants gathered in the big, shadowy, bleak stone church, like exiles. The archdeacon, great-uncle Henry, preaching one of his remote, fluting sermons that passed over everyone's head, let alone a small boy's. Analysing St Paul to the Corinthians or the true meaning of Isaiah's prophecies. No one expected to understand the sermon. But to be gathered there in the Church, huddled close under the pulpit, gave them a sense of kinship, of community. Outside was Ireland, outside were the Catholics, the sprawling, brawling, undisciplined, untrustworthy world of the Virgin Mary and Rome and Fenians and Shinners and shootings. Here was sobriety and Queen Victoria's ghost and the Empire and loyalty. How could one belong to that outside world? It had sunk into him in childhood and when he had grown older and realized that half of childhood's reasoning was wrong and the other half distorted, when he had learned that the Colonel hated the memory of Queen Victoria and quarrelled about her with great-uncle Henry, when he had realized that the people in the house whom he loved, Agnes the housekeeper, the maids; and old Tim, the gardener, old Tim's children and grand-children, and Mea Culpa, and Mr Shirley the breadman, and everyone, everyone except themselves, was a Catholic; that old Tim and Mr Shirley had been Shinners, had been in the I.R.A., and that all of them loved his grandfather and liked him both for himself and as his grandfather's grandson and that no one was going to shoot anyone else, no one cared anything about the British Empire or the King of England, and that legally he was as much Irish as old Tim's grandchildren; even then he could never feel that he truly belonged, that he could be part of it, unthink-ingly and matter-of-factly as old Tim's grandchildren were, as all the Catholics were who streamed every Sunday towards their ugly nineteenth-century imitation Gothic chapel.

But for Kate none of that mattered. Perhaps she wasn't even aware of it. Or else she thought that it was because she herself had been born in England, and she pushed the feeling into the back of her mind, out of sight, persuading herself that with time it would vanish, would cease to be true. That she had only to throw herself headlong into Ireland, into romantic, idealistic, never-never Ireland, dive deep enough, and it would accept her, welcome her, open its great green heart to her and take her for its own.

'I'm half afraid to go on,' she said. 'I keep expecting it to disappear. Or something to happen.'

They smoked a cigarette and felt very close, as they always did after a quarrel. 'We are fools,' she said. 'I'm glad you gave them the money.'

In another quarter of an hour they were home, turning into the long avenue between the stone gateposts, the one on the left still leaning slightly outwards from the times that the Archdeacon had run into it in the Austin; both gateposts topped by stone cannonballs from the war of 1689, when the old castle had been burned. The elm trees. One fallen in the years since they had left.

Someone, old Tim, had begun to trim off the branches and given up, leaving an axe driven into the trunk, the blade rusting. Three cows grazing in the meadow that sloped down to the river. Beyond the river the wood. The avenue curved and they could see the house, the gravel sweep in front of it, the low stone parapet of the terrace. A dog came running out from the stable arch beyond the house, hearing the sound of the car. An Afghan.

'Suki!' Kate cried, and had the door of the car open before they were come to a stop. 'Suki!' She was half out of the car, her arms flung wide. The dog backed away, barked, recognized her and came in a long bound, its huge, feathered paws on her shoulders, tongue licking her face. The front door opened and Agnes was there, another dog with her, another Afghan, black as midnight, watching the strange performance its mother was making with surprise and disdain.

'Miss Kate! Master John!'

A maid they didn't recognize, young and red-faced and blushing, pulling the luggage out of John's hands. Old Tim hobbling out of the stables. The young dog barking. Patch trotting up, fat and asthmatic and full of rheumatism. Home. The big hall, almost cold in spite of the summer, the worn rug, the door open into the drawing-room, full of sunlight, the brightness of chintz and polished wood and silver.

'How is he?' Kate said, when it was possible to say anything.

'A bit worn out with the excitement,' Agnes whispered, dropping her voice as if it was a secret that no one but Kate and John should hear. 'I don't think he's slept a wink for nights thinking of you coming, and now hasn't he fallen asleep just an hour ago? I think you should leave him sleep till he wakes and I'll have tea for you in the drawing-room just as soon as you've washed your hands.'

'She thinks we're still twelve,' Kate said when they were alone. Suki at Kate's feet, Patch dragged off protesting to the stables, because he had rolled in something and was smelly even at the best of times, the black Afghan Shah still suspicious of them, looking at them round the edge of the drawing-room door. When the tea came he followed the maid in, to be shooed out again by Agnes, bearing the silver teapot.

'All he wants is a ham sandwich, the thief. My goodness, the pair of you.' She shook her head, pouring out for them. 'Married! And not a word to any of us.'

'We wrote——'

'That you'd be married by the time we got your letter! My goodness, the Archdeacon is cross. He won't forgive you too easily, I'll tell you that.'

'How is he?'

'Like a cricket. Not a day changed, God bless him.'

'And still driving the car? I see the gatepost has survived. Was it him knocked down the elm tree in the avenue?'

'Master John! If he heard you! But it's a wonder if he didn't. Hadn't he nearly poor Mea Culpa killed outright only last week, coming down the hill behind him the way he does so you wouldn't hear a whisper of the car till he's on top of you.'

'He's not still freewheeling down the big hill?' Kate cried.

'He is surely.' The Archdeacon had begun freewheeling his car down hills during the Emergency, to save petrol, and when the war was over he had continued, in order to save money. 'Mea Culpa only saved his life by throwing himself and his bicycle into the ditch at the last second.' Ham sandwiches, and egg and tomato and watercress sandwiches, and potato scones and brown bread and home-made jam, and currant cake, and cups and cups of tea that grew stronger and stronger on its brass trivet by the fire. Gossip about the archdeacon. About Mea Culpa. Thos Kelly, Jobbing Builder, known as Mea Culpa because whenever something went wrong with anything he had built, or tried to repair, he beat his breast with a big cement-stained fist and said, 'Mea culpa, mea culpa, but sure to God what can you expect with the class of bricks they do be making these days?' Or the class of timber, or the class of cement.

'Did he ever fix the dining-room chimney?'

'Does Easter fall in June? Sure hasn't he had us all driven mad with it since nineteen and forty-one, or was it forty? It was only last summer he had it practically rebuilt, and merciful heavens if you try to use it the smoke would choke you.'

And the old bishop dead, mostly of chagrin at the archdeacon refusing to retire and give up his archdeacon's house. 'And where would he live, the poor man, if he did? But the old bishop wouldn't give himself rest nor peace about it and now he's dead, God rest him, and the new bishop . . .' She folded her lips to indicate that there was much to tell which was above her station to repeat. Although she would undoubtedly repeat it, given a little more time.

The maid, Mary Ellen, old Tim's grand-niece, came back to say that the master was awake and wanting to see them. They went up, feeling suddenly guilty, all the years falling away, children again who had done something terrible and were creeping upstairs to be scolded and sent to bed, or worse. The portraits on the long landing frowning down at them. Pistol Lennox, whose white face and sardonic eye had terrified them both on dark winter evenings, like a ghost at the stairhead. The old General with his gold-hilted sword, taken from Ayub Khan's own treasury at the looting of Kandahar; Suki's ancestor beside him, darkened into a brown shadow by time and varnish. All the others.

The bedroom was almost stifling with the fire burning and the windows shut, and yet there was a chill under the thick warmth. The Colonel lay in the big walnut bed like a doll, hardly lifting the covers with his thin old body, his cheeks faded from red to an unhealthy pink under the whisps of white hair. It seemed monstrous that they had let him grow so old by himself and they stood on either side of the bed not knowing what to say.

'So ye're married?' the Colonel whispered. 'In spite of all of us, eh?'

John nodded, and Kate knelt down and took one of the knotted old hands lying on the fold of the sheet and kissed the back of it. It was cold and slightly damp under her lips like the hand of a man already dead.

'Registry office too. M'brother's furious.' For a moment the thought of the archdeacon's anger brought a spark of warmth into the faded blue eyes.

'How's yer mother, Kate?' The voice like a feather, barely stirring in the thick atmosphere of sickness.

'I'm going to tell her to come. She's very well.'

'Tell her to stay where she is. Nothing to do here.' He lay quiet, regathering his strength, his shallow breath rattling very softly in the bony chest. 'Best thing for her. Remarrying. Nothing here. Bloody country going to hell. Republic! Damn fools in Dublin ruining everything.' His voice a cobweb of sound, ghostly. 'You'll have to sell up.'

'Colonel! Don't!'

'Stop snivelling, Kate. I've had a long innings. Time to go.'

They drew chairs up to the bed and sat with him, not talking, because he had shut his eyes and they hoped he was asleep. After half an hour Agnes came in on tiptoe and made them leave. 'Please God he'll sleep easier now you're home,' she said. 'I'm heating the water for your baths. And I've a lovely shoulder of lamb for your dinner that won't take any time at all to be roasted so no lying on in the bath like you used to.'

The rooks still cawing in the elms as they ate their dinner in the big dining-room overlooking the terrace and the meadow and the wood beyond; the tall windows open to the summer evening, the air so soft and quiet it was like old wine held in a bowl of lead-grey crystal. They fell asleep in the quietness, feeling it reach into them from the meadow, and the trees, from the empty stables and the walled garden, from the fields. A living quietness, full of distant sounds that needed to be listened for; an owl, sounds in the wood, the tap and creak of old timber in the roof as the air chilled. Sleep.

At four in the morning they woke to hear the dogs howling outside the Colonel's door. He was dead.

4

De Rigo Buildings rise up like cliffs of Victorian brick out of a
desert of concrete. Fourteen blocks of flats for the industrious
working class, built as a charity long ago by the De Rigo Trust,
each block named after an important De Rigo of the nineteenth
or eighteenth century. The Earl of Beswick block. The Lord
Tintagel block.

Willy Doyle, Francis O'Rourke's ex-ganger from England,
with two months' wages in his hip pocket and a new fibre
suitcase, turned into the echoing cave-entrance of the Lady
Augusta De Rigo block, smelling the familiar smells, hearing
the familiar echoes as he hefted the suitcase up the cement staircase, his shoulder brushing the tiled wall. Third landing, flat 86.
His smallest brother that he only remembered as a baby opened
the door.

'Ma in?' Willy said. He was small and dapper, with a new blue
suit and pointed brown shoes, his hair oiled into a quiff over
sharp blue eyes that were full of humour and satirical knowledge
of the world. His ten-year-old brother Micky stared at him, his
own eyes equally sharp, full of suspicion, like a ferret staring out
of its hole.

'Who you?'

'Yer brother Willy.'

Micky hesitated and then let him in. 'Ma's out.'

Willy dumped his bag in the middle of the tiny living-room.
The impulse that had brought him back to Dublin on the heels
of his boss was already wearing off. 'Where's the old feller?'

Micky shrugged, 'Gone t'England.'

'Sending anything home?'

Micky shook his head. His face, his eyes, were too old for ten
years old.

'Where's Maureen?'

'Gone t'England. She sent us a quid last week.' He looked at
the case. 'What you bring?'

'You wait till Ma gets home. Where's Denis?'

Micky gave a thin smile. 'Inside.'

'Inside?' Willy said, his voice rising. 'You mean in the nick?'

'Six months.'

'I'll kill him,' Willy said. 'I'll bloody kill him. What did he do?'

'Cigarettes. Him and another feller knocked off a load of cigarettes from a caff. Thirty-two thousand.' He said it with a degree of pride at the quantity.

'Jesus,' Willy said. He sat down in the hard little armchair by the empty grate. A plastic statue of the Infant of Prague on the mantelpiece. The picture of the Sacred Heart over the door. 'He didn't get probation?'

'Denis?' Micky said scornfully. 'This is his second time in. The judge said next time it'll be years not months. He's a real hard case.'

'He's a bloody head case.' His voice became a squeak. 'What did he do it *for*? The second time in? Oh, Jesus. What a bloody thing to come home to. Does Da know?'

Micky shrugged again. 'He hasn't writ. Ma wrote the address we had but we didn't get no answer.'

The door opened and Mrs Doyle came in. A small, stout woman with her hair dyed blonde under a green felt hat and a black feather boa round her neck. 'Willy!' she screamed, and then, 'D'you hear about Denis?'

'Why didn't you write me?'

'We didn't like to worry you.' She put sausages and bread and half a pound of butter on the table and flung her arms round her son. 'You've always been so good I didn't want you to think we were asking for anything.'

'Dad sending nothing?'

'We got a Christmas card, but it hadn't got no address on it. From Birmingham.'

'I'd like to do him.'

'Maybe he hasn't got nothing to send,' she said defensively. 'But what we doing all standing up like this? Micky love, go and put the pan on, isn't it lucky I brought some sausages,

I'll make you a lovely fry, are you hungry? When d'you get home?'

'Don't be fussing,' he said. 'I brought you home a few bits.' He began unpacking the presents, leaving the pipe and tobacco for his father at the bottom of the case with the silk dress for his sister Maureen.

'I got a lovely job since Da went,' his mother said, not wanting to seem too eager for the presents, or to let him think they'd been in any hardship. 'With the Knights of St Brigid. I'm head cleaner for 'em in their house, you never saw anything so lovely, acres of linoleum, a great big house up on the Green, I don't have nothing to do hardly except see the other cleaners do their work proper.'

She opened her first parcel and a fountain of pink nylon sprang out. 'A niglijay,' Willy said. And a diamante powder compact and a hundred cigarettes and a half-bottle of gin. A pistol and a cowboy belt for Micky. Denis's parcel also stayed in the case. 'When does he come out?'

'Saturday it'll be four weeks.'

'I'll kill him.'

'He's bigger'n you,' Micky said.

'And it won't take me a minute to fetch you a belt on the listener either. Are you going to school?'

'Course I am.'

'No miching?'

'We won't talk about nasty things today,' Mrs Doyle said hastily. 'Oh, I'm so glad to have you back. Are you going to stay?'

'If I can get something.'

His mother's face fell. 'Things is pretty bad,' she said. 'That's why your dad went.'

'That bastard,' Willy said. 'If he'd seen a job he'd have run from it.'

'I won't have you speak like that of your father. And in front of Micky.'

'Get away, Ma. D'you think I don't know what he's like?'

'Micky!'

Willy sat eating his sausages, trying to feel glad that he was home.

* * *

In London, in St George's, Hanover Square, Lady Honoria Wyntoun, only daughter of the Earl of Lomax, once of Lomax Castle, Banff, and now of Pineapple Lodge, Falmouth, Jamaica, was becoming Lady Honoria Gandon, bride of Cecil Prendergast Gandon of Bassett House, County Dublin. On the bridegroom's side of the church there were ranks of Gandons, none of them enthusiastic about the wedding, but at least dutifully there. Also nervously there, looking between the spread fingers of praying hands to see what this girl was like that that imbecile Cecil had managed to pick up at the horse show and get engaged to in spite of everything that any of them had been able to do. Her stepmother a negress? An ex-cook? It didn't bear thinking about, and a good many of the Gandons gave repeated surreptitious glances at the brides' side of the church to see if the black Countess had sneaked over from Jamaica at the last moment to embarrass them all.

But she was still safely in Jamaica, kept there by the merciful poverty of her disreputable old husband, and in fact at the very moment that her stepdaughter was promising to love honour and obey her bridegroom Cecil, the Countess was cooking breakfast for the Earl, slicing ripe Julie mangoes over the dish of pimento rice and baked sunfish, with waffles on the side.

Outside the hut the Earl was sitting bare to the waist under a mango tree, composing rude telegrams to his daughter that he couldn't afford to send. He read them out in his cracked, cackling voice to Marcia, through the window of the hut, and she shrieked with laughter. 'Heh heh, Lawdy God, dat tell her off for de bitch dat girl is. Tell her too if she come back here wit' her airsy graces I give her tail a right warming wit' a powful cane.'

Lady Honoria came down the aisle like a white kitten dressed in oyster satin by Dior, her golden fairytale hair hidden under a veil of Brussels lace, her red lips parted in the half-smile of a kitten who sees the window of the larder left six inches open.

She was Lady Honoria Gandon. It had taken the last of her mother's legacy to land him, but she had landed him, and now the whole, immense, immeasurable world of the Gandon wealth lay spread before her, like a sea of milk. She laid her sharp-nailed little hand on Cecil's arm, and he gazed down at her, his mouth open, one leg of his morning suit contriving to look longer than the other, his stoop, that had managed to survive two years in the Irish Guards, making his six feet of willowy thinness seem bent protectively over her white purity.

Lord Alfred, active head of the Gandon concerns now that the old Earl of Beswick was a permanent invalid in the enormous villa outside Mentone, said the 'Our Father' through clenched teeth and prayed that in spite of all indications this girl would not turn out to be one more of 'that kind'. There was still a Countess of Beswick, the old Earl's third wife, floating round the world on an aircushion of alimony, and lavishing herself on a succession of lovers from Rio de Janeiro to Antibes. Every generation of Gandons seemed to be given at least one such woman as its penance, and Lord Alfred was grimly prepared to find that Lady Honoria was theirs.

The wedding reception was at the Dorchester, after which the bride and groom flew to Venice, to spend a month in the Gandon villa near Iesolo, where the family was developing some land as a holiday resort. Afterwards they were to fly on to South Africa, where Cecil was to become acquainted with some of the family's African undertakings. Lord Alfred had written privately to his cousin Julius, managing director of Tintagel Holdings (Pretoria) Ltd, that he would be most grateful if Julius could by any means induce Cecil and his bride to remain in South Africa indefinitely.

* * *

In Dublin, in the offices of the *Sunday Freeman*, where they were making up the society page with large pictures of the Gandon wedding and a rather romanticized version of the bride's background, supplied by the bride, Felicity O'Connor was trying to get a job.

'How do you know I can't write?'

The chief reporter looked at her with middle-aged, sardonic eyes. 'Go and write something,' he said. 'Impress me.' And then, because he was a kind man when he could afford to be, he said, 'Look, this isn't a job for a girl. And if you were a man there still wouldn't be a job. *There isn't any work.*'

A reporter, and two or three of the subs from the sub-editors' table beyond, lifted their heads to look. Her again. The fat girl from Connemara. She stood by the chief reporter's desk looking down at it, one hand resting on the edge of the scarred, ink-stained wooden top. She didn't even know why she wanted to write, what she wanted to write. Except that she did.

'They said in school I wrote the best essays of anyone.'

The chief reporter shaded his eyes with one hand and scribbled with the other. 'I'm sorry,' he said. 'There isn't anything.'

'Couldn't I be a sub-editor?'

'*Go away.*'

She began to cry, not as blackmail, but because she couldn't help it. 'If I showed you some of my essays——'

The chief reporter threw his pencil down and it rolled on to the floor. She picked it up and gave it to him with tear-stained humility. He looked at her and sighed, thinking of his own children, who in not many years' time would also be looking for work and getting snarled at by ill-tempered, underpaid men.

'I need a drink,' he said. 'If you promise me not to come back here for at least a week I'll stand you a cup of coffee and tell you what a horrible, lousy, rotten life this is.'

They went out together and the sub-editors and the only other reporter who was in stared after them with astonished eyebrows and then a snigger.

In the bar she asked for a gin and orange and sat trying to look sophisticated as she sipped it, not really listening to anything he said. A bar. A journalists' bar. She sucked in the atmosphere as if she was a sponge. The little old man in the corner like a dwarf in a black hat, like a leprechaun. The fat man with the red nose. The man who was shouting that Peadar had had it coming to him. The man in the long mackintosh reading a book as if he was alone, instead of being surrounded by people almost standing on top of him with their elbows in his face.

Dublin. Writing. Journalism. She felt her heart beating, pushing up into her throat. She thought of Drifin. Of the bar there, like a desert island most of the time, unless some of the fishermen were in from Inis Beag, or Tim Bourke the ferryman was collecting groceries to take across, or one of the sheep farmers was down from the hill trying to court Mary Lowry, or her father was home, staggering in with a couple of drunks he'd picked up in Galway or Leenane, telling them that everything he had in the world was theirs, they only had to name it and they could have it. With her mother standing white-faced at the top of the stairs, gripping the poker in case he was at the violent stage.

She felt the need to write like a physical need inside her body, like the kind of feelings she and Eithne and Dymphna had talked about in school, that made the blood come like a hot tide into her face, even into her hands.

'You don't understand,' she said.

'I've got to get back,' he said. He shouldn't have brought her here. He hadn't thought of her as anything except a fat girl, almost a child. But a couple of men were looking at the pair of them when they thought he wasn't noticing, and the next thing someone would be ringing up Janet and telling her he was off boozing in pubs with a pick-up. If she wasn't so fat she might be quite a good-looking girl. Brought up on potatoes, and bloated out like a balloon. But that wouldn't stop some of these bastards imagining things.

'How does anybody get started,' she said, 'if no one'll let them try?' She was crying again. Someone was going to come over if he didn't get her out of here.

'For God's sake stop snivelling,' he said. He stood up, shielding her from the rest of the bar as well as he could. 'All right, I'll give you a chance, only come out of here.'

'Wh . . . wh . . . what——?'

'Go on one of these diets,' he said, cruelty breaking through against his will. 'Go on one of these beauty courses,' he amended it to, 'you know, gymnasium, face-do, you see them advertised all over the place.' He was getting himself in deeper and deeper.

'How—how will I pay for it?' But the tears were vanishing, giving place to an incredulous wonder.

'Tell 'em to send us the bill. Up to ten quid.' The editor would kill him, lacerate him. Ten quid! 'Try to keep it around five.' Oh God. He steered her out. Half a dozen men he knew took pains to say, 'Hi, Jim! Introduce us?'

'My cousin,' he lied grimly. 'Up from the country.'

'What will I do then?'

'Write it up for us.' They were standing in the summer dark, neon signs flashing for sausages, for beer, Failte, An Tostal, Fly Aer Lingus. Suddenly, before he could stop her, she had grabbed hold of his shoulders, lifting herself on to tiptoe, and kissed his cheek. Then she was running up the pavement away from him, her heart choking her throat. She'd begun, she'd begun. Felicity O'Connor, Dublin Journalist. She'd begun.

5

The day after he had seen the house in Chesterfield Square Francis O'Rourke arranged to buy it. He called not on the auctioneers, seeing no point in paying a commission if he could avoid it, but on the solicitors having carriage of sale; Messrs Montgomery and Strood of Baggot Street.

A woman in her sixties with iron-grey hair coiled over her ears and a disapproving expression sat knitting behind a glass hatch. She wore grey woollen mittens and her hands scurried over the shapeless length of grey wool like fat little moles on a grey lawn. When Mr O'Rourke tapped on the glass she went on knitting, not even looking up, her lips moving as she counted the stitches.

'Yes?' she said at last, holding the knitting suspended.

'I've come about a house in——'

'Have you got an appointment?'

'No, I——'

'Mr Montgomery doesn't see anyone without an appointment.' She started to close the hatch.

'Mr Strood then.'

'Mr Strood is dead.' She said it with something like triumph. For years after the old gentleman's death she had been in the absent-minded habit of sending clients up to his waiting-room where they had sat with elderly patience for as much as an hour before a kindly messenger boy or passing clerk told them that Mr Strood had died in 1947. But if she no longer sent people up to Mr Strood she had not yet brought herself to send anyone in to his successor, Mr O'Hara, Mr Strood's grand-nephew, young master Johnny. And she was the more determined not to because she didn't approve of him. He was, if she had permitted herself to describe him at all, 'coarse'.

'You'll have to write for an appointment,' she said firmly, and shut the hatch tight.

Francis O'Rourke lost the last of his patience and shoved the hatch open again. 'You've got a telephone there,' he said in what he thought was a quiet, controlled voice. '*Use it!*'

Miss Frewen dropped her knitting and screamed. A youngish, powerfully built, low-sized man came out of the office across the corridor. He hadn't heard the scream, which was a small, genteel gesture of alarm and disgust rather than a real cry for help, but he saw that the man at the hatch was on the point of doing Miss Frewen some kind of injury, and tapped him on the shoulder. Francis O'Rourke swung round, his face scarlet with rage.

'By God!' he said. 'I come here to try and buy a bloody house——'

'Master John!' cried Miss Frewen. 'This—this man—he——'

'All right, Miss Frewen, I'll take care of it.' He steered Mr O'Rourke into his own office. He had not yet been allowed to take over Mr Strood's vacant suite of offices on the first floor and had been given instead the cubbyhole that had once belonged to Mr Fortescue the Head Clerk, who had died in 1941 and had not been replaced.

'Our Miss Frewen,' he said apologetically. 'What can we do for you?'

Mr O'Rourke sat down, his temper cooling slightly. Across the desk he saw a man that he found himself liking on sight, which was unusual enough to astonish him. Most people he dealt with in any kind of business he regarded as opponents to be beaten into the ground on first encounter. If you don't kick them fast they'll kick you. Weak opponents he regarded as bloody fools and went on kicking them. Strong opponents he regarded as chancers and bloody crooks, and might, after several struggles, come to respect. But to like someone on first meeting was almost unique. Johnny O'Hara watched him with a sardonic eye and smile as if he knew exactly what was passing through Mr O'Rourke's mind. He too liked what he saw well enough. A self-made tough. He was himself so sick and tired of dust-laden gentility, of Miss Frewen, of old Mr Montgomery, of the memory of old Mr Strood and old Mr Fortescue, of the traditions of the firm and of the idea of having to wait for Mr Montgomery to die before he would be allowed to make any decisions of his own that anyone capable of pushing his head and shoulders through that hatch and threatening Miss Frewen was like the sight of a human footprint to Robinson Crusoe.

'Number 38 Chesterfield Square,' Mr O'Rourke said. 'What's the price?'

'Nine hundred. But haven't you been to the agents?'

'I'll give you five hundred. And what the hell have the agents done to earn a commission?'

Johnny O'Hara put his head back and laughed. He had a pale, meaty, boxer's face, and a long slash of a nose that had been broken more than once in several years of playing rugby. 'They haven't done a bloody thing,' he said, 'but they'll have to get it just the same. Eight hundred.'

A quarter of an hour later they closed on five fifty plus commission and the usual fees and duties.

'We'll treat you right on the fees. And I'll see if I can talk Moberley and Gunn into taking a cut on their commission. As a matter of fact I'm meeting Paddy Gunn for lunch if you'd like to come.'

Francis O'Rourke's first impression of Patrick Aloysius Gunn was 'spoiled priest'. And for all the years they were to know each other that basic impression never changed. He came to respect him, but never to like him. There was something catlike, feminine, old-young about him, in his quiet, persuasive voice, his smile that always suggested that he knew more than he was willing to tell. He couldn't be more than thirty, the same age as Johnny O'Hara, and nearly ten years younger than Francis O'Rourke, but already there was an agelessness in his face, in his almost colourless, nondescript hair brushed carefully sideways from the ruler-straight parting that lay almost along the centre line of his narrow nondescript head. It was impossible to believe that he had ever done anything on the spur of the moment, ever lost his temper or shouted at anyone or had a fight. He seemed to have been born to live in the hushed, intriguing, watchful corridors of the Vatican, rather than a Dublin auctioneers'.

'He gives me the bloody pip,' Francis said later to Johnny O'Hara.

'He can give you a lot more than that if he wants to,' Johnny said. 'He's a lad to watch. Knight of St Brigid. In with all the right people. If you want to go into business here you couldn't do better than cultivate Paddy Gunn. He's still at the stage where he's flattered if people want him to help.'

'Are you a Knight?'

Johnny shook his head, smiling. 'Not my line. Are you?'

Francis O'Rourke also shook his head, but not with Johnny O'Hara's tolerant amusement. Rather with a kind of savagery. Bloody codacting, craw-thumping bloodless bastards that were half eunuchs before they started, dressing up in robes and swords and saying Novenas to get rich. Not that he knew anything about the Knights, except that they were religious, but that was enough. He'd had religion by the bloody bellyful as a poor little sod of an orphan with the Brothers, and it'd last him a lifetime.

'What a.e you going to do with the house when you've got it? Rebuild?' Johnny said. He had a habit of massaging his broken nose between his forefinger and thumb and the gristle inside it made a strange squeaking sound.

'Maybe,' Francis said.

'To live in yourself?'

Francis shook his head. 'Just an investment.' The vision of the brass plate drifted through his mind, made him feel defenceless and embarrassed under Johnny O'Hara's cool, permanently cynical stare. *Contractor. Limited.* He felt himself almost flushing, almost getting angry. 'I . . . we were thinking of coming back here to settle.' He hunched his massive, bull shoulders and squinted his eyes challengingly at Johnny, expecting to be told that he was out of his mind. But Johnny simply looked thoughtful, reflectively massaging his nose as if he was trying to mend it, see how badly it was bent.

'Depends if you can afford to hang on. As far as buying is concerned there won't ever be a better time. That house you're buying for five fifty. If you wanted to build it today it'd cost you ten times that. At least. And the site. Thirty feet by close to two hundred. Nearly the middle of the city. It'd make you laugh if it didn't make you cry. This town's not down on its knees, it's lying flat on its face.'

'What do you mean, "afford to hang on"?'

'It can't stay like this. It just can't. Things have got to start moving sooner or later, and there isn't anywhere for them to go except up. All it needs is a few things to happen——'

'Like what?'

'Like the Long Fellow shifting up to the Park and letting Sean Lemass take over. And some smart money starting to come in. This Common Market everyone's talking about. In a few years Europe's going to be one country. If property's cheaper here than anywhere else like it is now, people will come and buy it. Germans, French, Dutch, English, anyone who's got money.' He raised his flattened outstretched palm to show things going up. 'And if you're in on the ground floor.'

It was the first of a lot of meetings. Francis O'Rourke found himself telling Johnny O'Hara things he'd hardly told himself. The things he was working for. Something beyond money that he could scarcely put into words. Even the brass plate. And in spite of their difference in background Johnny O'Hara understood what he was talking about, what he meant. He might laugh at it, but he understood it, and behind the mockery he wasn't really laughing.

Francis also saw more of Paddy Gunn. He still didn't like him but he felt drawn to him like being drawn to a closed door, wanting to know what lay behind it. The sale of the house went through, and Paddy found him a house in Terenure to rent for five pounds a week, full of antique furniture that Maura never stopped complaining about. The dusting and the polishing. He had Johnny O'Hara in for drinks, and Paddy, and Johnny's brother Seamus, the T.D.

'Poor old Seamus,' Johnny said. 'As thick as a bloody post. But everybody likes him because he's too stupid to be any competition. Paddy Gunn says Seamus'll finish up as Prime Minister while all the others are killing each other.'

Another time Seamus O'Hara brought along Marty Mullins, Government T.D. for North Connemara, a fat, asthmatic, breathless man with little, shrewd eyes over sagging cheeks and big jowls, and a tightly bulging stomach under a greasy waistcoat with a thick gold watchchain looping across it. There was also Jim Hegarty from the *Sunday Freeman* and a man called Knowles in the Corporation. They talked about business, and what a man could do with a few thousand pounds if he knew his way round.

There were even one or two concrete suggestions, qualified by warnings that while this or that stroke might make a quick few hundred, anything bigger than that would need to be looked at as very long term.

'We aren't going to see anything of a change this side of five years,' Marty Mullins said. 'Depression everywhere. The Long Feller thinking the Irish Language is more important than keeping people alive. Not that'—he raised a pudgy, short-fingered hand quickly in warning and qualification—'not that the language isn't important, mind you. Ireland Gaelic, Ireland free. I'll give place to nobody in favour of the language, don't mistake me, Johnny. Don't get me wrong, Mr O'Rourke.' He shot a quick, cunning glance round his audience from his bright, boot-button eyes, assessing the need for caution. He was not at his ease in a room like this. In Moriarty's Bar, or any corner of his constituency, he didn't have to draw breath to know the tone to take, but here, separated from his hat that someone had hung up for him in the hall, and sitting in a softly upholstered armchair, instead of on a bar-stool or a hard kitchen chair, he felt unsure. But Francis O'Rourke's red face reassured him. This wasn't the kind of man that went round acorgering and mishlemashing.

'I don't yield to a living sinner on the question of the language,' he said, 'but a man has to eat as well as talk, and if we all want to eat three times a day there'll have to be changes, there'll have to be priorities. And by God we won't see any of the right sort of changes while the Long Feller is in the driver's seat.' He said it comfortably enough, because even under Eamonn de Valera's puritannical régime he had managed to eat his three meals a day and something besides, but it was a matter of principle. And like a lot of the others in the party he was getting impatient with the old shackles. 'A great man, God bless him. We'll never see a greater. But he's out of touch with realities, you have to admit it. Although, of course, the way things are, this is the time to buy. If you've got the money.' He smoothed his bulging stomach with a fond expression, the heavy gold chain clinking softly under his small, fat fingers, the breath wheezing in his chest.

'That's what I've been telling Franky,' Johnny said.

'I've me eye on a bit of a deal down my part of the world,' Marty said carelessly. 'Your part too, if I'm not mistaken, Mr O'Rourke. But it needs a bit of backing, if you take my meaning. A bit of the ready. . . .'

Francis began to get the feel of Dublin, although none of it was immediately encouraging. Maura was already nagging at him about going back to England.

'And get caught for eight thousand quid tax? Are you bloody mad?'

'What are we going to do here? What are we going to live on? How much have you spent since we came back?'

'You mind your own bloody business.'

'And who helped you make any money in the first place? Who told you you were mad working for Morgan's instead of for yourself?'

'And what do you think I'm doing now? Working for De Valera? I've got to get started somehow, haven't I? I'm making contacts, putting out feelers.'

'You're having a good rest as far as I can see.'

'All right, all right. I'm having a rest. The first bloody holiday I've had in five years. Do you mind?'

'Three months of a holiday. D'you think you're a gentleman, living on your rents? Four pounds ten a week out of that old wreck of a house in Chesterfield Square.'

'And if I bought ten houses like that? Twenty houses? Ninety pounds a week. Do you think the only way to make money is the way you start?'

'I know the way to lose money. And that's to stop working.'

'I haven't stopped working since I was fourteen. Leave me alone.'

But for that conversation and several like it he might never have listened to Paddy Gunn's suggestion about Castle Lennox. 'It's just come on the market,' Paddy said. 'Down near your native county, Mr O'Rourke. One of the nicest parts of Mayo. What we house agents like to call a Gentleman's Residence.' His soft, monsignorial voice laid the lightest of stresses on *Gentleman's Residence*, and the corners of his mouth twitched for a moment with a dry, priestly smile. But by now Francis knew him well enough to recognize these half-smiles, these small clerical half-jokes as overtures of friendship, rather than as mockery. It was as near as Paddy Gunn could come to intimacy with anyone. 'It really is rather fine too. Early Georgian. And about ninety acres. Woodlands and a small lake, I believe, but they say there's some excellent grazing and a bit of arable. I think you really might find it a very interesting proposition.' Again the smile flickered at the corners of his mouth, hinting that he meant something quite different to, or much more than what he was saying. And also, though without intending to, that inside the spoiled priest, behind the smooth façade, the careful parting of the hair brushed resolutely, unadventurously sideways, there was quite a different kind of man, tougher, harder even than someone like the pirate Johnny O'Hara. A pirate's chaplain. 'You too, Mrs O'Rourke,' he said, turning his smooth face towards Maura. 'I think you might really lose your heart to it.'

They were having dinner in the house in Terenure, the children already in bed, the four of them sitting at the candlelit table; Paddy Gunn smiling softly; Johnny O'Hara looking down his long nose at his brandy glass as if he could see secrets in it, his eyes narrowed, ironically reflective; Maura opposite Francis, glowering at him whenever she thought that the other two men weren't looking at her, nervous of both of them. She had held her own with a lot of Irishmen in her time, kept them in order with nothing more than a lift of her open hand or even a raised eyebrow and a hard stare. But not this kind of man. Both of them, in slightly different ways, made her feel a fool, as if just from the fact of being a woman she must be a fool. Whenever they were there she felt as if she was going to drop things, or say something stupid, or burn the dinner. What in the name of God did Frank see in people like them, letting them butter him up like a stuffed turkey? It was easy enough to guess what they saw in Franky, though. Ninety acres! Early Georgian! And in Mayo! Did they think Franky was mad? She looked at him, a terrible suspicion flickering into her mind and out again. He couldn't. He couldn't be such a fool.

'We don't have those sort of ideas, Mr Gunn,' she said.

Paddy Gunn contrived to look at one and the same time as if he was deferring to her position as his hostess, and as if she had said nothing at all. 'You'd probably get it for about four thousand, you know. It's almost laughable when you think of what it ought to fetch.'

Maura closed her mouth in a hard line of hostility, not actually snorting but conveying a snort.

'What in the name of God would I be doing with a place like that?' Francis said, but Maura's expression and that inaudible snort made him say it with a different inflection to the one he had meant to use. A gentleman's residence. He thought of Drumleague, of his mother's cottage, of the Mangans, of the Feeneys, of the Brothers of Compassion and the Industrial School where from the age of five until he was fourteen he had been raised up in the fear of God and the strap. Ninety acres. Woods. A lake. It was bloody mad even to think about it, but at least it wouldn't cost anything to look at it. And they were about due to go down and see his mother again anyway. Let Maura look after the bloody kids and leave business to him.

That was Thursday. On Saturday the deal that Marty Mullins had begun to describe to him a couple of weeks before, and that he had gone into without telling Maura, brought in three hundred pounds cash profit.

He arranged a party to celebrate the deal, asking Marty and the others to bring anyone else they wanted to. Before Maura could start complaining about the extravagance of having a dozen strangers in, who'd think nothing of emptying a bottle of whiskey apiece before the evening was out, let alone asking them round without giving her more than a couple of hours' warning, he smacked the bundle of notes down on the dressing-table in front of her.

'Three hundred pounds,' he said. 'How's that now?'

She shrugged her still magnificent shoulders, screwing her mouth up to put on lipstick. As the weeks in Dublin had gone by, and become months, she had recovered some of her old dominance, at least when they were alone together.

'Three hundred pounds?' she said. 'In over three months? You used to pay a good labourer more than that.'

He crushed the wad of notes in his thick fist, wanting to smack it down like a hammer on to the dressing-table, but something in her eye stopped him. There had been a time when she had swung as heavy a fist as his, and not been afraid to use it.

'You'd better give me that,' she said. She held his eyes for a long moment in the mirror and at the end of it he was the one who looked away.

'God almighty!' he said. 'Any other bloody woman would be grateful.'

'For being hawked out of her home at a minute's notice and brought back here?'

He threw the money down in front of her with an inarticulate snarl and stumped away into the bathroom to relieve his feelings. It was so long since Maura had really stood up to him that he had forgotten what it was like. If she wasn't bloody careful he'd give her such a thump she wouldn't forget it this side of Christmas. But he went downstairs without going back into the bedroom, and busied himself arranging the drinks and the glasses until the first of the guests arrived.

Half the people he didn't know. Eddie Knowles brought his brother, a priest, and his brother's friend, also a priest, a Father Herbert Tracey, the two of them on their way to Rome. They were both young, with that peculiar, skinned youngness that newly ordained priests have, as if their nerve-ends were nearer the surface than laymen's are; laughing too heartily at jokes and too eager to please. Father Tracey in particular seemed mentally and physically raw, as though every word said to him, every glance at him, caused him pain. Paddy Gunn surrounded the two priests with a cocoon of attention, bringing them drinks and biscuits—lemonade for Father Tracey, whiskey for Father Knowles—deflecting awkward remarks and people.

Johnny O'Hara nudged Francis, narrowing his eyes to sardonic slits, like splinters of dark glass, nodding towards Paddy Gunn and his charges. 'He's nursing the young vines,' he said. 'Baby bishops. When you see those two lads again you won't recognize them.' He made a sleek outline in the air to indicate a well-filled soutane. 'From the way Paddy's acting they must be marked out for big things.'

Jim Hegarty had brought a girl. 'Interested?' Paddy said, nudging Francis again, half an hour later. 'Also a Culchie.'

Francis felt his face going red, as if his thoughts had been visible. 'If she was a daughter of mine,' he said, 'and she went out in a dress like that I'd smack her bottom.' More bloody bosom than dress and so tight on her you could practically see her navel. Before he could stop him Paddy had brought the girl over.

'Felicity O'Connor,' Paddy said. 'Francis here thinks that what you need is a smacked bottom.'

It hadn't been an easy start to a conversation and the thought of Maura seeing him talking to the girl didn't make it any easier. 'Don't you like my dress?' she had said. She had a queer, husky voice that seemed to give more meaning to what she said than the words themselves. 'Or do you believe girls shouldn't drink?' She had a glass of whiskey in her hand and gave the distinct impression that it wasn't the first or second of the evening.

'Arrah don't mind Paddy,' he said uncomfortably. 'What d'you do?'

'I'm a journalist actually.' There was already a layer of Rathgar over the original Connemara. She was still at the stage where everything about Dublin impressed her: accent, people, sophistication. Later again she'd take some trouble to get rid of all the Dublin refinery and go back to being more Connemara than she had ever truthfully been. It would take a long time for the pendulum to settle down where it had begun. She had a rush of honesty. 'Well, I've just begun being a journalist.' She told him about the make-yourself-a-new-woman Beauty Course that had started it all. 'D'you know, I lost two stone!'

You kept it in the right places, he thought. He could practically see down between them. God Almighty. He kept watching for Maura out of the corner of his eye, but Paddy had nailed her on the far side of the room, playing up to her and flattering her. The thought crossed his mind that she might even be taking Paddy seriously. She certainly looked as if she had begun to like it. And after all she'd said about him these past months. It made him feel restless, remembering years ago, before they were married and all those bloody fly-by-nights in Ma Cooney's hanging round her. Didn't she know what age she was?

'I think I'm boring you,' she said.

'Of course you're not.' What the hell did Maura think she was at? The girl put her hand on his sleeve, almost leaning on him.

'Could I do an article about you? About how you made your money in England? The Returned Emigrant?' She still had a way of looking at men as if she thought they were wonderful simply for being men. It was a long way from being genuine. And equally a long way from being a 'come-on'. It was a defence. But it made her seem suddenly warm and close and defenceless to Francis O'Rourke.

'When I've made any money I'll tell you,' he said roughly, but he couldn't help sounding pleased. 'And who the hell'd want to read an article about me?'

'Lots of people,' Felicity said huskily. '*I* would.'

'My leg doesn't pull as easily as that,' he said, and at the same moment Paddy Gunn brought Eddie Knowles and his brother over to him to say good-bye and someone else got hold of the girl, and soon afterwards Jim Hegarty took her away, saying that he had to get to work. But he found himself thinking about her several times that night, and during the following days, and she was still occupying a corner of his mind as he drove the family down to Connemara, with a detour to look at the place that Paddy Gunn had recommended to him.

It was her voice that he remembered, husky and somehow helpless, as if she needed to be looked after. And the same kind of helpless look in her eyes. Don't hurt me. Maura had never had that kind of look. He smiled at the thought of it. The sound of the children squabbling in the back of the car—no longer the hired Buick, but a big American Ford that he'd bought cheap because it was too big for anyone but a taximan or a madman to want—the squabbling of the children about who had kicked who first broke through his thoughts and he shut them up with a growl that reduced them to mice. Maura stared sullenly out of the window. She didn't want to visit his mother. She didn't want to see Castle Lennox. And they had had another argument about going back to England. She was getting too big for her boots altogether.

She always had been, except for the last few years when he'd had the contract work really rolling in and there wasn't anything she could shout about. His mind went back a long way. A man was a bloody madman to get married. Ma Cooney's in Camden Town, where Maura had been a servant. The smell of cabbage and hash and fried snoek. Even then, during the war, Ma'd been so fat she could hardly move. Maura running the place. Banging the mats. Getting the lads out of bed that had to go on an early shift. And any of them that tried to grab her when they woke getting a thump on the ear that would have stretched them if they hadn't already been lying down. She'd been a bloody handsome lump of a girl in those days, there wasn't any arguing about that. A bust on her like a Christmas dinner. And a way of looking at you as if she didn't care if you lived or died that in those days had made a lot of men mad eager to make her care.

It was almost why he'd married her, that feeling that she wouldn't remember his name if he stayed away from her for a week. And that Norwegian. The only time he'd ever seen her look really interested in a man—except himself of course—was that fellow. He looked in the driving-mirror without thinking what he was doing and caught a glimpse of his older son, Joseph, big and blond and smiling, sitting happily in the middle of the back seat, having let his sister and his baby brother take the window seats just as he'd let anyone take anything else rather than fight for it.

It was a bloody mad thing to think of. They were married a good ten months before the kid was born and the Norwegian had gone back to his ship two days before the wedding. Mad. It was only the colour of his hair really, and lots of people had kids with hair a different colour to theirs. If only the boy had a bit more inside his head, whatever about what he had outside it. If he didn't start showing a bit more gumption soon he was going to spend his life getting walked on. He wanted to shout at him but there was nothing he could think of to shout at him about. It was bloody unnatural a kid being like that. Christ, if he'd been like that he'd have been dead by that age.

He thought of the school, the skin of his fingers crawling in remembrance of chilblains breaking, of being hungry always, summer and winter. Being frightened always. Until he learned that the only thing to do if you were frightened was to go up to whoever frightened you and give them a smack right between the eyes. And then kick them. Except that you couldn't do that with the Brothers.

Or with old Mrs Mangan afterwards, when the Brothers got him a job. Two and six a week and his keep, and Christ between him and a thrashing worse than he ever got from the Brothers if he so much as took an egg or a couple of slices of bread extra to fill himself when she wasn't looking. Her hands like a pair of wooden wash-paddles and her voice like the wind shrieking over a ridge. 'Franky! Did ye feed the calf! Did ye dig the potatoes? Where's the eggs I left on the windy sill? There's one missing! C'm 'ere ye villain till I teach ye what stealing means!'

'Missus I didn't, Jesus——'

'Swearin' and cursin' on top of stealin' is it? Where's me stick till I teach you something and I a poor widow woman takin' you in for charity to your poor widowed mother.'

It had taken him two years to save enough money to run away

from her. Enough to buy trousers and a jacket and a pair of boots, and his ticket to Liverpool. It was a long time now since he'd worn a pair of boots. But he could remember the feel of them as if they were still on his feet. The leather stiff as iron, cutting into his ankles. Like iron weights. And the ring of them on the road. He must have looked like some kind of a Mickey Mouse going down to the station, more boots than boy. But they'd done him well enough. Better. They'd won him his first fight in Liverpool.

Outside the Labour, and a big feller from Mayo who was on for chasing him away as a Connemara brat. 'Get home to a feed of seaweed you little black runt.' He'd got in under his guard and given him a kick on the kneecap that had stretched the big Mayo gom like a telegraph pole hit by a tractor. But he'd thought it wiser not to stay in Liverpool after that and gone down to London and a job on the White City foundations. Swinging a pick as heavy as himself till the head of sweat on him blinded his eyes and he thought the stomach would fall out of him. Jobs on the roads. Airfield runways. Trenches for cables. Pick and shovel. Callouses coming on his hands like cobbler's leather. Sending his mother two pounds on a Friday night and the rest drunk by Monday. Drinking in the Irish pubs, where only the Irish labourers dared go drinking and then only if it was a pub that was favoured by their own county. God help the Connemara boy that wandered into a Mayo pub. Coming out staggering, the drink in his brain like a dark volcano, his stomach in a black knot of vomit. Gaol cells and policemen's boots, and the shaking horror of Monday morning and the trench going up and down as he tried to hit the earth with his pick.

Navvies' digs, ten beds in a room, a pound a week per bed, and sleeping with his boots under his pillow in case they were stolen in the night, or a man filled one of them with urine.

Thickening up and out until he wasn't a boy any more, not a scrawny crow-haired starveling who had to kick and run, but a man built like a tree stump and as hard to shift. When the war came he'd been a ganger, because he could read and write and fight as well as knowing the job. It was that that had first brought him back to Ireland, looking for men. He'd been working for Morgan's, who depended almost entirely on Irish labour to keep going. But a man could only stay with them for six months before he was liable for call up for the Forces. So every six months men left and had to be replaced. He started going over to Dublin for the week-end to comb the pubs. Morgan's gave him his expenses and five pounds a man and the lodging-houses gave him another pound per customer.

Not Ma Cooney, who kept herself several cuts above the navvy trade. He stayed there himself by then, except on the job. About the third time he stayed with Ma, it was Maura who opened the door to him. A fine, big girl half a head taller than he was, with white arms and a white throat, like milk, and a red mouth and the richest, thickest hair he had ever seen.

He stole a look sideways at her in the car. By God, she was still a fine woman if she'd only keep her bloody mouth shut. He felt an absurd temptation to put his hand on her knee and squeeze it, but she'd think he'd lost his mind, particularly in front of the children.

'Shut up!' he shouted automatically, and the children, who had been squabbling so softly they hadn't believed they could be heard, shot bolt upright like electric rabbits starting out of a trap.

'Can't you leave the children alone ever?'

Baby Dermot began to fidget, and then to snivel.

'What is it lovey, what is it mummy's precious pet?'

'I want to do a wee-wee.'

'Jesus Christ, is it a hot-water bottle he is instead of a child?' He jerked the car to a stop so suddenly that all three children slid off the back seat into a heap on the carpeted floor.

'Can't you look what you're at, nearly breaking our noses and flinging us through the front?'

He sat glowering as first Dermot and then everyone else got out for their necessities. He realized furiously that he wanted to go himself, but out of sheer obstinacy he wouldn't. 'Jesus, Mary and Joseph,' he said as his wife clambered back into the car. 'Do you want to be showing yourself to the whole damn townland?'

A rear end on her like a bus. She sat sullenly furious and they went on, the need to stop again growing on him by the second. Ten miles to Ballycare. And this place of Paddy's two miles farther up another fork of the road. He'd hold it if it killed him. He should have come by himself. Or—the edge of a thought trailed through the back of his mind that it might have been no harm to bring somebody else. For company. And for an instant a husky voice whispered in his mind, '*I* would.' Round face, plump little throat, that bust on her, that dress. The way a bloody woman should be instead of shouting and roaring and telling a man how to run his own business and sticking her great big backside in the air round a furze bush like a cow backing through a gate. He was going to burst.

They passed a cottage with a licence sign. 'I'm going in for a drink,' he said. Again everyone slid forward, their noses on top of the back of the seat in front, or in Maura's case with her head nearly through the windscreen. Before Maura could collect herself to complain he was out of the car.

'I want a glass of water,' Baby Dermot said, still too young to know about Coca-Cola.

'I want a lemonade,' Venetia said.

Francis came back into the small dark bar from the yard at the rear buttoning his trousers, to find his entire family trooping in after him. 'God Almighty!' he said. 'What the hell do you all want?'

'Isn't it natural they'd want something to drink and they sitting hours and hours in that hearse afraid to open their mouths, and the day boiling them?'

'There's nothing natural about those bloody children.'

An old woman, in a shawl despite the boiling of the day, crept out of somewhere and took their orders, so much dust on the lemonade bottle that it looked like a vintage wine from a cellar. 'We're going to be late,' Francis said sourly. 'We're supposed to be there at four o'clock.'

They were half an hour late, after taking the wrong fork. Stone gateposts, one leaning awry. An avenue of trees. Cows grazing. A big square grey house.

'I suppose we're going to buy this as an investment?' Maura said. Francis gritted his teeth and said nothing. A big dog like a shaggy greyhound came bounding out in front of the car. Gravel crunched under the wheels. A man came through the open front doorway; down the two stone steps. Thickset, broadshouldered, the polo-necked sweater under the old sports jacket making him look like a boxer with his short neck and padded cheeks under the shock of dark brown hair. Where had he seen him before?

'Mr O'Rourke? I'm John Lennox.'

The boy at London airport. God almighty. The same bastard. Who'd taken the last taxi at Dublin airport the same afternoon. Jesus. A slow feeling of triumph began to spread from his stomach through his whole body. So he wanted to sell this place, did he? Gentleman's residence and ninety acres, and no gentleman's income to keep it going. Well, they could have a nice gentlemanly half-hour discussing it together, and at the end of it he would have great pleasure in telling this haw-haw bankrupt what he could do with his Georgian ruin and his ninety acres of bog.

'Mrs O'Rourke?' John Lennox was saying, holding out his hand. Baby Dermot was pulling at his mother's skirt, shifting from one small foot to the other.

'I want to do a wee-wee,' he whispered. 'Mammy, Mammy, I want to do a wee-wee.'

Francis felt the veins in his head swelling. He'd kill him, he'd give him such a belting he'd never forget it if he lived to be ninety.

'Oh dear,' Maura said. She had meant to keep an icy silence for as long as they were in the place, but that was hardly possible in the face of Baby Dermot's agitated whispering and plucking fingers. 'I am sorry, Mr Lennox, but you know what children are. And it's been such a long journey.' If she could only get hold of Frank and kill him. The shame of it.

'I'll call my wife,' John Lennox said. 'If you'll bring him in.' He seemed to Francis to be concealing a smile of malice and of triumph at an enemy's humiliation.

I'd give a hundred quid to belt him one right in his teeth,

Francis thought, following the straggle of his family through the front doorway of Castle Lennox. Like a bloody mother duck with a load of ducklings. Baby Dermot detached himself from her hand and stood still.

'Pick him up,' Francis shouted. 'Pick him up, dammit.'

But it was too late.

'I'm doing my wee-wee,' Baby Dermot said with pleased surprise.

6

There had been neither malice nor triumph in John Lennox's smile. If there had been anything there beyond a thin attempt at politeness it had been anger and humiliation. They had been waiting for the O'Rourke family since half-past three, sitting in the drawing-room without talking to each other, each of them pretending to be reading. The time for talking about it, even for quarrelling about it, had long gone by. They had already had three months of that, waiting for probate of the will. The house, estate, immoveables and moveables, to my grandson John Lennox to dispose of at his absolute discretion. Also the residue of money left after the few bequests. Fifteen hundred pounds to Kate. Five hundred to Agnes, the housekeeper. Seven hundred to old Tim, the gardener, who had spent his entire life at Castle Lennox. Some silver to the Archdeacon. Some silver and a painting to Kate's mother. Some small oddments to old friends, most of them already dead.

'I wonder what we'll get for the place,' John had said, and that had started it. The long, irrational argument descending into a bitter quarrel. 'How can we keep it? How? Selling eggs? How would we pay the rates? Wages? For God's sake try and be reasonable.'

But she wouldn't, couldn't be that. Not about the place she had thought of as her home. 'You weren't even born here.' Perhaps that was the reason. Born in London, living in army married quarters in Aldershot, or Catterick, until she was eight years old. This house had been the first real home she had known and she had loved it twice over because she had known what it was like even as a child to have no real home, not even a real country. Evacuated because of the war, seeing Ireland at last, the magic Ireland of her mother's and father's casual conversation. The word *Mayo* like fairyland, out of a storybook. She had thrown herself into being Irish, into living in Ireland, with a childish and yet somehow unchildish passion that John had never been able to understand.

Where he had learned Irish under protest, because he had to, at school, she had learned it for love, just as she had learned Shelta, because it belonged to Ireland, to the West.

She had found her tutor in the Colonel. His own sense of passionate Irishness had sprung from a different cause, from the romantic nationalism of the 1880s and 1890s that had drawn as many Protestant gentry as Catholic working men into its enthusiasms. The kind of enthusiasms that in Yeats and Martyn and Lady Gregory and Synge had created the Irish theatre, and in Douglas Hyde had created the Irish nation. For the Colonel it had led no further than learning Irish and compiling a manuscript history of Mayo in one hundred and forty-three exercise books. It had not prevented him volunteering for the British army on 7 August 1914, at the age of forty-five, putting himself down as twenty-nine, but it had made him friends among the local Republicans, and when he had returned to Mayo in January 1919 he had come home not as a demobilized British officer but as an open Republican sympathizer. During the next three years he and Castle Lennox had been in more danger from the Tans and the Auxiliaries than from the I.R.A.

During the next thirty years he had seen the ideals he had believed in turn into hypocrisies, seen them bought and sold and made indecent by men like Marty Mullins, but he had still believed that under the gombeen crust of Eire there still burned the pure fire of Erin, and he had tried to pass this belief on to his grandson and his grand-niece. It had always made John slightly embarrassed or impatient, or amused. But Kate had drunk it in as gospel.

The more so because her own family background was 'old Irish', Gaelic, her father an O'Donnell, her mother an O'Connor, her mother's mother an O'Malley, of the stock of Grace O'Malley, or so the Colonel claimed. When they had been children she had more than once attempted to squash her cousin John by reminding him that he came of planter stock, settled a mere three hundred years in the country. To which he had replied that at least his ancestors had been born Protestants, while hers had converted. 'For soup, probably.'

But those had been children's fights that flare into the open and vanish ten minutes later. This one hardly broke into an open fight at all. There was nothing rational to fight about. And on the afternoon of the O'Rourkes' arrival they had merely sat not talking to each other, or being painfully polite about trivialities, while John swore to himself that if this man O'Rourke or whatever his name was didn't make him an offer he'd go back to England next week and leave the keys with old Tim. And if Kate wanted to stay here, let her. The agents could sell the place over her head.

It was only when he heard the car come up the avenue that the phrase 'sell the place' suddenly changed its significance from getting rid of something he didn't want to having his home taken away from him. And for a second he felt exactly what Kate had been feeling for three months. But before he could tell her the car was on the gravel outside and he had to go to the door.

He loathed Francis O'Rourke on sight. He loathed his brick-red face and ragged black moustache. He loathed his tweed suit and his silk handkerchief and his yellow silk tie with a horse on it. He loathed his enormous motor car glittering with chromium strips like a perambulating jukebox. He loathed his enormous wife in her satin dress and her pearl necklace and mink scarf. He loathed his children: the big boy like a tow-headed doll; the girl like a ferret in glasses with her father's black hair sticking out on either side of her head in tight little pigtails tied in green silk ribbons; the small boy with his sister's spiky nose and the same thick glasses and his sailor suit.

That these people, these monsters should be thinking of buying his house, parking that chromium hearse in the stables, putting up pony jumps in the meadow and telling their unspeakable friends that they lived in a 'Cassell'. He was not in the least surprised when the small boy stopped in the hall as if he'd arrived at a public lavatory, and wetted the floor. He wouldn't have been surprised if the father had done it.

'It doesn't matter at all,' he said icily. 'The floors had people walking on it for a couple of hundred years. I'm sure it can survive that.' He caught Kate's eye and tried to give her an understanding smile. To his fury, she began to overwhelm the O'Rourke woman with kindness. Not politeness, but kindness, laughing at what had just happened, making a joke of it, hurrying the mother and the child up the stairs to the bathroom, starting to tell some entirely fictitious story about what she had done at the same age when her mother had taken her to tea with the General's wife in Catterick. 'I wasn't satisfied with parquet floor, I'm afraid. The sofa!'

He would kill her. He would strangle her when he had her alone.

'Bloody kids,' Francis said. Venetia was plucking his sleeve. 'Christ. All right. Go after her.' He turned a mottled face to John. For the last time for many years their eyes met not as enemies, but as fellow men, linked by the common humiliation of being married. But it only lasted a moment.

'Nice place you've got here,' Francis said, grinding the words out.

'We've liked it,' John said. He leaned against the hall table, crossing his ankles and looking down at his shoes. The attitude of his shoulders said as clearly as he could make them say it, 'This is all a stupid waste of time. This isn't your kind of place, and if you did make me an offer I wouldn't accept it.' He was not usually a snob. He was not conscious of ever being one. He had simply hated Francis O'Rourke on sight, as the classic image of the kind of man he loathed most: the gombeen man, the peasant who had made good by treading on other peasants' faces; the kind of man who before 1921 would have made his living as bailiff for an absentee landlord. 'You sound as if you come from the West.'

'Connemara,' Francis said. 'But I've been away a long time.'

'I guessed that from the car.'

And you grudge me every wheel of it, Francis thought. But he said, 'I like a big car. Big houses too. Give the family a bit of space to spread out.'

John looked reflectively at the puddle on the parquet and smiled.

'And then when you buy an old place,' Francis said, 'it's got a bit of character about it. You can imagine the people who've been there before you.' He looked at the line of portraits climbing the stairs. 'Are you selling the pictures as well?'

'No,' John said, although they'd probably have to sell the best of them. There was a Sargent, and a Reynolds, and one or two more that should make a couple of hundred each.

'That's a pity. It's nice to keep these old places together if you can.' Francis was moving round the hall, adopting something of the manner of a cattle-buyer at a fair. All he needed was an ashplant stuck at a jaunty angle under his left arm. He was enjoying himself again. 'All these old bits and pieces.' He tapped a bronze bowl at the far end of the table and it rang softly, like a muffled gong. 'They go for nothing at an auction.'

'I don't know,' John said. 'I've never auctioned my house before.'

And never have one to auction again, as likely as not, Francis thought. 'Family been here long?' he said.

'Since 1650. But the house is only 1730-ish.'

'Ah,' said Francis. He managed to put a great deal of meaning into the *Ah*.

'You can't see him from here, but in the dining-room there's the portrait of the chap that came here first. They used to call him Henry the Hangman. He was a judge.'

'That was an unlucky name to leave behind him.'

'He lived with it long enough. He died the day after his eighty-fifth birthday, drinking his sixth bottle of claret of the evening. I believe the people lit bonfires when they heard he was dead.'

Kate and Maura and the children came down the stairs, Kate saying, 'Have you been getting acquainted? Mrs O'Rourke loves the house—or the bit she's seen of it.' Her voice was determinedly bright. They began a tour of the rooms, downstairs and up, cellars and attics, making small talk. Or rather, Kate making small talk and John trailing behind with his face dark as thunder and getting darker. Once, as the O'Rourkes were clustered together looking at the view from a bedroom window, Kate came back and whispered to him savagely, 'You bloody bastard.

You're the one who wants to sell the place. Don't be such a filthy snob.'

'Me?' Before he could go on the O'Rourkes were rejoining them.

'You've some nice cows there,' Francis said. He was remembering the Widow Mangan and her cows. He could see himself walking out of the front door here of a summer morning and the cows knee deep in grass. Poking one of them in the flank with his stick.

'They belong to a neighbour,' Kate said. 'We just rent them the grazing.'

John turned away to the door, kicking at a torn edge of carpet. What the hell was the bloody use? Let the bastard buy it, and find out afterwards that there was dry rot in the roof and that in winter it cost about five pounds a week even to keep the main rooms from having icicles in them. They went and had a look at the grounds.

'How much d'you want for the place?' Francis said. Maura dug him in the ribs and he knocked her hand away with his elbow.

'Four and a half,' John said sullenly.

Francis smiled. 'If you said three and a half.'

'It's getting late,' Maura said. 'Your mother——'

'Or even three seven fifty.'

They were standing at the entrance to the walled garden. Half an acre of what had once been a flower garden, and then a vegetable and herb garden, and was now run to every kind of seed, the paths grown with moss and tufts of grass. But the walls of red brick still held the warmth of the sun and there was a stone pedestal with a sundial and a garden table sheltered by old fruit trees, pear and apple and plum. Even Maura felt touched by its pleasantness for an instant or two. The quietness round them, the evening closing gently like a book, the peace. And then the very fact that she had been touched made her terrified of what Francis might do. 'Francis!' she whispered.

Kate turned away and looked at the trees behind them. The temporary relief of being polite, of behaving well while John was behaving abominably, had disappeared. He was going to sell, and there was nothing she could do about it. Nothing he could do about it. And it didn't matter much if it was now, to these people, or next month to someone even more awful. The half-hope she had had that no one would buy at all, that they'd be like some of the places she'd heard of recently that were waiting for buyers for two and three years, had vanished as she looked at the walled garden. She had known beyond doubting it that she was seeing it almost for the last time as its mistress. As if it had told her. When she and her mother had come there first she and John had never been allowed in the walled garden in case they broke the flowers. There had always been something magically forbidden about the old wooden door with its wrought-iron handle.

'If I said four thousand,' the man was saying.

Four thousand pounds for this. She was going to cry. She wanted to scream: No! *No! John, please!* She felt the tears coming, she couldn't see anything clearly, the trees only dark shapes seen through water running down a window-pane. Everything that she wanted to remember about her life was like a tight knot in her stomach, making her feel ill. Days, sun, picnics, reading a book, the small sitting-room, the dogs. Where had the dogs gone?

'I'm going to look for the dogs,' she said in a choked voice. 'The road . . .'

There was hardly any traffic on the road at the bottom of the avenue and they were probably in the stables, but it was an excuse to get away. She walked and then ran, half blind and stumbling over ruts in the drive. There was no sign of them. She stood by the leaning gatepost, looking down at the scar on the stone where the Archdeacon had almost knocked it down. He had come to lunch yesterday, neat and pink and silver in his beautiful dark grey suit that made him look like an old doll.

'I can't understand why John wants to give up the house,' he had said. 'A man should never give up his home.' Armoured by age and selfishness against all explanation, all intrusions of reality. He did not want to hear of people not being able to afford things and was still indignant that his brother had left him only the George II tea set. Since he already had an even finer one of his own Kate had thought that he was intending to give it back to them. Instead of that he had spent a long time explaining how badly off his own father had left him, because he had entered the Church. 'He thought a clergyman didn't need money, my dear,' the old silvery voice chuckling crossly. 'How very wrong he was.' Perhaps the whole performance was only to prevent John asking him for a loan. She felt as if her heart was being wrenched out of her body. As if everything was changing, crumbling, everything she had thought was unchangeable, like the hills, like summer. It had always been here, safe, eternal. When she was away in school. In London. In Kenya. It had still been here. The trees, the house, the garden, the river, the Connors in the wood; the dogs—where had they gone?—as if they knew what was happening. The rooks and Sunday tea and the log fires and Jenny, and Agnes making pastry and the scullery maids, always changing, but always looking the same, fat and laughing with wet red hands and chilblains and shoes that didn't fit. Old Tim. The Colonel. Her mother. Even living in Kenya with her mother and stepfather it had seemed in some part of her mind that her mother was really still here, doing futile things in the walled garden while old Tim followed her round undoing them; or embroidering the cushion cover that never got finished and that Patch ate in the end. Even the Archdeacon. Preaching on Sundays to the congregation of seven. The four of them from Castle Lennox and the two old old Gibson sisters, and Mr Burke who was deaf.

Like that for ever. She leaned against the stone gatepost topped with its cannonball from William's war with James and found she couldn't cry any more. As if she was too tired. She went back up the drive, dragging her feet. A lot of leaves had fallen. The dogs came bounding, first Shah, his mouth bright with rabbit blood, then Suki, finally Patch, fat and breathless and old. Thirteen. Looking at the world through clouding, milky eyes. She bent down and touched him. 'Oh, Patch, it's all over. Everything, everything is gone.' When she got back to the others they had agreed on four thousand and were having an awkward cup of tea in the drawing-room.

'You're wise to accept,' Francis was saying, ownership already written in his expression, the tone of his voice, the way he sat on the couch, his leg stuck out towards the fireplace as if he was already warming his foot at his own fire. She noticed he had a thickened sole to the shoe, as if one leg was slightly shorter than the other, and it gave an added sense of brutality to the man that made her want to shiver. 'It isn't everyone's taste, a place like this,' he was saying. 'And if you change your mind about the pictures, let me know. It needs something on the walls.'

Mrs O'Rourke sat by her husband, her mouth tight with fury, and at the same time with unbelieving terror. The children began to torment the dogs, and Shah snarled.

'They'll have to get used to animals,' Francis said tolerantly. 'I'll buy a couple of ponies and teach 'em to ride.' He looked sideways at John, who was leaning against the big stone mantelpiece, his face grim. You with your little hat and your big head, Francis was thinking, you're not shouting so loud now. Nor won't in future if I'm any judge.

He got to his feet with a slight grunt, thick and rough and bristly as a tree stump, shoving out his hand to say good-bye. John shook hands as if he was touching something unpleasant. Kate could barely see the man as he took hold of hers, and as he looked into her white face Francis guessed what he had done to her and felt suddenly ashamed. And then angry because he had been made to feel ashamed. 'Thanks for the cup of tea,' he said. 'We'll fix the rest through the agents.'

They all went out on to the gravel and the Lennoxes watched the O'Rourkes drive away. Shah ran a long way down the avenue, barking after the big, shiny car.

7

Within three months of agreeing to buy Castle Lennox, Francis O'Rourke had resold it at a net profit of twelve hundred pounds, to the Sisters of the Divine Suffering. Like the house itself, the Sisters came to him through Paddy Gunn, of Messrs Moberley and Gunn and Co., Auctioneers, Valuers and Estate Agents, established 1871.

'Suppose I don't want to sell?' Francis had said, feeling his heart racing. Paddy had smiled his gentle, religious smile, and said nothing. 'Well?' Francis said aggressively, his heart coming up into his throat. 'I'd want to make at least fifteen hundred.'

'Twelve hundred,' Paddy said, still smiling. 'It isn't bad, you know. You haven't had to pay for the place yet, except the deposit. You're better than doubling your money. He lifted his hand gently, as if he was already holding the cheque between his clean white fingers, preparing to drop it so cunningly that it would waft of its own accord into Francis O'Rourke's wallet.

'My wife'll be broken-hearted. She was looking forward to living there.'

'We could always find you somewhere else.'

'Why didn't they buy it right off? Why did you offer it to me first?'

'I wanted someone to hold it for them. They had to get permission from Rome before they could buy.'

Francis swallowed, undecided whether he ought to be furious or grateful. With the profit hanging in front of his eyes he thought it best to be grateful. If this didn't shut her up nothing ever would. He had already gone back to England to restart the digging contracts, and even that hadn't pleased her, because he hadn't brought her and the family with him. How could he? How the hell could he have them over there when any minute the income-tax could be down on top of him? The only way he could feel safe as it was was shifting from digs to digs every couple of weeks, and from one end of England to the other between contracts. He'd just finished one north of St Albans and was going back to another in Yorkshire when he'd collected a new gang. Four and a half miles of trench for a new electric cable. Fifteen, sixteen weeks of work. Seven thousand four hundred pounds to pay the men and himself. With a good gang, and luck, like not striking a mile of rock where it was supposed to be sand according to the surveyor, he'd have half of that as profit, less his own living expenses. Say three thousand five hundred clear, in three and a half, four months. And she still wasn't bloody well satisfied.

'I don't know what she wants,' he said to Johnny three days later. 'She's got my mother with her. She's got the kids.'

'Buy her a fur coat.'

'She has a fur coat.' He took the Sisters' cheque out of his wallet. 'What could I do with this? Could you use it for me while I'm away?'

'Long term or short?'

'Either. Long if you like. There's no real hurry now I've got that place off my mind.'

Johnny O'Hara laid his finger alongside his twisted, know-ledgeable nose and squinted at it. 'Maybe there is something. There's a couple of houses down by the North Quays, Oxman Street. I think we'd get them cheap for cash. And if we went about it the right way we could buy the whole block that they're in for a few thousand.'

'And then what?'

Johnny brought his thumb up to massage the other side of his nose, making the broken gristle squeak gently and complain-ingly.

'Develop it. Right smack in the centre of Dublin. You could throw a stone from there and hit the G.P.O. That house you've bought up in Chesterfield Square, O.K. it's cheap, it's worth it, you're getting four pounds a week rent out of it. It's a good site. But it isn't a quarter as good as Oxman Street—if we could get permission.'

'Let's find out first.'

Johnny smiled. 'And tell everyone what we're doing? Franky, please. You go talking about "development" and those houses would cost you ten thousand each. Say that you're buying them as an investment, to collect the rents, and you'll get them for a few hundred a time.' He took the cheque. 'Leave this with me and I'll do the best I can. At the worst you'll get enough rent to give you better than interest rates. And at the best . . .' He spread his hands. 'It could be very big if you're willing to wait.'

'And if things get better.'

'They've got to. They can't get any worse. And where the hell else in the world would you buy a four-storey house in the middle of a city for six hundred pounds?'

The next day at the airport, on his way back to England, a throaty, husky voice had said just behind his shoulder 'Hallo, Mr O'Rourke. Are you going to England too?'

He turned round, knowing who it was even before he saw her face, the round, plump, wicked little face under the thick brown hair, the white soft neck and the bosom and the tight dress. The girl at the party. The journalist. He searched for her name. Fil . . . Felicity. O'Connor. The brown eyes smiling at him, admiring, saying, You're a Man! A Man! He took the hand she was holding out to him and it was warm and soft and yielding, like a caress, making him feel almost embarrassed, as if they shouldn't be touching each other in public. And at the same time sending a tremor up his arm, into his body, a soft current of electricity. His mouth felt suddenly parched.

'Manchester,' he said. 'Are you . . . ?'

She nodded. She went on leaving her hand in his as if it belonged to him, as if the fact of their meeting like this had created a bond and she was now waiting for him to tell her what to do. She said rather breathlessly, 'I'm going to Manchester too.' She smiled, but her mouth trembled. 'I've got an introduction to a newspaper. Jim—Mr Hegarty—gave it to me.'

'Come and have a drink,' Francis said. His mouth was still dry. His voice sounded unnatural in his own ears. He let go of her hand but she walked up the stairs beside him so close and submissive that he could feel the warmth of her shoulder through both her coat and his. A thin, cheap tweed coat not thick enough for a day half as cold as today. His own coat was blue Melton. He felt very big and protective. What the hell was he feeling so queer about? Just a girl he knew vaguely, giving her a drink at the airport.

They both had whiskeys, and then another. 'It's my first time in an aeroplane,' she said. 'Will we be all right?'

'Of course you will. I'll hold your hand when we take off. That's the worst bit.' He patted her knee to reassure her. 'Have you got fed up with Dublin?'

She made a mouth and shrugged. 'The grass over the hill. And I wasn't getting anywhere.' She looked away from him at the sky through the window. 'There are lots of newspapers in England. They must want people, mustn't they? I mean new people.'

'Of course they must.'

'You don't know any editors, I suppose?'

'Not my line,' he said, feeling slightly diminished at having to say it. 'If you wanted a trench dug.'

'A trench?'

'For electric cables. Sewer pipes. Anything. I'd be your man for that.' He smiled, holding the glass up, trying to convey, besides the joke, a sense of force and achievement and import-ance in the grip of his red fist on the glass, the angle of his thick forearm in its expensive layers of cloth. They sat together on the plane and he held her hand both when they were taking off and on landing. During the flight and on the bus into the air terminal he told her about himself, about the new contract, the gang he'd just hired, Willy Doyle who had come back to him the minute he sent for him.

'Asked for his cards and got on the next train. A fine wee feller, faithful as a dog. Do anything for me. Anything.'

'Why do you always want wee fellers?' she said. 'You said you'd just been looking for little small men this past week in Dublin.'

'So they fit in the trench without bashing their knuckles off the sides when they're swinging a shovel. You get one of these big clumsy gobs from the mountains and they spend half the time sucking their hands. You can't afford to waste time on this sort of work. What you want is little muscley lads like jockeys. They last all day when the big lad is gasping for a drink.'

He went on telling her things, his mind caught by his own stories, remembering other things. The accident to his leg. When he had seen the big mechanical digger start to tilt sideways into the ditch and he had tried to hold it. He had held it. For thirty seconds, that felt like thirty hours. And then it had fallen on him and smashed his left leg in five places, leaving it permanently stiff in the knee and half an inch shorter than the other leg. Or the time the big Galway man that they called the Basher said he was effed if he was going to work overtime on a Friday night. Coming out of the trench like some kind of a prehistoric monster, cheekbones on him like railway buffers and hands like a pair of crane grabs. 'C'mon lads, blow-up and let's get down to the boozer.'

He hadn't shouted, or tried to argue. He'd just lifted the nearest shovel and swung it, catching the Basher flat across the side of the skull with the blade of it, six pounds of steel blade on the end of a three-foot handle. He'd stretched him back in the trench as flat as a kipper, blood coming down over his ear like an ear muff. It had taken twelve stitches and a week in hospital to get Basher on his feet again, and it had cost Francis a hundred pounds cash to keep him from going to the police, but it had been worth every farthing. For years after if he so much as laid a hand on the shaft of a shovel every man on the gang started digging as if he hoped to reach Australia before blow-up. The story was passed on from gang to gang, and contract to contract.

'You must be very strong,' she said huskily, her small warm hand finding its soft way into his, and he felt a foot taller and a stone heavier. He didn't know that he was taking the place of Jim Hegarty, whose wife had finally been told that her husband was seeing a good deal too much in every sense of a girl who always seemed to be dressed in something two sizes too small for her figure and who obviously had designs on Jim. Although truthfully she had had no designs on Jim Hegarty, and had none on Francis O'Rourke, except to be protected. She was like a hermit crab looking for a new shell, crawling softly and terrifiedly across the ocean floor in search of shelter and safety. Francis took her admiration at its simplest face value, and warmed to her as he had never warmed to any girl in his life. The admiration was so simple and so innocent that it made his reactions innocent as well. She needed looking after, he could see that.

No one could say a word if he kept a fatherly eye on a girl that needed protecting. Saw her into decent digs and so on. 'I'll help you get fixed up with somewhere decent to stay in Manchester if you like,' he said. 'You need to watch out in a place like that. There's places and places.'

'If you knew how scared I am,' she said. 'I was scared enough in Dublin.' She had already told him a bit about herself. The Bar in Drifin. Her father. 'He doesn't mean to be bad. It's just the loneliness, I suppose. And the drink is right under his hand, day and night. There isn't anything to do except go fishing. I used to read all night in bed, until four in the morning sometimes.'

'It's a great thing, reading.' He let her go on talking, without listening very much. Manchester airport, the bus. A taxi. He'd come a hell of a long way since he first saw this bloody town. He held her hand and it already seemed to belong in his. Why not? Why not for Christ's sake? What was wrong with doing the girl a good turn? The image of Maura hovered in the back of his mind, making him uneasy and at the same time resentful. As if he could hear her giving out even when she wasn't bloody well there. Who started you off on the contracts? Who told you you were mad to be working for Morgan's instead of for yourself? Who started you on the way up so you can buy houses and travel in taxis and not give a damn if the fare is five bob or a quid? All right, all right, who said any different? What am I doing wrong? One day our own kids, Venetia—yes, Venetia'll be out in the world and maybe need a helping hand. But he knew that that was the most vile hypocrisy and changed his mental tack. What the eye doesn't see the heart doesn't grieve over. If it was in Dublin now he wouldn't put a step wrong, he wouldn't be seen with this girl, he wouldn't give any living soul the chance to say a wrong word that'd get back to Maura's ears. But in Manchester, dammit, what the hell did it matter what he did in Manchester? He covered her hand in his with his other hand, patting it reassuringly.

'I know a nice quiet hotel where they won't charge you too much. They'll do anything for me, you see. They'll treat you like a queen.'

It was not strictly true. They barely remembered him, but they had two single rooms and didn't look surprised at him arriving with a single girl. 'We'll have a spot of dinner,' he said. 'And then I'll show you the sights.'

It was two o'clock when they got back to the hotel and they stood waiting on the doorstep for the night porter to come, warmed with whiskey and wine and dinner and the taxi ride and a long rather blobby kiss just at the end of it, and he felt his heart hammering in his chest as if he was twenty instead of nearly forty and three times a father. He helped her in through the doorway, and once the night porter had shuffled out of sight again he put his arm round her soft waist and helped her up the stairs.

'I've had too much to drink,' she whispered, leaning against him. 'You muss—muss think I'm a very—very bad kind of girl.'

'I don't think anything of the sort,' he promised her. She was soft and heavy on his arm, giggling as her foot missed a step of the stairs. 'Upsadaisy.' The childish word of encouragement to bed made it seem all right. 'Up we go.' His own heavy leg thumping stiffly on the carpeted stairs like an echo of his heart beating, thudding in his chest.

'Up to the white gable,' she crooned. 'I've had sush—sush a lu'lly evening.'

They came to her door and he put the key in the lock for her, still holding her round the waist with his free arm, feeling for the light. Small, anonymous room. Wardrobe too close to the bed. Cotton curtains. Strip of carpet. Linoleum. She looked at the bed and then looked at him, her eyes muzzy with puzzlement and the beginnings of fright. 'You won't . . . I . . . I'm not——'

'No,' he said heavily. 'I won't.' He felt at that moment that he couldn't, that he had never meant to. But it still left him feeling heavy in the heart and dulled, as if life was not what it had briefly promised to be. He bent his thick neck and bristly face an inch towards her and kissed her on the cheek. 'G'night,' he said. 'Sleep tight.'

She put her arms round him, clumsily, not in an embrace but only to hold him, to stop him from going immediately. 'You . . . you're not angry?' He shook his head. She put her face down against his broad chest and clung to him, the thick softness of her hair under his chin, against his mouth, warmth coming from it like a thick scent. 'It seems so lonely,' she whispered, her mouth muffled in his coat. He sat her down on the bed and sat beside her, his leg stuck out, heel resting on the floor, his hand stroking her hair, her face, her side, finding its way under her arm, where her body was so warm that it was like a heater under her coat. Dammit dammit dammit, he thought, a man can stand so much. Her hand was cold and she put it under his overcoat and his jacket and held it flat against his chest, cold as ice through his silk shirt.

'Lovely shirt,' she said. She didn't want to be raped. She didn't, she didn't. Not taken advantage of. Not made love to. Just made love to nicely, not left alone in the strange room in the strange town, far away from Ireland, faaaaar away. She found a button of his shirt and twisted it with her fingers, feeling the warmth and strength of his body through all the cloth. She was so frightened of tomorrow that if he left her alone she wouldn't be able to sleep, she would lie in this horrible little bed wide awake until morning.

'D'you think I'll find a job?' she said. She wasn't feeling dizzy any more now that they were sitting down. Just a bit woozy, things sort of slowly undulating. 'I'm not drunk,' she said. He had her coat undone and his hand under it. Her hand under his coat. His hand under her coat. That was funny. Very. She laughed. 'I never let Jim, you know.' She shook her head. 'Not properly. He tried.' It wasn't true, not completely true, but it had only been once. Well, twice.

Dammit dammit dammit, Francis cried in his soul. Why the hell should I stand it? He had his hand on her skin, soft fullness of flesh between brassiere and girdle, softer and smoother than anything he could ever remember touching, warm and yielding and elastic, so exciting that his blood drummed in his ears, drowned out his conscience, remembrance of Maura, of his own daughter who might one day sit on a bed like this with a strange man; drowned everything but the desire to push his hand farther, discover more of this warm and hidden wonder. He leant forward so that his fingertips just reached the light-switch, the dark falling on them like a blanket.

'Wh—what you doing?' she whispered. But she couldn't see what he was doing because her face was tight against his chest and her eyes were shut. Burrowing into the darkness like a hermit crab that had found a big, comfortable shell. The darkness, the wine. As long as she held him she didn't feel lonely, she didn't feel afraid.

He woke at six in the morning with the first clatter of dustbins under the window, two storeys down. Her head lying on his shoulder, her hair in a thick mass touching his cheek, her body soft and warm and yielding, moulded against him, clinging to him, the bed so narrow that if either of them had moved a couple of inches in the night they would have fallen out. He could feel her breathing, feel her breast move very slightly with each breath, the breath itself warm against his bare chest. His arm was round her, holding her in the bed. In the room it was still dark, still night outside the thin, shadowy curtains. But the sounds belonged to morning. Early traffic. The kitchen below.

He stared at nothing, not sure how he felt. The first time in eleven years. Well, nearly the first. One or two of the usual kind, but nothing like this. His fingers touched the skin of her back, very gently, afraid, his fingertips so rough that they might hurt her skin. Nothing like this. All the quick words went through his mind. No better than she should be. He didn't owe her anything, didn't need to see her again, Maura'd never know about it.

He laid his hand very gently flat against her shoulder-blades, held her closer. She stirred and whispered, moved her own hand so that it lay on his chest, heavy with sleep. Her breath blew warm and fluttering on his throat. No better—no better than she should ... All her body stirring against his, warm and pliant, moulding itself, leg and soft stomach and softer breast. Nothing ever like this. He moved his other hand to touch her hair, move the mass of it upwards until he could feel it on his mouth. He blew through it and some of it fell away. Never. Never in his life.

He held her so tight that she woke up completely, giving a small grunt from being squeezed. He expected her to say something, to be shocked, pretend to be shocked, try and push him away. Or else to be brazen. But she was neither. She lay very quiet on his shoulder, looking at him. He couldn't see her eyes but he knew that they were open and that she was looking. He strained his head sideways, squinting down. Her mouth was smiling and for the rest of his life he remembered that smile, could see it whenever he wanted to, simply by closing his eyes and thinking of her. The full round of her cheek, the brown fringe of lashes, the brown eye, the brown cloud of hair just showing one small ear, the side of her throat; and her mouth smiling, the lips dark and full and curving, almost parting, and in the smile what seemed like her whole soul and heart, waiting for him to say something, do something; trusting him, believing in him.

Afterwards it caused him so much pain to remember it that he tried not to except very occasionally when he was feeling more than usually lonely and sorry for himself, or was taken unawares by some other memory that led to this one. But now, looking down at her smile, at the one brown eye that he could see, he knew that this was what he had dreamed of all his life without knowing it, something he could never have hoped in a thousand years could ever happen. And he had one of those still, suspended moments when everything in a man's mind and body is caught in what is almost a pain of gratitude, unbelieving, humble, for that one second utterly sincere. That this gift could have been given to him. He didn't know what he felt except that he wasn't going to let her go, that he wanted her, that she was what he had always wanted. But he couldn't tell her. Only hold her tighter, with hands that were rough as sandpaper on her skin. She didn't mind. Only smiled, safe in her new shell.

They stayed together for a year. To salve his financial conscience he called her his secretary and gave her a weekly salary, and in fact she did his correspondence for him, such as it was, on a portable typewriter that he bought for her in Leeds. She also did a lot of writing of her own. One of his memories of that year was of all the paper: wads of screwed-up pages scattered across the floor of whatever room they were staying in as Mr and Mrs. In Leeds, Sheffield, Barnsley, back down in St Albans. Sheets of paper scattered across the bed when he came back in the evenings, or from a trip to Dublin to get more men between contracts. The sound of the typewriter.

'Just practising,' she'd say. 'Messing about. Trying to learn to be a writer.' A couple of times she sold articles to the Manchester paper she had had the introduction to. And she got letters into other papers and nearly sold an article to one of the London Sundays. The day she got the rejection slip with a personal note from the Features Editor saying he couldn't use what she'd written but he'd like to see her if she was ever in London, he came back to find her as happy as if she had really sold something. She had a bottle of wine on the dressing-table, and two wine-glasses, and supper laid; stuff from a delicatessen laid out on paper plates on the bed and a Thermos of coffee. Sitting waiting for him, wearing the red quilted dressing-gown that she had bought him as a present out of the first salary he had given her. It didn't meet across his chest and so she had taken to wearing it herself, looking small and brown and half lost inside it, the sleeves turned back and the collar up round her ears.

'I don't want to go out tonight,' she had said. 'Let's stay home.'

And the word twisted something inside him. Because this room, any room with her in it, was coming to be his home. Not the big, characterless house in Rathfarnham that Paddy Gunn had found for him, where Maura, and his mother, and the children waited for him like strangers. This room. This girl.

'What are you doing to me?' he had said, trying to sound rough. She put her forehead against his stomach and held him, rubbing her head sideways. And the thought that she wanted to be alone with him twisted that something inside him—his heart? his conscience?—twisted it still more until it hurt, and he didn't know if it was more pain than pleasure. She loves me, he thought humbly. He had no real illusions about himself as a lover for a young girl. Rough and fat and forty. He couldn't talk to her about anything except his work. Tell her stories about the men. He couldn't ever talk to her about the things she knew about, books and writing and articles, he didn't know any of that. He couldn't make her speeches or even tell her that he loved her. Only hold her like this, his hands holding her head. So little he could crush it if he closed his hands together. The thick spring of hair like a cushion, soft, warm. The back of her neck. Why couldn't he tell her that he loved her? He tried to make his hands tell her, the calloused fingertips making a small rasping sound on the velvet skin. But she knew.

She wanted to be alone with him, instead of going out and spending money the way any other girl would have done. She loved him and she knew that he loved her and there wasn't any point in thinking things out, what to do, how to go on. Maura and the kids in Dublin. Fil here. It'd work out. He lifted her up until her face was on a level with his. The red dressing-gown, the warm body, soft as a cat, almost slipping out of the silk. Naked under it. His heart thudding.

'I love you,' he mumbled, not looking at her, looking past her at the scatter of typewritten pages on the bed. Sweeping them on to the floor, just pulling the covers back and all the pages fluttering, sliding down to the floor like leaves. Falling in autumn. It was autumn too. Six months together. Then nine. Christmas. Christmas in Dublin, trying not to think. The New Year in St Albans, not thinking, not wanting to think. In a week or two they'd have been a year together.

Back to Dublin for another bunch of men. A week at home,

that stretched into a fortnight, to let him clinch the deal over two more houses in Oxman Street and set up a Limited Company to own them. He owned five houses there now, and if they were going to buy any more at a reasonable price it was better not to let his own name enter into the negotiations. Johnny also wanted him to meet a man called Clancy who knew a lot about finance and had some money to invest.

And all the time he was at home in Dublin, with Maura and his mother, listening to the kids talking, or with Johnny O'Hara, or with Paddy Gunn, or meeting old Jo Clancy, or down in the usual pubs looking for the right kind of men, he was thinking of nothing but her; of the room in St Albans; her sitting by the dressing-table, lying in bed, moving round the room in the red dressing-gown, her hands lifting her hair off her neck, the dressing-gown falling open. Smiling. Waiting. And his heart would thud and he'd forget what he was doing, what he was saying. He could feel her skin under his hand. Hear the throaty, husky voice whispering, 'Hallo, Frank.' Waiting for him. Writing her nonsense. Pages of it scattered on the bed, screwed up on the floor. Waiting for him to come back.

He got away from Dublin on the Thursday evening. Maura's complaining anger still echoing in his head. 'What kind of life d'you think this is for me? What good's money if I haven't got a husband? How long are we going to go on like this?' His mother trying to soothe her down. 'Isn't he good to you now, Maura? Isn't there many a woman would be down on her knees night and day to have such a husband?' Which only made Maura worse. And the children saying, 'When you coming back, Da?' Except for Joseph, who only smiled, calm and quiet as if it was no matter to him whether his father was there or not. Not like a son. Every bloody time he saw him he looked more like that Norwegian and less like himself.

By God, if he ever found that that was—— In a way it was as if that was what had made him—as if there was something in Maura that had never belonged to him, never. Held back. Or given to someone else. And now, with Fil, he was finding what it was, what a woman should be, could be. Giving. Nothing held back. Like her body. Christ almighty, it wasn't just body a man wanted, as if he was a kid up against a wall. Something else, inside, to feel he was ... feel he was loved, that he was everything, that there was nothing she wouldn't do for him, give him. And as he thought of her, sitting in the narrow seat in the plane, with someone's elbow dug into his every time he moved, he had one of those instants of gratitude: still and hurting and so humble that it was like praying. In another couple of hours.

It would be late when he got there. After midnight. Into London from the airport, across to the station, the train to St Albans, the taxi. She'd be asleep. He'd open the door very quietly. . . .

He climbed the stairs as if he was a burglar, hoisting his stiff leg carefully, gently, almost holding his breath, his heart banging his ribs so hard that it seemed to hurt, his case knocking against his knee. And he already knew. Half his mind knew. Opening the door, softly, gently, lowering his case in the doorway and feeling for the light-switch, hesitating with his finger touching it, as the dark flowed round him out of the empty room. Empty. He knew it before he had opened the door, as if the emptiness, the cold silence had reached him through the wood.

He switched on the light and stood there. An empty room. Nothing. Bed made, dressing-table clean and empty, even the blue plastic waste-paper basket empty. Only the white envelope with his name typed on it, tucked into the mirror. He held it in his hands for a long time before he opened it, sitting on the made bed. The rough skin of his fingertips made a small rasping sound on the paper, backwards and forwards, backwards and forwards, touching the envelope without opening it, holding it, as if while it stayed unopened he could keep himself from believing.

8

'At last, a new Synge out of Ireland. And this time it's a girl,' cried the *Daily Express*. 'Smash hit for a playgirl of the western world,' said the *Daily Mail*. 'The biggest dramatic debut since *Look back in Anger*.' 'A great gust of belly laughter from the Ould Sod.' 'Miss O'Connor's tender, funny, furious, rumbustious play, *A Girl is Made for Loving* is the best thing that's happened to the London theatre in the past ten years. Bring your Aunt Edna, but she may need a stiff Irish in the intervals.'

Felicity O'Connor was famous. In the newspapers, on television, in the women's magazines, her round, slightly puffy face under the unruly mass of dark brown hair, the quizzical eyes under the swollen lids, the soft, longing mouth, became hauntingly familiar, driving large numbers of elderly men to write offering her various comforts and others, of a more conservative sort, to write and tell her that she should be ashamed of herself. Quite a few suggested that if her mother had done her duty with a wooden hairbrush some years earlier, the English theatre would have been spared this filth, this loathsome rubbish, this unprintable unprintable.

She turned all these letters over to John Lennox, with whom she had been living for more than a year before her play opened. Not living with him in any sense that the letter-writers would have understood, but simply as his and Kate's guest, half friend, half working companion for Kate. They had come together through the *Sunday Star*. John had been working as a junior reporter for the *Star* for nearly a year and the Features Editor had told him that an Irish girl had been persecuting him with suggestions for articles for months past.

'You're Irish. Go and see what she's like. She's in St Albans, according to her letters. The last idea she's on about sounds as if it might be something for the Irish edition. What happens to Irish country girls in England.'

'Why can't she come here?'

'If I tell her to come here I'll have to commission something and we'd never get rid of her. Take a day over it and see what you get.' The Features Editor had leered at him mechanically, trying to suggest what a devil of a lad he had been himself when he was twenty-five and a junior reporter. Still might be if he got the chance and wasn't so busy.

What John had actually got was half a bottle of the absent Francis O'Rourke's whiskey, the story of Felicity's life, her ambitions, and the first act of her play, in typescript. And although they had spent three hours together in her room it hadn't occurred to either of them that they might spend them in bed. For Felicity, it had never so much as crossed her mind. All she saw in John was a path to a newspaper. For John, it might have crossed his mind very briefly, but she was not his type and at that first meeting she talked so much, so breathlessly, that he hardly had a chance to think; simply to listen. And going back to London in the train, reading the first act of what was then still titled *The Sad Girl from Connemara*, he had seen that the thing which really mattered about Felicity was not her body but her mind.

He was the first person who had ever seen it, and he saw it with a passionate clarity that for the time being drove all thoughts of anything else out of his head. The following day he brought Kate to meet her with the idea already in both their minds that they could find a better home for a would-be playwright than living with a middle-aged Irish labour-contractor, in a succession of scruffy hotel rooms.

They never realized that the name Francis O'Rourke was more than an odd coincidence. 'It'd be bloody funny,' John said, but both he and Kate thought of their Mr O'Rourke as living in Castle Lennox with his unspeakable family. After a third meeting they invited Felicity to take the spare room in their flat in Hampstead. Clean the flat in the mornings, in return for her room and meals, and spend the rest of her time completing the play.

It was only after they had given the invitation and it had been gratefully, almost overwhelmingly, accepted, that they discovered they had known each other as children, thirteen, fourteen years before. Even though Felicity had told John Lennox the story of her childhood she had never mentioned the name of her village, and since every Irish village has a public house that is also a grocer's shop, it had meant nothing in particular to him.

And then a couple of days later, when she had already joined them in the Hampstead flat, she had said that she ought to be writing to her mother in Drifin, she hadn't written to her for ages. 'Drifin?' Kate had shrieked, and they had both, Kate and John together, remembered the fat, suspicious child in O'Connor's Bar, staring at them from behind the counter, making faces. Afterwards, when they had got to know each other better on that summer holiday of years, of centuries ago, she had given them free bottles of lemonade and told them that she was not really the daughter of the house, she had been stolen by the tinkers from a castle in Dublin and sold to the people who called themselves her mother and father for ten bottles of whiskey and a hundred cigarettes. When they didn't believe her because children couldn't be sold like that she had said perhaps it was a million cigarettes, she couldn't remember.

After that recognition the idea that Felicity was there to do anything except write her play faded into nothing. If anything, Kate looked after Felicity rather than the other way round, and as time went on the flat itself, and Kate's and John's spare time, began to centre on the play and getting the play finished. Both of them, Kate and John together, seized on the play, and on Felicity, almost fighting over who should give most, who was giving in the right way, what was the right way; as if Felicity was pregnant and they were sheltering her until her child was born. They both knew that there was something part silly, part hysterical, almost unhealthy in what they were doing, and at the same time felt that it was saving them from something much worse, much unhealthier, a complete break. Neither of them was happy in London. Kate thinking of Ireland, John thinking of Africa, each secretly blaming the other because they were not where they wanted to be, and afraid to bring the quarrel into the open in case it got out of hand, they said too much, went too far.

Because the real quarrel was not about a place, although that entered into it, but about a relationship, or lack of it. They even tried to quarrel about not having a child, as though even that was a better subject than the truth. But they were too intelligent to fool themselves with that for long and they remained polite to each other, considerate, too considerate most of the time, skirting round their inner unhappiness. The watchful, sombre unhappiness of those inner selves of theirs that maintained their distance one from the other, never let themselves go in passion.

The worst of it was that the passion was there and they both knew it. Only that they couldn't bring it alive together. He'd lie beside her in the dark after their nervous, almost timid love-making, wondering why he couldn't touch her, couldn't touch the hidden self locked inside her, wondering what she would be like if he was someone else. Derek Waters? Christ no. But someone, someone unknown. Who could release her. Like rock with water locked inside it, a fountain, a spring of water, that only Aaron's rod could unlock, could bring rushing out. And he lay humiliated, wondering how she felt, what she felt, was she also lying humiliated and unsatisfied, feeling that if she was someone else he would be the lover he ought to be.

And he still loved her, loved her more than he had when they got married, loved her so much that it was painful to see her sometimes, like seeing a lover beyond one's reach, forbidden. Her carved, smooth face that managed to hold so much life in it without any visible change of expression, simply a changing of the light in the eyes, the smallest smile. He saw her and he wanted to die, wanted to make some tremendous gesture of love, throw down walls, kill giants, bring her to bed as if the bed was paradise. And all he could do was light her cigarette, pour her a drink, touch her hair.

And so they both seized on Felicity and her play like something dropped from Heaven. Spoiled her, mothered her, flattered her, coddled her, emotionally exploited her, and Felicity sat in the middle of it like a plump kitten lapping cream. Anyone more sensitive than Felicity might have gone mad and run away from them, but outside of her writing Felicity had the sensitivity of a sandbag. She ignored the emotional storms that lay behind the coddling, and took all the spoiling, the flattery, the half-submerged squabbles of her neurotic nurses as a warm protection, a reassurance, a wall of comfort between her and the terrors of life, and almost as important, as a way provided by Destiny for her to bring her firstborn play into the world in comfort and in safety.

And this certainly it was. She read the play to them page by page, tried out scenes and speeches and lines and alternative versions on them. They remembered Irish jokes together, acted out dialogue, screamed with laughter, fought over changes, invented fantastic life histories for the characters, lived in the play, watched it take shape and grow, until it was a part of their lives. Until it was almost their life.

For Felicity it was probably the happiest year she would ever spend. Certainly it was the happiest she had ever spent. She felt completely sheltered, secure, liked, loved even, and even more wonderful, admired. To be believed in, to talk to people who thought that it was perfectly natural that she should write a play was like lying in a warm bath. The only thing she missed was sex, and only for the first couple of months. At a party in the flat she met a middle-aged theatre director whom the Lennoxes had brought to talk to her about the play and for the rest of the year she met him on most Wednesday and Sunday afternoons. He was bald and short and soft and passionate about cooking and he used to tuck her up in an enormous Chinese silk shawl on his white satin couch and leave her there with a box of liqueur chocolates while he scurried about his kitchen in a flowered apron and a chef's hat.

They ate from a gilt and glass supper trolley, and afterwards he joined her on the couch for an hour of softly placid love-making, interrupted by apologetic belches. Within three months of meeting her he had pledged himself to put on the play.

They tried it out in Birmingham to a mixed reception, rewrote the first and last scenes during the try-out fortnight, brought it to London with more prayers than hopes, and sat stunned, hidden in the dark of a box—Felicity, John, Kate and the producer, Michael Merryweather—as a sophisticated first-night London audience fell to pieces with laughter under their eyes. They had believed the play was funny, but they had never dared to dream that it was this funny; and after Birmingham they had hardly dared to think that London would find it funny at all.

London found it hysterical. Reaction in Ireland was predictably different. Only the *Irish Times* noticed the opening, giving a résumé of the reviews, some account of Felicity herself and a prophecy that in the unlikely event of the play ever reaching Dublin the least that could be expected would be the kind of clerical thunderbolt that three years earlier had closed *The Bishop's Bonfire* after four nights.

It was only when Fidelma Virtue of the *Sunday Freeman* quoted the play in her Advice Column as a horrible example of what might happen to a girl who went to England and neglected her religion that the floodgates opened. Letters poured in from furious readers signing themselves 'Disgusted', 'Mother of Ten', 'Catholic Mother', 'Old-Fashioned', 'A Catholic Father'. The fact that most of them had not seen the play or even talked to anyone who had seen it made no difference. They knew that the play was filth, pornography, a shameful scandal, a libel and slander on the purity of Irish womanhood. Some of the letter-writers thought it was a book. Some of them thought it was on in Dublin. A good many of the suggestions as to what should be done to Felicity were so startling thay they could not be printed. The letter columns not only of the *Freeman* but of all the other Dublin and provincial papers were studded for weeks with savage attacks on 'that woman', 'this girl who drags the name of her country in the English mud', and even more savage attacks on the handful of people foolish enough to try and defend her. One parish curate who had served in a northern English parish, and tried to defend her in a sermon on the grounds that from what he had heard and read of the play it was a work of literature, was obliged by his parish priest to preach a retraction the following Sunday and warned that if he was ever so immorally stupid again he'd find himself preaching to the sheep on Clare Island.

In Drifin, Felicity's home parish, the priest cried such woe for the immorality that unbeknownst to them all had grown up among them like a viper among little chicks in a nest that half a dozen of the lads went that night and tried to burn down O'Connor's Grocery and Bar, with Felicity's mother and father inside it. Fortunately the men were so drunk and the night so wet that they did very little damage, but the next night Felicity's father got drunk in his turn and went and threw stones through the priest's window.

'Come out to me, ye crawthumping old villain. How much d'ye pay Sean Farrelly for grazing your cow in his best field? How much did ye spend on yer new motor car, come out and tell me, ye robber. I'm not afraid of you, shoutin' at girls that aren't there to answer ye. Me daughter's the best effing daughter any man in this parish ever had. Me daughter, me darlin' Fil. Better for you if you had a daughter yourself, instead of yer niece down in Galway. Niece how are you. Don't think I don't know.'

Two men passing by and attracted by the noise had come into the priest's garden and started to beat Jim O'Connor senseless, and the priest had had to come shivering out in his nightgown to separate them and prevent worse bloodshed. In a panic his housekeeper had already called the Guards and they arrived from six miles away to find a threatening crowd gathering outside the presbytery, shouting that they'd lynch Jim O'Connor if they got him outside, the priest and Jim reviving each other with a bottle of whiskey and the housekeeper saying her prayers on her bare knees in the hall, with the door bolted.

First a local and then the Dublin papers heard the story, it reached the wire services and within forty-eight hours a fantastic-ally distorted version of it was in the world's headlines. Jim O'Connor's beating turned into 'attempted murder', two drunken men into a night-riding gang of hooded Catholic vigilantes, a Connemara Ku Klux Klan. The sodden attempt at burning the O'Connors' Bar and the three broken window-panes in the Presbytery became a religious riot, a new Albigensian Crusade. Reporters from America, England, even France and

Germany, not to speak of Dublin, headed for Drifin by aeroplane and hired car, seized on local informers, filled them with
whiskey, sometimes filling themselves at the same time, drained
them of every scrap of information and misinformation, fought
with each other for the use of the one public telephone, persecuted
the parish priest, the O'Connors, the Guards, the men who had
been in the crowd, the men who said they had been in the crowd;
their wives, for their opinions of Felicity, of the priest, of his
housekeeper, of their own men; squeezing, searching and
bribing for any smallest scrap of sensation that would justify
their expense accounts when they got home. For three fantastic
days Drifin felt itself to be the centre of the world. Television
cameras arrived from London. A second TV team arrived from
Boston, with a Boston–Irish crew of cigar-smoking, hard-
drinking cynics who seemed mainly interested in finding someone, anyone, who would say to the camera that he believed in the
little people.

Eventually they found Sean Daly, down from the mountain to
see what all the excitement was about. 'Arragh sure to God,' he
said, blinking in amazement, 'of course I believe in thim. Why
wouldn't I believe in thim, and I seein' thim with my own eyes,
as clear as I see you this minute?'

Almost choking with the fear that this precious Irish gem
would disappear in a whisp of Celtic mist, the director asked
him, 'When d'you see them, Paddy?'

'Arl the time, sir, arl the time. They come runnin' and patterin'
beside me on the mountain, and 'tis great company they are and
I leadin' the lonely life I do be leadin'.'

For years after Sean Daly lived on the story of how he had
fooled the Yanks, describing with streaming eyes each of the
crew members, and how they had looked, and how he had kept
his own face as straight as a sheep's.

'That was no hard thing for you to be doing,' Tim Bourke had
said. 'How much did the gom of a Yank pay you for that
rubbish?'

'Fifty dollars, Tim. Fifty green dollars, sheep and all as I may
look.'

'And did you give the Good Folk their cut?'

'Arrah my pity for your head, Tim Bourke. D'you think I'm a gom entirely?' But in spite of his tone his face looked suddenly graver.

'If I was in your shoes I'd put five of those dollars under the big stone up by your place. They've small liking for being used and not paid.'

Late that night Sean Daly did as Tim had suggested, creeping out in the dark with the dollars in his fist. The next morning they were gone from under the stone, and all his life Sean Daly was never certain who, or what, had taken them, whether it was Tim, or the Ones they were intended for. And he could never ask.

The Drifin story, even backed up by Sean Daly's belief in fairies, died out of the world's television screens and newspapers after a few days. But in Ireland it went rankling on for months, and in some ways for years, the rankling and the bitterness centring on Felicity, the absent, smiling, mink-draped girl who had begun it all, flinging her childhood, her drunken father, her love affairs and her bawdy, saucy, sexy jokes on to a stage and daring to tell the English that this was Ireland. That Ireland was not the pious crust that Church and State and Establishment presented to the world; a crust made up of Victorian hypocrisy and sanctimoniousness.

Her play, however indirectly, cried out that under that ugly, lifeless crust there still lived the real Ireland, full-blooded, kicking, shouting, threatening to get out. The old Gaelic Ireland that the priests and the Civil Service had long hoped was dead. The Ireland of the Munster poets, drunken reeling wenching men with copper in their pockets and silver in their mouths. Men like Eoghan Rua the Spáilpín who sailed with Rodney and bought his freedom from the English navy with an English poem, poor, limping thing as it was, compared to the strong music of his Irish that he wrote and sang for his own people; Eoghan Rua Ó Suilleabháin who came home at last to teach school and drink too much and love too much and die of a beating from a land-lord's servants, whose master he had libelled. And even dying, hauled his young nurse into his bed and loved her with his last strength. Eoghan of the Sweet Mouth, whose poems are still remembered.

Tim Bourke of Drifin could remember them, and recited them sometimes, in his harsher, Connemara Irish. Seán Daly knew them, and old Mrs O'Malley out on the island, Inis Beag. Kate and John Lennox knew them, and as a child Felicity had heard them. Eoghan Rua's verses, and Sean Twomey's, Seán O Tuama of the laughter, who once kept a tavern for his fellow poets and fell on such hard times that he ended his days keeping hens for that hard woman Mrs Quinn, sister to Lord Dartry. Seán O Tuama, who when the great Seán Clárach died wrote of his vision of the Muses at that death-bed, 'Nine Brightnesses with nine lanterns in their hand', *Naoi soillse is naoi lóchrainn'na lámha*; these men and all their comrades in poetry, who whored and drank and begged their way about the dying embers of Gaelic Ireland, their poetry like fountain gushes of crystal out of their ragged poverty, but also out of their learning; a Gaelic learning that stretched back two thousand years into the dawn of cultured Europe; the strength and laughter of such men survived in Felicity O'Connor's play, and even to hear of it struck a dread into the thin grey minds of Ireland's moral governors, clerical and lay.

The play, and all the scandals attached to it, formed a strange, paradoxical watershed in modern Irish life. For those grey, Victorian puritans who for fifty years had held Ireland in their black-mittened grip, it was the first crack in the moral bastions, the first rent in the Green Curtain that sheltered Ireland from the immoral winds of the outer world. The beginning of the end. Fifty years of moral teaching, moral censorship, on top of fifteen hundred years of the Faith, and a young woman—Jesus, Mary and Joseph, a young *woman*—could write that filth—a young woman raised in the Holy heart of the True Green Holy Land, the West, where Blessed Poverty had aided Holy Mother Church to keep the inhabitants from evil thoughts. It seemed to cast the shadow of the guillotine before it; Devil's laughter came out of it; Atheism, sexual liberty, every horror that the mind of pious men could shudderingly imagine.

For the real Irish, poor, oppressed, deprived of their culture and their poetry, their language and their love of life—deprived of it twice over, the first time by the English in straight oppression and tyranny, and a second time by their new Nationalist masters in the name of a twisted parody of liberty—for those real Irish whose only true liberty had been to emigrate, Felicity's play was like the half-heard echo of a half-forgotten anthem, stirring the blood and soul. Like the sound of pipes and marching men, heard on a misty evening. They did not write letters about it to the newspapers, real people rarely do. But they felt it, and transmitted their feelings one to another like a whisper of laughter, like a promise of the green. Like thin blades of grass that find their way through concrete and are filled with a green joy to see the sky.

As if they sensed, in the mere appearance of that play that they would never see performed and never read in print, a promise that old laughter would come back again, the old world might be reborn. It was a foolish hope, but then it's a foolish hope to see the summer in one returning swallow. And yet the summer comes. If things were going to change for Ireland and the Irish they would change not on the stage of a London theatre, but in the Stock Exchange. And there, in 1957, Ireland's quotation lay very low and small. Yet, in the deepest sense of truth, the spirit means more than money, and the spirit was stirring. Perhaps because it knew, with the clairvoyance of the spirit, that very shortly the money would stir also. And little by little, year by year, the green blood of money would begin circulating in Ireland's veins. Which the good and moral would see as the end of virtue. And the immoral and the laughing would see as a chance of life.

Of those who actually saw the play, very few, if any, were conscious of that kind of interpretation. The English saw it either as a confirmation of what they had always thought that Ireland was, feckless, bawdy, immoral and drunken, or as a laughing belch in the face of their own Aunt Edna Establishment. The Irish who saw it, Irish immigrants in London who had done well enough in England to join the play-going classes, saw it either tolerantly as 'great gas' or intolerantly as a shocking insult to the pure land and chaste womanhood of their own pure childhood.

Francis O'Rourke first heard of it on television, sitting with Willy Doyle in the lounge bar of a public house in Bradford, working out a tender for a new contract. Her voice caught his mind like someone catching hold of his throat in the dark, her voice out of nowhere, suddenly reaching him out of the non-descript mutterings of the television set in the far corner. A throaty, husky voice with laughter in it, saying, 'I don't give a damn in hell what they say in Ireland. All I've done is tell the truth.'

And the interviewer's voice, English, cultured, neutral, 'An autobiographical truth?'

'If you mean have I ever been to bed with anyone, yes, I have.' The husky voice breaking into open laughter, and for a long second even the smoothness of the interviewer stopped in its tracks, the man struggling for the next question.

'I was thinking about the childhood scenes. Do these represent your own childhood?'

'I think that's as much my business as your childhood is yours. They represent a truth about Ireland as I see it.'

The same face; slightly puffed with too much sleep, or too little, the heavy eyelids over the sudden sharp glint of the eyes, the dark waves of hair falling untidily over the pale forehead, the smile, the soft, full throat, the soft, full bosom, the tightness of the dress. Except that now she seemed to have grown, to have grown up, to have come to a kind of strength and certainty. He sat staring, his thick body swung half-way round in the chair, his hand with the biro in the stubby fingers poised over the table, his mouth falling open. What in the name of God——? Fil! Fil on the telly! Felicity. Her. Holy Jesus! A man interviewing her on the TV. About what for God's sake? What were they talking about, her childhood, what in hell——? She turned her head and for a moment she seemed to be staring straight out of the screen at Francis, her smile directed at him, and he could no longer even think. When he had recovered she was gone and someone else was on the screen talking about the World Health Organization.

He found out about the play that night, and two days later he went to see it, feeling as awkward in the foyer, and then in his seat, as if he was carrying a pickaxe over his shoulder. Fil writing a play! All those sheets of paper! All that time. A play! He still couldn't believe it. A play. Maybe she was acting in it. But even that. And it had said outside *by Felicity O'Connor*. God above. *A Girl is Made for Loving.* Just like her. In spite of the pain he was feeling he could smile at that. He hadn't guessed how much pain he could feel. It had died away in the past year or so. After those first few days, when he had walked round like a man in a trance not knowing what he was doing. Drinking himself senseless each night so that he could sleep, and waking every morning to find again that she was gone, that he was alone, the loneliness worse than the hangover. Willy Doyle had kept him sane, drinking with him, listening to him, walking round St Albans with him looking for her.

'A chap in a sports car,' the woman who kept the hotel had said. 'A woman came too. No they didn't say where they were from. The chap looked like one of them flash boxers.'

He had never thought of the Lennoxes. They had never crossed his mind. A man and a woman. What had they wanted? He had thought of white slavery, of going to the police. But how could he? Maura, the kids. And her letter, the one she had left him. Just saying, *Good-bye. You've been very good, I'll always remember. But I have to go some time and it's best now. You've got your family. You'll have to go back to them soon. And then I'd be left. But thanks. I'm taking the dressing-gown to keep. Don't be too angry with me. It really is the best. Your grateful* FIL.

The pain had died down. Work, drink, money. Once or twice another woman, although only for a night, a couple of hours. New contracts. Trips home to Ireland. Home? Christ, what was 'home'? Where? All the word meant was one room, and warmth, and her lying there in the bed in his red dressing-gown, waiting for him to come in; the typewriter on her knees and a scatter of pages on the scruffy bed-cover; and her arms going out to him, soft and round and smooth, holding him, her mouth warm and moving against his ear, against the bristles of his cheek, 'Hallo, Frank.'

But the pain had died down. Money. Buying houses with it in Dublin, making himself believe that all of it still mattered, to become rich, powerful, build something that would last, that he'd leave behind him, to say, Francis Xavier O'Rourke was here. See what he did who began from nothing. He, or the company, owned nine of the ten houses in Oxman Street between St Olaf's Row and Marietta Street, and already they had bought one of the houses round the corner in Marietta Street. They owned almost half of the square block whose fourth side was formed by Slaughter Lane, and whose hollow centre was Aram Court. They were already making tentative, amateur sketches of what they could do with the site when they owned the entire block and got it cleared of houses. A supermarket and shops on the ground floor, offices above it, a tower above that reserved for themselves. The whole lot rising ten, twelve, maybe more storeys, dominating the centre of the north side, looking across the river to Christchurch Cathedral.

When he was in Dublin he could even believe in it, care about it. Even working in England he could care about it. But now, sitting awkwardly in his stuffy upholstered seat in the stalls, his stiff leg jammed under the seat in front of him, a fat woman beside him eating chocolates, a thin young man with no chin crowding at his other elbow, telling a girl what the message of the play was going to be, he knew that nothing in his life had ever mattered except Fil, and that nothing else ever would. And he sat like a man with a wound that can't be healed, holding it together with his hands, waiting.

But whatever he was waiting for was less than what he saw. Like the wound being torn open and the heart pulled out of him, bloody, beating, still alive, screaming with agony. The curtain rising on a stage set to look like a scruffy hotel bedroom in Leeds or Bradford. He hadn't bought a programme, he hadn't thought of it, but he knew where the room was, what room it was. A girl lying in bed. Typewriter on her knees. Red dressing-gown.

Papers scattered on the bed, on the floor. Bottle of whiskey on the dressing-table.

He thought for a minute, a whole minute, that it was Fil herself lying in that bed, and he couldn't listen to what she was saying for the pain of it. He sat rigid, nailed there with pain. The red dressing-gown, the pale, almost puffy face, the fall of hair, the husky, throaty voice. The Lennoxes had found an actress, a young Irish actress just making her name in England after an abortive year in films, who looked a little like Fil even before she had studied the part, and who after rehearsals and soaking herself in the script was her walking, throaty image. She came from much the same kind of background too and poured her soul into the play. For her, as for Fil, and in its different degrees for Kate and John, it was a shout of passion, for all that they loved in life, against all that they hated, against the crawthumping and the hypocrisy, and the men with dirty suits and bicycle clips who thought that Nationalism was issued by the Department of Education like a Leaving Certificate pass in compulsory Irish.

But for Francis O'Rourke, who was the Ireland that they loved and hated, the play was like crucifixion. He sat so stunned with pain that he was not able even to think of leaving, of getting up from that dusty, uncomfortable seat and pushing his way out along the row of knees, the laughing faces, already loud with laughter, sometimes at jokes they didn't understand, simply knowing that everything was funny; that outrageous girl in a man's dressing-gown lying in bed thinking of her man, of sex, of love, of food, of childhood, of drink and drunkenness, of being loved, held in a man's arms, protected from the world outside the cotton curtains of the bedroom. Funny not because she was making jokes, but because she was being honest, in her cracked, throaty, whispering voice that carried to the gods and the boxes like a husky echo. So honest that the only thing for civilized people to do was to treat it as a joke, for fear of being hurt. But Francis was not civilized and he was like Prometheus on the rock. How could she do this to him? And when his likeness came in, a black-haired, thick-set, shouting actor with callouses on his tongue and the red glow of whiskey in his eyes he thought he was going to die, his heart was going to swell and stop, choked and stopped with pain.

There was a moment in the first act that by some theatrical accident had become its climax. Fil had not thought of it even as funny, and neither had Kate nor John. For Fil it had simply been true, something that had happened, and that for her meant Francis, and his returns from Dublin, or a two-day absence in London or Birmingham. Coming in late at night with a bottle of Irish whiskey in one pocket and a pound of Irish sausages in the other. Coming in on tiptoe to see if she was asleep, stealing up to the bed, waking her with a whiskey kiss, and saying in loving tones, 'I've got the bangers, love, will I fling 'em on the pan?'

Whether it was the line itself, or simply the word *bangers*, or the way the actor delivered it, or the idea of a fat man waking his lover with a suggestion that he cook her a pound of sausages, the audience fell apart. Night after night. And after that line the evening was made, the audience was in the hands of the pair on the stage for the rest of three acts.

For Francis it was the death-blow. He got to his feet without knowing what he was doing, pushed blindly out past the knees and helpless laughter, heard the laughter as if it was pursuing him. He couldn't see, trod on feet, bumped and lurched his way to the aisle, only managed to head for the exit because it was in the opposite direction to the stage. Out through the swing doors into the cool, dispassionate foyer, the surprised doorman starting forward as he came to the outer doors.

'Are you all right, sir? Taxi, sir?'

Francis didn't answer. He lurched forward into the dark, drizzling street, wet pavements turned to gold by the lights of passing cars, stumbled anywhere, found a public house, drank, tried to get drunk, couldn't. As if his mind, his capacity for everything had been castrated. Fil. Every time the blessed feeling of drunkenness, of semi-anaesthesia came towards him like a curtain blown by the wind into a room, to fold round him, hold him, he thought of her, and everything fell away except the pain. He could see her, feel her, as if they were lying side by side in bed, naked, touching. Her round arms, white, soft, warm, enclosing; holding him; her warm mouth. And her teeth were in his throat and her fingers held a knife that was slowly peeling the living skin from his back.

They threw him out of the pub at closing time and he walked and limped half the night until at four in the morning he fell on to a bench down by the Embankment and a policeman arrested him for being drunk and homeless. Finding that he had money and was more ill than drunk they let him go in the morning and he went to the railway station and fell asleep again in the waiting-room, waiting for his train to Barnsley.

He was not cured. He never would be cured. But inasmuch as he walked and talked and got on with his work and thought about money and how to use it he was recovered from the worst. As time went by he thought himself that he was cured, or rather he stopped thinking about Fil at all for long periods together. A year went by, and part of another year. He and Johnny, and their third partner, old Joseph Clancy, with Paddy Gunn in the background as a consulting and guiding spirit, completed their buying of Oxman Street, of the four houses in Marietta street and the five in St Olaf's Row, and began what was to turn into the longest and most difficult part of the project of buying up the entire block: the purchase of the houses in Slaughter Lane and Aram Court. There were only four; two that were not much more than shells of houses used for storage at the back of Oxman Street and the two that faced into the courtyard and were known as Numbers 1 and 2 Aram Court.

The difficulties arose from the sudden and passionate enmity of Lady Honoria Gandon.

9

Lady Honoria had already seen *A Girl is Made for Loving* before
Francis O'Rourke saw it. She and her husband Cecil Gandon
had come back from South Africa after two years that Cecil had
thoroughly enjoyed and that for Lady Honoria had turned into
frustration, an increasingly irritating limbo. In the beginning it
had been pleasant enough, even exciting. The sun, space,
servants; and the respectful black faces of those servants like a
healing salve on the still unhealed wounds of her childhood
poverty in Jamaica, with its memories of jeering black children
and friendly contemptuous black adults. A big, cool Dutch
Colonial farm house in the hills above Cape Town, a pleasant
penthouse flat in Johannesburg, trips to Lourenço Marques for
the bullfighting season; roughing it on safari on the big Gandon
cattle ranch north of Zimbabwe, twelve hundred square miles of
it, bumping over earth roads in a Land-Rover, with the servants
and the picnic things in a couple of three-ton lorries behind them;
being entertained by the Governor in Government House, and
back in Pretoria doing the rounds of Embassy parties, inviting
some of the better-class attachés and third secretaries down to the
Cape with them for the wine harvest; hearing people talk about
the Gandon money with none of the European nonsense of
pretending that millions don't matter and that being very rich is
an awful bind anyway; hearing people talk about her husband's
family as it should be talked about, representing something
almost holy. All that was milk and honey and butter for her
paws.

But she didn't like Cousin Julius, she didn't like the way he
treated Cecil, as an imbecile to be half humoured and half bullied,
and above all she didn't like being overshadowed by the Oppen-
heimers and being considered simply one member of one rich
family. There were too many enormous fortunes in South Africa.
If Cecil had been a different kind of man, if he had been capable
of using his money and his connections, it might have beèn

different. And yet even then, she would not really have wanted to stay. She found herself dreaming of somewhere small and manageable, where she could be undisputed Queen. Somewhere like Ireland.

At the end of 1956 the Cecil Gandons returned to Europe, and to Dublin. They bought a pleasant eighteenth-century house in Merrion Square, perfect for small intimate dinner parties of a dozen or so, to which she was determined none of Cecil's dull and horrid family would ever be invited; and for visits to London the lease of a mews cottage in Knightsbridge. It was when they were moving some furniture into the Mews that they saw Felicity O'Connor's play. As a play it meant nothing to Lady Honoria. If she thought anything about it she thought that it was very lower class and very vulgar. But Lord John Somerville had recommended them to see it, and Lady Featherstonhaugh was so hysterical with laughter trying to describe the sausage scene that she was in tears for half of a dinner party, and Anne Bench the society portrait painter was actually painting the girl who wrote the play and calling her 'Fil', so that there was no doubt that one had to go to it. She contrived to meet the girl at Anne Bench's house in Chelsea, met the Lennoxes at the same party, and asked everyone back to the Mews. She was still not acting consciously, working consciously towards anything. She was simply like a kitten trying to rake sunbeams towards itself with lazy, playful paws. If it was warm and bright it must be hers to play with, that was the way life was. Since she had come back to Europe one beautiful thing after another had dropped into her small, joyful grasp, and in a delightfully different way to South Africa.

There, there was always Cousin Julius disapproving of things and talking about politics and the family's responsibilities and what so-and-so would think. And people had always thought of her as one of 'the family'. But here in lovely, lovely London, and darling Dublin, she was simply herself, Lady Honoria, young and beautiful and rich and unique. Some of the stuffy older people in Dublin also talked about 'the family' and said some of the dreary things that Cousin Julius used to say, but somehow it was easier to escape from them, laugh at Lord Alfred and blow him a kiss and go off to the races or fly over to London to get her hair done, or to Paris to buy a dress, or just sit in Jammet's Bar while people whispered, 'That's Lady Honoria, isn't she a peach?'

And gradually, out of this warm and gorgeous happiness there was growing the ambition to be more than just a peach; to establish her uniqueness on rocklike foundations; to achieve the queenship she had daydreamed about in South Africa when some millionairess with diamonds like headlamps had outjewelled her at a party. The Queen of Dublin Society.

For nearly half a century Dublin had had nothing that could really be called Society. The Viceroy and his Court had gone, and the Marty Mullins and their like had come. The well-bred, both Protestant and Catholic, had shuddered and fled to London, or stayed in their desolate country houses, if the Shinners hadn't burned them down. The great families, people like the Gandons and the Gardiners, the Beauchamps and the De Rigos, had become part of English society, regarding Ireland simply as the place where they had their businesses, or their estates, or their shooting-lodges and racing-stables. The Gandons more than most had kept some kind of roots in Ireland, and made a quiet display of the fact that they had kept them, but in their hearts their London houses were their real homes, and secretly they regarded their Irish houses and estates as being in a kind of rebellious colony. They had sound working relationships with the new rulers of the place (still 'new' after ten, and twenty, and thirty years) but they were purely working relationships and it would not have occurred to any of the Gandons, any more than to the Beauchamps or the De Rigos, that there could be any *Society* in Ireland. In Ireland, one worked, or shot, or fished, or hunted, or joyfully met one's friends at the Horse Show. But for Society, if one bothered with that kind of thing, one went to London. It was so axiomatic that one never thought about it.

It would be an exaggeration to say that Lady Honoria thought about it herself. She simply felt it. That like South Africa, London was too big. But Dublin was within her reach. Why shouldn't Dublin have a Society, and why shouldn't she be Queen of it? She imagined herself surrounded by all the Beautiful People whose pictures she saw in the glossy magazines. Or people like them. Well bred and rich and clever and talented and adoring her. Some of them of course not quite so rich, so that she could help them. Indeed some of them, particularly the talented ones, might be quite poor, so that she could guide their careers towards tremendous successes, and afterwards everyone would say, 'Without Lady Honoria so-and-so would be absolutely nowhere. She *made* him, my dear, absolutely made him.'

Again it was instinct rather than any conscious plan. It was obvious that Dublin Society would have to be different to London's, and centred not so much on wealth, or even birth, where in any event she was not really in favour of strong competition, but on some quality or qualities that she could influence. She could not make people rich. She could not confer titles of nobility or start an Order of Chivalry. But she could patronize talent. Young, handsome, well-behaved talent that would be adoringly grateful. Poets, painters, scholars, young lawyers whom she would encourage to become judges, architects whom she would nurse towards creating splendid skyscrapers and wonderful country houses. At some stage in her childhood an elderly French acquaintance of the Earl's had told her about Madame de Staël and the great French salons, and fractured remnants of the stories had stuck in her subconscious. A lovely woman lying on a beautiful, elegant couch; young men in satin coats on their knees beside her, reciting poetry and witticisms—the witticisms making fun of other, far less attractive women. As a small, angry child with a courtesy title and no shoes she had clutched that image to her bony little chest like a beautiful doll, until it became part of her being. To be rich, to be adored, to be admired and flattered and looked up to. As black Marcia's voice screeched after her in the scented Jamaican dusk, threatening her with woeful punishments, for whatever she had most recently done or not done, she dreamed of queenship, of being for ever beyond the necessity of having to wash her father's shirt, or scrub out the hut, or go down to the Post Office in Falmouth to see if the remittance had come.

To be Queen of Dublin. It was surely possible. As the young

and beautiful wife of the heir presumptive of the Gandons the title was almost hers for the asking. The Gandons had laid the foundations of their fortune at the beginning of the eighteenth century, speculating in land, buying up estates from Catholics who could not keep them without abjuring, and jobbing government contracts for timber and building stone. By the 1760s they were so rich they could afford to be half honest, and began to yearn for prestige. They were among the first and the greatest of the Dublin developers, leasing enormous tracts of land from the Crown on the south side of the Liffey, and trying to rival the Gardiners and Fitzwilliams in laying out streets and squares of handsome Georgian houses that would make of Dublin one of the finest cities in Europe.

By the end of the century they were so rich they could even afford patriotism and instructed the six members of the Dublin Parliament who owed their seats to Gandon influence to vote against the Act of Union. Two betrayed them for English pensions. One died of apoplexy at cards the night before the vote. The other three did what they had been ordered to do, and the Gandons were enshrined in Dublin legend as 'a fine family, the rale thing, rale old gintry'. And to do them justice they kept faith with their city. What they had built and laid out they protected. And even when the Gandon Estates and properties in Dublin became very much a secondary matter for the family, and their main financial interests lay in London and South Africa, they saw to it that no unscrupulous leaseholder spoiled or exploited their part of Dublin. No one could alter or build or rebuild or demolish anything without their Estate Offices' carefully considered permission, and every leaseholder was bound by severe penalty to maintain his property in good condition.

Dublin owed a great deal to the Gandon family and even after a generation of 'Independence' resentment of the Gandons as Anglo-Irish snobs and West-British God-Save-the-Kings was balanced by a vague recognition, a half-remembrance, that they had done something for the city. But if Dublin's recognition of what the Gandons stood for in Irish history was vague and shadowy, Lady Honoria's was non-existent, and it was purely accident that she stumbled on 'Evictions' as a Cause, a means to her end of becoming Dublin's Madame de Staël. During a long and atrociously boring dinner party she was obliged to sit beside an elderly architect who insisted on telling her about Aram Court, and the abominable sins of the Dublin Developers who were obviously going to destroy it, along with the rest of eighteenth-century Dublin.

By the end of the dinner she would happily have burned Aram Court to the ground with her own hands. It was only afterwards, telling the story of the dinner party and all the boring details to which she had been forced to listen to some artistically minded friends, as a sample of the kind of thing she had to suffer from the Gandons' idea of social life, that she realized, from their unexpected reaction, that here was indeed a Cause, and that these particular friends, who hadn't yet grasped the point of her story, were electing her its leader. 'Darling Honoria, how brilliant of you to know so much about it all. Those poor, poor people! Where will they go? What will they do? I mean, they'll be put out into the street. If only the Gandons could stop these awful Developers?'

It took her barely a second to change the point of her story from resigned boredom to passionate, Queenly indignation. 'The Gandons?' she said. '*I* shall stop them.' The Society of the Friends of Aram Court was born half an hour later. And did indeed deserve to be born.

The two houses in the courtyard were truly unique; the last remaining pair in Dublin of Dutch Billy houses, built at the end of the seventeenth century, with cross-ridged roofs, leaded windows, overhanging first and second storeys, and a third storey in the attics, lit by small, square-leaded windows tucked into the shallow triangles of their gables. The Georgian developers of the middle and late eighteenth and early nineteenth centuries, who had swept away most of Tudor and Jacobean Dublin to make room for their own neo-Classical ideal of a city, had overlooked them, or not been able to buy them up, and had built round them, hiding them behind the mid-Georgian façades of Oxman Street.

Because of their discreetly hidden position they had been bought in 1759 by a wealthy Dublin Catholic and used as both a Convent for French nuns and a Mass house. After the Catholic Emancipation of 1829 they had been willed to the Catholic Archbishop of Dublin as homes for indigent clergy and had been kept for that use until 1903, when they had been sold to a Solicitor. The Solicitor's hand-painted sign, *Scrivener & Attorney*, still hung in one of the windows. His grandson had been interested in the theatre, and from 1931 until 1958 the two houses had been used to store costumes, to rehearse homeless plays, and sometimes to shelter homeless actors and hangers-on of the theatre.

Now, emptied of most of the costumes and occupied only casually and occasionally by some 'fit-up' players whose travelling lorry and caravan were parked in the courtyard, the houses were for sale by Public Auction, the auctioneers being Messrs Moberley & Gunn.

And but for the accident of that dinner party and two of her friends misunderstanding the point of Lady Honoria's rather long story and where her actual indignation lay the auction would have gone off as quietly as everyone else had intended it to, and the two Dutch Billy houses would have changed hands for a few hundred pounds apiece. As things turned out, they were to become one of the *causes célebres* of Dublin, and would make auctioneering history as well.

'Those poor, helpless little people,' Lady Honoria cried, genuinely moved by her own fineness of spirit. 'They'll lose their homes over my dead body!' Or at least over Cecil's overdraft. Because as even she had realised from what the elderly architect had told her, the two houses in Aram Court were right in the middle of the Developers' planned new building. Without them their whole scheme would be paralysed. And she would paralyse it. She would simply buy the houses in Aram Court herself.

10

The auction of Numbers 1 and 2 Aram Court, desirable city investment properties to be offered in one or two lots suitable for storage facilities or site development, solicitors having carriage of sale being Alloway, Barnacle and Truett, was advertised to take place at the salerooms of Messrs Moberley & Gunn, of Lucy Street, at 3 p.m. on the first Monday in November, 1959.

At five minutes to three there were six people in the property saleroom, a medium-sized, nondescript, dirty back room furnished with two dozen rickety wooden chairs and a large wooden table with two rather more substantial wooden chairs ranged behind it. On the table were a water carafe and a glass. Lady Honoria sat in the middle of the front row of chairs, her black sealskin coat swung back from her green woollen dress, her hands fiddling nervously with a small ivory leather notebook and a gold pencil. Beside her Valentine Carthew of Wellingborough, Otis and Carthew, Cecil Gandon's solicitors, sat fiddling equally nervously with the small tight knot of his Guards tie, his small mouth shaping tentative words under his beaky nose.

'N–n–nearly t–t–time, Lady H.,' he said. His accent cried out like a plea for recognition: I was at school in England, a simply splendid school.

'I know,' Lady Honoria said. 'Where the hell is Cecil?'

'I–I–I–I'm s–s–sure he'll b–b–b–be along soon, L–L–L–Lady H.'

Of the other four people in the room one was an old man in a dirty overcoat who looked like a ragpicker, also sitting in the front row. His nose was red and dripping and every now and then he coughed into a handkerchief so spectacularly filthy that Lady Honoria had to look at it. Every time it came out of his overcoat pocket, blackened, streaked, unspeakably decorated, she found herself hypnotized by it, incredulous, like being drawn by sheer horror to look at the victim of a street accident. It couldn't be true, and against her will she waited for the next paroxysm of coughing, the next dreadful apparition.

Behind the old man sat a fat woman with a shopping basket, whose bus was not leaving for another hour and who wanted somewhere to sit down in the warm. Two rows behind Lady Honoria sat a man with a sniff. Behind him again, tilting his chair back until his shoulders touched the wall, sat Johnny O'Hara, solicitor and partner to Francis O'Rourke and old Joseph Clancy, squinting down his long, slightly bent nose at the sports pages of the *Irish Press*. Once or twice he lowered the paper to look at the back of Lady Honoria's beautiful head with its little black sealskin hat hugging the golden hair. And poor Val Carthew, God love him. This was going to be a grim half-hour for poor Val. He went back to the article about the Triple Crown prospects. A very grim half-hour judging from what he had heard, with Lady Honoria threatening him with destruction if she didn't get the houses, and the Gandons threatening him with worse if she did.

'Psst. Psst.'

He looked round to see shadows behind the glass panel of the half-open door. Jo Clancy's big, flaccid face came round the edge of it, jerked to beckon him out. Jo Clancy and Franky O'Rourke in the corridor, Jo almost wringing his hands already, Franky sweating, chewing at his black moustache, his thick, bull shoulders hunched as if he was going to charge through the door head down.

'Relax.'

'Is she in there?'

'Of course she's in there.'

'Fifteen thousand,' Jo Clancy moaned, actually wringing his hands. 'It's madness, it's madness, I won't go on with it.'

'Don't be a bloody fool,' Francis said. 'What the hell is fifteen thousand? I'd go to double that if I needed to.'

'Frank's right,' Johnny said. 'It's nothing. It's the luck of God the Gandons aren't willing to back her on this. If they were . . .' He bunched his fingers, kissed the gathered tips and let them fly apart.

'It's all right for you,' Jo said, his mouth shaking, his sagging, flabby cheeks an unhealthy mauve colour. 'You've hardly anything in this.'

'I've more than I can afford to lose,' Johnny said, 'and I don't intend to lose it.'

'How do you know the Gandons aren't backing her?'

'A chap in Lord Alfred's office. I got my brother to drop a few words around that anyone who sticks his finger in this will get it bitten off. In fact Lord Alfred has done his damnedest to get Lady H. to pull out of it. And they've screwed down the clamps on Cecil's Trust Fund. The absolute max they could possibly go on this according to another chap I know in Cecil's bank is fifteen.'

'Oh, my God!' Jo Clancy whimpered, holding his heart. In pity for him Johnny O'Hara clapped him on the shoulder, soft and old and sloping and rheumatic under the thick blue overcoat.

'Don't worry, Jo. They won't go anywhere near fifteen. It'd mean them leaving themselves without their pocket money till Tib's Eve and selling everything they can lay their little hands on. I bet you they won't go over five, if they bid at all.'

'Pocket money!' old Mr Clancy moaned. 'You call fifteen thousand their pocket money? Oh, my God. This'll be the death of me, I know it.' In reality he was looking far beyond the cost of Aram Court to what the purchase was leading to; to the astronomical costs of the building that would take its place and the place of all the other buildings they had been buying in Oxman Street and St. Olaf's Row and Marietta Street and Slaughter Lane. O'Rourke's Folly. Or Jo Clancy's? It would be the death of him before it was done, they would have him dead and buried and in his grave. Why hadn't he stayed retired, minding his roses?

Paddy Gunn, who was to act as auctioneer that afternoon, and his clerk, came down the grubby corridor from the front office, the clerk carrying a sheaf of papers, Paddy with the faint suggestion about him of a priest hurrying to say Mass, at once busy and devout. And yet there was nothing obviously priestly about him, about his expensive tweeds, his pale mauve silk shirt, his dark mauve silk tie with silk handkerchief to match, his hand-made brogues, his sensible eighteen-carat gold Rolex. He smiled at the three conspirators, nodding briefly, the nod and his expression letting it be understood that as far as this afternoon was concerned they were on opposite sides of the altar rails and intimacy was out of place.

They all went in, Johnny making the others wait a moment or two so that they didn't appear to come in together with the auctioneer. Clerk and auctioneer settled themselves behind the table, their backs to the tall, dirty window, so dirty that it was impossible to see through the grey, crusted panes into the courtyard behind.

'Good afternoon, ladies and gentlemen.' Paddy Gunn smiled, his warmth equally distributed between Lady Honoria and the fat woman waiting for her bus, Valentine Carthew and the rag-picker. He looked at his watch, the second-hand ticking towards the hour. 'A thin house,' he said, smiling more broadly to indi-cate a joke, 'but thick wallets, I hope?' Valentine Carthew tittered politely. Lady Honoria glanced sideways at him, chilling the titter into a nervous twitch. Even in the past few weeks of chairing meetings of the Friends of Aram Court she had begun to put on authority, to show the first indications of the *grande dame* she would one day become. And Valentine Carthew had his own reasons for nervousness, as Johnny O'Hara had already heard.

'Where the hell has Cecil got to?' Lady Honoria whispered for the fifth time. Her husband had been sent to make a final, very reluctant attempt over lunch to melt his Uncle Alfred's heart: to get both his approval for the Friends of Aram Court and their ambitions, and his permission for Cecil to draw on his own capital to buy the houses, if the price went higher than the few thousand Cecil and she had in their current accounts.

The harsh fact was that despite her budding air of authority she was suddenly and painfully frightened. She had defied Lord Alfred: all his hints; all his kindly-gruff 'advice'; all his increas-ingly irritable requests not to get 'mixed up in things', not to do anything that might 'embarrass the family'; and finally his direct order not to go any further with 'any more of this damn Pre-server nonsense'. It was to get this order rescinded, as well as to get permission to use his own money, that Cecil had gone, driven and bullyragged by her like a sheep being driven to the slaughterhouse, to face his uncle over an office lunch, a ritual plate of cold beef and tomatoes and Guinness's stout in Lord Alfred's private dining-room in the Kildare Street Estate Office.

All that had been humiliating and frustrating enough, but it had been a private humiliation and frustration that no one else needed to know about. Now, almost for the first time, she was realizing what would happen if Cecil had failed. Facing the next meeting of the Friends of Aram Court not as their Queen, their champion, their Lady of Victories, but as a silly, futile girl who had talked and talked and achieved nothing, who hadn't even been able to buy two miserable, rotten little ruined sheds in a Dublin slum. She couldn't, couldn't face them like that. She'd kill herself first, leave Dublin, pretend she'd been taken ill—why didn't he come? Where was he? He couldn't have failed. She wished with a desperate misery that she had never heard of Aram Court, never started the Friends. Stupid, lickspittle hangers-on, toadies, social climbers, why in the name of God had she ever bothered with them? The shame of it!

The clerk was reading the documents, droning on and on about leases, God knew what. If he didn't come she would kill him. The door opened, steps shuffled and slithered towards her. Cecil folded himself down into the vacant chair beside her, between her and the ragpicker. The ragpicker began a paroxysm. Cecil watched it apologetically, half-thinking he must have caused it by jostling the poor old fellow or something. He saw the handkerchief come out and stared at it, not believing what he saw.

'Good God!' he whispered. 'I mean—don't look, but gosh . . .' and then: 'Am I late, m'love?'

She was keeping her eyes tight shut with tension, afraid to look at him, afraid of the answer she was going to see in his help-less, chinless, witless face. Why had she married him? Why wasn't she dead? 'Is it—is it all right?' she whispered. It had to be all right. He was going to say, 'Yes.' She willed him with all her soul to say, 'Yes.'

'Got to get me breath,' he wheezed. 'Gosh I'm puffed—couldn't get parking—miles away—whew . . .' He twitched his nose and one eyebrow discreetly towards the ragpicker, whose clothes were indeed beginning to hum gently in the heated, stuffy room.

'Is—it—all—right?' she hissed, stressing each syllable. She had once seen Marcia, her stepmother, fell her father the Earl with one tremendous sweep of an iron frying-pan. If she had had a frying-pan, or anything else solid and heavy enough close to her hand at that moment, she could imagine herself doing the same thing.

'N–n–n–n–not s–s–s–so l–l–loud, L–L–L–Lady H.' Valentine Carthew pleaded. Why had he come, why had he allowed her to make him come? He was even a Friend of Aram Court, she had made him pay a pound subscription. The Gandons would never forgive him. Those ruffians O'Rourke and O'Hara would never forgive him. He was ruined whatever happened. 'P–p–p–please k–k–k–keep y–y–y–your v–voice down.'

'Shut up, damn you,' Lady Honoria whispered savagely, her whisper almost drowning the clerk's droning monotone. 'What–did–Lord–Alfred–say–Cecil?'

As a defensive reflex Cecil himself began to stammer. 'H–h–h–h–he s–s–said no. Awfully sorry, m'love.' Apart from the fact that Honoria was obviously going to be pretty peeved for a bit, he was really rather relieved. He hadn't the slightest interest in Aram Court, and had never understood Honoria's. And the idea of quarrelling with his uncle over two rotten old ruins in a slum had been making him break out in cold sweats for weeks past. The awful thing was that he had to face Honoria more often and more concentratedly than he had to face Uncle Alfred. He was still shuddering slightly at his uncle's advice after he had tried to explain to him the problem of coping with Honoria when she set her mind on something.

'Beat her,' Lord Alfred had said with surprising earnestness. And venom. 'Give her a damn good hiding. But whatever the blazes you do she's not to buy those blasted houses. That's the last word on the matter, Cecil. Have some port and then go and tell her.'

'He couldn't have said no!' Lady Honoria whispered, her whisper again carrying above the bluebottle droning of the clerk's mumbled reading.

'Sssshhh,' Valentine begged her, his eyes shut with professional pain. Behind them, Johnny O'Hara squinted down his nose with sardonic mockery. Francis O'Rourke laughed aloud, opening his ferocious mouth under the untidy ragged black moustache. It was the sound of that loud, harsh, vulgar and triumphant laugh that decided Lady Honoria to go on, in spite of Lord Alfred, in spite of Cecil, in spite of Valentine Carthew and everything and anything that 'the family' could do to her. Nothing and no one could make her back down and humiliate herself after a laugh like that.

She began to recalculate in her mind the sums she had already worked out half a dozen times a night as she lay awake thinking about those beastly, filthy little houses. Cecil's half-year allow-ance that had just been paid in. The shares left over from his grandmother's will, that he hadn't sold yet. Two insurance policies they could cash in. Fourteen, maybe fifteen thousand. Nothing would make them add up to more, and in common sense they couldn't dream of spending all of it together on any-thing, let alone Aram Court. What would they live on for the next half-year if Lord Alfred wouldn't help them? What would Lord Alfred say? More frightening still, what would he do? But she was beyond fear and far beyond common sense. She could think of nothing except that jeering, vilely triumphant laugh, and hear it repeated and repeated, in different tones and degrees of subtlety, by all her friends, all her acquaintances, all her enemies; one enormous, gathering wave of laughter that would not only destroy her position at the head of the Friends of Aram Court, as claimant to the vacant throne of Dublin Society, but would sweep her out of Dublin altogether.

And anyway, as common sense insisted on trying to get its nose round the door of her closing mind; houses like those couldn't possibly, conceivably go for anything like fifteen thousand. Val and Cecil had had her half-way persuaded that they could, that men like that odious creature O'Rourke would pay any money, would think nothing of spending five, ten, fifteen thousand if they needed the site for development; but it couldn't be true, she wouldn't believe it. Fifteen hundred was more likely.

The drone had come to a stop. Paddy Gunn the auctioneer lifted his eyes to the room as if he was about to begin preaching, shot his cuffs and said briskly, 'Right, ladies and gentlemen. There are the details. You all know the conditions of sale. Twenty-five per cent on acceptance of bid. Now. Who's going to begin? Who's going to start me off for these two exceptional properties? I'm not going to insult you by offering them separately. Who'll start the bidding for the two together?'

No one spoke. The man in the dirty overcoat beside Cecil Gandon choked, took out his handkerchief and buried his face in it. Cecil looked away, met his wife's dangerous eyes and looked back at the handkerchief like a man probing a sore tooth. His face turned slightly green. He was trying to make up his mind whether it was better to try and get his wife out of the room now and risk her making a scene, or sit there in terror that she would lose her mind and start bidding. On the far side of Lady Honoria, Valentine Carthew cracked his knuckles miserably and stared at the ceiling. Lady Honoria tried to control her breathing and the beating of her heart. Fifteen hundred. Should she say it now? Startle them all with one solid bid? She could go to two. Or three. Her mouth was dry and her throat seemed not to be working. That O'Rourke man couldn't rationally go above five, it wasn't possible.

The man behind Lady Honoria sniffed loudly in the silence. 'Eighteen hundred,' he said. He was a stout, comfortable man and he had a stout, comfortable voice that said very clearly, I know what's what. Them houses are worth eighteen hundred for the two and not a penny more. He looked round, challenging anyone to be so stupid as to outbid him. The man choking into his handkerchief raised his streaming nose to say in a desolate croak, 'Eighteen fifty.'

Paddy Gunn stared at him indulgently, wonderingly, as if he did not know that such innocence existed, and had put it down to consummate cunning. 'Sir, please, let's be serious. For two properties like this? Eighteen fifty? Now, I know it's a cold, miserable afternoon and we're not warmed up yet . . .' He went into his auctioneer's patter, like an actor trying to put life into a matinée audience, and yet curiously never losing for a second his priestly gravitas, the hint of eternal truth behind the commercial trivia. 'Now, who's going to start me with a serious bid?'

Lady Honoria crouched like a greyhound waiting to be released from its trap, her fingers shredding her gloves, her throat paralysed. Eighteen fifty. If she said, 'Nineteen'? Someone would say, 'Two thousand.' She couldn't bear it, she was going to be sick. It was not two wretched little houses they were bidding for, it was her life, her pride.

'Two thousand,' she whispered, and then, afraid the auctioneer might not have heard her, she said , '*Two thousand!*' much too loud. People sat up. Beside her Val Carthew flinched as if she had hit him. Old Mr Clancy shut his eyes. She was in. It had started. They wouldn't be content until they saw him collapsing with a heart-attack. 'M'love,' Cecil beseeched her, whispering out of the corner of his mouth. 'We can't. Lord Alfred——'

Her whispered answer was so shocking in its ferocity and vulgarity that he stayed looking at her, his mouth slowly falling open.

Behind them the comfortable man sniffed, allowing it to sound like laughter. The ragpicker blew his nose. Johnny O'Hara rustled the pages of the *Irish Press*, made a casual business of folding them. When everyone's attention was caught by the sound in the hushed room, he sighed gently and said nothing, smiling.

'Two thousand?' Paddy Gunn said at last in a pained voice. 'Two thousand? For investment properties like these? Have you seen them? I ask you, have you been to view them?'

'They're collapsing,' the comfortable man said. 'That's what they are, collapsing. Done. Finished.'

'Two two,' the ragpicker said, peering sideways at Cecil and Lady Honoria over his handkerchief.

'Two thousand five hundred,' Lady Honoria whispered. Valentine Carthew went rigid in his hard, uncomfortable chair. He was going to get up and leave. He was going to disassociate himself from the whole thing. He wouldn't remain a second longer. He'd be able to prove that he wasn't here, that he hadn't stayed. But he didn't move. It was as though he couldn't trust his legs to support him. The thought of Lord Alfred, that should have strengthened his resolution, seemed to paralyse it. Cecil opened and shut his mouth, trying to say, 'M'love, m'dear.' Nothing came out.

Paddy Gunn, from behind his auctioneer's table, gazed fondly at Lady Honoria, enfolding her in beneficence, his expression suggesting very slightly, almost imperceptibly, that he was on her side, that given the slightest chance he would knock these superb properties down to her for half of what they were really worth. And he really was happy to see her bidding. The higher she went the higher Frank and Johnny O'Hara and old Jo Clancy would have to go, and the higher would be Moberley & Gunn's commission. It would be nothing directly into his private pocket, but all things being equal a larger profit for his own firm never came amiss.

The silence stretched, became almost somnolent. Lady Honoria forgot to breathe, sitting still and tensed and huddled inside her sealskin coat, not daring to believe that she was going to win, that she was going to get the two houses for two and a half thousand, that she had beaten them all.

'I have two and a half on my left,' Paddy Gunn said, wearily, a man seeing the illusions of a lifetime crumbling into ashes. 'It's against you, sir,' he added wheedlingly, looking at the ragpicker. The silence deepened. 'Surely, surely someone here realizes what they're being offered?'

Shut up, you fool, Lady Honoria wanted to scream. She dug her nails into her palms. She was going to win. She was going to win. Why didn't he say it was over, knock his hammer on the table or whatever they did at auctions? Come on! Come on!

At the back of the room the door opened and a small, bent man with wisps of grey poking out from under his old, greasy felt hat, and a drip on the end of his long red nose, crept in like a caricature of Fagin. An ancient grey raincoat flapped round his ankles, almost touching the broken tops of his shapeless, almost colourless shoes, and his hands hung large and red and raw in front of him as if he had just found them and was not yet sure what to do with them.

But curiously enough that was the one thing that he did know. He was Walter Bouchier, the painter, and one of the first Friends of Aram Court. Long before Lady Honoria, or Frank O'Rourke, or any of the other principals in the matter had so much as heard of Aram Court, he had known every stone and brick and window-pane in the two houses, as he knew all the oldest corners of Dublin, from the archways leading off the Quays to the door-ways of Crampton Court to Winetavern Street to the Ha'penny Bridge. He had painted them all, with a love and passion that in any other city might have made him rich, or at least famous. In Dublin he had been lucky not to starve. But he had heard of the Friends of Aram Court, as everyone in Dublin hears everything that happens, often before it happens at all, and he had come to the first meeting with a carefully folded pound note that might otherwise have made him happily drunk for a week-end.

Something to Lady Honoria's embarrassment and much to her friends' amusement, he had insisted on being enrolled, and had immediately presented the new organization with a painting of Aram Court itself, which painting now hung in the basement passage in Merrion Square leading to Lady Honoria's kitchen. He saw it there quite often, because whenever he called at the house to inquire timidly how the salvation of Aram Court was progressing, Lady Honoria, who was basically very kind, had sent him down to the kitchen for some tea and a slice of cold pie or whatever cook had available. And in return poor Walter Bouchier had developed for Lady Honoria a tongue-tied but passionate devotion.

Of all the Friends, of all her wide acquaintance, he alone saw her as she herself wanted to be seen, the Queen of Dublin, superb, supreme, raised on a golden throne of wealth and loveliness above the common ruck of mere humanity. He wished with all his heart that he had one quarter of the talent as a portraitist that his friend and drinking companion Seán Ó Conaire possessed, so that he could reveal some fraction of his vision of her on canvas. Instead he could only bring her small gifts of his Dublin paintings, which she kindly took from him and gave to one of the maids to stack away in a cupboard or in the attics.

He crept into the auction-room now in a kind of ecstatic terror. She had told all the Friends that none of them were to come to the Auction, on the excuse that the less fuss there was the lower the price might stay, and that anyway if they were there watching her they would only make her nervous and upset her bidding. The real reason of course had been sheer, instinctive terror that they would see her fail, that she would not only be humiliated, but humiliated right in front of her own supporters. Whatever happened, if they weren't there at the time she would have a chance to think of some kind of explanation afterwards.

For most of the Friends it was an order they were perfectly happy to accept. They had all begun to get rather bored with the entire project and had also begun to be extremely nervous that they might be asked to subscribe to the purchase price. But for Walter Bouchier it was not only a sacred command, it was a torment. How could he disobey her? But at the same time, how could he stay away? When his Queen, his Lady, was going into battle against the forces of darkness, young and beautiful and innocent, to face the monstrous men who wanted to destroy the heart and glory of Dublin. How could he stay away? And so he crept in to watch her fight for Ireland against Mammon, for all old, beautiful, threatened things. If she was furious with him, that was the penance he would have to pay. He stayed huddled at the back by the door, his eyes fastened on her, swimming like old shelled oysters behind his thick, pebble glasses.

'I have two and a half on my left,' Paddy Gunn repeated. 'Against the remainder of the room.' He lifted his auctioneer's gavel. Lady Honoria thought she was going to faint. She wanted to reach out beside her and grip hold of Cecil's arm, half for support, half in triumph. But before she could move her hand Johnny O'Hara had refolded his newspaper with the air of a man who has allowed the children to play long enough and said, in his slightly nasal, cynical-sounding drawl, 'Three.'

Cecil, who had been thinking for a long, agonized minute that his wife was going to be left as the highest bidder, let out his held breath in a sigh of pleased relief. Even Valentine Carthew managed to look happier. She'd have to stop now.

'Four thousand,' Lady Honoria said quietly. If they wanted a fight, let them have it. The blood of thirty generations of Highland Wyntouns and Lomaxes flowed like an icy torrent of rage through her narrow, beautiful blue veins. Let them have it.

'Five,' Johnny O'Hara said in the bored voice of a man whose patience is very long, but not inexhaustible. Old Mr Clancy sagged inside his big blue overcoat as if air was slowly leaking out of him. He saw a steeply descending path in front of him towards his inevitable heart-attack. Nothing could save him.

'Six,' said Lady Honoria. Valentine Carthew tried to say something. 'L–L–L–L. . . . Cecil leaned forward, tried to catch her eye. There was going to be a scene, a most frightful scene. He thought longingly of his uncle's advice. If only it was possible.

'M–m–m–m–m'love.' Damn Val and his bloody stammer, it was catching. 'M'dear, for pity's sake——'

'Shut *up*,' Lady Honoria hissed at him. She raised her gold pencil six inches in the air like a tiny dagger and brought the point sharply down an inch behind Cecil's kneecap. He folded forward in agony, clutching his knee, and for almost a minute he was blind and deaf to what was happening, the tears running out of his eyes with pain and the effort of not showing what had happened. When he came back to ordinary consciousness his wife was saying, 'Twelve thousand,' in much the same kind of voice that her ancestors had used at Flodden and Bannockburn, calling the clans to charge. Cecil choked in agony. Valentine Carthew was sitting helpless, whispering 'O m–m–m–m–my G–G–G–G–God' over and over again, and then 'P–p–p–p–p–p–please L–L–Lady A–A–A–A–Aitch.'

'Fifteen,' Johnny O'Hara said, contriving to sound like a

sardonic computer. By the door Walter Bouchier was clasping his big red hands together as if he was praying. For him any sum of money over ten pounds was enormous, and anything over a hundred was unimaginable. He could scarcely take it in that these figures flying about the room actually represented money. They were simply battle-cries and the largest, loudest battle-cry would win. Come on, he prayed silently for his beloved. Higher, higher! You're going to win!

'Sixteen,' Lady Honoria said. Scots, wha ha'e wi' Wallace bled, Scots, wham Bruce has aften led, welcome to your gorie bed, or to Victorie! Beside her Cecil tried to believe that he was losing his mind, that none of this was happening.

'Eighteen,' Johnny said.

'Twenty thousand!' Lady Honoria cried. Or to Victorie!

Old Joseph Clancy moaned inside his overcoat, struggled out of it like a turtle overturned on a beach, 'I won't allow it, it's madness——'

'God dammit!' Francis O'Rourke roared, crashing across the beginning of Johnny's following bid. 'Twenty-five thousand.'

Before Lady Honoria could open her mouth again Valentine Carthew from the right and Cecil from the left fell on her like the pillars of the temple crashing inwards on Samson, gripping her arms and half lifting her out of her seat, in absolute concert, as though their two stricken minds had worked by telepathy. 'You've got to shut up,' Cecil whispered, something of the Gandon heritage waking in his anaemic veins. 'That's enough.'

'T–t–t–t–too m–m–m–much,' hissed Valentine Carthew. For Lady Honoria it was like being rudely woken from a trance, a dream of battle, of herself with kilt and claymore laying the hated Southrons low. She almost needed to ask 'Where am I?', her eyes dazed and unfocused as her two escorts half-lifted, half-urged her out of her seat and hurried with her, awkwardly and shamefacedly, along the row of chairs, down the long, narrowish room towards the door, and through the doorway, as the unbelieving, stricken-faced Walter Bouchier opened it for them.

'Sorry ... sorry ... 'scuse me,' Cecil kept whispering to no one in particular, and then more passionately to the crimson-faced Francis O'Rourke as they passed him on the way out. Cecil half expected to be arrested on the spot, to be made to prove that he could have backed up his wife's bids with cash; to be sued for whatever her bids had cost Francis O'Rourke. He didn't feel safe until they were out in the gathering greyness of the afternoon. Walter Bouchier crept after them in dejected misery, and went and got very drunk on credit.

11

The plans of Brefni House went into the Corporation late in May 1960, Brefni House being the name they had eventually hit on for the new building in delicate allusion to an entirely imaginary relationship between Francis O'Rourke's humble ancestors and the great house of the O'Rourkes of Brefni. The roughly rectangular block of houses bounded by Oxman Street, Marietta Street, Slaughter Lane, and St Olaf's Row, with Aram Court hidden in the middle, was to be razed to the ground and in place of the nineteen derelict houses was to rise Francis O'Rourke's dream. Or at least the beginning of it. A long glass and concrete monster of a building, eight storeys high and at one end a tower rising a further eight storeys.

Andrew Fane had designed it, creating a honeycomb effect of heavy precast concrete units to frame the windows, making the building at once massive, almost threatening, and at the same time curiously light, aerated. In his 'artist's impression' it soared up from the slum surroundings like a twentieth-century castle, as enormous, domineering, challenging, as the Norman Castle across the river had been when John of England had it built in the thirteenth century, to glower down on the mud-and-wattle cabins and ramshack timber stalls and houses of his subjects of the Pale.

When Francis saw the plans first, just after Christmas, he had become gripped again by the idea, not simply as a way of making a lot of money, or even as a challenge, but as an ideal, a dream. As if this was what he had been born to do, and for a second the curtain had been ripped aside and he had seen his own purpose in life, what he had to achieve, had to leave behind him for the future. Old Jo Clancy was with him and all he was interested in was the cost. Andrew Fane had lifted his hand theatrically, pushed back his lock of white hair, waited his moment and said, 'I'd say'—lifting one eyebrow to consider the effect—'a fraction over a million. About that.'

'Jesus, Mary and Joseph,' old Jo had whispered. He had put his hand up to his heart, pressing the fat, rheumatic, knuckleless fingers against the thick cloth of his coat. 'You can't mean it.'

'It's approximately a hundred thousand square feet of floor space. And at ten pounds a square foot, for the kind of building you want, with ten per cent for contingencies, you can say one million one hundred thousand.' Andrew Fane put down his elegant, slender, manicured fingers on to the artist's impression. 'And, gentlemen, no million that you ever spend will be spent to better effect.'

He had been Johnny O'Hara's idea. The second that he had heard that Lady Honoria was organizing against them he had pushed their existing, hack architect, old Jo Clancy's choice, into the background, and grabbed Andrew Fane. 'He's culture,' Johnny had said, 'and we're going to need culture by the bloody bucket if that bitch starts acting up.'

Jo Clancy had known from that moment, if he hadn't guessed it long before, that he was getting out of his depth, that if he had any regard for himself he'd pull out of Jofran Ltd, the company they had formed to buy up the sites for the new building, do what he had been meaning to do four years ago when young Johnny O'Hara had brought him along to meet Francis: retire, grow roses, look after his health, have more time with his son Victor, read books, go on a cruise. It still wasn't too late.

But it was. He was already too deep in. Nearly all his capital was in with Francis and Francis would never let him out. Never. Not now. Andrew Fane! Over a million! Oh my God, oh my God, he wasn't going to live to see the end of this. Like a premonition. Waking in the night and feeling his heart going faster and faster and the pain coming under it like a knife, like a hot knife, red hot, stabbing him. If Franky knew, if he knew how bad he felt. He felt it coming on him now.

'Ring my son,' he whispered. 'Ring Victor to fetch me, I'm not feeling well.'

'Get away out of that,' Francis said. 'You ate too much bloody lunch. Look at it. Look at it.' The tower. It was the tower that caught his mind. An office at the top of that. Sixteen storeys high.

Windows all round it. Like flying. He could see it. Big desk. Like a bloody tennis court. Mahogany. Five, six, seven telephones. Or maybe no telephones. A girl to do all that. And for a second he thought of who the girl might have been, the pug, puppy face, the hair, the dressing-gown, the sound of the typewriter, and the pain was almost like Jo's pain, under the heart, stab and twist, and he actually stiffened, half lifted his hand. Big couch, he thought mechanically, his mind gone leaden. Leather, two or three of them scattered about like islands. Black, white. 'It's a wonderful building,' he said humbly.

Andrew Fane looked at him, surprised. It was strange how one could reach even people like this with a real work of art. He adjusted the paperweights and silver cigar box and silver cigar-lighter on the corners of the plans to keep them from rolling up, and nodded. 'Yes,' he said. 'I gave it my best.' That unspeakable woman Lady Honoria attacking him for treachery, 'artistic pornography'. In her own house!

'My dear,' he had said, 'on pornography everyone must defer to your judgement. On art I think you will find that most people in Dublin would rather defer to mine.'

He looked almost fondly at Francis O'Rourke. Not the client he would have chosen, perhaps, but now, if he had to choose again between him and that unadulterated vixen—was *unadulterated* the word to use in her case?—there wasn't any choice at all. A cross between Lady Macbeth and Lucrezia Borgia.

'I think that not only you but Dublin will be very proud of this building. If I say it myself, it has the spirit of the times.' But even he looked strangely sobered, the thought of Lady Honoria weighing on him, not as an active pain but as an unhappiness, a Hamlet sense of ill about the heart, a feeling against reason that ill would come of all of this.

She had begun organizing her counter-attacks within a few days of the auction, almost within twenty-four hours. After the first shock of failure had died down, she had realized that losing a battle needn't mean losing the war. No surrender, the blood of the Lomaxes cried in her. Run away? Admit she had been humiliated by a fat, red-faced peasant like O'Rourke? She would rather be burned alive in St Stephen's Green, be publicly be-headed in the courtyard of the Castle. Scots wha ha'e wi' Wallace bled! On, on! Charge! Cecil and that snake-in-the-carpet Valentine Carthew might carry her physically off one field of battle, but unless they chained her up they wouldn't stop her reaching the next battlefield. Friends of Aram Court, fellow soldiers in the Army of Culture, we live to fight again! She saw herself in battered but still beautiful armour, a tattered banner of exquisite embroidery fluttering above her lovely golden head against a blood-red sky and coal-dark storm-clouds. Scots wham Bruce has aften led, Welcome to your gory bed, or to Victorie! As she saw the vision in her mind's eye she almost wept for the beauty and the pathos of it. If Cecil, if Valentine Carthew, if that old pig Lord Alfred couldn't see it, then damn them. And as far as Lord Alfred was concerned she felt she no longer had anything to lose. He had already pulverized Cecil, and jolly good luck to him. Cecil could do with a bit of pulverizing. As for money, Lord Alfred had locked up Cecil's capital for the next Heaven knew how many years. But she still had Cecil's allowance and no one could take that away from her. She had Cecil's insurance policies and his grandmother's shares, and what more did she need? This was no longer a battle to be fought with money, beyond the essential few hundred here and there to keep things moving. This was now a war of wits and hatred, and if she hadn't got more of both of those than a handful of bogtrotters like O'Rourke and his lot, she didn't deserve to win. What was needed was pub-licity, a campaign to show the people of Ireland what these brutes were like, what they were daring to try to do. Public meetings, letters in the newspapers, deputations to important people.

She started with letters to the newspapers, from the Friends of Aram Court, from herself, from almost anyone of substance or reputation she could cajole or blackmail into helping. A timid little professor of Economics who in person would have fled from a duck in St Stephen's Green, but in print was a Bayard. A novelist who had written his last novel so long ago that he was now accepted by the cultured as a great artist. Poor Walter Bouchier, who had his letter written for him by Kate Lennox, while he sat in the kitchen drinking stout, his hands shaking, having just had a violent quarrel in McBain's with Seán Ó Conaire who had threatened him as a slieveen and a lickspittle, a kitchen scrounger. An elderly Senator who had known W. B. Yeats wrote to say that the destruction of Aram Court was a national disgrace. A German refugee architect mentioned the Nazis as also the kind of people who preferred skyscrapers to unique, irreplaceable houses, pregnant with the history of their city and their people.

A French architect of enormous reputation was flown in from Cannes at Lady Honoria's—or perhaps more accurately Cecil's—expense, wined, dined, flirted with, flattered, and introduced to the Press at a small cocktail conference arranged by the Friends of Aram Court. 'These gentlemen that are wishing to assassinate these beautiful old houses, I hope they are able to sleep well at nights. For I could not if I was contemplating such crimes.'

Behind these skirmishers and forward patrols Lady Honoria prepared her main attack. She was finding that she had a flair for intrigue and leadership and was growing in cunning almost by the day. Somehow, by the dropping of a word here and getting someone else to whisper a not-to-be-repeated-secret there, she managed to get it to be widely believed, in spite of all Lord Alfred's increasingly angry protestations, that somehow the Gandons themselves were involved, and that they would be very glad if planning permission was refused. In July 1960 planning permission was refused. The tenants of the nineteen houses stayed where they were. Any of them who had been willing to move out into Corporation flats or houses found that they couldn't, because from the Corporation's point of view they were already housed, at least after a fashion. And a second kind of voice began to add itself to the attacks on the Developers. A political voice, that they were slum landlords, exploiting the poor, taking rackrents from the helpless, and at the same time subjecting their tenants to dreadful conditions, unwilling even to mend a lavatory or a window-pane.

'Christ,' Johnny had said. 'If we mend anything down there,

we'll have to mend everything. And for what? The better we make those damned houses the harder it'll be to get an appeal through. Leave things the way they are.'

The House the People Committee entered the war, and joined forces behind the scenes with Lady Honoria. Denis Farrell, long-time Communist, veteran of the Spanish Civil War, came to her with his gentle, grey, clerical face and his grey, gentle voice. 'We are both interested in the quality of life,' he had said. 'You more in the quality, I more in the life perhaps'— smiling softly at his joke. 'But when it is people against profit then I think that we are both for people. Isn't that true?'

They were in the big drawing-room of Lady Honoria's beautiful Georgian house in Merrion Square, with its high windows, and great famille-rose vases of tulips and hot-house carnations. They stood together by the Adam fireplace, Lady Honoria with her back to the windows, seeing out of the corner of her eye her own head and shoulders in the deep Venetian mirror: green velvet against swan white skin, the gold necklace from Cartier thick and heavy round her creamy, lovely, some-how still childish throat, the gold of the necklace echoing the yet more gorgeous living gold of her hair, caught back by its simple green velvet band, and she thought without affectation that she had never seen anything so beautiful in her life. It was as if the presence of this soft, grey, shapeless man had heightened her beauty by sheer contrast. And a Communist! A real live Bolshevik! Inside herself she shuddered with a kind of delicious terror, like almost touching the nose of a wild animal through the bars of its cage, offering it a piece of chocolate. And here there were no bars, there was nothing between them except the width of the marble fireplace. No one even within call, except Alice the parlourmaid and cook down in the kitchen.

'Both for people?' she said dreamily, touching her necklace. Suppose he tried to tear it off her, what would she do? What a funny phrase. And he was wearing mittens! Actually wearing grey woollen mittens. The absurdity of it gave her a small spasm of laughter inside her throat, overcoming her nervousness, making her feel suddenly warm and protective towards this silly, grey little man. How could he be a Communist and wear mittens? He reminded her somehow of Walter Bouchier the painter and she wondered if he was hungry, if he would like to go down to the kitchen afterwards and eat something.

'Of course I'm for people!' she said, and thought with a sudden flush of joy of crowds of people loving her, cheering. Hurrah for her Ladyship, hurrah, hurrah! 'What else is there in life except people, and helping them and making them happy?' She lifted her chin with great pride of generosity, noticing in the mirror how beautiful the green velvet looked against her skin, against the necklace. Far better than that awful yellow thing she had just bought in Paris. She might give that to Alice. 'I live for people,' she said.

'I know that, Lady Honoria. That is why I have come to you. You are very kind to receive me.' He lifted one of his mittened hands in a soft gesture of gratitude. He wore the mittens because long ago five of General O'Duffy's Blueshirts had taken him to a cellar and smashed all his fingers with an iron bar.

'You won't be writing any of your Bolshy filth with these for a while,' they had said, and that had been true. Now, after nearly a quarter of a century, both hands were crippled with arthritis in the damaged knuckles and he had to type whatever he wanted to write, painfully, with two hooked fingers. But he wrote quite a lot. News-letters, broadsheets; ill-printed, grey-looking pamphlets explaining Communism and its veering path to the handful of the faithful, telling the poor in a grinding, dialectical, Party prose quite unlike his own soft voice that they were the masters of Ireland, they were Ireland, that out of their hunger the rich fed fat; that out of their children's emigration the children of the rich rode horses; that out of their humility and patience the powerful grew proud.

All his adult life he had written this, begged and pleaded for the poor to listen, spoken on rainswept corners, been beaten by the police, the Blueshirts, the outraged sons of the middle classes enrolled in the Legion to keep Ireland Catholic. He had grown grey and shapeless on bad food and too little sleep. He had worshipped Lenin as given a different twist in childhood he might have worshipped Christ; served Moscow as he might have served the Vatican. His mother had hoped that he would be a priest. But his labourer, trade-unionist father had followed Larkin in 1913, and been one of the few in the Labour movement to fight against the betrayal of Labour in 1919, when the movement bowed out of active politics, leaving the field clear to the Nationalists and the Right-Wing Republicans. From the time he was nine years old he had been selling pamphlets and ephemeral Communist news-sheets on street corners, and he had been writing them since he was twenty, when his father was already long dead of tuberculosis.

In 1939 he had been in Moscow, and again in 1951, and those two visits had kept his faith alive like a sanctuary lamp, still and red and motionless and burning, the centre of his life. He knew what had happened in Catalonia in '36, and in Hungary in '56, and it made no more impression on his faith than liberal chatter about the Inquisition would make on a Jesuit's. And if he could use Lady Honoria he would use her as willingly and lovingly as he would see her shot. What mattered was the poor, the future, the coming of a generation that would not be warped by hunger, enslaved by ignorance, by mindless obedience to the priests and to the rich, but made free and glorious. He would be dead, but his dead body, his grey dust would be a fraction of the ground they stood on, upright, singing, masters of their world.

'We can make this several kinds of test case,' he said. 'When you are talking and writing about art and culture, about what these buildings represent as architecture, very few will listen to you. Even fewer politicians. But if you add to art and culture that people are suffering, people are being made homeless to make room for offices and in the meanwhile are being forced to live in filth and squalor, then very many people will begin to listen.'

'We'll make them listen!' she cried. In her imagination she saw mass meetings of the homeless cheering her, old women struggling forward on their knees to kiss her hands. God bless your ladyship! May God reward you for your goodness! At that moment if Denis Farrell had asked her to join the Communist Party she would have joined it, as leader naturally, and worked for the Revolution. She had never heard of Rosa Luxemburg, or La Pasionaria, but that was how she felt. 'We'll fight shoulder to shoulder!' she said. 'And win!'

They didn't meet often again. There was no need. They simply exchanged information, and co-ordinated their campaigns, of letter-writing to the papers, public meetings, pressures on T.D.s and Corporation officials, spreading rumours and dropping inspired whispers into the ears of the more receptive journalists. There were quite a number of these, and there was no need for any ignobly snobbish or subversively political motive for their receptiveness. To see the conditions in which the tenants of Oxman Street were living was to be appalled. The fact that all over Dublin thousands upon thousands of families had been living like that and worse than that since Dublin began was neither here nor there. Articles expressing honest horror about Oxman Street and its neighbourhood began to appear so frequently, and so persuasively, that politicians had to take notice. In April 1961 the Minister for Local Government turned down Jofran Limited's appeal against the Corporation's decision on Brefni House. The which was greeted by nearly all concerned as a tremendous victory for the forces of Light. The fact that by itself it did absolutely nothing to improve the living conditions of the miserable inhabitants of Oxman Street and St Olaf's Row and Marietta Street occurred to almost no one.

Jofran in the meantime, which is to say Francis O'Rourke and Johnny O'Hara actively, and old Jo Clancy passively, like an unwilling passenger on a ship he is sure will sink at any minute, had been gathering their own support. Johnny's brother, Seamus, had already moved up a rung or two in the Party and was Parliamentary Secretary to one of the ministers, making friends on all sides with his jolly laugh and frank blue eyes and his locker-room jokes, but these friends were mostly the younger men in the Party and unwilling to get involved in something that had the smell of too much power against it, the Gandons, big money. They were realistic young men, which was why they had joined the Party of Reality, and if they were going to back anyone in a thing like this they would back the Gandons.

'But they're Anglo-Irish,' Seamus had complained, bewildered at such unnational feelings. 'West British. And anyway, they're not really in this, it's just that woman.'

'Ah sure, I know, I know, but leave me out of this, Seamus boy. If it was anything else now, if it was something down my part of the country, by God you wouldn't have to ask me twice. Why not try so and so, he knows the Minister's cousin pretty well, and his father was in the Flying Column with the Old Man. . . .' Only Jer Mullins was any help, and against all expectation, because he was the junior T.D. for Oxmantown, and if anything his political profit would have seemed to lie in opposing the Developers. But he was a lot shrewder than that. He had a long, bent nose like Johnny O'Hara's, and a capacity for sniffing future profit like a truffle-hound's for truffles.

'I'll ask my uncle,' he said. 'Marty.'

'We haven't been too friendly with him for the past few years,' Johnny had said. 'I don't know if——'

'Water under the bridge,' Jer answered. 'Leave it to me.' He was still very young, still at the running stage of eagerness to please, thin and quick and jerky, like a ventriloquist's puppet, all stick bones and twitching wires inside the expensive suits that always seemed four sizes too big for him, as if he had bought them knowing that he would get fat; that very soon the twitching and the jerking and the running errands would pay off in perks and promotions and tips on good things, ending up with a State Mercedes and a nice little property down in Meath with a couple of racehorses and a smart mistress. But now he was still at the running stage, willing to run anywhere for anyone, providing of course that they were powerful or useful, and he was a familiar sight dashing up and down the stairs of Leinster House, dashing out to the car-park with a wadge of documents in his hand for some elderly forgetful member of his party, running to the telephone, to his own car, to open doors for the Old Man or a minister, or a coming colleague. What Seamus O'Hara with his big face and his blue eyes was getting by telling jokes and being so nice that he frightened no one, Jer Mullins was getting by doing favours, by being quicker and cleverer and sharper than anyone else. And he was still so young and insignificant that no one was frightened of him either. Yet. And he had Marty behind him. Marty of Connemara.

The quarrel, not even a quarrel, the coolness between Francis and Marty had begun the year after they met, and over the most absurd of things: old Mrs O'Rourke's pension. Not her widow's pension, or her old-age pension, but her I.R.A. pension, that for more than thirty years she had been proclaiming to anyone who would listen was due to her for the death and sufferings of her blessed husband Jim, that saintly man, that fighter for Ireland, and for her own sufferings and battles as his wife and widow, against the Auxiliaries and the Tans and the massed forces of evil and Empire and Lloyd George in the dark days of '20 and '21. Aye and before that too, when the whippersnappers and the bandwagon-jumpers and God-Save-King-Georgers were still touching their hats to the R.I.C. and saying, God bless you, Constable, and God keep us all safe from the Shinners. Oh be the Holy, she knew them, and they knew her, and they had known Jim, Republican, Fighter, Patriot, Martyr, shot up yonder in the big field the night of March 19 in nineteen and twenty-one by a lorryload of Tans, come up from Galway on purpose to get him. Up there yonder under that hedge, where he was lying with his Mauser pistol and surrounded by empty cartridge-cases, and the big murderer of a Tan captain emptying his Thomson sub-machine-gun into Jim's poor twisting body the way you'd gaff a salmon. Arrah before Jesus and His Blessed Mother if any man in Drumleague, if any man in Connemara, if any man West of the Shannon deserved the Martyr's Crown it was James O'Rourke. And by the same token if any woman in the same area deserved an I.R.A. pension as the widow of a hero, it was herself.

The person to get it for her, who else, was her elected representative in the Dail, Mr Martin Mullins, T.D., the other T.D.s for the district being Opposition slieveens, men with no more national feeling nor understanding than turnips, almost West Britishers, hangovers from the Redmondites.

'Arrah Marty man,' she had said, having known him from childhood, and seen him grow into the great man, the Caesar of

Connemara that he now was, 'what about getting me that little bit of an I.R.A. pension that's due to me? Who else would I turn to if it wasn't yourself?'

They had been standing outside her cottage at the far end of the grey, drab village, under the mountain, and he had nearly had a seizure trying not to laugh in her face. Even then, and that was a long time ago, her wish for an I.R.A. pension had been a joke. It was as well known to Marty Mullins as it was to everyone else in Drumleague that Jim O'Rourke had been shot as an informer. He knew the man who had shot him, and drank with him often enough in Moriarty's up in Dublin. Anything Jim O'Rourke had ever done for the I.R.A. he had done so that he could tell the R.I.C., the Royal Irish Constabulary, about it. And any dealings he had with the Tans had been for the same purpose. He had died under that hedge, true enough, and he may even have fired his Mauser pistol in self-defence. And also true enough, there had been a lorryload of Tans there; but they had come to save their man, and arrived ten minutes too late.

The story that the Tans had done the killing had been put round simply as a smokescreen to confuse the British authorities, and protect the real executioner, and everyone who needed to know the truth, either to be pleased by it, or frightened by it for the good of their political souls, had known very well what had really happened.

For twenty years Mrs O'Rourke had contented herself with simply describing her husband's heroism and patriotism. And because villages can be kind as well as cruel, no one had bothered to contradict her. God help her, the poor creature, and what fault was it of hers if her man was one of that kind? What harm if she had her illusions?

But to get her an actual pension for being the widow of an informer was a different thing, and from the early forties when she first started badgering him to get it for her, 'up above in Dublin', to 1955, when Francis O'Rourke brought her to live in his big house in Rathfarnham and keep Maura company, Marty Mullins kept putting her off with a bluff and kindly hypocrisy that had begun to wear thin after ten or twelve years.

'Ah sure, Bridie, who deserves it better than yourself now? But wisha, them pensions is the devil and all to get. It's like gettin' teeth out of a crocodile makin' them fellers pay up for the poor widow of a patriot like Jim.'

'And how did Lucy Mangan be gettin' hers, then? And Jenny O'Callaghan? And Peter Burke that says he was in the Post Office with Pearse, God forgive him for the lie. How did they be gettin' it?'

'Sure some things is simple and some things is complicated, Bridie, but God is strong, and maybe the old ass'll get there before nightfall. We can only go on trying.'

'That fat omadhaun,' Bridie would say when he was gone again from the village on his grass-roots tillage round his district. 'Do you see the flesh he's puttin' under his waistcoat up beyond in Dublin? I don't know what we do be havin' elections for at all, puttin' the likes of that porter barrel on our backs.'

Marty had put it down to one of the small penances of political life, but at least he only ran into it the few times a year when he was passing by Drumleague on his way to somewhere more important. But when Francis O'Rourke moved his mother up Dublin it became unbearable. He couldn't visit Francis without being badgered about it, and then the old woman actually got Francis himself to face him with it in Moriarty's. He gave Francis a slightly impatient answer, one word borrowed another, and ever since there had been a coolness.

Jer Mullins put an end to it. He let Johnny O'Hara understand that if Francis went to Moriarty's at a certain time, Marty would be there with all old sores forgotten. Moriarty's, a public house strategically placed near Dail Eireann, plain and simple enough to be democratic, and yet not so scruffy as to be beneath the dignity of a member of the Irish Parliament, was Marty Mullins's office, his club, his meeting-place. Every worth-while constituent up from Connemara for any reason knew that he could find Marty there at the right hour of the day. When Francis turned into the public bar, Marty was already installed, sitting on a high stool with his back to the counter, his overcoat, his coat and his cardigan undone to show his bulging waistcoat, with its heavy looped gold watchchain hung with hurling medals. His large black politician's hat was on the stool beside him, his bald, pink head was shimmering with comfortable, companionable sweat, and he was listening to a small, urgent, ferrety man with a raincoat down to his ankles and a dilapidated felt hat crammed on to his head so tight that his ears stuck out from underneath it, turned at right angles to his skull.

' 'Tis due to me,' he was saying. ' 'Tis owing to me. Didn't my two cows take sick on me there before Christmas and divil a sup of milk either of them have given me since and the pair of them eatin' a rick of hay between them and not a pound of fat to show for it. And even the small small patch of potatoes I do be havin' goin' against me with the fungus. If it isn't a man like myself should be gettin' the postman's job who in the hell is it and I votin' for you as religious as a fanatic every time there'd be an election?'

And Marty's wheezing, asthmatic voice answering him, like rusty water drawn from a reluctant, yet still tolerant and patient roadside pump. 'Arragh God mend your head, Maggot, and how would I be gettin' you the postman's job and you not able to read nor write? Sure there's scholars in for that job, scholars, man.'

'But do they have their cows gone sick on them like me, and their potatoes ruined on them and their mothers drawin' the blind pension and expecting to be smoking the best tobacco like a blessed chimney? Three Nuns she was asking me for. I amn't tellin' a word of a lie. Three Nunses tobaccy, the divil, and I roiled and murthered with the effort of payin' the vet, and the rates, and buyin' milk from the neighbours, my own two creatures bad luck to them bein' gone as dry as——'

'Aye, aye, the two of them taken sick on you, God spare you more trouble, but how in hell would you deliver the letters, man?'

'You mean you won't help?' the Maggot said incredulously.

'And who said that, God love you? Sure amn't I here to help you, what else for? But 'tisn't easy, man, 'tisn't as easy as you might be thinkin' and you down there sittin' by the fire and gosterin' with your poor old mother. It's me that has to go to the Minister, and God says he, how in hell will that poor fellow be deliverin' the letters says he, and the marks on the envelopes meanin' day nor night to him? Jasus man the Taoiseach himself couldn't get a job like that for you. It's something else entirely we'll have to be thinking of. Lave it with me, Maggot. Lave it with me. God is strong and he won't see a good man suffer beyond his patience.'

'Maybe he won't, Marty, but does He know how little patience there is left in me, and both of my two poor cows with no more milk in their dugs than I have?'

Marty came off the high stool with an asthmatic wheeze, but at the same time like a king coming off his throne, his large stomach and his pint mug of porter held before him in such a way that the Maggot had to back swiftly away or get overlaid. 'Lave it with me, Maggot, lave it with me, boy, we'll think of something. Francis man, 'tis a long time. How's the care?'

The Maggot, unwillingly recognizing a final dismissal, backed two steps further, mumbled something, and made for the door with curious, bouncing strides, the skirts of his tattered raincoat touching the sawdust between the bounces. At the door he turned again, lifted a hand in farewell and said tragically, 'Me patience is near gone, Marty. I've me nephew Tadgh who could read the addresses for me.' But his interview was over and he knew it, and went out into the summer night.

'Come into the snug,' Marty said. 'There'll be less fear of interruptions. They have me persecuted. Persecuted. Is the old lady keepin' well?'

'Middling,' Francis said. 'Middling.'

For five minutes or so they talked of indifferent things, Francis unwilling to humiliate himself by asking for help outright, and Marty amusing himself by waiting, and also unwilling to offer help before it was asked for. But it was Marty who mentioned the matter of Brefni House first.

'This bit of a building of yours? How's things going?' Marty wheezed.

'Slowish,' Francis said, and then with a bitter rush, unable to contain himself any longer: 'We'd have the damn thing built twice over if it wasn't for that bloody Gandon whore.'

'Indeed and you might. And again you might not.' Marty rapped the heel of his empty porter tankard on the ring-marked table-top and a curate popped his head through the hatch. 'The fill of this for me and a Jameson for Mr O'Rourke. Sure, dammit man, why didn't you come to me in the first place when you ran into a spot of bother? Why did you leave it so long? Relying on boys like Johnny O'Hara and young Seamus, and Jer there. Boys! The milk still wet on their mouths, man. What do they know? Now, if you'd come to me then . . .'

Francis knew that this was his penance for the long coolness and gritted his teeth to listen, forcing himself to nod with something like humility at the right moments. And Marty in his turn knew not to spin it out too much.

'But sure, what good is history except to forget it? What matters is now. Turned down by the Corporation. Turned down by the Minister. The Culture Vultures screamin' at you day and night in the papers. It's bad, man, bad enough.' He took a long gasping pull of his pint. 'But not so bad it can't be mended. What are ye doin' in the meantime? I mean, that bit of a buildin' isn't your only iron in the fire, or is it?'

'Pulling the divil by the tail,' Francis said. 'But we're getting by. Jo Clancy knows a bit about building land and what's worth buying, and we've done some deals.'

'So there's a bit of money in the kitty yet?'

'So so.'

'Ah.' He took another long pull and emptied his tankard. It was Francis's turn to rap on the table-top. When they were refilled, Marty wheezed casually, 'Did ye ever hear of the Guardians?'

12

The leaning gatepost had not been straightened, it was gone. The gateway itself had been widened, and the avenue was broad and smooth: tarmacadamed, glistening from recent rain. Except that it was no longer an avenue. The trees, the elms and the great beech trees, were gone, even the stumps gone, dynamited out of the ground. The tarmacadamed drive swept broad and naked up to an unrecognizable Castle Lennox, guarded by a gigantic cement statue of Our Lady painted blue and white, her foot planted on the head of the Enemy, the Tempter who might destroy the innocence of the holy Sisters of the Divine Suffering and their pupils. The house was still there, but flanked by a large and modernistic chapel, the tall, narrow windows made of chunks of thick, coloured glass set in grey cement. On the other flank of the house stood the school proper, two storeys high, flat-roofed, grey and clinical and anaesthetic, dormitories and classrooms uniformly lit by large, dull windows in subtly wrong proportions, so that looking at the bleak façade was like looking at a row of short-sighted men in thick, flat glasses.

'God, what have they done?' Kate breathed, as John let the car roll to a slow, stunned halt beside what had once been their own front door. They looked down towards the river and again it was unrecognizable. The wood was gone, every tree that had been worth selling had been felled, and lopped, and dragged away. But there the stumps had been left, as too expensive to dynamite. Scrubby undergrowth and sucker shoots from around the stumps were making the ruins look not better, but worse. Like a no-man's-land.

Girls' voices chanted the responses of Benediction from the chapel, fell quiet again, leaving only the sense of an alien presence. It was as though all the strength of the land had been sucked into that squat concrete silo of religion to feed those sexless voices. Kate felt herself wanting to scream. She gripped John's wrist and said, 'No, no . . . oh, John.' He didn't answer. There was nothing he could say. He hadn't wanted to come back here. He had half-guessed, half-known what they were likely to find. He had heard that the man O'Rourke had sold out to the nuns, and it was a racing certainty what nuns would do with a place like Castle Lennox.

'Do you want to go in?' he said. The black Afghan in the back of the Zodiac had woken up and was stretching and yawning. It began to whine. 'We'll have to let Shah out.'

'I can't bear it,' Kate said.

'It was you wanted to come.' He got out and the dog followed him, over the back of the front seat and down on to the gravel. He hadn't thought that he would mind. Until he realized that for years he had thought of Castle Lennox as it had always been, thought of it still here, even old Tim still here, Agnes, the maids. Where were they? Working for the nuns? The dog ran in a wide circle, sniffing the tarmacadam, whining softly, puzzled by the half-familiar, half-unfamiliar feel and smell of the place. Ignoring John's call of 'Here, come here, Shah' he ran to the white iron railings that separated the tarmac sweep from the meadow, and cleared them at a bound. The meadow was better, all familiar, and yet still strange, strange. He ran with his head lifted, seeing rather than scenting, missing something, vague shadows out of his puppyhood floating in his narrow, beautiful black head, his long tail quivering with familiarity and strangeness. What he was missing were the trees.

The singing rose again, ended, the dog ran like an arrow for the river. Kate got out of the car. She started to say 'Why——' and stopped herself. The doors of the chapel opened and the girls came trooping out, a look of unnatural piety in their downcast eyes. When they were past the two nuns at the chapel door the look vanished. They saw the car and the two strangers and stared, whispering. More and more girls, bigger and bigger as the chapel emptied, the senior girls last, shooing the smaller ones on past the strangers towards the schoolrooms. When they were all gone by one of the nuns came up, hands hidden in large sleeves; a small, plump, dumpy woman with an air of authority.

'May I help you? Have you come about one of the pupils?'

'No, Sister,' John said. 'We used to live here and we ... we simply came by——'

'Mother,' the nun corrected him. 'Mother Veronica. I am the Headmistress. You must be Mr Lennox?' She said it with a slight air of condescension. 'And you would like to see your old home?' She shook one wrist free from her sleeve and glanced at a large silver wristwatch. 'May we give you tea? I have a French class in a few minutes but one of the Sisters will look after you. Mrs Lennox, I presume?' She swept them both towards the front door without visible effort.

'The dog,' John said. 'I'm afraid our dog is——'

'He can come in too,' Mother Veronica said. 'All are welcome.' She gave a light metallic laugh. 'We are quite a modern school, you know. You'll notice some changes, I have no doubt.' She turned and clapped her small fat hands, and by some miracle of telepathy or coincidence, Shah turned and came bounding back towards them. 'Beautiful, beautiful fellow,' Mother Veronica said. 'I'm afraid he will find the floors rather slippery.'

Everywhere linoleum, thick, expensive, hygienic, ice-smooth. 'This is our parlour,' Mother Veronica said. 'Indian tea?' She rang a bell beside what had been the drawing-room fireplace. The hearth was still there but filled with an electric radiator. The floors shone, the walls were white, with a gigantic crucifix above the mantelpiece, flanked on one side by the large oval sepia photograph of a nun and on the other by an equally large portrait of Pope Pius IX.

'Our Foundress, Mother Mary of the Holy Wounds. She was blessed with the Stigmata. His Holiness Pope Pius IX granted our Order its privileges. But I mustn't stay chattering while my pupils are waiting. Do you have children yourselves?'

'No,' Kate said.

'There's plenty of time yet,' Mother Veronica said. 'Where is —— ah, Sister Philomena, we have guests. The old owners of Castle Lennox.' She gave bustling instructions for tea and milk for this beautiful fellow here, why, making friends already, and disappeared with a slight whisper of black robes brushing the linoleum.

'How could you, Shah?' Kate said when they were alone. Shah lay on the floor and looked ashamed. 'How can we get out of this?' But there was no getting out of it short of running away, and they went miserably to the windows, back to the fireplace, to the long mahogany table with its light burden of religious magazines, and two or three holy books. *A Life of Mother Mary of the Holy Wounds*, by Sister Theresa of the Assumption. *A Chaplet of Prayers for Meditation*, by Father Eustace Keenan. *The Monthly Recorder; Mother Mary's Aspiration*; the quarterly publication of the Sisters of the Divine Suffering.

The tea came, and polite, whispering answers from Sister Philomena. Eighty pupils. Eleven sisters. Including Mother Veronica of the Holy Cloth of course. Such a beautiful old house, truly beautiful. Had they seen the chapel? After their tea, no, no, she would be having her tea at another time, thank you, thank you. But after tea they must indeed see the chapel, designed by such a wonderful architect, Mr Fane, had they ever heard of Mr Fane the architect, they believed that he was most famous. His uncle was Sir Egbert Fane, the builder, who had built the chapel for them. It had cost eighty thousand pounds, she had heard. Which was why they were so deeply in debt. And another forty thousand pounds for the schoolrooms and dormitories. She would indeed love to show them those also, but they would understand, the pupils, term-time. The girls were so happy here, so happy, such beautiful air. And did they know, there had been a Mr O'Rourke, she did not know all the details but she had heard that it was Mr O'Rourke who had actually sold them the house and land—his daughter was here as a pupil. Such a clever child.

Sister Philomena of the Annunciation was thin and young, so far as Kate or John could tell, nuns' wimples making most Sisters look much younger than they are, and the thick habit muffling almost any kind of figure into shapelessness. But her leather girdle seemed to outline a narrow waist, and there was the suggestion of a young bosom under the folds and ruches of black cloth and the starched white neckpiece. Her voice came soft and gushing, a rushing whisper of eager answers and volunteered information as if her words had been dammed up inside her for silent months, years, and she found it astonishing, dangerously exciting almost, to be talking to strangers. She took them into the Chapel, genuflecting with such loving familiarity that both Kate and John felt wretchedly awkward as they stood beside her.

'I love this chapel,' breathed Sister Philomena. 'One feels so at peace. Even with all the children. Or because of them. The beautiful windows.'

The inside of the chapel was blond wood, broken into patches of red and blue and golden yellow by the light through the coloured glass of the windows. The Stations of the Cross were simple sketches, almost cartoons in charcoal. 'By quite a famous painter,' Sister Philomena breathed, 'Seán ... Seán Ó Conaire, yes, Ó Conaire. Did you ever hear of him? Such a strange man! Like a great big bear! Mother Veronica told us'—she dropped her voice still further into a horrified amusement— 'that he *drank*. The poor, poor man. And she made him promise that if she gave him the work he was not to touch a *drop* of whiskey the whole time he was here. And every evening for his supper she brought him a bottle of stout. Isn't she wonderful?'

For Kate and John, brought up in the Low Church protestantism of the Church of Ireland as interpreted by their great-uncle, Archdeacon Henry, and long since become agnostics, the chapel was meaningless. Their idea of a Catholic church had been gained in Chartres and Notre-Dame and at a Catholic friend's wedding in Brompton Oratory, and if they had not been told what it was they might never have guessed that this chapel also was Catholic. Sister Philomena seemed to sense their feelings.

'It's so modern,' she said when they were outside on the drive again, 'it used to worry me at first, I found it quite hard to say my prayers. But one grows to love it so, the simplicity. As if there is nothing between you and ... no barrier——' She blushed suddenly, a wave of crimson coming up from her throat to her forehead. 'I'm such a chatterbox. Mother Veronica would have a fit if she heard me. It was so nice to be able to show you our chapel. I do hope you feel we are making good use of your old home.'

Shah had been locked in the car before they went to the chapel, and greeted them with lazy, loving stretches of long front legs. The car swung in a wide circle past the schoolroom windows. Venetia O'Rourke, staring dreamily out of the window during the last moments of Mother Veronica's French class, saw it go. To freedom, to freedom.

'*Je vous* en *prie*. You notice here the use of *en*.'

Silly old Face Wipe. Silly old French. Where were they going? Dublin? Anywhere except awful here. Were they married? They had been quite old, probably thirty at least with dozens of awful little children they were going to send here, poor brats. Mother Face Wipe smarming over them, you could bet that.

'Jennifer Adams, give me another example of the use of *en*.'

'*M'en*, Mother? *M'en Dieu?*'

Come on bell, ring. Thank God for tea. Old marge and stewed tealeaves but at least it was something and she had the other half of her Kit-Kat safe in her locker. They must make a fortune here. I'll be getting my period tomorrow, I'm sure of it. If I had a bath tonight and made it come very badly maybe she'd let me stay in bed tomorrow and miss the match. Jennifer fainted the last time, actually fainted. Mary Healey said she found a sanny down the nun's lav. I bet it was Sister Philomena's.

She began dreaming in an odd, almost hostile way about Sister Philomena. She had hugged her once and she had a real bosom, not all hard and flat or huge and floppy, but like . . . like . . . the woman with the car had had a real bosom too. He hadn't been bad-looking for someone his age. Sort of battered. By life probably. Sister Philomena's mother was a widow, she had had eleven children and four of them were nuns, two were priests, one was a Christian brother, one had been killed in Korea and the others were in America. It was hardly worth having children if that was what was going to happen to them. Jennifer said it was the worst agony in the world having children, worse than toothache, worse than the period, worse than constipation, worse than anything. She had heard her sister scream. Actually *scream*. Did Sister Philomena mind not having children? In the Middle Ages she might have been seduced by a lewd monk. And if she said anything about it she would have been locked up and tortured because the monk would say she was possessed by the Devil. What would they have done to her? Taken all her clothes off first. And then——

'Come on, come on, tea, you idiot.' Everyone clattering desks, Face Wipe gone, Jennifer pulling her arm. 'What are you dreaming about?'

'Religion. You wouldn't understand.'

'Have you anything left in your locker?'

'Not a crumb.' She fought for a second with her conscience. 'Well, only the tiniest crumb, it's almost mouldy.'

'Mary Healey's had a parcel. If we threaten to douse her in the lav again she might divvy up. For Heaven's sake get your books together or we won't get any cake.'

* * *

An hour later the Lennoxes drove down the far side of the mountains into Drifin, Felicity O'Connor's home village, a bleak grey cluster of cottages flung down like a handful of stones between sea and mountain. There was an air of dead-end about the road, except for one newly built, startlingly modern house at the entrance to the village. Fifty years ago the herring and the mackerel brought shoals of silver into Drifin, and smoked and salted fish from Drifin went to America to feed the immigrant poor of the New World. But after the First World War and the coming of refrigerator ships the market for salt fish vanished overnight and Drifin was ruined. The men who had made the real money out of the trade locked their bank accounts and went away, rather than invest their profits in refrigerator plants, and Drifin sank into ruin.

The island of Inis Beag, four miles out from the harbour and lying like a sleeping whale on the horizon, was ruined with it. Where fifty currachs and pookauns and a dozen Galway hookers had once filled the harbour and the sea with movement, now only half a dozen currachs lay upside down on their trestles in front of O'Connor's Grocery and Bar. The village seemed to live in a long dream, broken only at intervals of years by brief excitements. The Dalys leaving Inis Beag, and settling on the mountain above. The Traceys and the Black O'Malleys following them a few years later, was it nineteen and fifty-four, or was it fifty-five? The year the O'Connor girl up and left for Dublin beyond. Fifty-four so. Her, the strap. Be Jasus no loss in her. Arrah now, arrah now, don't be too hasty. Did you ever hear tell or see with your own eyes what she wrote? Did ye now? No. Then how can you be talking so certain? Ach my pity for your head Paudeen Og, do you take me for a gom entirely? How wouldn't I be knowing what she wrote and Father John preaching her down from the altar himself? Would he do that if he didn't know the kind she was? Agh so? Agh so? Faith is a wonderful thing, boy, and charity is another wonder.

The excitement of the play, and the television crews, and the newspapers, had died down in four years. The rain out of the Atlantic and the length of days had softened and damped down the ferocity of talk and it was now beginning to melt into the local folklore, like the night of the big storm in forty-eight, and the time the curate from the next parish was found dead in a ditch with his bicycle on top of him and a broken whiskey-bottle in his pocket. That had been in nineteen and twenty-six, no, twenty-seven, no, twenty-six because that was the year that Cait O'Malley's son Donal was drowned off the Black Rock, d'you remember? Arragh God be good to the old lady and they say they're for taking her off the Inis at last, the White O'Malleys is for coming into the mainland and she'd be left there by her sole self. God and she'd stand it. I'd say that there'd be no shiftin' her even so.

The Lennoxes pulled up by the bar and went in, the bar dark and cool, a shade musty, after the warmth of the late September sunlight. Advertisements for Guinness, Jameson, Hennessy's Brandy, Tullamore Dew, Sweet Afton. Black settle benches round the walls that somehow suggested damp. Two plastic-topped tables and half a dozen chromium and plastic chairs, remains of a drunken spree of Jim O'Connor's in Galway a year or so ago. He had gone down with a wallet full of money to pay the arrears of rates, drunk his way unsteadily round the City of the Twelve Tribes with a long session for each Tribe, ordered himself three hand-made suits, a set of golf-clubs and an electric power saw, with a refrigerator, a new electric cooker, and a suite of bedroom furniture for his wife Eileen. The plastic tables and chairs had been an afterthought. Make th' place bewful, upper-date. Right? Gotterkeepupperdate in bus'ness or Kerrassh, finish. Bankrupt. Right? He had come back to Drifin blind drunk and fighting, had given Eileen a black eye, fallen into bed, and two days later when he staggered upright he couldn't remember even having been to Galway. It was a complete bewilderment to him when packing-cases began to arrive Cash on Delivery with impatient and then angry men demanding to be paid not only for the goods but for cartage.

They had got rid of most of the things, but Eileen herself had liked the tables and chairs, thinking they gave a touch of class to the bar, and they had kept them, paying for them out of the money put aside for the electricity bill and Eileen's false teeth. Sure God, the old ones had done her long enough, couldn't they do her a bit more even if they did slip up and down? And anyway couldn't she get them out of the money put by to pay the arrears to Guinness's?

'Is anyone home?' John called. Shah was out on the mole, smelling the sea. Kate hitched herself on to one of the wooden bar stools, leaning her head back against the cold wall, beside last year's calendar. The sea. It was never the same in Dublin, nowhere else in the world. Damp, draggled, crumbling, and yet so beautiful it stopped her heart. The pain of Castle Lennox was easing. As if coming over the mountains had separated her from it, from that victory of the outside world, and she was home again, in the real Ireland, the real West. The silence, the feeling that no one would ever hurry. Stillness. Outside Shah barked at a seagull. The seagull lifted on contemptuous wings and drifted away.

'Anyone at home?'

Slippers coming. Eileen O'Connor came through the doorway behind the bar, spectacles down her nose, a library book in her hand—'A terrible one for the reading that woman, sure God I heard she locks herself in the lavatory readin' to keep out of the way of himself when he's violent.' Her hair had gone even blacker since they saw her last, and her mouth was outlined with a startling shade of lipstick. It was as much defiance of the parish as any personal vanity.

'John!' she cried. 'Kate!' And then, not so loud, almost breathlessly, 'How—how's Fil?'

'She's not with us,' John said. 'Just sends her love. And this.' He put a small parcel on the counter from his coat pocket. There was a barely detectable sense of relief about Felicity's mother on hearing that Felicity was not here. She had suffered too much from her daughter's fame, or infamy, to think of her coming back in person without flinching. The anonymous letters, and some not anonymous, were still coming occasionally, even after four years. She could identify them now without so much as opening the envelope. Dirty, crumpled envelopes usually, often with the stamp in the wrong corner, or upside down, and the address straggling downwards, ill-spelled and irregular. Inside, one sheet of notepaper folded smaller than necessary: DEAR MRS O'CONNOR, your daugher is a WORE, she is MUCK, I especkt this minute she is sleeping with NEGREOS i hop she will cash SIFLIS she is sutgh FILT you are wunding or Savour the way you bring her upp yors fathfuly a CATHOLICK MOTHER P.S. She nede the STRAP. That had been the last one, only a month ago.

'Where did you spring from the pair of you?' She put on her more refined accent to greet them and adjusted her old green cardigan round her thin shoulders, preening slightly. 'If I'd known you were coming——'

'You'd have baked a cake,' Kate said, coming forward and taking both her hands. 'And aren't you the smart woman entirely, Mrs O'Connor, made up to kill? Are you expecting a boyfriend?'

'Go away with you, you bold girl. And not caught yet, eh?'

She nodded at Kate's stomach and Kate flushed very slightly. 'Let me look at you both.' She dipped her head and looked over the rim of her glasses, like a thin, chirpy bird with a red beak. 'Are you on holidays?'

'In a way. We may be coming back.' When they were together in Ireland it was almost always Kate who answered the questions from third parties addressed to both of them. When they were in London it was the other way round. 'We've just been to Castle Lennox,' Kate said, her voice hardening. 'Have you heard what they've done to it? All the trees gone, and they've built an enormous chapel, and schoolrooms——'

'Don't be talking,' cried Mrs O'Connor, 'don't be talking, the place is gone mad entirely with the building. Did you see the new house as you were driving in, the two-storey one, sure how could you miss it? Germans, no less! Didn't Festy Bourke sell them his field on the cliff because his cow fell over it and he wouldn't spend money on fencing—well didn't this German come and buy it from him for three hundred pounds—three hundred pounds! Festy thought it was seven Christmases come in February, and the German goes and builds that place there and they say he imported every stick of furniture and even the electric stove from Germany, nothing Irish good enough for him, the creature, nor even English. German furniture! And now he has fences round the place that'd keep soldiers out. But heavens above here I am talking your heads off and not asking do you have a mouth on you at all. You must be droughty with the thirst coming all that way. From Dublin? Today! God love your energy. Sure it's all I can do to drag myself to Galway in the one day.'

It was ten years since she had set foot in Galway and then only on an afternoon excursion, but she had a reputation to keep up in the parish as a travelled woman, and not only travelled but also a foreigner, having been born in Barna and only come to Drifin on the unfortunate occasion of her marriage to Jim O'Connor.

'How's Jim?' John said. Like Kate, although in a different way, he had felt the atmosphere of Drifin like a kind of homecoming,

but against his will and against his common sense. In spite of
Kate's enthusiasm they had never known the O'Connors or Drifin
all that well. A few times each summer in childhood they had sat
in this bar, waiting for Tim Bourke the ferryman to be ready, or
had come back from the Inis for the afternoon with one of the
boats for what was fondly supposed to be a treat, in spite of the
fact that they usually got sick; sitting with a bottle of lemonade
while the men got steadily drunker before rowing home again
to the island, or playing solemnly on the mole outside with the
small fat child Felicity.

Since then they had been here only twice; once, miserably,
when they were waiting to sell the house and had left Castle
Lennox in desperation, each hoping the other would see more
sense if they got out of the house for a few hours; and once
almost dramatically, not long after Felicity's play had begun
echoing round the civilized world, to try and persuade Eileen
to leave her husband and come with them to London, to join
Felicity.

'Ach sure, how could I leave him?' she had said then, over and
over. 'He needs me.' It had been a frustrating visit, and even more
frustrating when Felicity, who had begged them in tears to go,
said, 'Thank God,' when they told her tragically that her mother
couldn't be budged. 'I was dreading it,' Felicity said, 'but I felt
I had to make the offer.' She had gone off to Ibiza then, leaving
them in London with their holiday fortnight used up, and she
hadn't even sent them a postcard.

It irritated him now to hear Kate talking, acting—and acting
was the right word—as if Eileen O'Connor was her long-lost
fairy godmother. And she'd be the same with old Mrs O'Malley,
crying half the night in broken Irish. And yet in spite of his
irritation he felt sucked back into something—home? childhood?
a kind of lying nostalgia, a false sentiment that he knew was
false and that still gripped him, so that he could half see himself
like a ghost, a small shadow, sitting on the settle under the
window there, lemonade in front of him, listening to Tim Bourke
and Festy and the others shouting over their pints, trying to
pretend that his own lemonade was black porter and that he was

a fisherman himself. That he belonged, that he was one of them. And the smell of the sea going back to the Inis, the small slap of the calm summer water against the skin of the currach, the suck of the sea at the bladeless oars, the creak of the wooden rowlocks and Tim shouting suddenly, 'Be aisy there, Festy you omadhaun, is it to put us all in the water you're trying?'

'The divil run off with you, Tim, is it out for catchin' crabs you are? D'you want to be drownin' the children?'

Lobster for tea, and strong tea itself and potato cakes, and the smell of the turf fire, and old Cait O'Malley like a black witch beside it, a queen of witches, her nose high and sharp and her eyes like splinters of dark blue glass under hair as black as horse-hair from a sofa. Christ, he thought irritably, I'm as bad as Kate, and made up his mind that hell or snow she'd never get him back here to live. He hadn't heard what Eileen had answered about her husband, but it didn't matter. Either he was on the batter, or had recently been on the batter and was lying sick upstairs recovering, or was recovered and therefore due to go on the batter again almost any minute. Kate was giving the most recent news of Felicity.

'... did you not hear from her about the new play? It's fantastic, really fantastic, better than *A Girl is Made for Loving*— there's almost no comparison, she's grown up——'

'Jesus, Mary and Joseph,' Mrs O'Connor whispered, her face paling a little. 'Another one?'

'It's about an Irish girl in London and this middle-aged man——'

'Oh, Mother of God, not again!'

'No, no, no, it's completely different, this is a sophisticated man—actually it's based on a real character that we both know, but that's completely off the record and I haven't said a word. I'm afraid he may be rather angry about it——'

'Oh, my God. Will they hear about it here?'

'Everybody will hear about it. It's going to be a sensation. Lionel Fring is putting it on. In fact she's with him in Rome at the moment, a sort of business holiday——'

'I can imagine,' said Mrs O'Connor, folding her mouth rather thin. 'It's time that girl got married.' She had opened the small packet John had given her. An ounce of French perfume in a heavy crystal flask, wrapped round with a gossamer silk scarf. As a matter of strict fact Kate had bought them both the previous afternoon in Bond Street. 'For God's sake get her something, darling,' Felicity had said as they were seeing her off to Rome. 'Something that looks extravagant, I've been meaning to write to her for ages. God bless, there's my taxi and Lionel goes frantic if I keep him waiting.' Scent and bosom and tight silk dress and crooked stockings and her raincoat left behind so that they had to dash down four flights of stairs with it to catch the lift.

'You might even see it on TV,' Kate was saying. 'Can you get the B.B.C. here?'

'That'd be all I'd need. It's been my daily dread that it'd be on the wireless.'

'You know you're getting TV in Ireland? John's getting an audition for it when we go back to Dublin, they're testing people for jobs already.'

'Don't pay any attention to her,' John said. 'The whole thing's her idea, not mine. She had seen an advertisement in *The Times* and made him answer it. *Irish Television is looking for experienced journalists, preferably with some knowledge of television requirements. Irish journalists now working in England will be given particular consideration.*

He had answered it more to keep Kate quiet than for any interest, and had not expected or really wanted to hear anything in return. 'Anyway I'll never get the job. For one thing I've never set foot inside a TV studio.' But he had been given an interview in London, and very much to his surprise a fortnight later had had a telegram telling him that his audition was at ten o'clock the following morning in Dublin. Could he be there?

'They must be mad,' he said, but after a telephone conversation that cost him a pound they had fixed on a day in October for the audition and since his expenses were being paid they had decided to come over for a holiday beforehand. And in a weird, sentimental way it was almost pleasant to be back. To be out of London. And to think that someone in Ireland was at least interested enough to want to interview him.

'Have the tinker Connors been by at all?' Kate was asking. 'We wanted to ask for them at Castle Lennox but there wasn't any point once we saw it.'

'I haven't seen them in years,' Mrs O'Connor said stiffly. 'I never knew what you saw in them. The whole thieving rascally race of them ought to be swept away if you ask me.'

'Eileen, Eileen!' Kate put down her empty half-pint stout-glass with its rings of pale brown foam all the way down inside it. God, John thought, she'll be wearing pampooties next. 'They were the sweetest, darlingest family—and as honest as——'

'Foxes,' Mrs O'Connor said. 'Vermin and thievery, that's all your precious tinkers are, and if they never come by again good riddance to them.' It had annoyed her for years that the Connors had almost the same name as herself, and since the matter of Felicity's play Una Bourke, Festy's sister, had pretended to discover that the Connors and the O'Connors had been the one family, only a couple of generations ago.

'Go away out of that,' Kate said. 'You'd be the first to give them something if they knocked on the door now.'

'The back of my hand.' She started dramatically as the door opened. 'Oh, my God.' But it was Tim Bourke, the ferryman, if a pookaun with an outboard motor could be dignified by the name of 'ferry'. He was a huge man, so tall, so broad, so enormous in his turned-down sea boots and great, sagging banin sweater that he seemed built on another scale to that of ordinary people. Winter and summer he wore the same clothes, the same boots, the same small woollen hat like a greyish-white pimple on top of his white start of hair, as thick, and springing and coarse, as a white furze bush.

'God save all here.' His voice was harsh, speaking the guttural English of a native Irish-speaker, as different in accent from the soft English of those parts of the West where Irish had been lost as North German from Austrian. 'I heard you were by,' he said, taking first Kate and then John by the hand with an awkward, shy formality. He looked John up and down. 'I think it has prospered with you?'

'Fair enough,' John said. 'And yourself? You haven't grown smaller anyway.' He nodded at Eileen. 'What are you having?'

'A drop from the little jug then, if you're insisting. Herself knows my taste.'

'And if I don't I should,' Eileen said.

'It's a long time and a long time, Tim Bourke,' Kate said in Irish. 'And how is with you all these years?' Her Irish was hesitant and she flushed as she spoke.

'Listen to her, listen to her,' cried Tim, also in Irish. 'You have the fine blas on you, you didn't lose it away yonder. The blessing of God with you, and you a grown woman now.' He lifted the whiskey-glass, his vast hand dwarfing the tumbler to an eggcup, his mouth opening like a cave, his throat swallowing once. 'That was a creamy drop. And did you keep the Irish yourself, Mister John?'

'Ten words and all rusty,' John said in English. If Kate wanted to make a fool of herself let her.

The big ferryman put his glass on the counter. 'Why would you keep it?' he said with a tone between sadness and bitterness, and speaking in English again himself. 'Much good it ever did any of us to have it and they up in Dublin thumping their breasts and bellowing like walruses about the great culture of it and the death that's on us all if we lose it. Little they do for us to keep it. Five pounds a year to us if we have our children speak it for the inspector and he coming round like the landlords of old trying to trap them into English. God damn their souls. And how do they think our children will be doing in Birmingham with the purest Irish of the great poets in their throats and no English?'

'Tim, Tim, don't be talking like that,' Kate cried, her Irish coming back like spring water rattling in a long unused pipe. 'Why should they leave? Why should they go to Birmingham?'

'Why did you go, my bright love?' He had held her on his huge knees while she spewed her heart up over the side of the currach and taught her how to fish for lobsters with a mussel tied to a hook on the end of a broomstick, and the endearment came naturally in Irish.

'It's easy telling you're on holiday,' Eileen said with a dry voice. She understood Irish perfectly, living on the edge of a Gaeltacht and half the men coming down the mountain for a night's drinking being more at ease in Irish than English, but she only spoke it under protest with a deliberately English accent. Her mother's parents had been native speakers and she was still ashamed of it.

'What do you mean?' Kate said fiercely. 'We're back because we want to come back. To live here. To work.'

'My pity for your head,' Eileen said. 'God above, and you able to live in London. There are some don't know how to count their blessings.'

'What in the name of God would you come back for?' Tim said. 'Sure, aren't they still leaving in handfuls? It isn't gold the streets of London is paved with, it's Connacht men.'

'And girls,' Eileen said with a sniff. 'They say every other prostitute in London is Irish.'

'Why?' whispered Kate, with a ferocity that startled herself. 'Why? Because this rotten, slieveen, gombeen government that you have here, that you've let sit on your necks for forty years, survives on two things. Keeping those that stay at home as ignorant as lumps of wood, and exporting the surplus population. Nobody makes trouble here because it's easier to go to London. And the pot-bellied gangsters and ignoramuses and pious craw-thumping hypocrites you've been voting for for forty years live up in Leinster House like African chieftans sitting on heaps of skulls.'

'I never voted for anyone in my life,' Eileen said indignantly.

'Exactly. And because you didn't, because people don't care a damn what happens here so long as they're all right, Tim Bourke's children go to Birmingham as navvies or waitresses in a fish-and-chip shop.'

'Oh, shut up, Kate,' John said, embarrassed. 'You don't know the first thing about what's happening here.'

'I wouldn't have said it myself,' Eileen said, drawing her mouth into a prim, puckered line, 'but I won't contradict you. We've done quite well so far.'

'Well? Well!' Kate spread her hands round helplessly, taking in the dank bar, and the desolation visible through the windows. 'You call this well?'

'Are you for going over to the old lady?' Tim said. 'Because if you are the tide is turning.'

And later, as he swung the nose of the pookaun out into the open sea beyond the stone mouth of the harbour, he said, 'You should leave poor Eileen O'Connor be, Miss Kate. She has enough of misfortune of her own without squabbling with her over Ireland's. Sure we all know the West is finished, but if it turned into Hy Brasil itself it would do that poor woman no good with the man she has.'

The sea had got up and slapped the bows, and it was not really a time for talking. Shah crouched in the belly of the boat, whining miserably as spray came over him. The world was sky and sea, the shore low behind them and the mountains blurred into blue shadows under sudden rain. The sky had clouded and a chill wind snatched and tore at the waves. Not the chopping wavelets of the harbour, but long ridges risen from the sea, white-fringed and rolling. When they dipped under the brow of one they could see neither mainland nor island. And then they lifted, high on grey-green water, foam-streaked like marble, the outboard racing for a moment as it cleared the sea. The Inis lay before them dark and far with white lace on its rocks.

'Are you sick, Miss Kate? Don't look at the water and you'll be fine.' Tim sat with a pipe between strong teeth like a horse's, his face dripping mahogany, one arm stretched on the tiller, the other along the gunwale, easy and tranquil, one eye watching the sky, the other half-closed and squinting. He gave the sense of being part of the boat, like a sea-centaur, Manannan. 'It's getting fresh.'

Neither John nor Kate was anything of a small-boat sailor. As children they had got used enough to the passage between Drifin and Inis Beag, if the water stayed half-way calm, but once it got up at all they had been miserable even then until by the end of a summer holiday they had got their sealegs. And four years as a deep-sea sailor had done nothing to give John the kind of stomach a pookaun in a stiff coastal sea demands. Now they were both beginning to feel the queasiness of stomachs coming adrift, that no one remembers until it comes back to them and then seems like the one reality of their lives.

'I'm going to be sick,' Kate said. Her hair was already down round her face in dark strings, drenched with spray, her face white as a white stone. John tried not to think, not to look at the sea, or at Kate, or at Shah, now lying in sodden misery like a wet hearthrug at his feet, and most of all not at Tim Bourke, blowing gusts of tobacco smoke into the wind. Now and then the wind veered, and plucked the smell of it across John's face, like sea-weed being burned, or rubber tyres.

'She's looking less than herself, the poor soul. You'd better see to her, Mister John. It's the city has her destroyed.'

John turned reluctantly. Kate was lying across the gunwale, retching, the water lifting and racing within an inch of her face, taking the spew out of her mouth. He looked at her for a second and then joined her.

'God almighty,' Tim shouted. 'Do it the other side, the pair of you, do it downwind.' But they were both beyond hearing him. They lay helpless until after a timeless misery the wind and sea dropped suddenly, sharply as closing a door, and the boat rode into the harbour of Inis Beag as softly as a bed rolling across a carpet. Even the sun had come out again, the clouds were a grey mass in the east, breaking themselves on the wall of mountains, and the curve of Inis Beag and the walls of the small harbour were round the boat like arms holding her safe. The fields of the Inis were bright green against the heather blue of the ridge that formed its whale-back and the cottages were white and welcoming. Two men stood on the slip waiting to help them in, their own currach just drawn up beside them.

The water round the easy-gliding pookaun was green glass, Mediterranean smooth. It was not possible to believe that a hundred yards behind them the sea still lifted.

'A fine day and welcome to you,' the men called to Tim, not wanting to show curiosity about the strangers. When John and Kate had been helped out and the dog lifted out to flop on the slipway again like a drowned spider, and when the two islanders had been told who the visitors were, they still pretended not to have seen anything, not to have noticed that the visitors had been sick. But one of them said to the other in English, ' 'Tis a poorish sort of a day and a nasty sea.'

'It is very poor. I am glad to be on dry land out of it.'

It made Kate, and even John, feel better and they were able to pull themselves together and walk up the stone slipway behind the men carrying their two suitcases and Tim carrying Shah. The dog rested his narrow, beautiful head on Tim's shoulder and looked at them reproachfully, that they had done this to him in the ninth year of his age. Kate put her hand in John's and lifted her face to the sun. The wind blew above the ridge, but down here by the harbour and in the village street it was no more than a breeze, drying their faces.

The house they were going to, White Kate O'Malley's, Cait Ban's, was at the far end of the street, the only two-storey house on the island and for that reason known as the 'big-house', or sometimes the 'house with stairs'. It was a great pride to the island and Cait Ban was forgiven much because of it. Arrogance in particular. Not that she cared whether she was forgiven anything or not. She lived on her own strength.

One or two women looked out of doorways, ducked their heads shyly at the sight of strangers dressed in city clothes, and one of the women held a year-old child in her arms, but before they were half-way down the street Kate and John realized that the island had changed out of recognition since they were last there, only five years before. Three-quarters of the houses were empty, the doors shut, the small deepset windows blank eyes. Five years ago the population of the island had been failing. Now it seemed almost gone.

Tim Bourke had put down the Afghan with a mixture of wonder and self-scorn. 'I carrying the creature as if it was a Christian itself, and it looking at me as if it expected no less. Use your own four legs, you great idler.' Tim had less of the island indifference to animals and their welfare, but he was embarrassed to be seen pampering a dog.

'Are the Black O'Malley's gone?' John asked, pointing to a long cottage.

'They are faith. And if it was next year instead of this the White O'Malley's would be gone after them and this place would be empty of every soul. Those two women we passed just now are for going this coming winter as soon as the weather turns.'

'And old Cait. Not her, surely?'

'If the others go how would she stay?'

'I can't bear it,' Kate said, who on the island would be known as young Kate, or Red Kate, if she lived there in sufficient intimacy.

They ducked their heads into Cait Ban's doorway, the two islandmen standing aside to let them in first, Tim calling out, 'Cait? Cait Ban? You have company this night.'

The old woman was by the fire, a black shape by the black hearth with its red eyes of embers, the whole kitchen dark as a cave after the brightness of the sunlight. The room smelled of turf and tea and tobacco and very slightly of cats and fish. Two kittens wrestled over a fish-head by Cait's feet and the edge of her long skirt, and the mother cat lay in an inglenook of the hearth, watching them with green eyes.

'God bless the house,' Kate Lennox said in Irish.

'Caitlin beag!' the old woman cried out. 'And Sean! Praise be to God who made Heaven and Earth. Put their bags there, Micilin, Paudeen, this is a great joy you have brought me, Tim, let me find glasses and the black bottle——'

The cat saw Shah coming in the door and arched its back, spitting for its kittens to beware of danger, and within seconds all formality went out of the door with cat and dog, Sean, Paudeen, Micilin and Tim giving chase to save the cat, or rather, in the case of the islanders, simply to see what would happen, the kittens getting under the dresser with tiny miaowlings of terror, Shah barking for victory, as if he was frantic to wipe out the disgrace of being sick and having to be carried up the slipway.

When the men came back with Shah securely tied by the collar with a leather belt old Cait and young Kate were by the fire, each holding a glass of poteen, old Cait smoking her pipe and young Kate a cigarette. They all sat drinking a welcome to Kate and John, until Tim Bourke said that he had to be getting back and Micilin and Paudeen said that they would go now and return later with everyone else who wanted to make the visitors welcome.

'Few enough it will be,' Old Cait said. 'There are only few in it.'

'But why?' Kate said. 'Why is everyone leaving the island? What is there on the mainland that you haven't got better here?'

'For me there is nothing on the mainland,' the old woman said. 'But for the young people there is nothing here either. Not even a school for the children now that there are so few of them. But sure the school was already shut the time you were here before.'

'What do the children do then?'

'What children? Sure God, a birth on the island would be a wonder. There's Finger Donal's wife with a young baby, maybe you saw her and you coming up the street? And Micilin's two small sons and Paudeen's last daughter that's almost beyond schooling, and two-three more, and they all go to the mainland in fine weather in the pookaun with Tim, and back again in the evening. And when they are landed by Drifin there is an old bus that will take them five miles to the schoolhouse in Carra. And again if the weather is bad on us it's no schooling for them till it clears. That's one reason why the young families have been going. I am the oldest, and soon by the look of things I will be the youngest also and I alone here with my cat and the hens. If your fine dog hasn't killed my poor Tibbeen.'

'She was well enough on the roof of a cottage when we last saw her,' John said. 'But you couldn't stay here alone.'

'Why not? What would I do beyond in Ireland? Sit by another woman's fire maybe, and make myself small and quiet when that woman would want to be raising her voice to me. Better be lonely in my own place. And I've company enough in my head, with all the thoughts I have of times past. But it's not talking of myself I want to be when I have visitors. Tell me your own news now.'

They talked on and on and it grew to be evening beyond the open doorway, the wind dropping into silence, and the sea only a murmur on the threshold of hearing. They told her about London, and Felicity O'Connor and her play, and about television, and she nodded her head, but none of it meant very much to her. The biggest town she had ever seen was Westport, and that had been forty years ago. She had never been to a cinema, even to one of the travelling tent cinemas that sometimes came to Drifin for a winter night or two. And yet this woman's stories and the purity of her speech were quoted in books, Cait Ban Ni Maille of Inis Beag, one of the last great storytellers, one of the last founts of the purest north Connacht dialect. She had had that reputation even when Kate and John were children, which was why Colonel Lennox sent them to Inis Beag to learn Irish.

She could speak English too, although for choice she never spoke it, only from necessity or for politeness, if a visitor came to her who had no Irish. Visitors had come to her from Germany and America, London and Dublin, to hear stories, to learn turns of speech and old usages of words, which was why almost forty years ago her husband, himself a singer and story-teller and blood kin of Grace O'Malley the Queen of the Islands who outfaced Queen Elizabeth of England; that was why he put a second storey on to his cottage, to accommodate the scholars who came. He died not long after, and then their son Donal drowned. She was left alone in the 'house with stairs' except for the people who came to talk to her, from Dublin and from Universities in half a dozen countries.

She sat in her black dress by the fire making tea for them, and the kittens, grown used to Shah, came out from under the dresser and ate their fish-head. Even John found himself speaking Irish again, halting and uneasy, and the past flowed back to him. Night fell and the others came in to drink poteen and strong tea and smoke tobacco and ask polite questions, until they got used to the strangers, remembering them as children—the visit of five years ago had only been for a couple hours while Tim was unloading groceries from his boat, and few had seen them then. Until it was midnight and the guests, the few that there were, hardly enough to crowd the kitchen, began going home.

'We'll walk up the ridge a little before we go to bed,' Kate said, and they walked out into the cool darkness, almost cold after the heat of the kitchen and the fire and the people and the poteen.

'Are you still glad you came?' John said.

She said nothing for a minute, and then in a hard voice, 'Yes.' They walked on up the ridge. A night bird cried suddenly, unnervingly close to their heads, and the wind sighed among the stones. A sheep woke with a start and hummocked away.

'Stay still, Shah,' John said, and the Afghan whined in his throat and fell to heel. There was the smell of the sea all round them, but the sense of home, of permanence, had gone and they both felt wretched. No one in the kitchen had talked of staying except Cait Ban and with her it was only talking. How could she stay?

'They can't just go,' Kate said miserably. But they would. Time and again this island had been emptied through the centuries, through the thousands of years that men had sailed here. When there was pressure on the land the island filled. When the mainland population dropped, the island emptied. Like a tide. But they couldn't think of that. The night was full of ghosts around them, themselves as children, running here, mindless with happiness, summer lasting for eternity; and the ghosts they had been told of round the fire; Donal himself who came back from the sea to his mother, holding out his drowned hands to her at the window, through the grey, misted glass, and Cait Ban's father who had been King of the Island and who had also drowned, with three of his brothers in a storm; ghost upon ghost; the white horse who rose out of the sea in time of trouble, the horse of the Famine, a white horse galloping at the water's edge, his hooves soundless on rock and shingle, his mane like a sea woman's hair; the ghosts of the Spanish sailors out of the big ship that had broken on Seal Rock, who had been murdered by the islanders for their gold earrings. Long, long ago. Other ghosts so old, from so long ago that they had no names; ghosts of seamen out of Gaul and Tartessos and Massilia, coming here for gold and deerhounds, or sheltering on their way north to Ultima Thule and Amber Land.

And the island itself a ghost, so old, so crouched in the grey sea, that human men were nothing to it, small, crying creatures running about on the rocks, dying, going away, while the island remained, locked in its endless warfare with the sea, listening to the songs of the sea women as they combed their seaweed hair, watching the horses of Manannan racing, white-maned, tossing their foaming heads to the glory of their master; listening to the stories that the seals tell, of the far seas and the golden beaches, of the great drowned palaces of the sea king's kingdom, far under the waves.

'They are walking on my grave,' Kate said.

He put his arm round her, feeling that the land itself was hostile to him, maybe hostile to all men, but particularly to him, who had no roots there, whose ancestors for a handful of centuries had sat loose in the saddle, indifferent, arrogant, and gone in the end as easily and shamefully as they had come.

'I won't take that job,' he said. 'Even if they offer it to me.'

She stopped and faced him, astonished. 'What?'

'We're not wanted here. We never were. Least of all here.'

She didn't answer him at once, but began walking very fast along the top of the ridge so that he almost had to run to keep up with her. 'Where the hell are you going?'

'To the hollow.'

It lay a half-mile along the ridge, half a mile of stumbling on rough grass and between boulders. Like a small crater, very deep and steep-sided and narrow, that Cait Ban said had once been a hole in the ridge right down from the crest of it to the North Cove, where indeed there was a cave that itself was blocked at the back, far in, by fallen boulders. In the bottom of the hollow lay the Stones, big white stones, egg-shaped, some of them mottled or flecked with black, each of them about as heavy as a woman could comfortably lift with both hands. The Cursing Stones.

Kate went slithering down into the hollow and he followed her unwillingly. The stones lay on a rough slab of rock like a table. They had been afraid of the stones as children, afraid even to touch them, until their last summer holiday on the island, that they had sensed was the last, was the end of their childhood. Kate had dared him to go with her to the Hollow in the dark, and touch the Stones, and wish.

'What'll we wish?'

'That we come back, stupid.'

He had forgotten that for years. 'D'you remember the last time we did this?' he said. Something of that childhood closeness was back with him, an unquestioning closeness. And he felt in that moment how much he loved her, wanted to love her, how little all the nonsense, all the surface play-acting and romanticizing mattered. Maybe if they did come back they could get close again, all the London smog that seemed to lie on their minds would dissolve, let them see each other clearly, let him see her as she really was. Ireland, England—it didn't matter which it was for any of the foolish reasons. Only that one rather than the other would let them come closer, find each other. And if it helped Kate to be here, to pretend, to think she was Irish, what did it matter? Let him find her. Let him find her.

Kate looked at him, her eyes strange in the starlight as if she could see things far away from them but could not see him, not the Hollow round her. 'I remember,' she said. 'May there lie a curse on the people who have done this to this island.' With her two hands she was turning the largest stone round and round leftwards, against the passage of the sun. 'The people who are growing fat while the West is starving, may their money rot them, my curse on them for ever. May there come a time when the poor of this land will own it, and no one will drive them away, no one will starve them away. May the man who refused a schoolmistress to this island see his own children leave him and hate him.' She rested her hands for a moment and then began to turn the stone right-about in the direction of the sun. 'May those who leave this island in sorrow come back to it in joy. May we come back. May we spend our lives for this land of stones. And my curse on either of us who goes away from it.'

'Kate!'

'Be quiet,' she whispered. 'What else is there for us to do? Where else do we belong?'

The still outline of the dog was dark above them on the rim of the hollow, black against the stars.

13

In October 1961 Francis O'Rourke, old Jo Clancy and Johnny O'Hara joined the Guardians of the Flame. It cost them a great deal of money: a hundred guineas a head entrance fee, a hundred guineas a head first year's subscription, and a joint donation paid in unequal shares in accordance with their shareholdings in Jofran, Ltd, of five thousand pounds. There was nothing obligatory about the donation. As Marty Mullins explained, 'Each of us gives according to his ability.'

'And gets according to his need?' suggested Johnny.

'Ah now, ah now,' Marty said, 'sure that's not the idea at all, there's nothing selfish about the Guardians. We're purely a patriotic organization, dedicated to Ireland and the Party, the Party and Ireland. What's good for one is good for the other, and the selfish man, let him emigrate or join the bowsies on the other side of the House.'

'What the hell do we get out of it then?' Francis said. He knew very well but he wanted to hear it spelled out, which was the last thing that Marty was going to do.

'A feeling of sacrifice,' Marty whispered, dragging the breath into his asthmatic chest. 'And sure what is the sacrifice but for to make the Party prosper? And if the Party prospers doesn't Ireland prosper? And if Ireland prospers don't we all ? Cast your bread on the waters, Francis boy, cast your bread.'

Just before Christmas it was discovered that Jofran's appeal against the Corporation's refusal to sanction the plans for Brefni House had gone to the wrong Department. Instead of the Department of Local Government, which had turned the appeal down, it should have gone to the Department of Economic Development. It was Jer Mullins, parliamentary secretary to the Minister for Economic Development, who brought this possibly hopeful news to Johnny O'Hara.

It was even more hopeful because the Minister, Paddy Noonan, was the founder of the Guardians and the Chairman of its

Committee. The five-thousand-pound donation of course would weigh nothing with him, but it meant that he was the kind of man who believed, naturally, in the Guardians' ideals, of prosperity for Ireland, and prosperity is impossible without Development. He himself was a young, driving man belonging to the post-Civil-War generation, and the new politics. His father had been on the right side in the Civil War, and he had done his share during his school days of blacking the eyes of boys whose fathers had belonged to the wrong side, but as a politician he knew that such things were secondary to economics. Ireland had had enough history to last it for a couple of centuries. What it needed now was money. In March 1962 he granted Jofran's renewed appeal and instructed the Corporation to pass the plans of Brefni House.

But at this point Lady Honoria, nudged and guided by Denis Farrell, played her next stroke. She got hold of Matt O'Carroll, who was not only Labour T.D. for Oxmantown, but also Councillor for one of its Wards on the City Corporation, alderman, ex-mayor and ex-President of the United Irish Workers' Union, and so played on his sense of the Corporation's independence from Ministerial fiats that he forced the Corporation to defy Paddy Noonan. No councillor, not even Party councillors, wanted to be seen as enemies of the Corporation's free exercise of its just powers, particularly in a case that involved housing the poor as against giving way to rich developers, and the Minister's order was sent back to him with a brusque rejection.

'Five thousand pounds!' Old Jo Clancy shouted, and then whispered it, afraid that by shouting he would raise his blood pressure to the danger level. 'What are we going to do, Franky?'

'Screw somebody's castors off him, starting with that old villain Mullins,' Franky said. 'Leave it to me.' They had a brutal interview in Moriarty's or at least one that started brutally, but Marty Mullins had faced too many situations like this in forty years of politics to be cast down so easily, and he managed to leave Francis with the feeling that the whole thing had been foreseen by him from the beginning, and that in a few weeks time

Francis would see it as a positive benefit to the Company. 'Arrah sure, Franky man, God is strong. As sure as there's a cross on the ass we'll come out of this on the right side and you'll be laughing at yourself, laughing at yourself man for all the worrying you've been doing. Lave it with me, man. Lave it with me.' Even choking with asthma he managed to sound in total command of the conversation.

A month later, out of the blue, and without so much as having applied for it again, old Mrs O'Rourke got her 'widow-of-a-patriot's' pension, backdated eleven years. It was only for fifteen shillings a week, and she spent almost all of it on masses for the soul of her dead husband and perpetual care of his until then neglected grave back in Drumleague, but as she said:

' 'Tis justice at last. 'Tis the Will of God to downface them ones like Lucy Mangan and Jenny O'Callaghan, flaunting their bits of dishonourable pensions in the face of the world and pretending that their Seaneens of husbands died for Ireland. And my widow's curse on that Marty Mullins the thief that kept me from my rights until this day.'

'Mother, mother, it was Marty got it for you, will you not give the man credit?'

But she wouldn't. 'A thief from his cradle. If I thought it was that ruffian, that omadhaun that gave it to me sure I'd . . . I'd send it back to them.'

A month later again a quite spectacularly profitable deal fell into Jofran's lap, involving a piece of land that was needed desperately by one of the Semi-State Companies. 'Now sure, doesn't God look after His own?' Marty said, and even old Jo Clancy had to admit that He did. Meanwhile the Government, properly incensed at the Corporation's defiance, set its lawyers to investigating whether the Corporation was entitled to reject a Ministerial Order. The investigation dragged through the summer and autumn of 1962.

'We're going to have to compromise,' Marty said, sniffing from a small plastic aerosol to relieve his breathing. Part of the compromise involved making Marty Mullins and his nephew Jer directors of Jofran, Ltd, which by now had become Jofran

Holdings, Ltd, with a cluster of subsidiary companies each with its own concern: building, land, house property in Dublin, a factory in Drumleague making office furniture, with a contract to supply several Government departments and one or two of the Semi-State bodies, and a new project of Johnny O'Hara's concerning trailer caravans, both building them and renting them out on caravan sites in well-known beauty spots. They already had four sites: one on the Ring of Kerry overlooking one of the most beautiful views in Europe, one near Killarney and two in Connemara.

The second part of the compromise involved agreeing to submit amended plans of Brefni House. 'It's that Gandon bitch,' Marty admitted. 'But for her you'd have got everything flying. But with all this culture talk and all the publicity even Paddy Noonan doesn't want to look like a black Philistine destroying the beauty and heritage of Ireland. And then again, you can't ask the Corporation to get down on its knees to us. Never rub dung in a man's eye if you can sell if for manure, Franky, remember that.'

'What kind of amended plans?'

'Sure, any kind. Something that'll let the Councillors off the bloody hook, man. They don't want to have the Minister gunning for them. And sure to God, we don't want them gunning for us, do we? We'll be needing them in the future. Get your fairy fellow to draw up another pretty picture for them. Something Georgian-looking.'

Andrew Fane swore that he would die, that he would withdraw from the whole project before he would sacrifice one storey, one concrete pillar of his work to satisfy the vulgarians in City Hall. But he came round in the end, prompted just at the right moment by his uncle Sir Egbert Fane, the builder, himself a man of Culture, but of the avant-garde kind. 'Dear, dear boy!' Sir Egbert had cried. 'Little we have in this life beyond our honour, grant I you that, but think, oh think of such challenge and opportunity as is offered to you by this strange dilemma of making that which is new appear to be consonant with that which is old, not to say ancient. This paradox of artistic inveracity! Think too of what imagination may do even behind and hidden by the dull and featureless façade of Georgianity.'

Persuaded by his uncle, and the thought that what he designed his uncle would undoubtedly be asked to build, with all the money that that involved, not to speak of his own commission, Andrew Fane submitted. In June 1963, after a great deal of subterranean bargaining between several interested parties, excluding only Lady Honoria and the out-and-out Preservers, new plans for a drastically altered Brefni House were submitted to the Corporation. The tower had gone, and the top storey of the main block, to avoid overwhelming the Four Courts as seen from the south side of the river. There were to be underground parking facilities for an agreed number of cars, which would add considerably to the expense, the site being so near the river and there being so much underground water to deal with. The honeycomb effect of massive concrete frames round deeply sunken windows had been sacrificed to give the exterior Georgian proportions, blending, so the Corporation hopefully thought, with the general appearance of Georgian Oxmantown. Almost everything, in fact absolutely everything, that had made Andrew Fane's original conception worth building, had been sacrificed. But as Marty Mullins wheezed at Francis O'Rourke, rubbing his fat old hands together in Moriarty's, 'Bugger the details, the point is to win. And we've won.'

At the end of August 1963, the plans of Brefni House were finally approved. All that remained was to get rid of the tenants, and demolish the houses, in order to clear the site.

14

They walked along Marietta Street staring at the tenements with a mixture of astonishment and contempt. The place was a total slum. Broken windows, filthy-looking slatterns standing on the doorsteps, even filthier-looking children playing in the street, screaming curses. The lid of a cocoa tin came rolling and Victor Clancy trod on it, squashing it flat.

'Look what yer doing, mister!'

They turned down Slaughter Lane, the wall of a warehouse on their right and the backs of houses on their left until they came to the opening into Aram Court.

'All the fuss about a dump like this!' Victor said. Joseph Anthony, Francis O'Rourke's elder son, didn't answer. He never did unless he was asked a direct question. He stared round Aram Court with polite interest, not wanting to remind Victor that it was Victor who had brought them there, but wondering if he could suggest their going for a drink. He was a year older than Victor but in everything that mattered Victor was the leader. He decided where they went, and what they did when they got there. He always had, ever since they first met six years earlier at Joseph Anthony's fourteenth birthday party.

'It's so lovely for the boys to be such friends,' Mrs Jo Clancy had said later to Maura O'Rourke, and both mothers had remained convinced of it ever since. So had their fathers. For all four parents it was one of the recompenses of life to see the two boys together. Their being together seemed to emphasize their bigness and their beauty: Joseph Anthony a fraction bigger, taller, more beautiful. And God knows, Francis thought, he needs every bit of it, the poor half-wit. He was always torn two ways by his elder son. By a kind of grudging, concealed pride at his beauty, and an equally concealed rage at the fact that year by year he looked less like any O'Rourke who had ever lived and more like the Norwegian sailor of Camden Town who couldn't conceivably have been his bloody father unless ... unless ...

The only thing he didn't need to conceal was rage at the boy's stupidity.

'The bloody eejit!' he shouted when he got his school reports. 'The boy's a bloody moron. What the hell do you do in school? Nothing! Look at it, look at the marks you get! Be Christ, if I'd got the schooling you're getting!' Joseph Anthony's great sky-blue eyes, pale as the summer skies of Norway, beautiful as a fjord between eyelashes like fringes of larch trees, would fill with large, slow tears.

'Look what you're doing to the boy!' his mother would shout. 'How can he help it if . . . They're not teaching him right!'

'*Could do better*,' Francis quoted furiously. '*Doesn't seem to try. What he needs is a few belts of the strap.*'

'You dare! If you so much as lay a finger on him!' As the years in Ireland had gone by and Francis had seemed to need her less and less she had found compensation in the fact that her elder son needed her more. Or at least she was convinced he did. Venetia, even Baby Dermot, seemed to grow away from her like their father, self-sufficient, closed in on themselves. But Joseph had needed her and she became a different woman when she was with him. The hard, almost hostile defensiveness she had adopted with her husband gave way to love for her son, the kind of love she might have given to Francis if he had been a different man.

The careless indifference that had first intrigued and then captured Francis before they married had been an exact expression of her feelings for him. She cared no more for him than for any of a dozen lodgers passing through the boarding-house week by week and trying to feel her leg on the stairs. It was only when her twenty-seventh birthday came round without her having ever met that piously hoped for Mr Right her mother had always said would arrive even if she spent her time sitting in the chimney corner waiting for him that she began looking around her not for romantic love but for simple rescue from Ma Cooney's, and decided that Francis O'Rourke was the best prospect in sight. There was indeed for a week or two a Norwegian sailor who fluttered her heart. But she had known that it was an irrational, dangerous flutter and that a Catholic Connemara man was worth a thousand Protestant Norwegians. And so she had fixed her beautiful eye and placid mind on Francis O'Rourke, and ever since she had been as good a wife to him as she knew how to be. If he was now rich and getting richer he owed a great deal of it to her. But she had never really loved him and he had never known how to make her love him, as the Norwegian sailor had known without even thinking about it. The O'Rourkes had lived together, and been affectionate, and felt some physical stirrings one for the other, almost frantic at times on his side, and tolerant on hers, and felt both stirrings and affection die down to an irritated indifference, until Maura had built a shell round herself, of which the outer expression was eating too much and taking a greater interest in religion. But her real passion, her only genuine passion, was Joseph Anthony.

She saw in him the husband that she might have had, if only Mr Right had come by; saw in him the lover she had never had, the man she had never possessed, and she poured out her love for her son like a pine tree pouring its life-blood resin over a trapped fly, to preserve him for eternity, motionless in amber.

Joseph Anthony received her love with a charmed easiness and tolerant indifference. He never resented it constricting him because he was scarcely aware that it did. But then, he never resented anything or anyone. Not his mother. Not even his father. Certainly not Victor who had long ago bullied and mocked him into obedience and who now took his obedience as much for granted as he would a motor car's. Anything they did together, and they had done a great deal more together than their parents ever dreamed of, was at Victor Clancy's instigation. It was Victor who had introduced Joseph to sex, to beer, to cigarettes, to their first woman, to stealing whiskey from Father Duggan's study, to introducing new boys to the same cycle of development. If he ever thought about it, Joseph Anthony expected the same relationship to continue for ever.

They had come down to Marietta Street and Aram Court out of curiosity. They had heard about these places for years until they seemed to take on an extra dimension that didn't really belong to Dublin, or the real world. They had both of them half expected to find something extraordinary. And all it was was a slum like any other slum. They walked farther into Aram Court and found that one side of it, that had been formed by the backs of the houses in St Olaf's Row, had disappeared. The houses there had been demolished, leaving a stretch of rubble-strewn mud thirty yards long by ten or twelve deep, and concealed from St Olaf's Row itself by a wooden hoarding, whose back was towards them. A man was leaning against the hoarding throwing something down on to the ground and picking it up again, time and time over. A small, thin, foxy, sharp-featured man in his early thirties, in a cheap, shabby grey suit and a dirty white shirt open at the neck.

He looked up as they came nearer. 'Hey, lads. Lookin' for a game?'

'A game?' Victor said.

'Pitch an' toss.' He spun the ha'penny, watched it fall between two broken pieces of brick and cocked his foxy head at the two boys. 'Heads or harps?'

'Harps,' Victor said.

'You win,' Denis Doyle said. He summed up their possible wealth with a narrowed, expert eye. 'Tanner a toss?'

'All right,' Victor said.

'How 'bout you, misther?'

'All right,' Joseph Anthony said.

'I been waitin' here for some o' the lads,' Denis said, spitting on his ha'penny. 'We always plays a game lunchtime. Your call, misther.'

They had each won five shillings off him before he produced the pack of cards. 'Yer too good for me,' he said. 'D'you know how to play stud?'

Twenty minutes later they had each lost two pounds. 'Double or quits,' Denis coaxed.

'I haven't enough left,' Victor said.

'Get away out o' that. Lads like you? You're stuffed with it, I can tell a mile off. Quality, that's what I said to myself when you come round there just now. Real quality. Young gentlemen on a tour of the sights, eh?'

'My father owns this place,' Joseph Anthony said, sweeping a vague hand round the site and Aram Court.

'And mine,' Victor said. The one thing he had never been able to drive into Joseph Anthony's head was that their fathers were equal partners; that if anything his father had a bigger share of the companies than Joseph Anthony's had. It gave him an odd feeling at times that his domination over Tony was not as complete as it usually seemed to be, and for that reason he never pursued the argument too far. Tony would simply smile at him and seem to accept what he was saying, and ten minutes, or an hour, or a month later would say again in exactly the same tone of voice, 'My father's company . . .' or, 'My father owns . . .' with a curious suggestion that couldn't conceivably be intended, and yet was maddening, that Victor's father was somehow an employee of Tony's father, and not his senior partner.

'Eh eh!' Denis Doyle was saying. 'Then you must know my brother. Willy. Willy Doyle. It was him flattened all these. Your dads' right-hand man my brother is. I been watching the site for him.' He ruffled the torn, greasy pack of cards between thin conjurer's fingers. 'So that's who your dads are, eh? Fancy that. Seeing as that's who you are there isn't any problem. Double or quits on credit. You win, I pay up. You lose, pay me when you can. The word of your dads' sons is good enough for Denis Doyle any day in the week. Hey, Mick, Petey, you know who these two genman are? The bosses' sons.'

The boys, one about sixteen and the other any age between a wizened fourteen and a shrunken eighteen, had come up behind Victor and Tony, shuffling too-large boots on the rubble. They all began playing. Three more boys joined them. Victor and Joseph Anthony found themselves eight pounds down apiece. They emptied their pockets and still owed close to eleven pounds. 'That's a real run of bad luck,' Denis said. 'But I never—truly I never seen any one take it better than you two. Is that right, lads?'

None of the five lads ever had.

'I suppose we'd better get you the money,' Victor said.

'That's my lads,' Denis said. 'Credit's all very well, but it never fed the soldier as they say. But I wouldn't like you to have the bother of having to come back here with the cash. Suppose I came with you?'

'There's a shop down by the quays,' Victor said. 'They'll give it to us. I don't know what my father'll say, but we'll have to make up some kind of story for him.'

'You'll think of something,' Denis said happily. Mick and Petey attached themselves to the party, the other three boys having to go back to work. They all went out into St Olaf's Row and turned down towards the river.

'We're a bit conspicuous,' Victor said miserably. 'I mean so many of us. The shop, it's one of my dad's shops, the manager'll think it's a bit funny——'

'You lads scarper,' Denis said to Mick and Petey. 'I'll handle this.' Reluctantly the two boys fell behind, seeing their share of sixteen pounds fading away. 'Scarper,' Denis hissed, and they scarpered. Denis and Victor and Joseph Anthony went on down towards the quays. They were in River Lane, behind River Street, and with the two boys gone there was no one else in sight. Victor caught Denis by the lapels of his grey, Italian-cut jacket and half lifted him against the wall.

Denis opened his mouth to shout and tried to hit Victor in the face. Victor brought his knee up between Denis's legs. Not hard but hard enough to cut the shout off and turn Denis's face green. 'You stay quiet,' Victor said, 'or you'll have a squeaky voice for ever. Take the money out of his pocket, Tony, inside his jacket.'

'You can't,' Denis tried to whisper, but he couldn't shape the words for the pain in his crotch. Joseph Anthony put his hand inside the coat, feeling it warm and greasy against his skin and wrinkling his nose in disgust. There was quite a thick wad of notes. He started to peel off the five pounds they had lost.

'Give it to me,' Victor said impatiently, letting go of Denis with one hand and grabbing the notes. He pushed the wad of them into his hip pocket.

'Jesus!' Denis screamed. Victor hit him in the stomach, still holding him against the wall with his other hand.

'That'll teach you to cheat, you little rat.' He dropped him and gave him a kick as he folded down on to the ground. 'C'mon, Tony.' They ran for fifty yards and then walked easily, getting their breath. Behind them Denis Doyle hung on his hands and knees, vomiting.

'He knows who we are,' Joseph Anthony said.

'What the hell can he prove?' Victor said. 'You think he's going to the Guards to tell them he got beaten up for cheating at stud? Be your age. And suppose he did, who are the Guards going to believe? Him or us? I caught him trying to pick my pocket and I thumped him. He'd get six months.'

They walked back along the river and across it to Grafton Street and into Daly's Lounge Bar. When they counted the wad of notes there were thirty-one pounds in it.

'We're going to have an evening,' Victor said. 'A real evening.'

* * *

A hundred and fifty miles from Dublin in the Convent of the Divine Suffering that had once been Castle Lennox, Joseph Anthony's sister Venetia was sitting cross-legged on the floor of her dormitory in front of a wide open window. She was naked except for her blue cotton drawers, the soles of her feet pressed against the insides of her thighs, her hands resting on her bent knees, thumb and forefinger making a circle, the other fingers lying relaxed against her kneecaps, pointing downwards.

'Om mani padme hum,' she intoned. 'Om mani padme hum. All is one. One is all. Unity. Unity. Om mani padme hum.' She was alone. Blessedly alone. Everyone else playing hocky or tennis, the nuns saying their Office. Their Office! Christianity! She thought of their fretful pieties with tolerant condescension. Om mani padme hum. The Path to the One. The Wheel turns. All changes and all is the same.

Feet came running and she tried to keep out the thought of intrusion. When one was really far advanced, of course, intrusion, the whole awful outside world, simply didn't exist.

'Face Wipe is coming!' Jennifer panted. 'Quick!'

Venetia turned her head, retaining the expression of withdrawnness so that Jennifer could see it, and appreciate the difference between them. Like a Lama. In the snows of Tibet.

'Get up!' Jennifer hissed urgently, slithering towards her like a skater across the polished expanse of dormitory linoleum. 'Get up, you idiot!'

But Mother Veronica was already behind her in the doorway, her eyes sweeping the room, taking in the girl squatting by the window, the other girl panting over her. The girl squatting was naked, the other one—— Her heart almost stopped for a second, seemed to check physically before beating faster. But it was absurd, impossible, thank God it was impossible, she had seen the girl running into the room only this instant. Whatever it was it was not that, blessed be Our Saviour, blessed be Our Lady, Our Patroness.

'Jennifer Adams,' she said, controlling her voice. 'Venetia O'Rourke, what are you both doing?'

Not completely naked, thanks be to Our Lady, not utterly naked. 'What are you doing sprawling on the floor in that disgusting condition, Venetia? Get up, child, get up, cover yourself at once.' She had not seen her own body in such a condition in thirty years. But this was a different age, she must constantly remind herself that everything, everything was changing and that one must not judge hastily.

'I'm not doing anything, Mother,' Jennifer said. 'I . . . we . . . were excused hockey——Sister Philomena said——'

'I did not ask you what you were not doing. I asked what you are doing. Jennifer, hand that dressing-gown to Venetia, and then you may leave the room. If you are not engaged in hockey practice go to the library and prepare tomorrow's lessons.'

Jennifer went, turning for a second to look despairingly at her friend from the doorway. The idiot. The idiot. She was going to get into the most awful row and she wasn't going to make the slightest attempt to get out of it. She looked as if she didn't even understand there was going to be a row. Her and her silly old yoghurt, she was mad, completely mad.

'I am waiting for you to leave, Jennifer,' Mother Veronica said, without needing to turn her head. May the Holy Spirit grant me wisdom, she prayed. 'Now, Venetia, tell me the meaning of this exhibition of yourself.'

'It wasn't an exhibition, Mother. No one was here.'

'Jennifer was here. I am here.'

'I thought I'd be alone.'

'I see. For what purpose?'

Venetia lifted her head and eyebrows infinitesimally, contriving to suggest that what she was going to say might be beyond Mother Veronica's comprehension. 'I was contemplating.'

'You were . . . what?' Mother Veronica, after thirty years of schoolgirls, was not often at a loss. But even before this she had sometimes felt with Venetia that the girl erected some kind of transparent barrier around herself, so that one could see her and hear her, but never reach her. If any of the other girls had said any such thing—not that any of them would, poor dears—she would have known exactly how to react, to laugh, or to look grave. But Venetia! Contemplating!

'You appear to have been contemplating yourself,' she said coldly, more coldly than she really felt, as if she too needed to erect some kind of barrier between herself and this extraordinary child.

'In a way you might describe it like that, Mother,' Venetia said, a shade loftily. 'And I was not sprawling. I was in the Lotus Position. Well, nearly. That's a Yoga position for contemplating.'

'I am aware of that,' Mother Veronica said. 'Have you been'—she searched momentarily for a neutral word, '. . . occupied with such practices for long?'

'All this term, Mother.'

'Do you . . . do it while other girls are present?'

'Sometimes, but they usually interrupt. It's better when I'm alone. That's why I got off hockey this week.'

'Why——' Mother Veronica began, startled. 'You mean Sister Philomena knows . . .' She checked herself. 'What excuse did you give to Sister Philomena?' Heaven knew, Sister Philomena was a scatterbrain, but not to such an extent.

'Well, I'm no good at hockey, Mother, because I can't see the ball, and I said I wanted to do my exercises by myself.'

'Ah. What you are really saying is that you gave Sister Philomena to understand an untruth. Am I correct?'

'No, Mother. These are exercises. Yoga exercises.'

'I do not propose to argue with you, child. You know very well that by "exercises" Sister Philomena understands physical jerks of the usual kind. Not sitting naked in front of an open window where you will cause scandal to anyone entering the room, and will also catch pneumonia. There have been several occasions over the past few terms when I have had the gravest doubts about your conduct. I am a broad-minded woman and this is a modern school. Not many years ago any young girl behaving as you have just behaved would have been instantly expelled. But even in a modern school there is a level of misbehaviour, of immodestly foolish behaviour, which I cannot in conscience tolerate, and I see that I shall have to take stringent steps to bring you to a more . . . a more becoming frame of mind. Your father is paying a great deal to have you taught not only the academic subjects of the curriculum, but to become a young lady, a Catholic young lady, with all the virtues and responsibilities that that term implies. I have already at times felt with you, Venetia, a despairing sense that I am failing in my obligations to your father in this respect. You are a clever child, Venetia, but that is not enough. Indeed, if not allied to other qualities, that may in itself present dangers in the development of character.

'As a first step, you will give me your undertaking, your solemn undertaking, that you will immediately, from this moment, cease all this nonsense of Yoga and of contemplation of your own body——'

'It's not my body I'm contemplating.'

'Venetia! How dare you interrupt me? I say you will give up this wicked nonsense at once. Since you apparently feel a need for additional spiritual exercises you will spend an extra half-hour every evening in the Chapel, kneeling before the Blessed

Sacrament. And you will explain to your dormitory companions, in my presence, that what you have been doing, and no doubt have been presenting to them as clever conduct, is in fact silly, immodest, and pagan. Is that understood?'

Venetia stood in front of her, seemingly even thinner inside the dressing-gown that in fact belonged to Jennifer, a much larger girl. She had begun to shiver, half with cold and half with nervous tension, while Mother Veronica was lecturing her. She could see the point coming a long way off, where she was going to have to decide. She clenched her teeth together to prevent any possibility of their chattering, her hands holding the edges of the dressing-gown together, lapped over across her middle.

'Is that understood, Venetia?' She felt suddenly sorry for the child, so thin, so shiveringly guilty. Really only a child in spite of her fifteen years. Oh dear, oh Blessed Mother of God how cruel one must be to be kind to young things. Did they ever realize in after years how much one suffered with them and for them? 'I am waiting, Venetia.' She would let her off the half-hour in Chapel after a week. If only she herself could find a half-hour, one blessed, blessed free half-hour to kneel there in the empty Chapel before Our Lord. And she must impose that precious gift on this poor child as a punishment. Dear Saviour, how strange this world is.

'I . . . I . . .'

'Yes, child?'

'I don't believe I've done anything wrong. And I'm not going to tell anyone that I think I have. It isn't just.'

*   *   *

The telephone call from the convent reached Francis O'Rourke at five o'clock the following evening, as he was stumping into the house in Rathfarnham from a meeting with old Jo Clancy, Johnny O'Hara, Paddy Gunn and Andrew Fane, and he was already tired and angry.

'Mr O'Rourke here.' What the hell did they want? Another bloody subscription?

'Mother Veronica here, Mr O'Rourke. I am afraid, I am very much afraid, Mr O'Rourke, that I must ask you to prepare yourself for an unpleasant shock——'

'What? Venetia? Is ... has something happened?'

'I'm afraid that it has.'

'Oh, Christ. Is she ... has there been an accident?'

'It is nothing physical.'

'What—the—bloody hell—are—you—talking—about?' He was holding on to the edge of his patience, and sounded like it.

'I will be grateful if you did not swear at me, Mr O'Rourke.'

'I'm not bloody well swearing. Christ, woman, what's happened? Has she ... is she ...'

Behind him Maura had come into the hall, hearing his raised voice, and her daughter's name. 'Frank, what is it? What is it? What's happened?'

'Shut up! No, not you, my wife. What the hell has happened?'

In her study Mother Veronica shut her eyes, holding the telephone with her fingertips as if it might contaminate her small, plump, immaculate hands if she grasped it more closely. 'Perhaps if I spoke with Mrs O'Rourke ...' she said, while across the room Sister Philomena stood with clasped hands and reddened eyes, her lips moving silently as she recited prayers. Mother Veronica thought for one wicked second, her mind escaping from its usual controls, that it would be an enormous satisfaction to smack Sister Philomena's face. She instantly repressed the thought, noting it for Confession. Oh dear, oh dear, how much damage that child had done already. But it simply confirmed her in her certainty that she had reached the right decision. The man was swearing again. With such a father, no wonder the daughter was unmanageable.

'I am deeply pained to have to tell you,' she said with a smooth rush in an interval of the swearing, 'that I must ask you to take Venetia away. I do not wish to describe it as expulsion. Simply that you should agree to remove her.'

'What! What the b——'

'Mr O'Rourke, if you continue to use bad language I must terminate this conversation and arrange for Venetia to return to you by train, under the escort of one of the Sisters. Would you prefer that?'

'What has she done?' whispered Francis, holding on to the telephone with both hands. His wife was staring at him, her face getting paler by the second, one hand held to her bosom, pressing into its soft bulk with an agony of questioning. 'Is she pregnant?' Francis said, his voice starting as a whisper and ending as a roar, a kind of shout of anguish. Behind him Maura sat down suddenly on one of the polished wooden chairs against the wall and sobbed aloud.

'I have said that it is nothing physical,' Mother Veronica said with cold distaste. 'If you will allow me to explain——'

'Allow you? I'll bloody well make you——'

'This conversation is becoming extremely unpleasant, Mr O'Rourke. I have had occasion to discipline your daughter for conduct that is perhaps foolish and wrong-headed rather than intentionally wicked, but that even in itself presented problems of . . . shall I say, modesty? Unfortunately Venetia has seen fit to reject all correction and to adopt an attitude of complete defiance. I gave her two hours for reflection, and when she remained obdurate I arranged for her to sleep apart under the supervision of one of the Sisters and to take twenty-four hours in solitude to contemplate the unwisdom and the un-Catholic nature of her attitude. I am very, very sorry to say that at the end of those twenty-four hours her attitude had not only not changed but appeared positively to have hardened. I have there-fore no alternative but to ask you to withdraw her from my school. I regret it deeply, and confess it as a failure. But some-times one does fail with pupils and when this happens it is wiser to recognize the fact before more harm is done. I have no doubt, I have every hope, that in some . . . some different kind of school Venetia may grow up to be all that you desire. But it cannot be here.'

Several times during the past minute Francis had opened his mouth to interrupt, but no sounds came out of it. Behind him he could hear his wife sobbing. If he wasn't holding the phone he'd hit her, he'd fetch her such a clout across the ear she'd have something to snivel about for a month.

'I'll come down and see you,' he whispered. 'I'll come to-morrow.'

'Tonight if you please. These things are best done at once.'

He bit off what he wanted to say. 'All right. I'll be down about nine. We'll talk about it then.'

'We can talk by all means, Mr O'Rourke, but I am afraid there is no possibility whatsoever of any such talk leading to a change of mind on my part. I wish your daughter to leave my school tonight.'

'I'll be down,' Francis said gratingly. 'I'll kill her,' he said to no one in particular. 'That effing bitch, I'll strangle her.'

'My little girl,' wept Maura, 'don't you dare touch her, don't you dare, Frank. Tell me the worst of it.' It was her own fault, all her own fault, she had never loved her enough, never showed her enough that she loved her. Oh the poor child, the poor little child, she had let her go, why? why? 'Why did I ever let her go away to school, oh my little Venny.'

'Shut up you stupid cow!' Francis shouted. All he needed was his mother to join in, and at that instant she came down the stairs, scenting rather than hearing trouble, because in the past year she had become very deaf.

'What's the matter, what's happened, who's shouting? What's Maura crying about, Franky, what's the matter?'

I'll go mad, Francis thought. I'll go bloody raving mad and kill someone. He tore his car keys out of his pocket and stamped towards the front door. 'I'll be back when I'm back,' he said. 'Christ almighty.'

In the Convent, that had once been Castle Lennox, Venetia sat isolated in the nuns' parlour, her luggage already packed beside her, her grey school overcoat folded across her suitcase, her grey felt school hat on top of it, tea, bread and butter, a boiled egg and a glass of milk on a tray in front of her. She touched none of it, her face white and pinched, her eyes behind the thick spectacles constantly on the point of betraying her by tears, her nose pink, her hands locked in her lap. 'I will not cry. I will *not* cry. I will not *cry*.'

From time to time Sister Philomena or one of the other Sisters opened the door, thrust anguished faces round the edge for a moment, to express compassion, understanding, good-will, or reproach, or all combined. In the school itself, in the classrooms, the library, the corridors, the stairs, the dining-room, the dormitories, nothing else had been discussed all the previous night, that day, and the present evening.

'Venetia! Naked! Abso-lutely *starkers*! Right at the window absoballylutely *starkers*! Face Wipe saw her from the gravel. She nearly died!'

'Stuff. She caught her in the dorm, she was in front of the mirror.'

'Sssh. There was much more than that, didn't you hear? Jennifer was there too. Jennifer! Yes, Fatty Adams.'

'What? What was *she* doing?'

'*That's* the big secret. That's the sixty-four-dollar question. What *was* she doing? What were they both doing? You don't think Face Wipe's going off her nut because Skinny Vinny was in her pelt in the dorm, do you?'

'What d'you mean?'

'What do you think I mean? *That*, of course.'

'What do you mean, *That*?'

'What do you think I mean, you ninny? What they're always on about, of course, what that priest was on about, the drippy one at the last Retreat. 'Meh deeah dorters, it meh at taimes occur that young people meh experience certain *feelings*—eh mehn young people of the same sex meh . . .'' *That's* what he meant.'

'Oh my golly, no.'

'Oh my golly, yes. I bet.'

'Then why isn't Fatty getting the push as well?'

'Because Face Wipe thinks she was the innocent party.'

'Because Fatty's uncle is a Bishop, you mean. Sssh, here's Philly, yes, Sister Philomena, we're just going to go up to the dorm now. Sister—Sister—is she . . . is she GONE yet?'

It was ten minutes to ten. A few minutes later a goggle-eared school heard the soft crunching of heavy tyres on the gravel sweep, saw the headlights throw brief shadows across white-washed walls, heard a car door thud closed and the bell ring violently. Hands hugged knees, eyes stared in the darkened junior dormitories. Senior girls tiptoed to the windows, peered out.

Francis found his daughter already standing in the hall, waiting, her suitcase beside her, hat and overcoat on, face paper-white from exhaustion and nerves, eyes swollen from tears that for the last hour had defeated all her efforts to keep them back. On the way down he had passed from rage with Mother Veronica, his wife and his mother, to fury with his daughter, and he walked into the school prepared to knock her down on the spot. And if he had seen her as she had wanted him to find her, cool, composed, defiant, a contemptuous, even an understanding victim of medieval injustice and reactionary stupidity he would surely have struck her then and there. But seeing her as she had become over the past hours of waiting, like a refugee, her thin shoulders bent with misery and tiredness, tears rolling from under her spectacles, he suddenly realized that whatever she had done, whatever had happened, she was his bloody child and no one was going to do this to her and get away with it. He had stopped twice on the way down for large whiskeys to strengthen him and calm his mind, which was why he was late, and when Mother Veronica, who had been watching for the car lights from her desk in the study, came out into the hall like a small black galleon to face him, he was in exactly the mood to face her.

'What the bloody hell have you been doing to my child?'

'I have been praying for her,' Mother Veronica said. She smelt the whiskey and her nostrils whitened. 'I had intended offering you tea after your journey, but I see that that would not be appropriate. And please do not raise your voice to me, or use foul language. This is a school for young ladies.' She lifted her small square chin, ready to fire another broadside if it was needed. Poor, poor, poor child. What chance had she with such a parent? But what else could she herself do? Her duty to the school, to the children, to their parents, left her no alternative, not to speak of her duty as a religious, a religious teacher, vowed and dedicated to the upholding of religious standards, standards of conduct and morality, obedience and discipline. Allow one brick to be removed from the wall, and all might fall to the ground in ruin. One could see it happening. Everywhere. Even in Ireland. Permissiveness. Disobedience to authority, questioning of God's priests and bishops. She could not in conscience allow any action of hers, any act of omission, any laxity, to do harm to the Church, however small it might seem, however cruel the remedy might seem to the offender. She had meant to attempt some explanation of this to Mr O'Rourke and to Venetia, so that whatever their feelings at the moment, they might afterwards come to realize the essential nature of her action. But any such attempt was clearly pointless.

'I am sorry for you, Venetia, and my prayers go with you. I shall always be pleased to hear of your future progress.'

Francis had been opening and shutting his mouth, choosing and discarding one curse after another as inadequate.

'Come out of here,' he said at last, 'come out of this bloody place. I was mad ever to send you here.' She tried to lift her suitcase, heaving it up from the linoleum, and he took it from her. 'Arrgh,' he said towards Mother Veronica. She bent her head in acknowledgement as if he had said, 'Good-bye.' Outside he threw the case into the back of the big Jaguar. 'Get in the front.' They drove away, the lights swinging again across the walls and windows, throwing shadows into dormitories, on to wide-eyed listeners. 'They're going, she's gone.' Some of the juniors cried under the covers, not knowing why they were crying. Sister Philomena was in the chapel, kneeling where Venetia might have knelt for her half-hours of punishment. Oh, Sweet Saviour watch over her, guard her from evil. Oh, am I sinful to have loved her? Sweet Jesus forgive my sin, forgive Your poor servant who is unworthy to be Your bride.'

In the car Venetia cried silently. When they were out of the drive and on to the road she said whisperingly, 'I . . . I'm sorry, Daddy.'

'That effing bitch,' Francis said, accelerating, as if the convent was on his heels. 'Have you had anything to eat?'

'N–no. I ... I couldn't——'

'There's a pub ten miles up the road. Jesus bloody Christ what a bitch. I'm glad you're out of there. We'll find you a proper effing school.'

Venetia pushed thin, tentative fingers under his arm, feeling the tweed of his jacket hairy and warm, like a rough animal. She felt so overwhelmed with love and gratitude that she could have died for him. The smell of whiskey filled the car. 'You see it was my Yoga exercises. She ... she wanted me to say—to s–ss–say——' Her voice shook with crying and she couldn't go on, her hand squeezing the thick tweed of his coat, her fingers clenching on his sleeve.

'Don't cry, lovey, don't cry any more. You can tell me about it when we're eating.' Memories of the Brothers came to him, floating on wings of whiskey, huge men, straps in their great knuckly fists, loud voices shouting, eyes terrible, a small, shivering creature that was himself in childhood standing snivelling before them, cold, hungry, terror-stricken, helpless. 'They're all the bloody same,' he said.

'Some of them were nice,' Venetia said, blowing her nose. 'S–S–Sister Philomena ...' As she thought of her she began to cry again. 'B–but I c–couldn't—it w–wasn't just.'

At the public house, the Angler's Tavern, they were given dinner in a small private sitting-room, because the dining-room was already closed. Venetia had mushroom soup, and fillet steak with croquette potatoes and fried onions and green peas, and two glasses of Burgundy, and ice-cream and coffee, and slept all the remainder of the way to Dublin. It was four in the morning when they arrived.

15

In November 1963 Jofran Holdings, Ltd, applied for eviction orders against the remaining tenants in Oxman Street, Marietta Street, and Aram Court. A good many of the tenants had already gone, willingly or sullenly, to other tenements, or to Corporation housing schemes on the far outskirts of Dublin, or to stay with relations, or to emigrate. Where houses were completely emptied by these evacuations Jofran moved quickly in and pulled the house down before anyone else could occupy it. In this way the whole of the small stretch of St Olaf's Row had been demolished months ago. So had two houses in Oxman Street and one in Marietta Street more recently. They had almost cleared one of the houses in Aram Court as well, but the night before Willy Doyle and the wreckers arrived Denis Farrell got six families to move in. They had been there ever since and three or four men with raincoats and a look of dangerous certainty about them had said to Willy and the workmen that the first man who laid a pickaxe to a wall behind which decent poor Dublin working-class families were sheltering was likely not to get home that night except on a stretcher. Willy Doyle went and got the Guards, and two young policemen came back with him, saw the young men, warned them against disturbing the peace, and went away. The young men remained, their hands in the pockets of their long raincoats.

Once again articles began to appear in the newspapers, with pictures of the houses, of broken lavatories leaking on to floors, of mothers with babies living a family to a dirty, rat-infested room with one water tap between six or seven families. One photograph showed Francis O'Rourke getting out of his Jaguar in Oxman Street, the site of a demolished house and timbers supporting the bulging wall of the neighbouring house in the background.

Francis would have gone bull-headed for everyone and everything at that point, including the Irish Republican Army, but old Jo Clancy insisted that they try offering money. Fifty pounds a family.

'If you offer them any more than that,' Johnny O'Hara said, 'they'll get the idea that there's a fortune in it and we'll finish up giving them thousands.'

A dozen families accepted the fifty pounds and another house came down. In December a reluctant judge granted the eviction orders with a stay to give the families concerned three months to find other accommodation. It was kindly meant, as judges' gestures often are, but essentially meaningless. Most of the families concerned were under rents ranging from five to eighteen shillings a week, even when they paid them, and if they could have got Jofran to accept them. There was no accommodation they could conceivably get, from the Corporation or anyone else, at less than two pounds, and it would almost certainly be several miles from where any of them worked, if they were working. Which meant at least another pound a week in bus fares. A workman's wages were about eight pounds a week.

In January 1964 Denis Farrell's Marxist Irish Republican Party, one of the many left-wing splinters from the Irish Republican Army and the Republican movement in general, organized a public meeting outside the G.P.O. It was not announced as a Marxist meeting, or even as a Republican meeting, but as a meeting of Dublin's homeless, organized by the House the People Committee. Denis Farrell was not there, but a number of the young men who worked for him were there, and one of them, Con Danaher, was the first speaker.

The son of a small shopkeeper in Galway, and a third-year student in U.C.D., he had already been a Republican for several years, and Denis Farrell's disciple for a year. He lived on cigarettes and coffee and fanaticism. No one who knew him had ever seen him finish a meal, and very few had ever seen him sleep. Even by daylight his face looked ghastly, greenish white, shadows under his eyes like bruises made by policemen's thumbs, his cheeks and forehead scarred by acne, his black hair at once lank and dry, his teeth and fingers discoloured by tobacco, dark yellow, black, burned. And out of the white mask of his face his eyes also burned.

As he climbed the tailgate of the lorry that was to serve as platform for the meeting the wind sliced through his shabby coat like a razor. He had no overcoat, no vest, no socks. He had nothing. Only a belief in suffering, and a mad vision of a world of summer. In front of him, pressed round the sides of the lorry, fifty or sixty people waited, shivering in the neon-lit dark of O'Connell Street, outside the historic building of the 1916 Rising, the General Post Office where Pearse and Connolly and Plunkett and a hundred and fifty men offered their sacrifice that for future generations Ireland might be free.

The small waiting crowd was made up of a very ill-assorted collection of people. Some were from Oxman Street, come in the faint hope that someone cared what happened to them. Some were boys like Con Danaher, left-wing Republicans, Communists, soldiers of the ghostly army of fanatics that has always been prepared to die for Ireland without ever having much idea of how to live for it. Some were old-guard left-wing Republicans, Marxists from the days of Connolly and Larkin; one of them an old man with crippled legs who had met Lenin and been beaten so many times at so many demonstrations that he was deaf and almost blind. But he came to meetings, dragging himself on crutches, and when the moment came he would shout, 'Long live the Irish Republic, long live the Workers' Republic, down with Dev.'

And there was an old woman, crunched into herself with rheumatism, who had nursed the wounded in the G.P.O. in 1916, and run guns from Glasgow on the boats in 1920 and 1921 and been pistol-whipped by a Tan officer and flung half naked into a gaol cell with prostitutes. And out of the prostitutes she had made patriots and lifelong friends. For forty years she had lived on bread and margarine and the memory of Connolly's last words to her, and the hope of Ireland's future. 'Oh my Mary,' Connolly had said. 'Ten women like you and we'd have won.' And then he had said, 'Five men like you and we'd have won.'

But the day would come when they would win. And she sheltered her cold old bones from the wind beside the big body of a man who in fact belonged to the Special Branch. There were eight Special Branch men there, quite easily distinguishable because they were all very large and well fed and well clothed and had contented faces.

Con Danaher began talking. He took minutes to get into his stride, and then a kind of self-hypnotism came over him and he took off. 'Who are the people of Ireland?' he screamed above the noise of the traffic, cars on their way to cinemas and restaurants, buses on their way to Finglas and Ballyfermot, Foxrock and Ballsbridge. 'Who are the people?' He stabbed his finger into the knots of upturned, shadowy faces. 'Ireland lives on the bodies of the poor. Your bodies, your sweat, your labour, your hunger and disease and misery.' Inadvertently he pointed at a Special Branch man who looked indignant. 'You are Ireland! And what do you get for it, what's your reward for being Irish? What's the freedom and the care that those men died to give you, there behind me? I will tell you the freedoms of Ireland. The freedom of the White Ship. The freedom to emigrate, to sweat your guts out in Birmingham and London, for your daughters to walk the streets of Liverpool looking for a pound; the freedom to——'

'You're a dirty Communist!' a voice screamed in answer. Unseen by the small crowd another group had joined them, consisting of religious young men armed with potatoes, eggs, tomatoes, and stones. A stone hit Con Danaher in the stomach, winding him, a tomato squelched on his face like breaking blood, fighting started. A woman from Oxman Street got trampled underfoot. Con Danaher and three young Republicans were arrested for disturbing the peace. The crippled Republican who had met Lenin was hit on the head with a baton and his glasses were smashed. Everyone else went home stimulated.

At the next meeting, the following Saturday night, Denis Farrell arranged for the opening speaker to be a priest, Father Herbert Tracey, social worker, already gaining a dubious reputation among the religious as a man wrong-headedly inclined to mix up politics with religion and to forget his proper function in life. But at least the religious young men could scarcely throw stones at him, and he was an even better speaker than Con Danaher. Reporters from the newspapers were there, with photographers, in the hope of a repetition of the previous Saturday night, and Father Tracey spoke to them as much as to anyone else.

'Half a mile from here,' he said, 'in the heart of Catholic Dublin, sixty-four families are threatened with eviction. A hundred years ago, under the tyranny of England, it needed a regiment of soldiers at times to evict one family from a cottage. But we have advanced. We have become free. We have thrown off the yoke of the foreigner. We can carry out our evictions for ourselves, and we need no regiments of soldiers. All we need is an Irish landlord, and an Irish judge, and an Irish bailiff, backed up by half a dozen Irish policemen, with Irish newspapers to report the event as a further step in Ireland's progress towards the millennium. But what millennium? Will there be anything Catholic about it, anything Christian? And what crime have these families committed that they are not to share in it?

'If they are poor, who has kept them poor? If they are out of work, who has offered to employ them? If they are ignorant, whose duty has it been to educate them?

'Their crime is that they exist. Your crime, yours and yours and yours, is that you exist. You occupy space. Space needed for the glittering buildings of the New Ireland, the Cement Republic, the Technocrat Republic. In these last years we have seen a revolution begin around us, and we are the victims of it, you are the victims. You have no share in it. For this is a revolution of the rich, the powerful, the well connected. A revolution of the gombeen men, the traders, the men of business. The same manner of men who crucified Our Lord. They have been unleashed from the shackles of morality and they are at your throats. All you can do is submit, go away to some quiet place where you can starve without offending their eyes, or let them bury you in the foundations of their wonderful new buildings. For new buildings need a sacrifice and you can be that sacrifice, your blood can bind their cement for them.' He paused, looking round him with feverish, haunted eyes. His voice dropped very low, creating silence in which it could still be heard, as actors' voices sometimes do at the height of a dramatic scene, speaking very softly instead of more loudly. 'Or . . . you can resist,' he said, as if discovering that truth himself for the first time. 'Yes! You can resist! For this is the strange truth about all revolutions. They seem inevitable, but they are not. They can be resisted. They can be overthrown. For who will carry out this great revolution? You. Not the rich. They will only give the orders. You will carry them out. If you are mad enough. If you are unchristian enough.

'Who will evict those sixty-four miserable families? Who will smash in the doors, carry out the broken furniture and throw it on to the pavement? You. Poor men. Workmen. Labourers. Men as poor as the Apostles. Who will demolish those buildings that once were homes? You. You. You. Who will dig out the foundations for the office block that is to take their place? You will, with your sweating, aching muscles, your hungry stomachs. You. And by the living God if you do it you deserve what comes. You will mix the concrete, lift it up, build your graves. Listen, listen, listen before it is too late——'

He flung his black arms wide in the dark, stood like another man fifty years before, crying out his heart to an unhearing people, resist, resist, rise up and smash your chains, break out of the prison that the rich and powerful have built for you, be men. If death must come let it find you standing, let it find you brave.

'What kind of Ireland do we want? Let there be green fields and sunlight. Let our children learn. Let the green come out again and spread on every side. And resist. Resist.'

It was exciting stuff to hear from a priest and a good deal of the pith of it got into the Sunday papers. Lady Honoria followed things up with meetings of a different kind and tone, in rented halls, one of them in the Mansion House, and another in the Temperance Hall. Father Herbert Tracey, a shade uncomfortable in these middle-class, squirrel-coated surroundings, spoke at both. Matt O'Carroll, the Labour T.D., put down a whole series of questions in the Dail, as to why the matter of the Oxman Street and Aram Court houses had been transferred to the jurisdiction of the Minister for Economic Development, why that Minister had overruled the Corporation, what steps he or anyone else in the Government proposed to take to rehouse these families if the eviction orders were allowed to stand, and so on.

Another T.D. on the Opposition benches was believed to have framed a question involving the Guardians of the Flame and the size of Jofran Holdings, Ltd's, contribution to them, but he was quietly told that if he started asking libellous and vicious questions like that not only would his constituency never get another road grant, school grant, bridge grant, or public telephone kiosk; the Ministerial files would also be thumbed through for evidence of various unsavoury things he and his friends had done a few years ago when they formed the Government. He was stricken with Influenza Diplomatica and went to bed for a week.

The three-months period of grace drew to an end, the eviction orders were reconfirmed and the proper persons were instructed to gain possession of the premises concerned, by force if necessary. Two days before the due date, a force of Republican students led by Con Danaher moved into the houses to reinforce the thinned ranks of legal tenants and extra-legal squatters. They brought with them bedding rolls, stocks of tinned food, paraffin heaters on which they could boil tea and soup, plastic containers filled with water in case the water supply was cut off, candles, torches, lanterns, wooden clubs, copies of the Proclamation of Independence of the Irish Republic, a Republican flag, the Plough and the Stars Socialist Republican flag, a Tricolour flag and several megaphones. Con Danaher was their leader, Father Herbert Tracey their chaplain, Denis Farrell their unseen éminence grise. One of the larger Trade Unions passed a resolution that none of its members should take part in any evictions and that if they were penalized for refusing to do so, this would be a cause for strike action directed at the authority imposing the penalty. Matt O'Carroll as ex-President of the Union proposed the motion. John Farrell, Denis Farrell's half-brother, and a branch secretary of the Union, seconded the motion.

The day before the evictions were to take place Denis Farrell organized a march from Oxman Street to Dail Eireann, to be led by Father Herbert Tracey, aided by Con Danaher, and made up of sympathizers and the unable-bodied tenants. The able-bodied ones were to stay put, with the squatters, to conserve their strength, avoid any danger of being arrested on the march, and help prevent any sudden swoop of the wreckers in their absence.

The march took place. A hundred or so people, men, women, children. Some of them shouting, some of them singing, some of them trudging sullenly against the chill wind blowing down the river from the docks and the Irish Sea, all of them poor, all of them, even Father Tracey, without any real hope that by marching they would do anything to improve their lot. But if Father Tracey and Con Danaher had done nothing else they had drummed it home to these dregs from the bottom of the Irish barrel that if they must be defeated they should first stand up and shout defiance.

They stopped for a moment on O'Connell's Bridge, where almost fifty years before the British cavalry had trotted gaily towards the General Post Office at the first hint of the Easter Rising, to retreat minutes later in bloody ruins before the gun-fire of the Volunteers, and Father Tracey turned to his followers who had begun to shrink together at the sight of some mounted police drawn up to meet them. 'If Christ was in this city this day, where would He stand? There? There with the Guardians of the Peace, the Garda Siochana on their horses? Or with us? Where would He walk? With the Guardians of the Rich, or the servants of the poor? Follow me, and we'll make the rich listen.'

'Look out for your heads,' screamed Con Danaher, but this was for the benefit of the television cameras and the newspaper reporters, not for any real danger. The police at that stage had no intention of using violence. They simply flanked the march, some on foot, some on horseback, hemming the marchers into the middle of the road, the marchers so poor and thin and ragged against the fine size and uniforms of the Guards that they seemed like a gang of nineteenth-century convicts on the way to the docks for transportation to Australia; and indeed in the sounds of the marchers' shuffling feet, the ringing jingle of the horses' bridles, the creak of saddles and the clop of hooves the ghosts of other sounds survived. Of Irish chains and English horses; after Emmet's Rising, and the Young Irelanders, and the Fenians of '67. Of men and women and sometimes children walking for the last time on Irish stones with bloody feet and breaking hearts and only the faith in their souls that one day Ireland would be free, that on one glorious morning the aisling would come true and all the five green fields would laugh with freedom, grow sweet with liberty.

The convoyed, guarded marchers reached Kildare Street, and turned up it towards Leinster House, Dail Eireann, the shrine of Ireland, and saw another and stronger phalanx of police ahead of them, blocking the way. 'Go for the bastards,' Con Danaher said urgently, but Father had been appointed the leader of the march for a number of tactical reasons, and he had sworn all along that his condition for leading it was that there should be no violence. He turned his back on the police again as he had on O'Connell Bridge, and faced his followers.

'We have a right to march,' he said. 'We have a right to protest. We have a right to carry that protest to our servants in Dail Eireann, and they have a bounden duty to hear it. Do not compromise our rights with violence, or any hostile act towards the Guards. They are doing their duty as they see it. Follow me. But follow me peacefully.'

They went on slowly towards the dark line of horsemen and foot Guards and tried to make their way through. 'We don't want any trouble, Father,' the Inspector said, a shade baffled by being faced with a priest on a demonstration. 'You can take your people down Molesworth Street and up to the Green, or back where you came from, but you can't come into Leinster House grounds.'

'We have a petition.'

Behind Father Tracey there was shouting, pushing, a few threats.

'You can hand your petition to me, Father. I'll see it's delivered.'

'I demand to deliver it in person.' As he said that a wave of pushing rippled from behind him, threw him against the horse on which the Inspector was sitting. The horse backed, still under control, but whinnying. Other horses stamped restively, one of them knocking into a foot Guard, sending his cap rolling. Men surged forward from the middle of the march, half a dozen or so men of quite a different stamp to the common run of marchers, more disciplined, younger, with a look about them of knowing what they meant to do. The Inspector brought his horse back into line and Father Tracey was sent stumbling.

'The Father's down!' someone screamed, and the fighting started. It was over as quickly as it had begun. An old woman trampled by a horse, Mary Kavanagh in fact, Connolly's friend, so old and rheumaticky that she couldn't get out of the way in time; a couple of bruised heads and some sore ribs; one Guard with his nose broken by a flying kick as he fell on his hands and knees in the scrum; half a dozen of the marchers arrested for disturbing the peace, for which they would later be fined a pound, or seven days in default. Nothing. Nothing at all as demonstrations go. And it would have been even less but for the presence of television cameras. Even a little violence goes a long way on a television screen, and it had been part of the business of the half-dozen young men to see that it got there, and in the most profitable way.

And they succeeded. Overnight, at a cost of seven pounds in fines and a few bruises, the Oxman Street affair became a national event, Father Tracey a national figure. Even better than that, the demonstration became a self-perpetuating affair, because news feeds on news. The following morning John Lennox began to round up people for his programme of the coming Friday, *Friday at Ten*, to be subtitled: 'Office Blocks or People'; Father Tracey, Con Danaher, Denis Farrell, who all accepted immediately; and through the succeeding three days, all the others who on Friday night at about nine-fifteen would be gathered in separate groups into different offices and waiting-rooms in the studio building to be entertained, prepared, made up, kept quiet, jollied, calmed, by various young people whose job it was to do these things every Friday night before the programme began.

At nine-forty they would be shepherded into Studio One for the confrontation that long before it began had become certain to turn into the ugliest brawl in Irish Television's short history.

16

John Lennox sat in his black swivel chair behind the studio desk, watching the guests file in, shepherded by girl researchers and assistants. He was a very different man to the one who had come back to Ireland two and a half years before. Even physically he seemed to have grown more solid, his shoulders broadening and thickening, his body heavier, his face fuller-cheeked and yet harder, more certain. Two and a half years ago he had been a man who received orders. Now he was a man who gave them, and found it difficult to remember that there had been a time when things were different.

He had taken to television as the hull of a destroyer in a naval boatyard takes to the water when it is launched, sliding down uneasily, slowly, timbers splintering, and then, as it touches water, suddenly right and perfect and serene. Every mental quality that he had, which all together had made him no more than a run-of-the-mill competent journalist, had suddenly taken on a new dimension from the first moment that he sat in a studio chair and faced into the small grey eye of a television camera. Studio lighting built his face into a new strength, giving his cheekbones and his eyebrows, the chestnut thickness of his hair, the hatchet hook of his nose a sardonic masculinity that was supported and echoed by the slight western, Mayo tang and rasp of his voice.

He found that he had the gift of talking to the camera lens as if he was talking to a friend, easily, intimately, thoughtfully, humorously; with whatever tone the occasion needed. And like a boxer he could think on his feet. Where other, probably more intelligent men had failed in their attempts at television because the cameras and the lights, the number of people around them doing separate, whispering things, the whole electronic, mechanistic jungle of the studio had destroyed their capacity to think, the same factors actually fed John Lennox's mind, brought out qualities he had never suspected that he had. As some men are born to act on a stage. John Lennox seemed to have been born to perform on a television screen. All that he had never been able to pour into marriage he poured into his work. This strange, exhibitionistic work that was almost like a love affair, not with one cool, difficult, unreachable woman, but with a thousand, a hundred thousand, half a million watchers; offering them everything that was in him, and yet in a way impersonally, dispassionately, risking nothing of his real self, uncommitted, uninvolved; like a man swimming in the sea, buoyed up by it, supported by it; only the slight danger of drowning to give excitement to the swimming. A love affair that left him untouched, never dulled by physical emptiness. Even his relationship with Kate had grown easier because now he needed less from it, no longer so bitterly missed what it failed to give him.

After six months he had been a personality. After a year he had been a national figure. Now, moving into the third year of television, and the second of *Friday at Ten* he was an institution. He had already passed far beyond the stage where he was a member of Lady Honoria's claque. In the beginning, when he was still finding his feet in Dublin, and had not yet realized his own power in and through television, he had once or twice allowed her to use him, and the magazine programme he was then working on, to publicize her crusade. One of her celebrities had come on the programme to say that Aram Court was unique. She herself had come on wearing a very handsome, boyish dolman with gold facings, like a young and beautiful hussar, to cry out passionately, 'Where is the Spirit of Countess Markiewicz in this dreadful, money-grubbing Ireland of Developers and Office Blocks?'

A couple of newspaper critics had made rather cruel fun of this outburst and the hussar's rigout, and afterwards Lady Honoria had blamed John Lennox for leading her into a trap and making her present herself in a wrong light. As a result for the past year or so they had been very cool to one another, and when John had seized on the affair as programme material it had been a genuine decision, and not taken in any way to please Lady Honoria. But she had thought that it was an attempt on John's part to get back into her favours and had taken the invitation to appear on the programme very coolly indeed. He watched her coming in now, beautifully dressed in black and white. Black wool suit that fitted her like a French glove; white silk blouse high at the throat and foaming over into a lace cravat that made her look like an arrogant, indignant boy, with her pale golden hair almost hidden under a tight velvet hat. He smiled slightly in welcome. Silly bitch. Father Tracey behind her. Smile again. One of the villains next. O'Hara? Yes, Johnny O'Hara. He looked at the cue card on his desk. Junior partner in Jofran. Solicitor. Brother of Seamus O'Hara the parliamentary secretary. In the Guardians. Thug.

Patrick Aloysius Gunn, sleeping partner in Jofran, auctioneer, well up in the Knights, a lot of friends in the hierarchy. Be careful. That last was Kitty Foyle's note, the head researcher. The rows filling up. The two women, tenants. Con Danaher. Farrell. Communists. Francis O'Rourke. Chief thug. John Lennox riffled the cards in the thin pile in front of him, smiled greetings, nodded to the Floor Manager. Fifteen minutes to air.

*　　*　　*

In Chesterfield Square Venetia turned into the doorway of Number 38. It was not much changed from what it had been like almost ten years before, when she had sat in the big black car and stared through the window at the dirty children and the Square. The hall still smelt like a damp cave, her footsteps echoing on the slate floor under the high, handsome ceilings. There were still the mingled smells of cooking, boiled napkins, urine, dry rot and dirt and poverty coming like a thin fog out of the peeling walls, the scuffed doorways, down the wide staircase.

The basement tenants had gone, driven out by the rats and the wet. Two of the back rooms on the second floor were empty, the floors gone through. When she had asked her father why he didn't do something about the house he had said vaguely, 'Don't be worrying me, child. I'll do something in my own good time.'

'But the people are miserable there.'

'They don't have to stay.' And then: 'Jesus Christ, haven't I enough on my lap down in bloody Oxman Street without you starting at me about that place?'

'Leave your father alone,' her mother had said, and upstairs Dermot had said, 'It's all in this book. Capitalism can only exist through the exploitation of the workers. It's pointless asking Dad to do anything about it or trying to do anything yourself to make those people happier. It'd just be a sop. It says here that the worse Capitalism is seen to behave, the better it is for the cause of the Workers. It simply brings revolution that much closer. You're just a sentimentalist, Venny.'

She thought of that now, going up the last flight to the studio at the top, carrying the chocolate cake and the tin of coffee and the cigar. She knocked and went in, bracing herself for the smell of drink. But there was none. He was sitting scrubbed and timid, like a huge, tame bear in a shirt and trousers, on the rickety wooden chair by the card-table that she had cleaned up for him weeks ago, and that had begun to recover its coating of paint smears and scraps of newspaper stuck into paint blobs and varnish rings. But he had covered the table with the cloth she had given him, pinched from the kitchen linen cupboard at home, and he had laid out the supper things, knives, forks, plates, cups, even saucers and teaspoons and a jug of milk.

'Hallo, Sean,' she said. She took off her hat and coat and he stood up awkwardly, all hands and anxiety, taking them from her, folding them on to the bed that he had made seem like a couch by spreading a torn purple drape across it. He had lit the stove and there was also an electric fire burning. Just before Christmas she had got Willy Doyle to rewire the room and put in a socket.

'What have you been painting today?'

'Nothing really. I've been getting ready.' He moved a chair up to the table for her, brushed invisible dust off it with his hand.

'I've brought you a few things. The cigar is to smoke while we're watching.'

He took the parcels and stood holding them, looking from the cake in its green and white cardboard box to the tin of Nescafé to the cigar in its silver tube. 'You shouldn't . . .' he began, and didn't go on, stumping across the room so that floor swayed and creaked, putting the cake box and the tin on the packing-case beside the gas ring. The television set was on a tea chest at the end of the bed. Ever since she had brought it in for him on hire, two days earlier, he had kept it at the foot of his bed and from the moment that it went on in the evening until Close Down he had lain and watched it, spellbound. He had done no work at all even during the day, wondering if it was time for the programmes to start again. But for the matter of that he had done no real work for weeks, months almost, since she had taken over his life and made him comfortable.

Arriving thin and spiky-faced one morning saying, 'I've come to have a look at the house. My father owns it.' Wrinkling up her nose and walking round the studio as if she didn't believe what she saw. He had been drunk the previous night and was feeling very delicate, and he had gone back to sit on the bed in his vest and trousers, only wishing that she would go away.

'Do you know it's twelve o'clock?' she had said. 'Aren't you up yet?'

He had simply stared at her.

'I thought painters had to paint in the daylight, and you're missing it all. It's a lovely day outside.'

'I paint inside.'

'That doesn't make any difference. Aren't you afraid of falling through the floor? That plank's got a hole in it.'

'It's a rat-hole.' It wasn't, but it might make her go away.

'I've seen lots of your paintings. I like them very much.'

'Thank you.'

'Although I don't know how you get anything done in a place like this. Doesn't anyone look after you?'

'No.'

'You obviously need somebody. You haven't even got any curtains.'

Within a month he had had them. She and her brother Dermot and Willy Doyle had brought them in and hung them, and scrubbed the floor, and whitewashed the walls and the ceiling and cleaned the windows, and put down pieces of rug and matting, and nailed tin over the mouse holes in the skirting and let in pieces of new wood into the rotten places in the floor timbers, and brought him an armchair that Venetia had bought for ten shillings in a junk shop, and rewired the room so that he could have the electric fire and a bedside lamp, and made him bookshelves out of a packing-case, and a pantry cupboard out of another and cleared out twenty years' accumulation of rubbish from the corners of the vast room.

'Why are you doing all this?' he had said helplessly as he saw his mental comfort being destroyed around him, his emotional cave-refuge of squalor being made into something alien and unrecognizable.

'Because my father's been taking rent from you for ten years,' she said, 'and left you in these terrible conditions. It isn't just. My brother says it's just a waste of time, it's just patching a rotten system. But you have to do something. And artists have to be looked after so that they can give all their time to art.'

'But I don't want to be cleaned up. I don't want the floor scrubbed and the bottles all thrown away.'

'You'll like it when it's done.'

Strangely enough he had liked it when it was finally done and completed, and he was alone in his unrecognizable studio, with the electric fire glowing and the curtains drawn and the card-table laid for his supper. The only thing was that he could no longer work. He realized that half the reason he used to work was to keep warm by moving about. There was no point in lying frozen in the bed once he woke up. But now he was warm all the time and he lay in bed most of the day reading detective stories, or staring vacantly at the whitewashed ceiling that made him think every time he woke up in daylight or with the bedside lamp still on, that he was somewhere else. Even drinking no longer had quite the same attraction and there were nights when he left at closing time without having to be thrown out, and made his way almost soberly back to the studio, thinking of the electric fire and the curtains and the transistor radio that he kept permanently tuned to Radio Luxemburg in case he couldn't find the wavelength again.

'You're ruining me,' he said to her now, opening the silver tube of the cigar and smelling it.

'It's five to ten. Turn the sound up. It'll be on in a few minutes.'

A programme was just ending. Advertisements began. 'My daddy's terribly upset about all this. Mummy says he hasn't been sleeping for nights and nights. He doesn't say anything but you can tell.'

'Will I make the coffee now?'

'You can put the kettle on. I'll make it for you in a minute. When are you going to paint me?'

He waved the cigar vaguely and miserably. 'Soon. Soon.'

'You've been saying that for ages. Will you do it before Easter so I can give it to Daddy?'

'I have to feel in the right mood.'

'That's imagination. You just have to start.'

He stood looking at the advertisement, a young man driving a sports car, a beautiful girl beside him, hair blowing in the carefully directed wind. Get with the High Octane Set. He felt himself being driven into a corner. He could see the portrait before he so much as primed the canvas. Glasses, spike nose, raggety black hair. Like a skinny rat. And she'd think he had done it to hurt her. Out of resentment at being in her debt. Or she'd just be hurt. And he didn't want to hurt her.

He felt old and clumsy and helpless, standing there like an old dancing bear being asked to dance again, his chain being tugged. Dance. Dance. But you can't dance to order. Not even for gratitude. I am of Ireland. Out of the Holy Land of Ireland. Come dance with me. Invest with the New Ireland Building Society, four and a half per cent tax free.

A girl on the screen. 'And now, our weekly late-night discussion programme—things people are talking about with John Lennox, on *Friday at Ten*.'

People marching, banners, faces, music crashing louder out of the television set; a priest, placards, a woman shouting. A dozen voices shouting. *Give us homes! ... Remember 1916!* echoing the placards. *Did Pearse die for Office Blocks?*

And a woman holding up a child, her screaming mouth like

a wound. 'Look at his face! Look at the rat-bites!' Hatred and anger driving out of the screen like an assault. Venetia covered her face with her hands. 'Oh, my Daddy,' she whispered. 'My poor Daddy.' As if suddenly in that scream of victim-fury she had understood what Dermot meant, what the books he had been reading meant, his precise, pedantic boy's voice condemning their father to extinction. Her father, with his warm tweed coat and his whiskey breath and his curses and his way of holding her suddenly with both his hands for no reason at all, squeezing her shoulders until it almost hurt.

The film on the screen meant nothing very much to Seán Ó Conaire. He had lived all his life in poverty, and rat-bites and tenements and furious women were the way of nature. But the sudden movement of her hands, the thin stoop of her shoulders and her voice caught at his mind. He touched her arm and she looked at him, as John Lennox s dark, sardonic face came on to the screen.

'What will happen to him?' she said bleakly.

He didn't understand what she meant, but he saw in her face how he could paint her, what was behind the thin, plain, priggish exterior, the glasses and the freckles and the white skin and the crow-black hair. He wanted to tell her what he saw, that one day she would be beautiful, but he was sober and he couldn't say it, and she might misunderstand him anyway, old and useless and drunken. And she would never be beautiful outside, like the girls in the advertisements. But something would be beautiful. As nuns can be beautiful, shining from inside.

'We'll start tomorrow,' he said. 'First thing.'

*   *   *

In Daly's cocktail lounge Venetia's older brother Joseph Anthony was also watching the programme, on a television set perched high up behind one end of the bar. He had a double gin and tonic in front of him and a girl beside him and he was holding her hand. Farther along the padded bench Victor was sitting with another girl. Behind the bar the barman in a white jacket and limp black bow-tie was polishing glasses. Victor's girl was dark and thin, with a red silk dress and a black glacé leather handbag, and a suggestion of shrewdness about her eyes; that she was not one to be put on or told tall stories. Her friend, Joseph Anthony's girl, was blonde and seemed softer and kinder. Her name was Eileen. Joseph Anthony had been told the other girl's name but he couldn't remember it.

'That's my dad,' Joseph Anthony said, trying to work up his courage to tickle the palm of her hand with his middle finger. Victor could do these things without even thinking about them. He didn't even need to do them. Girls simply knew what he wanted and gave it to him.

'Your dad does look cross.'

'And am I supposed to be looking after him?' Francis O'Rourke was shouting. 'What about his parents? What are any of them doing about it?' The stricken, frightened faces of the two stout women tenants filled the screen.

'I think your dad's quite right,' Eileen said. 'People should look after their own kids. Don't you think so, Tricia?'

Her friend smiled, a hint of condescension in her knowing eyes. 'Seeing the company we're in it might be rude to say what I think.'

'Oh, you're awful, Tricia. Don't mind her, she always wants to be different.'

'You say anything you like,' Victor said, sliding his arm along the black imitation leather padding of the backrest so that it was behind Tricia's shoulders. 'You couldn't say more about our old fellows than we say ourselves. Isn't that right, Tony?'

'Asso . . . absolutely.'

'I think you're just pulling our legs. You're nothing to do with them.'

'That could be a compliment.'

Victor and Tricia went on with their verbal sparring match. The barman polished more glasses. Joseph Anthony lifted Eileen's unresisting hand on to his thigh and held it there. It was soft and small inside his big hand and made him feel curiously important and protective. On the screen the programme became a quarrel, everyone shouting. His father shouting. But not at him. At someone else for once. That also gave him a pleasant feeling. It wasn't that he was afraid of the old man. Not really. But it felt so awful being shouted at. As if there was something wrong with him. And because the old man seemed to expect things to go wrong they went wrong, as though the old man made them go wrong simply by expecting them to, rather than he himself doing anything. Like being surrounded by a wall so that he couldn't get out and then people blaming him for not getting out. He felt sometimes that he was quite different to what everyone thought he was, even what Victor thought he was. Different to what Victor thought most of all.

'Don't you get on with your dad?' Eileen was saying, her voice mildly shocked.

'He's always saying I'm a bit stupid, and giving out about me not passing exams.'

'Are you still in school?' she said, wide-eyed.

'We're in college. U.C.D.'

'I'm sure your dad only means the best for you.'

He had worked his middle fingertip into the warm, moist palm of her hand. Suppose he just pressed. Along the bench Victor had his hand carelessly on Tricia's shoulder, his glass tilted in negligent fingers so that the gin was in danger of spilling down her dress.

'That's a damned lie!' Francis shouted from the screen, his eyes raging, furious, his face dark with passion, and Joseph Anthony flinched, tightening his grip on her hand. 'I think sometimes he hates me,' he said, not even sure he was saying it aloud.

'What a thing to say!' Eileen whispered, this time really shocked. She thought of her own father, who kissed her good night every night of her life if she was in before he went to bed, and who usually lay awake until she got in anyway. His voice calling from the dark bedroom with the door ajar, 'Are you all right, Eileen love?' and then her mum saying, 'Of course she's all right. Go to sleep, waking me up like that.' And then, sharply, 'What time is it, where have you been?' But her mum didn't hate her, her mum loved her as much as her dad did. If anyone hated her she would die. 'I'd die if my dad hated me,' she said. 'Or my mum. Of course your dad doesn't hate you. I'm sure he's proud of you really only he can't show it.'

Tony pressed his fingertip gently into her palm. After a few moments he realized that either she hadn't noticed or she didn't know what it meant.

'You are a funny boy,' Eileen said. 'You're different from your friend, aren't you?' It was funny, he was so big and handsome and yet he was really shy. 'My mum says I'm a great reader of character.' She settled her hand comfortably in his. Just a big boy even though his dad must be so rich. Her dad always said that riches didn't bring happiness and it was true. The barman had put another gin and tonic in front of her. 'I mustn't,' she said. 'That's the third! I'd be quite drunk!' But Tricia and the dark one, she didn't like the look of him somehow, not really, his eyes or something, like he was laughing at everyone; they were talking about something silly, about politics and the Government. That was the trouble with Tricia, she wasn't any judge of character at all and she thought she was so clever. But cleverness isn't any good if you aren't a good reader of character as well. She'd like to tell that to Tony, but it'd sound funny just saying that out of nothing, for no reason, so she went on holding his finger. Such a funny boy putting his finger into her hand like that. Like a baby, somehow. It was a very boring programme. Maybe they'd all go somewhere else soon and have something to eat. Somewhere really nice with waiters and a band.

'Do you like dancing?' she said.

* * *

In the Lennoxes' big, cool drawing-room on Mornington Road, Kate Lennox and Felicity O'Connor watched the programme together, their coffee growing cold on the long, low table in front of the huge couch, Shah lying asleep in front of the fire at the far end of the room. Because of the television set the room had two centres; one in front of the big marble fireplace with its brass fender and Georgian fire-dogs and fire-irons, the portrait of

Pistol Lennox supercilious above the mantelpiece, surveying the other relics of Castle Lennox with one dark eyebrow raised, his thin, elegant hand resting on the case of duelling pistols in front of him; and the other centre the white screen of the television set with its flickering shadow-life like cold firelight in a cave of ice.

'I can't get over it,' Fil said, adjusting herself gently on the big, sagging couch so that her girdle didn't pinch. 'Frank. After all these years.' She looked fondly at his hot, furious face, his small savage eyes that seemed to be staring not at her but over her shoulder at the sideboard behind her. Poor, poor Frank being tormented. He never had had an idea what was happening to him. She had never heard of him or seen him or seen his name since the day eight years ago when he had gone back to Dublin for a week and not come back on the day he had said, and she had left him. And it was like looking back through a telescope at something far, far away and forgotten, thousands of miles in the past. And suddenly the telescope adjusting, and a face starting out of the blur of shadows, so close you'd think you could touch it. And still a thousand miles away. He hadn't changed, hardly changed a bit. Maybe a bit fatter? She rested an unconscious, slightly reminded hand on her own stomach and burped.

'Don't let me eat any more chocolates, Kate,' she said, taking another one. She had brought them herself. Truffles from Switzerland, that she had bought when she was changing planes on her way back from Egypt. 'But they're so gorgeous. How the hell d'you keep your figure?'

Her own figure burst even more ripely out of her Dior dress than it had done years ago when she took in the backs of her Boyle's Store dresses herself. And her skin was even more like cream velvet. Her second play, *Why Are You So Scared of Me, Darling?* had not had the same kind of success as *A Girl is Made for Loving*, and then there had been the libel action that that poor idiot Lionel had taken against her and life had been quite a mess for a long time. But her third play, *What Makes You Think it's You?*, centred on a libel case and a homosexual producer having an affair with a woman playwright, had put her back on top of the world. Lionel had gone to America rather than face it, and Merryweather had forgivingly come back to her, and she felt rather the way the truffles tasted, coated with chocolate and full of cream. And there was poor darling Frank, like some kind of bull being tormented by John and all those creatures. In a strange way it made her feel even more comfortable.

'Would you mind terribly if I took my girdle off?' She hitched up her satin skirt and wriggled the elastic down and curled up on her end of the couch with a sigh of relief. It was like being back in the Stone Age coming back to Dublin. Nothing had changed. The same voices, priests giving out, everything.

'It hasn't changed a bit,' she said.

'For God's sake,' Kate said, astonished. 'You must be joking.'

'But it's incredible. Can you imagine in London a row like this with a priest in it? And people saying "Yes, Father" and "No, Father" just because he's a priest?'

'But don't you realize what it means, having a priest saying things like that?'

'Black beetles,' Fil said, having picked up the expression in Rome with Lionel and treasured it ever since. 'Of course they're still the same. D'you think my mother doesn't write and tell me what's going on? D'you think I don't see an Irish paper some-times? And every paper you see, year after year, there are the same awful articles, the same awful letters. My memories of 1916. Can the G.A.A. survive with the Ban? What De Valera really said in 1932. New scheme to revive the West. Is compulsory Irish damaging the language revival? Christ, if you took it seriously it'd make you puke. And the letters. Catholic Mother of Ten. Disgusted, Ballyfermot. All these young gerruls wearing trousers puttin' bad thoughts into decent lads' minds. I swear I read that exact letter a year ago, and practically the same letter ten years ago just before I left. Jesus, this place is pornographic. I think you're stark mad to live here.'

She felt so indignant momentarily that she took another truffle.

'That's why we're living here,' Kate said. 'Because it has to be changed. It is changing.' She pointed her finger at the screen, where John was starting again after the commercial break. 'That's changing things. He's changing them, helping to change them. Do you think ten years ago, two years even, we'd have had this kind of thing in public? You should be back here with us.'

'Doing what? Writing articles for the *Family Rosary*? Can you see the Abbey putting on *What Makes You Think it's You?* They'd have a fit. They still think Yeats is alive. What could I do here? If I tried to do anything I'd get burned at the stake. Look at Franky! And John is helping them burn him!'

'What on earth do you mean?'

'Look at him. Look at it. Listen to them all. For fifty years everyone's happy for all those people to live in a slum with their kids bitten by rats and that's wonderful, that's Ireland, that's Mother Machree, we're free from the horrible English with their filthy atheistic socialism and their wicked Welfare State. And then people like you and John get all socially conscious and say, 'It ought to be changed. It ought to be different, with nice Montessori schools and free milk in the mornings.' So Frank comes and wants to tear down the slums and build modern buildings and create some prosperity and you all turn round and kill him. And who's right in front of the lynch mob along with John? A priest! The same kind of self-righteous bastard who preached hell-fire for me down in Drifin and got Mother nearly burned in her bed by a lot of drunks.'

'For God's sake, Fil, how unfair can you get?'

'I can get a lot unfairer than that, I can tell you the truth. Christ, stop me eating all these truffles, I'm a pig. I have to say that four times a day at every meal, Fil, you're a pig, Fil, you're a pig. But honestly, you and John! What's that priest saying? Keep the slums. Keep poverty. Being poor and dirty and bitten by rats is the way to the kingdom of heaven. And making the country prosperous is the road to hell. Whatever he's actually saying that's what he bloody well means. And that hot-eyed little bastard next to him, what's his name, the one with the hair over his forehead——'

'Con Danaher,' Kate said coldly.

'Give a boy like that two chances and the whole sugaring lot of you are for the chop. You don't think he's going to let you go on living the beautiful liberal life when the revolution comes? I've seen his type in London and lots of places and they scare me stiff.'

'At least he believes in something.'

'And I don't? Hitler believed in something. So did Torquemada. Show me a man who believes in something and I'll show you a murderer. If people like you and John go on messing about long enough you'll find yourselves all hanging from lampposts.'

'What you're saying is, "To hell with poor little Ireland. It's a horrible place and no one can make it any better and I just want to forget about it." Is that what you mean?'

'Stop being snotty. If I meant exactly that wouldn't I have the right? Did you ever read any of the letters I get from my loving fellow-countrywomen? It's like getting letters from a zoo, worse than a zoo, from a cess-pit. God, I'm supposed to be an immoral woman. You should read some of those letters. I got one the other day, with shit smeared on it. I really did. Can you imagine that kind of mind? And that woman, whoever she was, had ten years of Catechism and compulsory Irish and probably goes to mass every day.'

'But Fil, Fil, this is what we want to change. That's why we're here. You don't think that's the real Ireland, do you, that woman? Or the education she got, or the slums those people are living in? What we want is to make Ireland what it should be, what it could be. We were down on Inis Beag and I could see——'

'For pity's sake. You're thinnking of lovely civilized picnics on Inis Beag on a permanent summer afternoon. What do you think that boy—what did you call him, Danaher?—what do you think he's dreaming about? Something like East Berlin. You're stark mad, Kate. I was in East Berlin. For the East European premiére of *A Girl is Made for Loving*. They were as nice as hell to me and I've never been so frightened in my life.'

'Apparently it didn't stop you taking their money.'

'No, darling, it didn't. Any more than it stops you and John taking all this horrible capitalist money that John's getting for laying the foundations of the Irish Workers' Republic.'

They had been following the programme with half their minds during the argument and they both seemed to feel at the same moment that if they went on arguing they would have got beyond the point where they could draw back. Perhaps they had already. 'I want to watch properly,' Kate said. Fil took another truffle and ate it slowly. She hadn't meant to go down to Drifin until next week, but she'd go tomorrow and get it over. Five thousand dollars for one article on how Drifin seemed after ten years' absence was a lot of money, but she wished she had never signed the contract to do it. Coming back even to Dublin was like getting into someone else's greasy bathwater. Drifin! And from there down to Shannon and to New York. Thank God for lovely, noisy, vulgar, capitalist New York, and with a shred of luck she'd be signing up for the film rights of *What Makes You Think it's You?* This awful, awful, awful little. country. Like a trap, making you feel that once you were in it you might never get out again. She finished the truffle and licked her fingers one by one. God bless Switzerland. God bless food.

* * *

Victor Clancy swung the big Jaguar sharply off the mountain road and turned down an earth track, the car lurching softly, the headlights picking out grey boulders, heather, a ridge of turf.

'Where are we going?' Tricia said sharply. 'Where are you taking us?'

'To the party,' Victor said. 'Like we promised.'

'Whass . . . whass the matter?' Eileen mumbled from the back of the car. Her head was against Joseph Anthony's chest, her mouth buried in the comfortable warmth of his sports jacket. She had had too mush . . . too much . . . mush too mush to drink. She wanted to tell someone but the words were too hard to say. Tha' was funny. Th'was very funny. She began to laugh. Joseph Anthony stroked her hair, his other hand under her coat, holding her bosom warm and captive in the palm of his hand.

'You're a nau . . . naughty boy.' Mush too mush.

'If you don't stop I'll scream,' Tricia said.

'Scream if you want to,' Victor said. 'I'm stopping in a minute anyway.' The headlights touched trees, the white wall of a cottage. 'We're here.'

Tricia pushed the heavy door open, started to throw herself out, expecting to be held. Victor got out the other side, unlocked the door of the cottage without even looking to see what she was doing. 'Tony, we're here.'

Joseph Anthony came stumbling out of the car, half carrying, half pulling Eileen with him. He had an arm round her and she stood blinking and stupid in the cold mountain dark.

'Wh–where's a party?' she said.

Tricia was five yards away from them up the earth track. 'Eileen! Run!'

'I'm cold,' Eileen said. 'I'm hungry.'

Inside the cottage Victor had lit candles and a Tilley lamp. It was an old farm cottage on land that Jofran had bought as a speculation and his father had given it to him as a birthday present. They had it furnished with an old couch, and an arm-chair and two beds upstairs.

'For Christ's sake come in and close the door,' Victor said. He was stooping down by the fireplace, aranging firelighters and sticks and turf. 'Tell that stupid bitch to stop shouting and come in for a drink.' In one of the deep niches of the fireplace there was a bottle of whiskey and some tumblers. 'Pour out the drinks, Tony. I wonder if either of them knows how to cook?'

'I'm hungry,' Eileen whimpered. 'Where's the party?'

'Have a drink,' Joseph Anthony said kindly. He held her mouth open with one hand and poured half a tumbler of whiskey into it with the other. She choked helplessly and he sat her down on the couch. 'Can you cook?' he said. The tears were coming out of her eyes and she couldn't breathe. Outside the door Tricia was shouting, 'I'm going to the Guards. I'm going to the Guards.'

'Then eff off,' Victor said. 'Up to the road, turn left and it's seven miles straight ahead. Some of it's downhill.'

'Eileen! Eileen, what are they doing to you?'

'Where's my friend?' Eileen sobbed. 'I want my friend.'

'I know what she bloody well wants but we're going to eat first,' Victor said. 'I wonder if these sausages are bad? Leave her alone and find the pan. *Shut up!*'

Eileen sat stiff on the couch, her mouth open to sob, her nose red, her blonde beehive hairstyle collapsed, the buttons of her dress half open. Outside there was stillness. Joseph Anthony went to the window-sill to get the frying-pan, black and greasy from the previous week-end, pieces of egg and bacon still stuck to it. Through the dark glass of the small window he saw Tricia's face like a ghost, white and staring, peering in at him, and beyond him to Eileen on the couch.

'I'm going for the Guards,' she whispered venomously through the glass. Joseph Anthony smiled and shrugged, making a gesture with the pan.

'Give her the bloody pan,' Victor said.

Joseph Anthony took it over to Eileen and put the handle in her limp, unresisting hand. 'Do you know how to cook sausages?' he said. She nodded and sniffed.

'But I'll spoil my dress,' she whimpered.

'Then take it off,' Victor shouted. 'I'm bloody well starving and you go yammering on about your dress. Cook something.'

Joseph Anthony lifted her up by the elbows. 'Do you want to take your dress off?'

'N–n–no.'

'Leave her alone!' Tricia shouted. 'I'm going to fetch the Guards now. If you dare touch her!'

Outside it began to rain, a fine, drenching mist sweeping softly across the bogland from the mountain-tops. Tricia started up the track. Before she was out of the shelter of the trees her hair was wet and one of her stiletto heels had turned on a stone, almost spraining her ankle. Seven miles. She'd kill him, kill them both, she'd have them in gaol for years. Her other ankle turned. The fine rain trickled down the back of her neck, under the collar of her thin evening coat, under her nylon dress, down her back. It grew heavier, the drops stinging her face. The moon was hidden, the stars, everything. Everything black. She could see a glisten of wet earth track for a yard or two in front of her, the dark silhouette of turf banks on either side of her and nothing else. And it was cold. One of her shoes came off and she began to cry with anger.

In the cottage Eileen was also crying, crouched sniffing and coughing over the smouldering turf fire. Damp, cold air hung in the chimney, driving the smoke into the room. Raindrops hissed on the sods or in the frying-pan. The sausages slowly turned black. A party! A lovely party they'd said. She had wanted to go somewhere for dinner. Oysters and Champagne and fillet steaks and port wine and chocolate cake. She had made up the menu long before they left that boring old Daly's and that horrible old programme on the telly. They were mad. A party! This! The smoke was getting in her nose, getting in her eyes, she was going to look so awful she'd die, and her mum would kill her, kill her, even her dad would be cross. It must be all hours. And how would they ever get home? She felt sick.

'I feel sick,' she said. Victor got the pan out of her hand in time.

'Well, that's the bloody fire,' Victor said. 'How the hell has she managed to burn the outsides and they're still raw in the middle?' And then to Eileen: 'Do you want some bread and sausage? It's all there is.'

There was a knock on the door. Joseph Anthony opened the latch. Tricia was standing there, her shoes in her hand, her hair in drenched strings round her face, her feet and legs splashed with mud to the knees. 'Come in,' Joseph Anthony welcomed her. 'Is it raining?'

'I'd like to see you both in gaol,' she said. Her teeth chattered, and as she stepped inside the doorway the rain began to run out of her like water from a sponge, gathering on the floor.

'Have something to eat,' Victor said, waving half a sandwich, better tempered now that he had had something to eat himself. Eileen was still kneeling by the hearth, holding her stomach with blackened, ash-covered hands, smears of soot on her face, her dress, her arms, her stockings, even her hair. The fire that she had almost doused by being sick on it smouldered acridly, filling the cottage with a strange smell.

'The pint of Jameson's is your only man,' Victor said, picking up the whiskey-bottle and filling four glasses. 'We're going to have a wonderful party. Take your wet things off and come and sit by the fire.'

'When are you going to take us home?'

'When we've all had a drink and you're warm and dry again. You'll catch pneumonia like that. Take your coat off and come and sit here and be friendly. Tony, hadn't you better take Eileen up to the bathroom? She's looking sort of puny.'

'Upsadaisy,' Joseph Anthony said, scooping Eileen into his arms. 'Lovely washes.'

'Where's he taking her?' Tricia said, starting up again. Victor held her down with a hand on her shoulder.

'For Christ sake leave her alone, she wants to get sick. What are you, her mother? Have a drink.'

Upstairs Joseph Anthony laid Eileen on the bed. It was covered with grey army blankets. His teddy bear sat on a narrow shelf over the bed where there had once been a statue of Our Lady.

'I want to go to the bathroom,' Eileen whispered limply.

'There isn't any bathroom,' Joseph Anthony said. He sat on the edge of the bed beside her and began undoing the remaining buttons of her dress. 'We'll be lovely and comfortable,' he said. 'Do you like my teddy bear?'

'I want my daddy,' she wept. 'Oh, oh, oh, oh.'

'There, there,' said Joseph Anthony. 'There, there, there.'

17

The reverberations of the programme had begun before the programme ended, with an interweaving of furious telephone-calls: from viewers to the studios, complaining about bad language, about people being allowed to attack a priest on television; about having a priest on television who was obviously not a priest at all but an agent of Moscow, a Bolshevik atheist; complaining about having communists on the programme, about having cut the programme off just when the workers were going to win their case; about having Lady Honoria on the side of the tenants.

'What does she know about the working man?'

There were complaints about having the programme at all, when what people paid their licence-fee for was entertainment, and why had there been no live transmission of a Gaelic football match for more than a month. The whole television station was an anti-national conspiracy of Reds. Obviously biased. In favour of the tenants of course. In favour of the rich of course. Why was nothing followed up about the Guardians of the Flame? Why was nothing followed up about corruption? Why did John Lennox allow all that discussion about corruption and the Guardians go on without interrupting it? What was Ireland coming to?

But the more meaningful telephone-calls were between people outside of television. Lord Alfred Gandon, his voice shaking with fury, tracked down a stammering Cecil at one o'clock in the morning, by telephone, and told him to have his wife present herself in Lord Alfred's office at ten o'clock that morning, or else. With less heat, but equal feeling, members of the Hierarchy spoke to one another by telephone, and then to the Father Provincial of the Bernardines. A white-lipped Father Provincial left word for Father Tracey that he would be pleased to see him at Father Tracey's earliest convenience after morning mass.

The Minister for Economic Development, Paddy Noonan,

woke the Director General at three o'clock in the morning to read him a blistering lecture on industrial sabotage, and demand that everyone connected with the programme be fired. 'Starting with that bastard Lennox. What the flaming hell do you think you're playing at, handing over the national television station to a bunch of communists?'

'You're drunk,' the Director General said, trying to gather his wits. He had only returned from London at eleven o'clock that night and had no idea that there had been a programme of any particular kind, or what it was all about.

'Don't you tell me I'm drunk, Sean, or I'll come round and screw your bloody knobs off. I want that effer fired, do you hear me? Did you see it? Then why the effing hell didn't you see it? What do you think we put you there for?' It was a very bad quarter of an hour for the Director General and one in which it was very tempting to bend before the storm. Behind Paddy Noonan's abuse lay everything that the Director General held valuable in life. Power, responsibility, ambition. It was very possible that Paddy Noonan could deprive him of all of them if he didn't give way. And if the Minister hadn't abused him, or had been content to wait until the morning and allow the Director General to find out what it was all about, things might conceivably have gone differently.

'I'm effing well telling you what it was about!'

'Don't shout at me, Paddy. It's three in the morning.'

'And don't effing Paddy me——'

'Go to bloody hell.' He put the telephone down, and when after a few moments it rang again he left it off the hook.

The quarrel committed him to nothing, except perhaps psychologically, but the following day that fractional weight was enough to tip the scales, and increasingly, as the day wore on with its salvos of telephone assaults, he found himself defending a programme in which he didn't quite believe, because he wanted to defend the Station itself, in which he did believe. All his training, all his career, all his ambitions for the future pulled him towards the group of Ministers who were swearing that the programme was one more proof in a growing series of proofs that Irish Television was falling into the hands of subversives, Reds, anti-nationals; men who wanted to destroy society. And that that bastard John Lennox was the ringleader.

'It was a fair, impartial——' It was not a moment for qualifications.

'Impartial my backside. It was bloody communism. How much longer has your contract got to run, Sean?'

'Long enough,' the Director General said coldly. By the end of the day he had offered his resignation and had the offer refused. 'Then *Friday at Ten* continues? With Lennox?'

'If you feel that it should. With a touch on the brakes perhaps.'

'If I feel it needs one.' Or if he could put the brakes on without seeming to be giving way to the pressures he had just resisted. He foresaw a lengthening avenue of crises in front of him and wondered with a beginning of hopelessness why he had ever taken the job. With a heavy mind he began to draft a series of guidelines for *Friday at Ten*. By the time he had filled a wastepaper basket he realized that whatever he said would seem to his staff like a capitulation to outside pressures. Suppose he broadened the paper to deal with all current affairs?

Another full waste-paper basket later he broadened it to comprise all programmes: *Principles of Broadcasting; Guidance for Broadcasting Personnel*; it was impossible even to find a title. He was still there at midnight.

John Lennox was already asleep in Drifin, unaware that there had even been any rows, apart from the abusive phone-calls to the Station, during and after the programme. But those were expectable, and their volume formed a rough guide to the programme's success. He had left Dublin at lunchtime, to drive Fil and Kate, reconciled after a night's sleep, down to Drifin to prepare Fil's article.

Father Tracey was also out of Dublin, in the Bernardine Retreat House in Roscommon, under obedience to remain there until more permanent arrangements could be made for his future. And not only to remain there, but to remain there without making any public statements whatsoever. If newspaper reporters attempted to question him by telephone he was to say that he was in the Retreat House of his own free will as a natural part of his religious life and as a member of the Bernardine community. He was to break off all contact with Lady Honoria, Denis Farrell, Con Danaher and the inhabitants of Oxman Street.

'There are times, Father, when the best of us need to be protected against our own excesses of zeal,' the Father Provincial had said. 'And when the Church itself needs to be protected from its most devoted servants. This is one of them. Go in peace. Pray for me.' It had not been a warm interview.

Lady Honoria's meeting with Lord Alfred had been even less warm. It had almost not taken place at all. At ten o'clock she was still in bed, reading the *Irish Times*, Cecil walking in increasingly agitated misery from bed to window, from window to door, downstairs to the hall in the pretence that he was going to his uncle by himself, and back again to the bedroom, biting his knuckles in despair and fright. At twenty past ten the telephone rang.

'Yes?' Lady Honoria said with simulated boredom and unsimulated distaste. 'Oh, it's you, Valentine.'

'Oh, L–L–L–Lady H. L–L–L–L–ord Alf–f–f–f–red——'

Lady Honoria turned back to the *Irish Times*, holding out the white telephone to Cecil without looking at him. 'It's Valentine having a fit,' she said. 'You'd better talk to him.'

The conversation went on for a considerable time, Cecil saying, 'No! Oh n–no!' at intervals, gradually catching more and more of Valentine Carthew's stammer. After five minutes he cradled the telephone in shaking hands and turned his pale, birdlike face to Lady Honoria. 'He's terribly angry——'

'Valentine?' Lady Honoria said, allowing herself to smile. She was wearing black silk and she couldn't help thinking what an extraordinary waste of time and pleasure it was to lie in a black silk nightdress and rose pink sheets on a sunny morning while her idiot of a husband sat listening to an even bigger idiot on the telephone. She held out a slender, beautifully manicured hand and admired it against the sheets.

'N–n–no! Uncle Alfred of course. He's threatening to do terrible things.'

'What can he do, the silly old man? Take your money-box away?'

'In a way, yes. He's also going to bring your father and step-mother over here.'

'What?' She sat up in bed as if she had been stung. 'He's what?'

'Val says he's been told to make the arrangements.'

She was already out of bed, tearing the phone out of his limp grasp. When she had finished, or run out of breath, Val said at the other end of the line, 'I–I–I–It's n–n–no g–g–g–g–g–g–good s–s–s–s–ssssssswearing at me, La–La–Lady H. He's abs–s–s–s–ssssolutely f–f–f–furious———'

They were in Lord Alfred's office at half-past eleven, Lady Honoria still swearing that if Cecil's uncle thought this, and if Cecil's uncle thought that, she would ... While poor Cecil trembled so much that he could scarcely drive. He did nothing to improve matters by not being able to find a parking-place for a seemingly endless five minutes, driving round and round a circuit of choked streets while his wife poured anger and contempt on him like steam out of a kettle.

But as they walked into the Gandon Estate office in Kildare Street, with its uniformed doorman who greeted them as 'M'lady, Master Cecil'; with its panelled hall, and waiting-room, that contrived at once to breathe an air of fustiness and of immense power, like an Egyptian tomb, a kind of nervous quietness fell on Lady Honoria. Cecil merely gaped at the pictures like a condemned man waiting to hear how long his sentence was going to be. Pictures of ancient sports teams mostly, such as the Harrow Cricket XI of 1889, Lord Alfred's father a small boy at the back in a peaked cap. A slow bowler of great merit. Sepia pictures darkened into indistinctness. Almost everyone in them long, long dead. They played their own part in throwing a weight on Lady Honoria's spirit.

They were kept waiting for ten minutes, until Miss Paxton herself came to tell them that Lord Alfred would see them now. She said it as if it was they who had applied to see his Lordship.

The interview was as grim as Cecil had feared it would be.

Lord Alfred was quite a small man, short and portly, with a white moustache and a pale blue eye; strangers often thought him a kindly and charitable old gentleman. But within five minutes he had reduced Lady Honoria close to hysterics, and when Cecil once tried to say, 'I say, uncle, I mean ... after all ——' he had blasted him where he stood, like an aspen tree struck by lightning. Lady Honoria felt like someone who carelessly pulls a shiny knob on a vast machine and finds giant pistons and flywheels crashing round him. She had no conception that so much powerful brutality existed in the world. For the first time she was given a faint idea of the real power that lay behind the Gandon fortune. If Cecil had been a different kind of man she might even so have survived the attack. But he was like a wet rag, and she saw herself with Cecil's income—his income! let alone his capital—tied up for years to come in a family lawsuit, her black stepmother and intolerable father brought to Dublin and hung round her neck like a pair of albatrosses; every journalist in Dublin and London given the most scabrous 'inside' stories of how she had abandoned them, neglected them, robbed them. She began to weep, artistically at first, and then helplessly. Lord Alfred watched her.

Nothing in his long life had so filled Lord Alfred with horror as that television programme. To see this cream-fed little vixen embroiling them, embroiling the Gandons, with the worst conceivable kind of Party ruffian. Sitting there beside a row of Reds, insulting men who belonged to the Guardians and the Knights of St Brigid, all of them Party members, and with brothers, uncles, cousins and God knows what, high up in the Party hierarchy—and half the country assuming that whatever she said, the family thought. He had thought that he was going to have a stroke, a fit. For forty years the family policy had been to treat the Irish authorities with kid gloves and a protocol as exaggeratedly courteous as King George the Third's ambassador presenting his credentials to the Chinese Emperor. The worse ruffians they were, the more one needed to flatter them. One needn't mix with them socially, but at official level, no word must ever be breathed to suggest that the Irish Free State, and later the

Irish Republic, was not a truly sovereign State of great virtue and importance. The fact that in private the Gandons might regard the entire country as a cross between a cattle ranch and a native colony had nothing to do with it. What mattered was what was said in public. And now this monster, this female Dracula . . .

He was a patient man. An immensely patient man. If he wasn't he would have strangled her years ago, when she first started this bloody nonsense about Aram Court. He ought to have done it. By God he ought. But he had almost come to tolerate that particular imbecility as this generation's version of the seemingly inescapable family curse, and a shade better than it might have been, than he had feared it would be when he had first seen her, just after that drivelling quarter-wit Cecil got engaged to her.

But his worst forebodings, the worst nightmares of the family at the time of Cecil's marriage had foreseen nothing like this. She might have taken lovers. She might have taken to drink. She might have lost fortunes gambling in casinos. She might have taken nullity proceedings against her husband on the grounds that he was incompetent in bed. Gandon women had done all these things in their generations. But none of them, not the worst, most perverted, vicious trollop of them all had ever gone on television to undermine the very cornerstone of the family's existence, its relationships with the Irish Government. In the dark hours of that dreadful night Lord Alfred had fore-seen the family having to move entirely to London, sell its Irish holdings and estates, disentangle its enormous tax and banking affairs, now as always hair-balanced to secure the maximum tax benefits, and face a hideous readjustment and the gruesome prospect of existence under a British Labour Government; or else attempt an even more complex transfer to Liechtenstein or Zürich.

Morning had brought calm and reason, and before ten o'clock he had begun a series of reassuring apologetic telephone-calls, and to work out the skeleton of a plan which might even draw advantages from the threatened disaster. But when he had realized that after all the damage she had done the girl was going to be defiant instead of abject, he had resolved to macerate her. And he had done it.

When it was finished he told her her sentence. It was really an extremely mild one. A mere six months in South Africa to let matters cool in Dublin. He would have liked to have made it six years, or better still for ever. But he occasionally needed Cecil physically present in Dublin or London, and it might be better to have the girl under his own eye. He thought of the damage she could do in South Africa if she was given long enough and shuddered. He almost regretted mentioning South Africa at all. But wherever she went might be as bad.

'Miss Paxton will get your tickets,' he said. He didn't offer to shake hands with either of them. Before they were out in Kildare Street again he was on the telephone to Moberley and Gunn, the auctioneers.

'Mr Gunn? Mr Patrick Gunn? Morning to you, Alfred Gandon here, that business last night on the television. M'nephew's wife gettin' carried away with herself—didn't mean a tenth of the things she said, of course, but that's no excuse for her saying them. Gave me a sleepless night, I can tell you. Hate any sort of rudeness. But I was wondering, 've been meanin' for a long time to make your acquaintance, heard a lot about you as a shrewd property man. There's a couple of property matters comin' up I'd value an outsider's advice on, to tell you the truth. If you'd be interested it might mean some business your way. How are you fixed for lunches next week? Any day that suits you, sooner the better. Monday then, one o'clock, just down the street from both of us, the Club, eh? Glad to have caught you, Mr Gunn. Another six-day week chap like meself, eh? Well, pleasant week-end to you. G'bye.' They both put down their telephones feeling very pleased.

18

The longer-term effects of the programme were less easily defined, but far more significant. Among the half-million or so viewers who had seen it, only one hundred and twenty-two reacted positively by telephoning the Station, or writing letters to complain about some aspect of it. Of the eight letters addressed to John Lennox personally, three told him that he was an atheist, a Communist and unfit to appear in front of a Christian people. Five told him with varying degrees of enthusiasm that he was the only courageous man on television, that he ought to stand for the Dail, that a man like him restored the writer's faith in democracy, that the undersigned was thirty-seven years old, possessed forty statute acres of good land and would like to meet him with a view to *matrimony*. 'I know we have a lot in common. I can tell from your eyes.' The fifth enthusiast was delighted that at last: 'some IMPORTANT PEOPLES like yourself is speaking up for the poor of this country. I am temporly unemployment and if I could raise Five Pounds it would be a grate help.'

The newspaper critics were equally divided. One condemned it as 'Trial by television':

Some of those appearing on the programme may be all the wicked things that John Lennox obviously thought they were, but it is a highly dangerous situation when any man can be dragged in front of the television cameras on the threat that if he does not appear he will be condemned in his absence and by his absence, and when he does unwillingly appear, that he can be found guilty in what amounts to a camera-head court martial. The sentence may be no more than public contempt and obloquy, but this alone is a heavy penalty and one which no television personality, however persuasive and professionally competent, should be allowed to impose. The phrase 'character-assassination' springs to the typewriter in such a context.

Another critic found it splendid television, full of life and fire, and exactly what viewers had come to expect from *Friday at Ten* and from John Lennox. A third critic found it full of sound and fury signifying nothing very much after an hour of travelling in circles:

> It has become a part of Irish Television's gospel that a good stand-up fight is essential to every studio programme. It is high time that someone should explain to those responsible that something else is needed as well—clarity and logic. We need to know what the fight is about. Anyone who gained more from Friday night's encounter than a general impression that the rich are wicked and the poor are always right must have been working by telepathy. This general proposition may even be true. John Lennox certainly seemed convinced by it. But speaking personally I would have liked to have had the proof demonstrated by an occasional fact.

Patrick Lacey, writing as 'Fidi Defensor' in the *Marian Weekly*, was even more hostile.

> Friday night's effusion, on the squatting campaign in Oxman Street, was one more striking example of what we have come to expect from this dedicatedly anti-Catholic and anti-National programme and performer. It was one more deliberate assault on the fundamental values and beliefs on which this State was built and on which, may God be thanked for His Mercies, it still rests. Let us ask ourselves, not as passive recipients of the Telly Effluent, mental sewer pipes through which Irish Television may pour what it wishes without comment or rejection, but as Catholics, as thinking, responsible Christians, citizens, parents, what the message was that this programme offered to us. It told us: (1), Property is bad; (2), To manage your own property to your own advantage is wicked; (3), To invade someone else's property is good if coloured with Socialist jargon. I.e., Theft is Good. This was its message about property, and I need not remind readers of

the *Marian Weekly* that the right to own property is a funda-mental tenet of both Church and State.

What was its message about Religion? (1), That priests and bishops are against the poor, i.e., they have not spoken in favour of Socialist techniques of forceable State acquisition of property; (2), That the Church is anti-social, i.e., that it owns land that it will not give to the State for housing people whose accommodation is the State's responsibility and not the Church's; (3), That the only good priest is a rebellious priest who indulges in Socialistic techniques and activities, e.g., marches and demonstrations, and who is in alliance with known Communists.

I could continue with such analysis much longer if the Editor was able to give me space. *It may well be that a publication devoted solely to such analyses of what television is doing to our society and religion is becoming essential,* and in future weeks I shall be returning to this issue. In the meantime I have one word to say to all readers. Be *vigilant.* You are under attack. It is a subtle, insidious attack. Sometimes it may even be per-suasive for those who do not think deeply. That is its *danger.* When you watch, *think. Compare.* Compare what you are told by the sophisticated performer on the silver screen with what you have learned from your Catechism. With what your priest tells you. With what your conscience tells you. *Analyse.* And have no doubt. The aim of a great deal of our so-called television entertainment is to turn this country into a Com-munist State.

Patrick Lacey was not a sophisticated man, and perhaps for that reason had a much clearer grasp of the effect of the pro-gramme on the vast, passive majority of viewers who neither praised nor blamed, telephoned nor wrote; who scarcely remem-bered a week later what the programme had been about, except that it was 'great gas' or 'boring', or that 'the chap with the big moustache seemed pretty angry' or 'it seemed funny seeing a priest taking that sort of line'. Imbedded subconsciously in that passive mass were all the impressions Patrick Lacey warned against. With an additional one that he had not bothered to mention: that politicians are bad, and that television journalists are good. I.e., as he would have put it if he had thought of doing so, that politicians are corrupt scoundrels, uninterested in people except to exploit them and make money out of them; secret, devious, undemocratic, afraid of the light of day; or else, as in the case of poor Matty O'Carroll, bumbling and ineffective. While television journalists are the reverse of all these things. And that true democracy, the voice of the people and the spokesmen for the people's will lie not in parliament but in a television studio. And he could have gone on analysing the implications of that for an enormous number of paragraphs.

Down in Drifin they had absorbed all those lessons, and received John Lennox as a hero, almost a local hero, who even overshadowed the excitement of Felicity O'Connor coming home. With Fil herself they were awkwardly courteous. Whatever they said about her among themselves; about the length of her skirts and the size of her bosom, the grandeur of her clothes and the shamelessness of her makeup, to her face she was 'Miss O'Connor, ma'am' or 'Felicity' said with an emphasis that stressed the speaker's right to be familiar. Children followed her round at a distance, staring from behind the corners of houses or hedges or stone walls. The parish priest found that he had to go up to Dublin for several days. The shock of her plays had worn off, leaving only a rather exciting atmosphere of wickedness and sin. If she had been by herself it might have been different. But protected by John and Kate, by obvious wealth, by the lapse of time since all the trouble, and by natural politeness, the three-day visit went off with scarcely a ruffle of feelings.

Jim O'Connor had sworn when he first heard of the visit that he would beat the girl within an inch of her life for being a strumpet and an ungrateful daughter and had got drunk on the prospect. When Festy Bourke reminded him of his promise he had called Festy an effing liar and said that if any man laid a finger on his flesh and blood, or so much as said an insulting word about her, not only would he kill him, but that man would never darken the doors of his bar again. He might do his drinking in Letterfrack. He might do his drinking in Leenane. For all James O'Connor cared he might do his drinking in Hell. But the one sure certainty was that no drop of drink would he ever get from James O'Connor's Grocery and Bar in Drifin. And that if Festy Bourke had had the spunk of a rat he'd have been married twenty years ago and would have more to occupy his dirty bachelor's mind with than other men's daughters. At that stage they tried to fight but were too drunk to find each other, and when Fil and the Lennoxes arrived, Jim O'Connor was in bed with a tremendous hangover and a gash on his forehead that he had got from falling on a pigswill bucket in the yard when trying to relieve himself after the quarrel.

The only other ruffle had been when Sean Daly had tried to get into Fil's bedroom upstairs in the bar the last night she was in Drifin. There had been a great send-off party for her in which all old sores were forgotten, the parish priest was cursed for a villainous old wretch that hated to see anyone enjoy themselves, let alone two people together, her plays were toasted in gallons of porter: her father staggered downstairs and fell on Festy Bourke's neck, kissing him; Fil's mother went to bed with a headache; and Sean Daly fell into the harbour. He was pulled out by Tim Bourke and John Lennox, and after being stripped naked of his sodden clothes was wrapped in a blanket and put in front of the kitchen fire to dry out, with a glass of hot milk and whiskey that Fil brought him from the stove.

'Arragh God,' he said to her, his teeth chattering and his mind shocked almost sober, 'you're the kind girl Miss Felicity and no doubt of it. I thought to myself and I coming to my senses in the depths of the water, I thought, as sure as there's a cross on the ass Sean Daly, you're a dead man this night. And then again I thought and I being pulled out of it, sure I'm scaped from drowning only to be took by the pneumonia. I could feel it starting in me toes, they were like stones on me. But the very sight of you would warm the pneumonia out of a corpse. Slainte.'

He downed the milk and whiskey, and when he was alone in the kitchen found the whiskey-bottle and emptied it into his mug. Five minutes later he was fast asleep by the fire and never woke until three in the morning. He was still drunk, but in the pleasantest possible way, warmed by the fire, refreshed by sleep, full of virile thoughts and his mind occupied by the one splendid vision of Felicity's bosom as she bent over him, her cleavage showing like the backside of the handsomest pig in Connemara, her face smiling tenderly at him like a nurse in a hospital.

'She loves me,' he thought with dizzy pride. He lurched upright, letting the blanket fall round his toasted feet. 'Be Jasus I'll have her,' he thought. And then, 'And be Jasus she'll have me as well. Where is she? Where are you, gerrul?' He staggered out into the bar. Darkness, the smell of drink, someone snoring. It's never her, he thought. He felt for the door behind the bar that led to the stairs, half crept, half fell up them, and pushed open the first door he came to on the landing at the top. More snoring. He felt gently over the pillow end of the bed. Two heads. 'Can't be her,' he thought, his fingers stroking Mrs O'Connor's curled hair. She woke with a scream.

'Sssshh,' whispered Sean Daly, ''tis only me, ma'am, Sean Daly, ma'am. Good night to you, don't be disturbing yourself for me, now.'

She sat petrified in the bed, listening to him fumble his way out in the pitch dark. 'Jim,' she said uselessly. Next door Sean Daly felt his way towards Fil's bed, touched bedclothes, sheets, Fil.

''Tis yourself,' he whispered passionately. 'Move over, gerrul, I'm bloody cold all of a sudden.' He ripped the covers back and threw himself in beside her. 'Arragh be Jasus 'tis a great thing to have a woman after a night's drinking.'

Fil's scream rang through the bar like a fire alarm. She threw herself out on to the floor on her hands and knees, bringing the bedclothes with her.

'What are you at, gerrul? 'Tis me, 'tis Sean Daly of the Hill. Didn't you give me the eye in the kitchen below? Come back to me with the blankets.'

John Lennox, Kate and Mrs O'Connor came running in, switching on the light. Sean lay stark and bony in the warm hollow of the bed where Felicity had been sleeping, blinking hazily at them, a foolish smile on his unshaven face, the idea beginning to seep into his mind that he had done something wrong. He waggled his fingers propitiatingly. Beside him, on the floor, Fil dragged the bundle of bedclothes round her, still half believing it was a nightmare.

'Get out of here,' John shouted at Sean. 'You're a bloody disgrace, man. What the hell do you think you're doing?'

'I . . . I was lonely,' Sean Daly said. He began to realize that he was naked, and clutched at the edges of the sheet he was lying on, trying to drag them over him. 'Sure you shouldn't be here at all, ma'am,' he said to Mrs O'Connor, 'and I in my pelt.'

'Get out!' Fil shouted. 'Get out of my bed, you drunken lout! God, what a place!' She stood up, bundled and furious. Kate suddenly felt hysterics of laughter coming on and had to run out of the room.

'Get him out of here,' Mrs O'Connor beseeched John. 'I'll call Jim,' she threatened to Sean Daly.

'How can I get out of here and you lookin' at me?' He had the sheet dragged over himself and lay now like an Egyptian mummy ready for burial.

John Lennox answered the problem by picking him up, sheet and all, like a corpse, and carrying him out, steering his bare blue feet with their gnarled toenails through the narrow doorway. In the passage outside he tried to set him down, but Sean had locked his arms round John's neck. 'Carry me,' he said. 'Carry me home.'

'I'll beat you bloody senseless,' John snarled. His own feet were bare and were becoming frozen on the icy linoleum.

'Beat me then,' Sean wailed in Irish. 'Sure to God what am I? Only a useless man, a poor man from the Inis that's lost his home, God help me, and is condemned to the mountains.'

'Will you let go of me, you devil?'

'I will not,' Sean cried. 'Come home with me where I live my lone life with the sheep and my poor dog and my mother dead on me this ten years. Who'd marry me? Who'd have me?' He thought of the lost beauty of Felicity and raised his voice in a great keen of bereavement. 'Sure God the great titties on her and

I not even getting to lay my head between them. 'Tis fifteen years since I went with a woman, d'you know that, Tim Bourke?'

'I'm not Tim Bourke. God damn you let go.' He got him down the stairs at last, and with Kate's and Mrs O'Connor's help got him partly dressed and out of the front door.

'I'm lost. I'm astray entirely. Where am I going?'

In the end John had to get dressed himself and take him half-way home up the mountainside. Two miles from Drifin, Sean Daly fell in a ditch and wouldn't get out of it, and John left him there, where Sean's old sheepdog found him in the morning. Back in the bar everyone fell asleep again, except for Jim O'Connor in his bedroom and Festy Bourke under the long bench of the bar, neither of whom had woken in the first place. The following afternoon John and Kate drove Felicity to Shannon airport, and saw her off for New York.

It had been a good three days on the whole, in spite of Sean Daly, and as John and Kate drove back from Shannon to Dublin late that evening they were surprised to find how heavy-spirited they both felt. In part it was saying good-bye to Fil, and in part meeting her again. She had changed and they had changed and all the friendship, the drinking together, the laughing together and talking about old times and London had a slight ring of falseness under the genuine pleasure. They had grown back into Ireland these last two years and Fil had grown away from it and it had been a shock to see Ireland again through Fil's hostile, contemptuous, sometimes furious eyes. It made them feel uneasy, and although she would never have admitted it it made even Kate question whether they had done the right thing in coming back. And yet where else, how else, could John have done as well? And where else could she herself have felt any sense of belonging?

'I wish we could have got over to the Inis,' Kate said. Each time they had wanted to go in the three days to see their piece of land and their cottage, that had once been old Cait O'Malley's, Tim Bourke had said the weather was turning; that they might get out but be stuck there for days with the spring storms, and the bad tides. 'I think he just didn't want to take us, he didn't want to go out there now that it's empty and the old lady's dead.'

She had died two years ago. She had refused that winter of 1961 to come in to the mainland. 'What would I do in Ireland?' she had kept saying, and because she stayed three other families had put off their leaving. In the February of 1962 the storms had cut off the island for nearly a fortnight and a child, Finger Donal's eighteen-month-old girl baby, had died of enteritis with no possibility of a doctor getting to her in time or of a helicopter landing to take her off to the mainland. The following month old Kate had died. She had been found early in the morning crouched at the bottom of the hollow by the Cursing Stones, blue and stiff with death and age and the freezing night, an old, crouched corpse in a black shawl like a body that might be found in a bog by archaeologists, two thousand years dead, preserved out of another time.

She must have gone to the hollow the night before 'to make a wish', Donal told the coroner later, and then on being questioned he became gruff and embarrassed, calling it 'nonsense of the old people, sure weren't they always wishing this and that, 'twas women's foolishness'. But whyever she had gone there, he said, it seemed obvious to him she had been unable to climb the steep side of the hollow again in the dark, if it was in the dark she had gone there, and she had died of the cold.

She had left a letter in her best teapot, dated a month earlier and witnessed by Finger Donal and Tim Bourke, saying that when it came time for her to die she wanted her cottage and her bit of land, eight acres at the south end of the island, and her grazing rights, to go to John Lennox and Cait Og O'Donnell, married to the same John. And since there was no one to contest the letter's wishes, the legal transfer was eventually made. But long before it was made the last families had left the island and it was well recognized by all of them that the old lady had brought about her own death, so that they could leave and she could stay, with no more trouble. The coroner had known this too, but he recorded a verdict of accidental death.

There was a scandal about the old lady's burial, because in the same letter that willed her land to John and Kate she asked to be buried on a headland of the Inis, looking out towards the Black

Rock where her son had drowned, the jagged splinter of stone like a shark's fin breaking the calmest sea with menace, always ringed and collared with white foam. *I will sleep there looking to my own,* she had written in her copperplate handwriting learned in another century from the De Vere Foster copying-books of her childhood. She had written her letter in English, as if at the end she had felt that the future belonged to English, or that no one might be left to interpret her wishes from Irish. Or simply that she had felt that in solemn, legal matters, only English would do. But at the end of the letter there had been one sentence in Irish for Cait Og. *Keep my grave, and let John lift one of the Wish Stones up from the hollow and place it for a pillow for me.* She had never used the phrase 'cursing-stones' even in speech.

The parish priest, who was responsible for the Inis as well as for Drifin, had begun to threaten a tremendous fuss about the old woman being buried out of consecrated ground. 'Then consecrate the bit where she wants to be buried,' Kate had said.

'It's paganism. Utter paganism. It would be a cause of scandal in the parish for ever.'

'It was her wish, Father.'

The priest found to his surprise that it was everyone else's silent but forceful wish as well. Tim Bourke suddenly discovered that the pookaun was leaking and couldn't be used. And the weather was not safe to bring the coffined body to the mainland in a currach.

When the priest talked indignantly to anyone about being defied, and the Laws of the Church and the ordinary decency of Christian burial for a Christian woman, the person he was talking to looked at the ground, or turned deaf, or said, 'Arrah, sure you're right, Father, you're right, faith, but 'tis the others.' And yet when pressed could never say what others, or what their thoughts were.

Even Kate never discovered the basis for the feelings, whether it was respect for the old lady's wishes, or an instinct that she should not be buried in holy ground. And since the feelings supported her own wish and the old lady's, she didn't press too hard to find out. Two days after the old lady's death, when the doctor had come and gone again and signed his certificate, Tim Bourke found that the pookaun was not leaking after all, and six men came out with Kate and John and a fine coffin ordered from Westport, and buried the old lady as she had wished, the priest refusing to the last to have anything to do with the matter and threatening excommunication on all concerned.

A few weeks later the last families left and Inis Beag lay empty. The following summer Kate and John spent a month on the island, exploring it as their own and making plans for furnishing the cottage and altering it, putting in a bathroom or at least a shower, and letting it to friends when they were not using it themselves during the fine months. Last year they had gone again, hiring a Galway hooker to bring over beds and tables, a couple of strong old easy chairs and the plumbing necessities for putting in a shower, and had spent a lot of their month's holiday rigging it up, and whitewashing and decorating and making bookshelves. But all through the month there had been an increasing sense of falseness about what they were doing, as if they were going against nature, playing at Irish Family Robinson.

It was not the loneliness. Tim Bourke came almost every day. Finger Donal or his brother Eoin came at least once a week because they had sheep grazing on the Inis for the summer, and sometimes their wives came with them for the day out and to talk to Kate. But there was no purpose in any of it. They were holidaymaking in a place that was not made for holidays; that had been shaped by the sea and peasant farming; and to play Mahler and Dvořák and Saint-Saëns on a battery-operated record-player seemed like whistling in the dark as the night closed in and the sea whispered and stirred like an enemy who senses victory. To play Irish music was worse; to play Ó Riada, or ballads, made all of Irish history seem no more than a shallow adventure against the great depth of the dark. They found themselves wanting to be back in Dublin, or in London or Paris, to be with people who were doing things, hoping, planning the future. The empty cottages down the street stared at them with blind doors and windows as if they were waiting for something, but nothing human. Shah felt it too and slunk about. There were still cats on the island, becoming proud and untamed, reverting as swiftly to wildness as the wind-bleached fields of the ridge, and Shah pretended to ignore them. He had grown old and rheumatic in the last year and liked to lie by the fire. A thousand reflections passed across his amber eyes but none of them were to do with Inis Beag. Castle Lennox. His mother, Suki. Dim, strange reflections of scorched rocks and sand, of mountains hung against a blinding sky, of horned animals that ran swifter than the wind and yet not so swift as the dreaming hunter, and in the black hunter's dreams the sound of the sea was a whisper from the north wind. Where is my dark child, it whispered, my beautiful swift courser?

None of them, not John, nor Kate, nor the dog, had any place on the Inis and they felt it, and each in their own way sensed that they might never go back, or at least not happily. The island belonged now to Old Cait and she could not share it with them whatever she had hoped before she died. How could she share it? The island would have to become another thing, the old times, the old ways would have to be swept and scoured out of it before any new people could be easy there.

'We really need our own boat,' Kate said, as they drove back to Dublin.

'Except that it seems a bit extravagant just for a few weeks a year. And Tim mightn't like it.'

'I was hoping we might have got Fil to buy one of the cottages and do it up. If we could get hold of a dozen people to make summer homes on the island we could keep a couple of boats between us.'

They talked about it for the rest of the journey, thinking of people who might buy a cottage, how much they ought to pay, what kind of boat would be needed as a ferry if people were going to be taking furniture and stores across as a regular thing, and what the problems would be. But even while they were talking about it they knew that it was something that was not going to happen and they reached Dublin tired and out of temper and strangely relieved to see street-lights and people walking about at one in the morning and neon advertisements filling the half-darkness with cheerful, multicoloured vulgarity.

'It doesn't mean we can't go away as well,' Kate said. 'I mean, your programme is off the air for nearly four months. We can go to France for June when the roads are clear, and down to the island for July or August. And maybe we'll have found someone to go with us by then.'

Strangely enough they were not the only people thinking of the island as a place for summer cottages. Moberley & Gunn had heard of the evacuation of Inis Beag from a local contact, and a month after Felicity and John and Kate had been down to Drifin, Paddy Gunn went down, was ferried over by Tim Bourke, spent an hour taking photographs and another two hours making rough measurements, was ferried back to the mainland, and that night and the next day made agreements with six of the fifteen families besides John and Kate Lennox who still had freehold rights on the island to sell their land and cottages for them. Of the remaining nine owners, seven were unreachable, being in America, or England, at unknown addresses, or God knew where. Two were making up their minds.

During the remainder of the spring and that summer, and autumn, and the following year, Moberley & Gunn sold twelve houses on Inis Beag, some of the owners having more than one to sell, and thirty-three plots of land, each of five acres more or less, around the shores of the island. The buyers included a German holiday syndicate from Hamburg which bought six of the cottages and five plots of land, three Frenchmen interested in shooting geese and wanting a shooting-lodge, two English lady artists, five Irish-Americans, an English film star who flew over the island by helicopter without landing and bought three of the five-acre plots surrounding a cove with a small beach where seals were playing on the sand, a Dublin businessman and a television executive from the B.B.C. who wanted somewhere to go in the event of nuclear war. By the end of the second year the price of a five-acre plot had risen from four hundred to two thousand pounds and the last vacant cottage, with a quarter-acre garden, was on offer at eighteen hundred, 'in need of small repairs and some redecoration', meaning that it needed a new roof and had no plumbing of any kind.

Forty acres were bought by Jofran's subsidiary, Caravan Holidays, Ltd, as a camping-site, at forty pounds an acre, this being one of the earliest deals, and taking in the whole of Sean Daly's holding at one sale. The following summer Caravan Holidays, Ltd, decided that the problems of servicing a camp-site on the island were too great and they put the forty acres back on the market, at a hundred and seventy-five an acre. An American millionaire bought the lot, 'In memory of John F. Kennedy, and my dear grandmother who came from that part of the world, the sweet green hills of Kerry'. The deal was done by correspondence and cable and it seemed too complicated to explain to the American that Inis Beag was not in Kerry or anywhere near it. And as in the event he never came to visit his purchase it hardly mattered.

But all this was only a very small portion of the business deals in which Jofran and Moberley & Gunn were involved following the programme about Oxman Street. Lord Alfred's peace-making lunch with Paddy Gunn was followed by other lunches, meetings, and proposals. Lord Alfred had recognized for a long time that Irish, and particularly Dublin, property prices were irrationally low in European terms and that as a matter of logic they must, in the not too distant future, begin to float up to something like European levels. Germans, Americans, Englishmen, French and Swiss buyers looking for summer homes, fishing-lodges, or simply for investment in land would drive up the price of small properties; and English and Continental money looking for tax relief and swift appreciation of values would drive up the price of Dublin building sites.

The need to placate the Developers turned this purely intellectual appreciation into a plan of action. After two or three preliminary dealings with Moberley & Gunn, which simply involved putting large commissions in Paddy Gunn's pocket, and also in Johnny O'Hara's as solicitor for the deals, Lord Alfred began placing some Gandon money at Jofran's disposal.

In October of 1964 the directors of Jofran Holdings, Ltd, at an extraordinary general meeting invited Gandon Estates, Ltd, to nominate a director to the Jofran Board. Lord Alfred accepted the invitation with pleasure on behalf of Gandon Estates and nominated himself, asking that his nephew Cecil be made Secretary of the Company at the same time, his nephew being on the point of returning to Ireland from South Africa, and having wide experience of the problems of property development. The proposal was agreed to unanimously. On a further proposal, from Paddy Gunn, Lord Alfred was elected Chairman. That too was unanimous.

When he had voted 'Aye' Francis O'Rourke sat looking out of the window as if nothing that had happened that afternoon had anything to do with him. He found himself thinking of his children. Why was he doing all this? What for? They didn't want it, they didn't understand it. Didn't understand the first beginning thing of what it was about. Joseph Anthony and this Eileen girl—where had he found her? what in hell did he see in her?—Venetia and her painting. Next year it'd be acting, or a boy, or God knew what, but it wouldn't be Jofran, it wouldn't be Brefni House or property deals, or the fact that the others were letting these Gandon bastards take everything over and were kissing their boots for doing it. Cecil! Jesus God! Cecil Gandon as company secretary! And Dermot. Baby Dermot. Telling his mother he was an atheist. 'Frank! He says he's a diabolical materialist!' Jesus.

He stared out of the window. He thought sometimes there was something wrong with him, he ought to take a holiday. He was tired. He had got a dose of the 'flu after that bloody programme, getting so hot under the lights and then going out in the cold without a coat, something. Christ, he was getting soft, like a bloody woman. 'I'm getting old', he thought, 'nearly fifty.' His leg aching nearly all the time. He hadn't ever felt well since that 'flu. Bloody murder. Since that programme.

He had thought at the time it had gone so well, he'd told those bastards a few things they needed telling, more than a few. And the next day Paddy and Johnny and Jo Clancy the old sheep all ringing him up and saying, 'Why did you do this? why did you say that?' like a lot of effing nuns. And the anonymous phone-calls, calling him a murderer and a Rachman and using filthy language. Even to Maura or his mother if they answered. His mother had nearly died of shock the first time and after that she wouldn't answer the phone at all, even if she was the only one in the house with him, and he had lain in bed shaking with fever or half under with drugs and listened to the phone ringing, ringing, thinking it was something important, the bank, Paddy, Johnny, something he needed to know. Until he dragged himself downstairs and a voice spat at him, 'Filthy bastard, I hope you die. May you lose your money and live with rats biting you yourself, you dirty bogtrotter, may you live on shit.'

After that the letters in the papers. Not the same kind of language but the same kind of hatred between the lines. Ten years ago, five, it wouldn't have bothered him. Straight man-to-man hatred wouldn't bother him now. If a man wanted to try and knock him down, let him bloody well try. Even thinking of it his fists clenched like red lumps of rock on the boardroom table and his face turned bull savage. But a wounded bull. Because the hatred wasn't man to man or straightforward or anything you could fight. Why? Why for Christ's sake? Like fog coming up from a swamp. Like poison.

And even that he wouldn't have minded, God you don't make money without sweating. But the kids. The feeling that the hatred somehow came out of them as well. Not out of Jo Anthony, God help him, not out of him. Nothing came out of him except some kind of dumb imbecility like this bloody blonde tart, she'd be pregnant next. But out of the other two, out of Venetia. Not saying it, not even looking it. But being kind to him as if he needed her to be kind. And Dermot not saying anything at all, just looking down under his bloody glasses like some kind of a judge. A kid of fourteen! Jesus, a touch of the buckle-end of the belt was what kids needed these days, and a bloody sin they didn't get it.

Marty had put his finger on it. 'Ah God they're not the same times they were, the pith has gone out of them, man. 'Tis too easy for a man to be well off.'

Marty had been the only one to give him any kind of ease of mind after that programme. When the others had been preaching doom, and saying that they couldn't fly in the face of that kind of publicity, and blaming him for leading them into it—him? Jesus, as if he had done it all and they hadn't agreed to it!—and saying that the Party and even the Guardians would leave them in the lurch over it rather than stir up any more stink, Marty had been like a rock.

'Arragh God,' Marty had wheezed, 'don't be soft. What does a bit of stink matter? Doesn't it clear the drains? The fellers that are doing all the shouting and roaring now'll have forgotten it in a month. They see it on the television and just seeing it there gives them the idea something's been done about it and they go on to the next thing. Give it a month and there won't be ten people in Dublin remember what the fuss was about.'

'But there's those bastards squatting in the houses.'

'Let them. Just cut the water off. They'll get tired of it soon enough.'

It had all happened the way Marty had said it would. The fuss had died. The young men in raincoats had livings to earn and other wrongs to right. Con Danaher went to a Student Congress in Eastern Europe. Father Tracey was long gone, first to Roscommon, and then to Nigeria, to the new Bernardine Mission in a place called Owerri. And with Lady Honoria and her money both withdrawn, the publicity campaign lost impetus and died away. Denis Farrell continued to write letters to the newspapers and to include Oxman Street and Aram Court in his own smudged publications as examples of Fascist Ireland's inhumanity, but the steam was gone out of the matter for everyone, and even Denis Farrell had to recognize it as a lost cause.

Tenants and squatters began to drift away. The fit-up company that was the only legitimate tenant of Aram Court had gone even before the trouble started. With the young men withdrawn and Con Danaher and Father Tracey no longer there to put courage into them, the other tenants followed. The squatters went back to their homes, or to summer holidays, and as each house fell vacant, Willy Doyle and his men moved in and nailed up the doors and windows. Now the last house was empty and next week Willy would be moving in with the demolition squad. In a month's time they ought to be starting to cut the foundations of Brefni House.

Only they wouldn't be calling it Brefni House. Gandon House probably, from the sound of this bloody meeting. If there was any portrait in the hall it'd be Lord Alfred's. The meeting broke up and he found himself going down in the lift with Jo.

'You're not looking so well, Frank,' old Jo Clancy said in a hollow voice, full of sympathy and pleasure. He had felt so ill for so long himself that he had come to think of healthy people as somehow unnatural and offensive, and he welcomed a pale, sweating forehead on a friend like a gesture of solidarity.

'It's the bloody weather,' Francis said. 'It gets at my leg.' He knew the old man wanted to be driven home and he ignored the signals; let him get a flaming taxi, he could afford it. The same damn performance after every bloody meeting. 'My boy Victor can't make it today, he had to take the car somewhere, would you mind if . . .' Well, he would bloody mind. He was sick of them all, sick of everything. If he could get on a plane and go somewhere and forget the lot of them. Go back to England and the contracts. Just dig a bloody trench, ten miles of trench, boss the men up, feel it raining, get down in it and swing a pick himself, feel sweat running on him that he'd earned. The only sweat he ever felt now was from the central heating. Get on a plane and go.

A husky, whispering voice said something at his elbow, and for a second his heart lurched, seemed to stagger in his chest. Her voice, the white face, the brown hair, the softness against his arm. But it was only a tinker girl begging. And her hair was yellow and she wasn't touching his arm.

'Spare us a few coppers, mister, we're terribly bad off.' There was a three-year-old child hanging on to her skirt with both hands, its face filthy. 'Just a few coppers to get food for the babby.'

'Get away to hell out of it.'

'I'll pray for you, sir, we're hungry, we haven't eat all day. It'll bring you luck, sir.'

'Oh, Christ,' he said, but it touched his superstition and he gave her a half-crown. Bloody animals.

'May God and His Mother reward you your honour,' she said, in a tired, mechanical voice, already moving towards another prospect farther down the street. The child stumbled and began to cry and she picked it up, murmuring to it in gamman. 'Is the krolusk at you mo sulyan? We'll eat soon mo gris, don't cry little heart's darling, we'll have lovely chips.'

Ann Connor of Mayo, Grunles, now married to one of the Gallaghers, and begging for him round St Stephen's Green. It was already getting dark but she was short of her money and daren't go back to him without it. 'Would you spare us a few coppers, lady, we're terrible bad off. Just a few coppers to get food for the babby. I'll say prayers for you, lady, we're terrible bad off, we haven't eat all day.'

'If you don't leave me alone I'll call the police. You ought to be ashamed of yourself.'

The woman hurried on, clutching her handbag, half frightened, indignant. There was never a Guard when you wanted one, never. Probably busy putting parking tickets on people's cars instead of protecting them from being assaulted in the street.

Grunles quickened her own steps, afraid that the woman had meant what she said about the police. She was still new to Dublin and afraid of everything, everyone. That was why it took her so long to get her money in the day. Her man had a right to be angry with her, she was no good of a wife to him.

'Spare us a few coppers, mister, we're terrible bad off. Just a few coppers to get food for the babby.'

On the other side of the Green, Francis had already got into his car and was starting home. Why had he thought of her like that? He hadn't thought of her for years. Like a pain in the gut. He stopped at a traffic light and for a second he shut his eyes and he could see her again, hear her voice, feel her hands touching him, sliding round his neck. Someone hooted behind him. Bloody bastard. Making the circle of the Green to head towards home he nearly ran over the tinker girl, carrying the kid this time, like a bloody rabbit in front of the car. He gave her a blast on the horn and she almost jumped out of her skin with the fright and nearly dropped the child. Bloody imbecile. But the fright in her face had made him feel slightly better and he drove home in a better humour. He ought to be singing really. The last of those bastards out of the houses. Getting ready to knock down Aram Court. He'd go down on Monday and watch them begin.

19

Walter Bouchier crouched on his antique canvas painting-stool like a garden gnome in a mackintosh. His nose and fingers were blue with cold and every few seconds he had to stop painting to blow on to his knuckles. It was not that the late October day was so cold, but he had been sitting in Aram Court since dawn and he had had nothing to eat or drink before he came there, carrying his easel and his stool, his huge wooden painting-box and the thick metal tube that held his brushes. The Death of Aram Court.

He had painted the Court a dozen —— he couldn't remember how many times he had painted it. The houses. The courtyard, the doors, the overhanging windows with their small square Jacobean panes of bottle-glass; children playing by the railings. In summer. In winter. Spring. And now the end of them. Inside the houses the breakers' men were having their tea. Big tin mugs of brown tea stewed in billy-cans over a brazier. They had been feeding the brazier all morning with timber out of the floors and stairs because they were wrecking the insides first. One of them, the one they called Mr Doyle, had asked him if he wanted to come over and warm himself, but he wouldn't answer, and they had left him alone after a bit. A few times one of the men had walked over to look at what he was doing but he hadn't spoken to them, he'd gone on working as if they didn't exist. Get it all down.

There would be a moment, he didn't know what it would be as yet but he would know it when he saw it, that would be the one. Until he knew what it would be he was doing two things: blocking out the houses as they were now on the canvas in front of him, touching in colours more as notes than anything else, shades of grey sky, cloud, the leaden light in a window, the sudden flash of sun like steel, like gold, the wounded look of the open door, the eye of the brazier inside the house, the shadows of men crouched round it—as he filled in the figures with swift strokes of umber he thought, Is this it? but not yet. And between concentrated spells on the canvas he was turning to a sketch-pad and pencilling movements, a man walking, carrying a pick, Mr Doyle standing with his hands on his hips and his head tilted back, looking at the roof of one of the houses. Or he pencilled fragments of house, window, cornice, door-frame. Like lovers touching hands, staring at each other's faces, before they say good-bye on a railway station.

But lovers return from railway journeys. He wouldn't think, he wouldn't let himself think. Except about the sketches, the painting. He would bring it to her. The housekeeper had said she would be back next week. He'd have the painting finished by then, he'd get a frame for it, everything complete. A returning gift. A sad gift to give her and she fighting for these houses and forced to go away and leave them. He didn't know why she had gone but she must have been forced, she would never have left the fight of her free will. Lady Honoria. Lady H. His heart beat, and he painted, painted, sketched and pencilled, dabbed, clenched his teeth against the cold and the hunger.

He became aware of a man standing behind him, but he ignored him. Mr Doyle came out of the house, looked, ran towards them.

'Mr O'Rourke, sir! Just having their tea-break, sir. We've got the back of the roof off and some of the back wall down.'

The back of the roof off! So that was what they had been doing. That was why the door looked like a wound, why the house looked in agony. He had thought it was that the house knew what was going to happen, not that it was already begun.

'What are you doing?'

He wanted to ignore the question, but Francis O'Rourke wasn't Willy Doyle or a workman. He hadn't a voice to be ignored.

'Painting these houses before you . . .' he wanted to say 'murder them', but he was too timid. He mumbled, ' . . . knock them down,' without looking up.

'Not bad,' Francis said kindly. 'I'll buy it off you when you're finished. For a souvenir.'

'It's not for sale,' Walter whispered. His heart thudded.

'I'll give you a fiver for it,' Francis said. Poor old bastard, he'd probably never seen a fiver. 'C'mon, Willy, get the lads moving, we haven't got all week. Mr Doyle'll take it off you when you're ready. Here's the fiver, Willy. You pay him. Mind you don't rub the paint when you take it off him.' They went towards the houses. The workmen began showing tremendous activity. On the upper floor a man shoved a pick-head through a window with a shattering of glass and lead strips, and began smashing out the remainder. To Walter Bouchier the sound was like his own glasses breaking, and yet he knew that this was the moment, this was the heart of the painting; that window coming out in screaming splinters, the workman like an enemy with a weapon smashing it, smashing his way through a house in a conquered town, the house shuddering with fear, lurching. Paint it, paint, catch it down on the canvas, sketch the man, feel it in bone and finger, feel it in heart and eye. He wept as he painted, the tears running down his nose to join the dewdrop permanently there. His stomach was in a knot of pain, indigestion, hunger, cold. The house cried to him, cried of all that was gone.

Cried out, *I am alive, let me live, let me go on living.* Cried out of all who had lived there, of the sober families who had feared God and honoured William, the merchant fathers and the honest mothers, of the children in their long doll-dresses who had looked out of those leaded nursery windows on the great growing city. Looked down to the Liffey before the Four Courts were built beside them, saw the merchantmen come up the river, spars and masts like winter trees, ships out of Holland, out of Bristol, out of the farthest places of the world, Spain and Africa and the Americas. Looked beyond the river to the distant hills, dark grey and frightening, where the Irish lived, naked and terrible. Papa and Mama said that they were dead and gone, all the bad Irish were dead and gone, following the wicked Catholic King across the water. But nurse said they were still there, nurse knew about them, nurse even spoke in Irish sometimes when the grown people were not there, said the bogey King would come if little girls weren't good, if they didn't eat their gruel, say their prayers, honour their father and their mother, if they told tales on nanna.

Old soldiers from the William war had limped by those houses, starving and crippled: a leg cut off by a cannonball on the steep hill slope of the Boyne; an arm cut off by the surgeons, the wound gone rotten because the Irish villains used witchcraft, used brass buttons in their muskets instead of clean lead ball like Christians. God save King Billy, God rot the Pope and damn the Irish into hell.

Dean Swift stumped by, his head full of Gulliver and growing madness. And the new city rose in all its grandeur, surrounding Aram Court, until the two Dutch Billy houses were almost hidden, and the priests came, worn dark cloaks and broken shoes and the mass stone and the chalice hidden in a box. How many masses said in half-secret in those Dutch Billy houses, may God in His mercy spare our land, may He look down on our poor suffering people. Ireland of the Penal times, and the carriages rolling in the new wide streets, and the Bucks swaggering and the prentices fighting, butchers against weavers, Catholic butchers hanging Protestant weavers' boys on meathooks by their tender jawbones, weavers houghing butchers with a knife-slash at the tendons behind the knee, God for the Butchers, God for the Weavers. Riot and murder, arrogance and beauty, and the priests in their hidden houses. How much holiness soaked into timber, into brick and slate and glass? And now all smashed.

A pickaxe came through another window, like an eye bursting, and Walter Bouchier felt it in his head, in the bones of his skull. He clenched his loose false teeth against screaming aloud, and painted with a delicate ferocity of hate and love and misery. All smashed, all smashed. Glass on the stones, dust falling, slates, brick, timber out of the gaping windows, great sweating labourers smashing down the helpless houses. Let us live, let us live, we would keep you warm, sheltered, we have stood two hundred and seventy years, is that nothing? have you no pity? We have served the town so long.

Until he could no longer stay there, watch no longer, paint no longer. He wrenched up his things, easel, stool, canvas and paint-box, metal tube for brushes, sketch-block and pencils, and went stumbling out of Aram Court, his nose running, his face mad. A child yelled, 'Look at the painter man! Look at the painter man!' Small child, too small to go to school, to learn worse hatreds. Soon half a dozen children were following Walter like Hamelin's children after the Pied Piper. 'Look at him, look at him, where yer goin', mister? Runny nose, runny nose!' He ran and stumbled and after a while they fell behind and left him.

Five days later he knocked timidly on Lady Honoria's door, the painting framed and finished, done up in old crumpled brown paper tied with bits of assorted string that he saved in a drawer. There was a new parlourmaid who didn't know him, and she took the parcel as if it was a bomb or something dangerously unclean.

'If I could see Lady H. Show it to her myself, I've things to tell her about—about the houses. She'll understand.'

Very doubtfully the maid took the message up to the drawing-room, with the parcel, to come down a minute or so later with word that her ladyship was out.

'Then—tell her I called,' Walter said. He could have sworn he had heard her voice. But perhaps she was busy, and didn't like to hurt his feelings by saying so. 'I'll call again,' he said.

'Like some kind of a tramp,' the maid said to the housekeeper. 'Calling to the front door like a visitor! The cheek of him.' The painting went down to the basement, still wrapped in its brown paper and string. Lady Honoria was already turning her eyes to other interests and if she had met Walter Bouchier face to face in the street she wouldn't have remembered his name.

And already, in Aram Court, the houses were levelled to the ground. There was nothing left. Timber burned, glass smashed, lead pipe stripped away and sold to tinkers—Luke Gallagher, Grunles's husband, came with a horse and flat cart and took the lead and metal for two pounds, paid to one of the workmen. A jobbing builder came with a seven-ton lorry and took all the bricks away for nothing, as dry filling for jobs he was doing himself.

The houses in Oxman Street came down, the winter dusk like a shroud for them, the houses themselves seeming to dissolve into dusk, floating, settling. Children picked among the rubble, threw half-bricks at hunting cats and at each other. Hoardings surrounded the entire site. Notices went up. *The site of Gandon House. Building Contractors, Egbert Fane and Sons, Limited. Architects, Andrew Fane Associates. For Jofran Holdings, Ltd.* Machines moved in, bit and clawed at the earth, carved out foundations down to the sea mud, that underlay the land.

Early on, one scoop of a mechanical digger lifted a clawful of rubble and dark earth, threw it to one side and let a spill of gold run out of a lump of earth at a workman's feet. He moved his boots quickly to cover it and stood there making a big business of lighting his pipe. Gold, be Christ. He was a middle-aged man and knew his way around. Sovereigns. A dozen stories flashed through his mind as he stood blowing and sucking and waiting for everyone else's attention to be elsewhere. Jackser Mooney that found thirty sovereigns in the chimney up in Drogheda. Billy O'Toole that found the bag of fifty sovereigns in the roof of the house over in Rathfarnham, along with an old rusty gun. There wasn't a house he worked on that he didn't have the hope in the back of his mind that there'd be sovereigns in the walls or the roof or under the floorboards. And now he'd got some.

He bent casually. Five, six, eight, there must be a dozen. Big coins. He kicked gently at the earth they had come from and the fragments of a leather pouch dissolved into damp mould, into nothing. No more. Kick and look, kick and look. He had the lot of them. Only a dozen. He squinted down into the cupped palm of his hand. Queer-looking sovereigns. Some of 'em bent. Maybe they weren't gold at all.

'What you got there?'

'What the——' He swung round, closing his fist. He hadn't heard anyone. Dinny Doyle, the gaffer's brother. 'Nothing, what you mean what have I got there? Me pipe.'

'G'way out of that. I saw you picking it up. Show us.' Dinny was dapper in a new suit, new pointed shoes, new tie, new hat. He looked a thorough gentleman and he wasn't going to stand any codacting from this zombie. 'Or shall I tell me brother?'

Grinding his teeth the workman showed what was in his hand. 'They're only bits of tin or something,' he said. 'Kid's toys or something.' If they had been sovereigns, if he had been sure they were sovereigns, he'd have fought about them. But he wasn't sure any longer what they were, and there was no sense getting in bad with the gaffer over what might really be only bits of gold-coloured tin.

Dinny tried to take one of the coins and look at it closer, and the man swung his hand away. 'They're mine.'

'O.K. I'll tell me brother.'

'Here, then. Don't get so bloody sharp. What do you think they are?' He said it placatingly.

Dinny Doyle took the coin and bit it, turned it over. A ship one side with a funny-looking geyser sitting in it with a crown on his head. Writing round the edge. 'I don't know,' he said. 'But it's not gold. They're pretty though. Give you a bob for them.'

'Get off.'

'If I tell me brother you'll get nothing. I'll make it five bob. Me brother's kid'd like 'em to play with.'

'But suppose they're gold?'

'Don't be stupid. Think I don't know gold when I see it? D'you never see a gold sovereign? Well, is that a sovereign? If it was a gold coin it'd be a sovereign, wouldn't it? It'd have to be. It isn't legal if it isn't a sovereign.'

'Then I'll give 'em to my kid to play with.'

In the end they went together to a shop that Dinny knew, down a side street. Small and dark, the window stuffed with watches, jewellery, old cameras, football trophies, second-hand typewriters, broken electric irons, dolls, walking-sticks, opera glasses, china jugs, religious pictures, a fly-whisk from Arabia, a gilt mirror. Dead flies lay like withered raisins along the bottom of the window frame. Inside there was furniture, dust, darkness.

An old woman in a blackish cotton dress, turning green with age, sat in a big armchair with horsehair and grey flock stuffing spilling out of its arms. She was nursing a black cat and sucking her gums, a cup of cold tea beside her on another chair, Sheraton, covered in dust.

'Dinny! What you brought me, love?'

'Beautiful stuff, gran, sovereigns, twelve of 'em, me friend found 'em. Real safe stuff. Nobody knows.'

The old woman took them one by one, squinting through her glasses and smacking her lips. She couldn't bite the coins because she had no teeth but she didn't need to.

'What kind of rubbish is this, Dinny? These aren't sovereigns.'

'Well, what are they then, they're gold, aren't they? They must be sovereigns.'

'Gold, gold. Rubbish is what they are, Dinny. What you want for them?'

'Five quid each,' Dinny said, swaggering to cover his uncertainty.

The old woman laughed so hard the cat jumped off her lap in disgust and went under a mahogany dining-room table piled with silver plate and dirty china.

'Well, give us a quid each.'

'I'll give you ten bob for the lot,' she cackled. 'Bits of tin, Dinny love, bits of tin is all they are.'

'Make it a quid,' Dinny said.

'Because I'm soft,' she said. She gave them the pound note and they went away and she sat holding the coins long after they had gone, holding them gently in her cupped, dirty hands. Five James the First Spur Ryals, an Angel, a Rose Ryal, three Charles the First Angels and two Unites. She didn't know that that was what they were. Only that they were gold coins, and very old, and almost certainly worth a lot of money. Who would she go to? Goby? Sam? Lovely things, lovely things. She stroked them with her wrinkled, dirt-lined fingertips. A hoard of gold. And the shadow of the man who had buried them hovered between her hands, small and far away, far, far away, digging in a soft breathless panic, his fur robe round his bony shoulders, his young wife asleep in the small room behind the shop, the baby in her arms. Digging in the earth floor under the counter of the shop, the bales of cloth on shelves around him, the apprentice gone to get news. News of the fighting, of the soldiers coming. Dig and dig, scooping the earth up with a black-handled knife and a pewter spoon, the savings of twenty years in the leather purse beside him. Push it safe in, smooth the earth. They'd take the cloth, take everything, but not the gold, they wouldn't find the gold.

He heard running, shouting, the apprentice coming, 'Run, master, wake the mistress, quick, they're coming, the soldiers are coming.' But it was already too late. The thud of heavier feet, a woman screaming, a sudden drift of smoke on the wind, the smell of burning, the brightness of steel.

'Why, master soldier, welcome——'

The knife-jerk into his ribs, body sprawling, covering the dug floor. Soldiers running, his wife, his wife—his old hands scrabbling, '*Matthew!*' '*Aaaaahrrrg!*' Dark.

But they never found the gold.

Who would she take them to? Goby might be best.

And in Aram Court they dug down and down. Below the time of the cloth shop where the old man had buried his gold. Down into the Normans' time, when all of this was Oxmantown, Eastmanstown, the suburb of the Eastmen, the Danes, the Baltic traders, descendants of the one-time kings of Dublin. An iron knife. A silver penny. A leather shoe preserved in the wet ground, still with its lace and its pointed toe. The man who wore it sailed to Iceland, taking wolf dogs and wine and frieze cloaks and timber, and brought back salted fish and tales of monsters.

Down further into the Danish time, the time of the Sea Kings and the Norsemen; men who sailed out of the fjords in their dragon ships to kill the weak and haggle with the strong; half merchants and half murderers; men with cousins in the Palace Guard in Byzantium, and brothers in the Orkneys and in Northumberland; men who came here like sea-eagles to build a pirate's nest in the broad, slow estuary of the Liffey, with its wattle ford and its black pool where they moored their ships.

A thousand ghosts stirring and whispering in the heavy ground as the jaws of the mechanical diggers tore and wrenched and gnawed and dug. To build a new Dublin for new pirates.

By the beginning of the following year the foundations were going in. Paddy Noonan, the Minister for Economic Development, laid the foundation stone with a silver trowel presented to him by Lord Alfred on behalf of Jofran Holdings, Ltd. 'A symbol of the new Ireland,' as the Minister called it.

'As I lay this foundation stone,' he said, 'I see in my mind's eye much more than a new building, handsome as that building will be. I see a new Dublin rising out of the old. There are some who have expressed a sentimental regret at the passing of the old. May I remind them, with respect, that we cannot live by the past alone; we cannot allow our city, our capital city, to be shackled by nostalgia and the sentiments of the museum. A city and its governors, servants of the public, must look not to the past but to the future. And I see Gandon House as a symbol of that future, a symbol of the new Ireland that is bringing prosperity to our people, a promise of a deeper and richer life for all. And yet, sentiment still has a place in our minds, and it seems to me fitting as I lay this foundation stone for a fine twentieth-century building in the heart of what was once eighteenth-century Dublin, that the name of this great new monument to our commerce and economic development should echo the eighteenth century, and the great name of Gandon.'

'I know how you feel,' whispered Marty in his old, asthmatic voice to Francis after the ceremony. They had become close friends of late. 'Lord Alfred strolling in an' taking the icing off your cake. But we need him, Frank. We need the respectability. You and me do something, and it's highway robbery. He does it with us and it becomes high finance. Did you hear what he's promised Paddy Gunn? A chapel for the Knights and a meeting-hall and God knows what all on the top floor. Penthouse religion no less, and him a Protestant.' He laughed wheezingly until he had to fumble for the asthma inhalant in his bulging waistcoat pocket and fight for breath.

'The top floor?' Francis said in a dull voice. First the tower gone altogether. Now the top floor for the Knights. If he was lucky he'd get a room in the basement along with the cars.

'He's a long-sighted man is Lord Alfred,' Marty said when he could speak again. 'There's lads in the Knights wouldn't go along with any of our ideas about business, and they've been putting the brakes on Paddy here and there and as like as not speaking to the bishops to keep an eye on us. And there's a group of craw-thumpers in the Party gathering round you know who that'd be only delighted to start a purity campaign if they get the chance. If God was abolished in the morning them lads'd still be religious if it was only to dish Paddy Noonan.'

'Dish him?'

'Where are you at, man? Of course there's some wants to dish Paddy. The Boss man isn't going to last for ever, and who's in the running to take over from him? Who else but me bould economic developer Paddy, darling of the Party, founder of the Guardians, the man that put the Party's finances in the black? Unless he falls over a brick in the dark. Haven't you heard all the whispers going on? That he's making a mint out of speculating? That he's buying up pubs with his illegal gains, and all that class of claptrap? That's he's a lot too thick with the like of us? And all the old talk about his girl-friends? The daily communicants are ganging up on him before he can get too strong for them, and pumping it into the papers about how Holy Harry is the man that doesn't believe in corruption. Who d'you think that one was aimed at? Paddy of course.'

'Harry Mahon?'

'Of course. Harry for Taoiseach. The nun's best friend. And if Harry gets the top job, good-bye Marty, good-bye me nephew Jer, good-bye to Jofran Limited getting some nice fat government contracts for office space. You won't get a permit to build a pigsty.' He squeezed the plastic bottle under his gasping nostrils like a tiny bellows.

'I've a bloody mind to go back to England. I'm sick of all this.'

'Get away out of yourself, Frank. It's eating and drinking, this class of stuff, this is what politics is about, man. We're

going to sink Holy Harry forty feet deep with his rosary beads
tied round his ankles, don't worry. It's the old dogs for the
hard road. This is why Lord Alfred is buttering up the Knights.
With the Knights of St Brigid behind Paddy Noonan half
of Holy Harry's steam is gone before he gets started. Argh
sure, it's a great country if you don't weaken. How's the old
lady?'

'Fair enough.'

'And the youngsters, what's this I hear about Joseph Anthony
getting married? You'll be a grandfather before I am.'

'Don't be annoying me.' He thought of Eileen's foolish,
boiled-sweet eyes, and the little mincing walk of her, defying
him to say a word. She had the family sized up all right, for all
the chicken brain of her, and Maura doting on her as if she was a
Christmas present that Jo Anthony had bought for her. God, to
rear a son to marry that.

'And how's Venny's painting gettin' on?'

'She'll grow out of it.'

*　　*　　*

And almost at that same minute in Sean Ó Conaire's studio at
the top of Number 38 Chesterfield Square she was saying, 'My
father thinks I'll get tired of painting. Will I, Sean?'

She had fallen into the habit of asking him strange, illogical
questions about herself, as if he could tell the future.

'I've been tired of it for forty years,' Sean said, 'but it didn't
stop me going on.' He was sitting for her. Not drunk, but not
completely sober. They had a bargain together, that he would
work in the mornings and he would teach her and sit for her in
the afternoons in return for a quarter-bottle of whiskey and the
promise not to lecure him.

'God above, child, if I killed myself with the drink tomorrow,
who'd miss me?'

'I would.' Careful, careful stroke. 'Don't move.' She had
painted five portraits of him. In the evenings she went to drawing
classes at the College. Sometimes she knew in her bones that she
was going to be very good. Sometimes the work stared back at

her dead and hopeless, and she knew that she would never be any good, she would never make work live.

'Will I be good, Sean?' Shadow the left cheek, a kind of mauve shadow, a beautiful, beautiful colour if she could capture it, feel it on to the canvas.

'You will.' He lifted the quarter-bottle out of his lap and emptied it, giving a long sigh and smoothing the back of his hand across his lips, almost kissing his knuckles, licking the last drop of moisture from the corners of his mouth. He felt the warmth run down like red tongues into his throat and stomach, the blackness lift from his mind. He wanted to lie down.

'That's enough, child.' He lurched out of the chair. It was a queer thing. He used to be able to drink a bottle of whiskey and after it he could walk a straight line like a tram on its tracks. And now a couple of mouthfuls and it had his legs shaking and his head going round. 'I want to lie down,' he said.

'I was just getting something.'

'Tomorrow.' He felt rotten suddenly. He put his hand on her shoulder to support himself. 'But stay here. Don't go away.'

She helped him to the bed, staggering under the weight of his hand. He let himself fall on to it and she lifted his legs, one at a time, and took his shoes off.

'You'll have to stop altogether,' she said.

'You promised. No lectures. Clean your . . . clean your . . .' His mind drifted. She cleaned her brushes slowly, carefully, one by one and laid them on the sill of the easel. Her own portrait, the one Sean had done of her, lay against the far wall, looking at her with troubled eyes. Her mother had hated it and her grandmother had threatened to burn it, and in case they carried out the threat she had brought it back. She still thought it was beautiful.

Not beautiful the way her mother wanted, like a chocolate box or a photograph. And how could even a photograph be beautiful when she didn't look beautiful herself? She knew what she looked like. But he had made a painting out of her, put things into her eyes that she hadn't known were there, into her face, until she didn't recognize herself. Her eyes, her mouth, her chin, her hair. And yet someone else.

'Is that me?' she had said, and he hadn't minded, he had known what she meant.

'Maybe not now,' he had said. 'What you will be. If they let you. Fight them off, child. Don't let them tie you up in ribbons.'

'What will I be?'

He had been half drunk and he had taken her face in his big fingers that always smelled of turpentine and turned her head this way and that. 'You'll be a good woman,' he said. 'You'll fight for what you believe in.' And then: 'You'll have your own kind of beauty.'

'Like that?' The portrait, with its troubled, troubling eyes and its haunted mouth and the shadows in its cheeks. 'My Gawd,' her mother had said. 'It makes the child look as if she has T.B.'

'Like that.'

It was after that she had started painting, trying to paint. She looked at the portrait she was doing. Clumsy. Awkward. And yet something about it was right. 'I think I'm getting something,' she said. She picked up a cleaned brush and the palette and began touching at one corner of the mouth, deepening the down curve, the line beside it, sunk into the heavy, mottled cheek. On the bed behind her Sean made a strange noise, the breath gasping in his throat.

'Ahhh ahhhh,' he said. The bed creaked under his weight. She had it right, she had it right. One more touch of brown, maybe dark red? Mix in some blue, a kind of purplish effect. Suddenly it made the protrait like a death mask, frightening.

'Ahhhhhhhh,' Sean whispered behind her, so close that she thought he had got up to look over her shoulder at what she was trying to do. 'It's dreadful,' she said. 'I'll change it to-morrow.'

The room felt oddly silent, cold. She turned to look at him. He lay on the bed with one arm hanging, his mouth open, his eyes wide, staring at the ceiling.

'Sean!'

He didn't move. She went very slowly and unwillingly towards him, reaching out a hand to his arm, stooping so that she could lift it back on to the bed. 'Sean,' she whispered. The arm was so heavy that she couldn't lift it. 'Oh, no,' she whispered. 'Oh, no, oh, Sean.'

20

It was the Easter of 1966 before Gandon House was ready for the grand opening. *Lord Alfred Gandon and his fellow directors on the board of Jofran Holdings Limited have great pleasure in inviting ——to a cocktail reception at 6.30 p.m. Wednesday April 20th, to mark the opening of Gandon House.* The guest of honour was Patrick Gerald Noonan, Minister for Economic Development, and the guest list included diplomats, other ministers—although not Harold Mahon, Paddy Noonan's rival and enemy, darling of the conservative and pious—T.D.s, Aldermen, Councillors, business leaders, journalists—including John Lennox accompanied by Kate—newspaper editors, the Director General of Irish Television, Cecil and Lady Honoria Gandon, architects, artists—of the smarter, modern kind, invited on the suggestion of Sir Egbert Fane, their patron—a Japanese businessman, an American airline executive, three university professors and a number of people who were only there because they liked free drinks and distinguished company.

At Paddy Gunn's suggestion the reception took place on the top floor, in the huge area that would in the near future become the conference hall of the Knights of St Brigid; a modern setting for a modernized, post-Vatican-Council Knighthood, socially conscious, ecumenical, forward-looking, outward-looking, businesslike. It was very probable that at the next annual conference Paddy Gunn would become Chief Knight. It was his influence that had inspired the Knights to agree to move from their antiquated headquarters in St. Stephen's Green, and as Knight Treasurer for the last three years he had already swung the Order decisively in a new economic direction, shaking the cobwebs out of their share portfolio. At the reception he acted as Lord Alfred's right hand and memorandum pad, bringing him round to meeet obscure T.D.s—who might one day be less obscure—presenting him to the right journalists—getting the right photographs taken, making it clear to all that Protestant

West British Lord and Catholic good-national Knight were one flesh and one currency. In that year and season of sentimental national nostalgia, of Remember-our-famous-dead, Ireland-abu, 'Fifty-years-ago-in-the-G.P.O.', it was more than ever essential to remind English and all foreign capitalists that Ireland was a sound investment; that all the nationalist oratory was no more than green froth on a pint of porter. Lord Alfred when he went to London for any of the dozen board meetings he sat at most months must carry with him the right impression. Of a country that had put bombs and guns and revolutions and hot-headed talk where they all belonged, in the national attic, and that to do business in Ireland was as sensible as doing business in New Zealand or Denmark and more profitable than either.

Any lingering feeling Lord Alfred had that he was still regarded in some ways as an outsider must be firmly banished. At a convenient moment Paddy Gunn contrived that Paddy Noonan, Lord Alfred, himself, the American executive, Sir Egbert Fane and the Japanese businessman were all by one of the windows looking across the river and down on the huddle of mean roofs that surrounded Gandon House. Already, here and there across the townscape, a new kind of building was beginning to break the monotony: square, uncompromising, glittering with glass, eight, ten, fifteen storeys high, the new office blocks.

'There's the real Irish revolution,' Paddy Gunn said. 'I'm second to no one in honouring 1916, but this is 1966, and thanks to you, Minister, and to people like Lord Alfred, it's as important a year in its own right as 1916 ever was. I hope you'll tell your friends in New York, Sam, that we're not looking back fifty years, we're looking forward fifty. And you, Mr Noguchi.'

'Pleass,' Mr Noguchi said, nodding soberly. He didn't like the sandwiches very much and he could not understand anything that anyone said. Perhaps they were speaking in Gaelic.

'We've come a long way in fifty years,' Paddy Noonan said, with Ministerial solemnity.

'We've come a long way in five years,' said Paddy Gunn. It was exactly five years since Paddy Noonan entered the Cabinet.

'I remember five years ago, the emigration figures, the unemployment figures, the feeling in the country—like despair. Nothing had ever happened, nothing ever would. And now—now, look at it.'

There was really nothing to look at except half a dozen rather bad modern buildings, but his Irish hearers knew what he meant. That in the streets below there was money, there was hope.

Lady Honoria came up to them, trailing Cecil behind her. He was carrying a flat parcel done up in brown paper and Lady Honoria wore her new smile. She had done a great deal of thinking in the long six months of exile and had come to realize that she had been too impatient, too confident that she could manipulate affairs by her own unaided strength. What was needed, she had come to realize, was finesse, intellectual jujitsu; to use the Gandon name to her own advantage; not in spite of the Gandons but with their willing co-operation. What she must become was not a maverick Gandon but the quintessential Gandon, the heiress apparent, the 'best man the Gandons had'. And in a family that had Cecil as the leading light of its younger generation by God that shouldn't be hard. For the past year she had set herself to win Lord Alfred's confidence, and even his affection. And she had gone about it with subtlety, not making foolish, flattering approaches to him himself, but to causes he held dear, beginning with those on the outer fringes of his interest. The Decayed Parsons' Widows Association had been the first.

'Maybe I was wrong about that gel,' Lord Alfred had once said recently. 'Maybe all that was wrong with her was a bit of idealism in the wrong quarter. Maybe she'll make a man of Cecil yet.'

She came now on respectful feet, a mere woman approaching a group of rich men. But a beautiful woman, bringing the tribute of her beauty. And something else. 'Minister!' she said, after an apologetically requesting glance at Lord Alfred. 'I know—Lord Alfred has told me—how much you did to make this building possible, and how much you did to make sure that it was in the best tradition of the old buildings it replaced. . . .'

Paddy Noonan looked suddenly watchful like a man who hears footfalls behind him in the dark.

' . . . I know at one time I was rather against what you were doing. But then I didn't realize what you were—what we were going to get in exchange for what we were losing . . . '

Lord Alfred felt an inner glow, almost of holiness. A Gandon! By adoption, marriage, accident, but, by God, a Gandon.

' . . . and—my husband and I—we'd like to offer you a very small token—a memento of Aram Court——'

With a rehearsed flourish Cecil whipped off the brown paper and held out Walter Bouchier's canvas, the last painting that had ever been painted of Dublin's last seventeenth-century houses. He held it out to the Minister, who took it in puzzled hands, still not sure whether it was going to explode.

'We had it done specially,' Lady Honoria said. 'You see? They're beginning to break the old houses down to clear the site for . . . for Gandon House.' Family pride trembled in her voice.

'That's . . . that's very kind,' Paddy Noonan said. He was suddenly touched. And it was easy to be touched by Lady Honoria. Her simple black suit by Chanel, the small sable hat, the thirty-two-carat diamond ring that Cousin Julius had had made for her in Johannesburg, the Patou perfume, the soft loveliness of her hair, washed and set by Vidal in London twice every month—all this made him realize in an unformulated but deeply felt way what it was that he stood for, what the revolution that Paddy Gunn had been talking about was really for. That Ireland should move, had moved, was moving, out of the pigs-in-the-parlour, red-petticoat and long black shawl mythology of the past into a future in which the type and symbol of everyday Ireland would be not Old Mother Reilly but Lady Honoria, soignée, beautiful. Not Kathleen ni Houlihan weeping on the desolate hillside for the men of '98, but Lady Honoria stepping out of her Rolls-Royce. No longer the image of defeat, but of victory.

'I'll hang it in my study,' Paddy Noonan said. He held it up so that the others in the group might admire the painting

Fortunately no one there was particularly sensitive, and they looked at the picture with satisfaction as a nice likeness of houses that they hardly remembered if they had ever seen them with conscious eyes. The window bursting outwards like an eye, the scream of pain, left them unmoved, unnoticing.

Lord Alfred put an avuncular hand on Lady Honoria's sable-stoled shoulder, warm as an animal's living fur in that warm room. 'This young lady's turning into a great patroness of art, Minister. You're honoured that she's sacrificing a picture out of her collection.' He patted possessively. A real Gandon.

As if drawn by instinct that the word *art* had been said in his neighbourhood, Sir Egbert Fane came over to them, holding a cocktail glass in one elegant hand and a smoked-salmon biscuit in the other, both with an air, a gracefulness that no one in Ireland, not even his nephew Andrew, could match. He saw the back of the canvas and went round to look at what was on it.

'Ahhaaa,' he said, initial enthusiasm dwindling away into polite contempt. 'A souvenir of bygone days, one observes.'

'Not your kind of thing, Eggy,' Lord Alfred said. They had become quite thick over the past year.

'Noooo,' Sir Egbert agreed with a thin smile. 'One wants, one desires—truthfully to say one *expects*—from the graphic artist in these days more . . . shall one say it . . . more *empathy* with the times.'

'Well,' Paddy Noonan said bluffly, 'I'm not one of your connoisseurs.'

Sir Egbert, who was so rich that he did not need to belong to the Party and actually voted for the Opposition, said, 'Ahhhhh.' And then, in pity for a man still inhabiting artistic darkness, and with the simple pride of a patron, he swept all of them away to see the three large Miglos that he had presented to the building: one in the central area of the fifth floor, the second two floors below, and the third in the entrance hall.

'Is it not a magnificent statement?' Sir Egbert said, of this third, and most prized painting of the three. It was twelve feet long by five feet high and was entirely black, except for one thin white stripe roughly two inches wide that ran from side to side of it, two feet from the lower edge. 'So . . . so *masculine* don't you think, Minister? Such harmonious interspatial formulations, such fulfilledness of intention, do you not agree?'

'It's a very big painting,' Paddy Noonan said.

Mr Noguchi, who had followed everyone down, said, 'Pleass.'

'Size is not every consideration—far from it when one thinks of much that has been accomplished within small compass—but where the statement calls for the broad and spacious gesture, then size is indeed of import, and in stating the bigness of this picture, Minister, you do indeed compliment it. I congratulate your penetration.'

'Ahhh,' said Paddy Noonan. He had often wondered if Sir Egbert was right in the head and he wondered it again.

Up on the sixth floor Francis O'Rourke went through into the unoccupied Knights' Chapel. It had not yet been consecrated but there had been a feeling that it should not be used for the reception and it was cool and empty; the lights were on because it had been shown to people, but they had all gone out again to the warm familiarity and chatter of the conference-room with its long white tables and its smell of whiskey and smoked salmon and hothouse flowers. Francis went to the farthest window and stared out. It was getting on for nine o'clock and the sun had set. He could see the red peacock's fan of the sunset in the west and the dark of the night coming from the east, up from the river mouth and the sea. It suited his mood and he went on looking at the sunset, islands of cloud turning black and crimson against the dark rose of the sky, but it seemed to him sombre rather than beautiful, an ending. What was it all for? All the fighting and clawing and struggling. Twelve years. He had spent twelve years of his life fighting and scheming towards tonight. His dream. O'Rourke House. Brefni House. Something permanent, something to leave his mark behind him. And what had it become? Lord Alfred's Georgian Public Lavatory. Gandon House. Down there in the streets, who in hell knew about Francis O'Rourke? Who'd ever know? That he'd been poor and become rich. That he'd set out to do something and done it. He might as well have stayed digging trenches for the Electricity Boards in England.

He belched and touched his stomach. Soft. Soft flesh over the belt. Not sleeping. Indigestion. His bloody leg aching all the time now. He was only fifty and there were times he felt older than old Jo Clancy. He didn't like to look at himself in the mornings. Bagged eyes. A bloody ruin. For what? For Gandon House. And after that? Lady Honoria House? Fifty. It wasn't old. How old was she now? Thirty-two, thirty-three? He'd seen a picture of her the other day in a magazine and she was putting it on as well. But it suited her. He leaned his forehead against the glass, holding the tumbler of whiskey in his hand like a half-brick.

'Dreaming of the future, eh?' a voice said. Lord Alfred. He didn't turn his head. 'New worlds to conquer? Young Johnny was roughing it out for me,' Lord Alfred went on. 'Buy up all of that that we can get, eh?' His stubby finger gestured downwards at the whole of Oxmantown, what had once been Oxmantown. 'It's a big project. Take a lot of capital.'

Francis grunted something that could be taken as a reply. It wouldn't be his capital. Any more than it was his capital in Gandon House. Money from banks, insurance companies, he hardly knew where the money had come from, that was Johnny's and old Jo's end of it. And now Lord Alfred's. It came to him with a slight sense of chill that there was no longer anything very much that he was adding to Jofran Holdings. He had his shares, he went to board meetings, he . . . what else did he do? Talk, listen, argue—he hardly listened any more. He didn't understand half of it when he did listen.

This business of the new project. In a sense it had been his idea from the beginning. To build not just one block, one building, but develop the whole area, like building a new centre inside the old decaying heart of Dublin. He had seen it in his mind. Like a . . . he hunted for the word, those things in Arabian stories, that men saw in the desert—a *mirage*. Big towers, white and shimmering, pushing up from the slums. If a man could leave that behind him. But it was the kind of dream that could be changed out of recognition by reality. Twelve years to make this building a reality and it wasn't worth twelve months, twelve weeks of a man's life. What would the other reality be? Lord Alfred would do it. Or Paddy Gunn after him. Or some young Gandon who was still in short breeches. Someone would do it. With money from London and New York and Zürich. And some fellow controlling the finances that had never set foot in Ireland. They'd do it some time. And if he was still alive he'd be at the opening reception and a few people would say 'Who's that old lame geyser?' and nobody would know and his chauffeur would take him home and he'd go to bed with hot milk and a sleeping-pill. Oh Christ oh Christ.

'I can see it all,' Lord Alfred said.

In the conference-room Paddy Gunn had brought his drink over to Kate Lennox—orange squash and tonic water—and was offering her a cigarette, smiling his soft, religious, auctioneer's smile. 'And how is the beautiful Mrs Lennox?'

'Armoured against flattery,' Kate said untruthfully.

'I'm especially glad to see you and John—may I call him John behind his back?—I'm truly glad to see you both here tonight. It makes me feel the war is really over.' His glance went briefly to Lady Honoria. Paddy Noonan had gone long ago, swept off in his Ministerial Mercedes to some other reception, and Lady Honoria was being beautifully impressed by the airline executive. Paddy Gunn's glance suggested that Lady Honoria's conversion was one thing, but the Lennoxes' peace-making was on a different level of importance altogether.

'I never thought of it as a war,' Kate said, keeping her tone as cool as was permissible in a guest. 'Simply a difference of opinion about values.'

'The old versus the new?'

'Or Money versus People,' Kate said.

Paddy Gunn smiled more winningly still. 'Aren't you doing yourself an injustice? I'm sure you never wanted people without money?'

'You know very well what I mean.'

'Of course I do. As the newspapers put it, "The Developers

versus the Preservers". A nice, simple, emotive contrast. But quite a false one, in our case at least?'

She raised her eyebrows, even more coldly. Of all the opposition forces she had always found Paddy Gunn the least attractive. With some of them there was at least the amusement of outright, open villainy. But villainy with a sheaf of arum lilies had a kind of horror about it.

'Come, come, Mrs Lennox, don't pretend to be dull. We are all developers, you and John as much as Francis O'Rourke and Lord Alfred. And your strange allies, Mister Farrell and Mister Con Danaher and their like most of all. Except that they want to develop us out of all recognition. And I don't think you do. We all of us, except for those last two, want to preserve the good as well as developing the better. There's no real difference between us. And do you know something? If I was asked to pick out the man in this room now—or any time this evening—who was the true revolutionary—do you know who I would choose?'

She shook her head.

'Your husband. There's no man in Ireland, Paddy Noonan included, who is doing more to change the country in the way that matters most. In its thinking. Compared to your husband we are all Preservers.'

'I'm sure he'd be flattered to hear you say so.'

'There's no flattery involved, I assure you. He's a powerful man. And I give him credit for attempting to use his power responsibly, whatever my friend Mr Patrick Lacey says about him.'

'Patrick Lacey?'

'One of our more reactionary Knights.' Paddy Gunn nodded towards the chapel. 'You've possibly heard that we're forming an auxiliary order. . . .' He smiled briefly, like a cat. 'Someone has suggested the title 'The Squirearchy', I'm not sure how seriously. But an auxiliary wing of the Knighthood that will be open to all men of good-will—and women, of course—regardless of denomination.'

'I hadn't heard.'

'Perhaps you'd mention it to John. This is a time—there are

grave problems ahead of us, Mrs Lennox, and there will soon be more serious choices for public men to make than whether or not to preserve an old building or construct a new one—much more serious. It will be time soon for those of us who love Ireland and its—I won't use the word Catholic—its *Christian* heritage—time for us to close ranks against a threatening future. Would you mention to him that we were talking along these lines?'

'I don't think his mind works along that kind of line.' She began to disengage herself, looking over Paddy Gunn's shoulder at a non-existent beckoner.

'I must let you go. But one other thing. I believe you own a small property on Inis Beag——'

'Yes?' Kate said, surprised. They had been talking of it only the other day, with a frustrated fury at what had happened to the island, when they were thinking of the coming summer.

'If you ever think of selling out——'

'I don't think . . .' she began, and stopped. Last summer the island had been full of Dutch boy scouts, an English sketching club, and a Spanish Shooting and Sporting Society. Someone had already removed all the Cursing Stones and the Hollow had been half filled in with rocks. The intention apparently was to fill it in entirely and build a bungalow on the resulting site.

'I won't be mysterious about it,' Paddy Gunn said. 'We've had an approach from an American hotel consortium. They're looking for a really fine site on the West coast or on an island with good landing facilities. They're planning to build something that really fits the environment, something in good taste, and they're prepared to buy out any bad development near by to preserve or restore the real beauty of the surroundings. There's a lot of money involved, and truthfully the price they pay for the land is almost unimportant.'

'I don't . . .' Kate began again, and stopped again. 'We . . . we've not really thought . . . I don't know if——'

'For a site like yours we were thinking in terms—approximately, purely approximately—of ten thousand pounds.'

'Ten th——' She stopped herself firmly. Ten thousand? Ten

thousand! And last summer if one of the Germans had offered them a couple of thousand for the lot they'd have jumped at it, after three nights of listening to Spanish guitars trying to drown out Dutch folk-songs and a long afternoon of rescuing an English lady sketcher who had got stuck half-way down the North Cliff. 'There was this beeeeautiful clump of anemones.' When she had been rescued it was found that her sketch-book had been left behind on a ledge of rock and she had wanted John to go down again and fetch it for her. It turned out eventually that she thought that John and Kate were the island's caretakers, employed by the Government to look after visitors.

'I told you you shouldn't wear pampooties,' Kate had said afterwards. But the whole holiday had left them sombre, and almost the only thing that prevented them from putting their land and the cottage on the market immediately was the thought of old Cait's grave. They had even talked about a price. At their most optimistic and thinking of prices they had heard mentioned they had thought of asking five or at least four. But what was driving them away would probably horrify anyone else. Who'd pay four thousand pounds to hear 'The Girls are Pretty in Amsterdam' twenty-five times a week?

'Think about it,' Paddy Gunn was saying. 'Perhaps I shouldn't be telling you this, but I don't believe my clients would quibble about improving on that figure—within reason—for a quick sale.'

'I'll talk to John about it.'

'And you won't forget—the Squirearchy?' The smile flickered. It no longer reminded her of a cat. When she was already two steps away from him she wanted to go back and ask if he really meant it, if he was making them a firm offer. Ten thousand! Improving on ten thousand! Eleven? Twelve? Where the blazes was John? She mustn't seem to be looking for him, not in a hurry. To seem in a hurry could cost hundreds on the eventual price. Ten thousand! It was unbelievable. Where could he have got to?

He was out in the central area by the lifts, with Matt O'Carroll, the old Trades Unionist, Labour T.D. Matt was at the reception because this was his constituency, however much he disliked the idea of Gandon House in the heart of it. 'I'm getting old,' he had said to John. 'I won't be fighting another election if I can help it. It's pipe and slippers and the garden for me.'

'Go away, Matt, you've a long run yet.'

'No, no. All I need is someone I could recommend for my shoes. There's a lot of young lads'd like to take them but they wouldn't fit. I've nursed this district for thirty years, Council and Dail. There was a time when I knew pretty nearly every family by name and most of their troubles as well. The youngsters don't want to put that kind of groundwork in any more. They want instant politics. They want to be statesmen before they've learned to stick up election posters.'

'Anyone but you would lose this seat at the next election anyway. Every slum family that got cleared out of here was three or four votes Labour was losing.'

'Do you think I don't know that? What the party needs here next time out is a man with . . . with . . . charisma.'

'God almighty, where did you get that word?'

'You've got it, John. The Kennedy touch.'

'Me? You must be joking.'

'They know you. They know you're on their side. They look up to you. If you stood for Oxmantown you'd top the poll. Make John Lennox your number one. You couldn't lose. Lennox for Labour.'

'Come off it, Matt.'

'I'm serious. This isn't off the top of my own head, John, we've been talking about it a while back. The big man thinks a lot of you, John.'

'You can't be serious. And what would I do—suppose . . . suppose you were right—just for a second suppose you're right and I got in. Give up television—I earn a lot of money, Matt.'

'A deputy's pay isn't too bad.'

'It's worse than mine.'

'Pay isn't everything. At least I didn't think you reckoned it was.'

'Maybe I don't. But being a deputy isn't everything either.

What would I do? Sit on an Opposition bench for the next ten years shouting, "What about the workers"?'

'Why does it have to be the Opposition benches?'

'You mean . . . ?'

'The Party of Reality isn't going to be there for ever, John, whatever they think. The country's getting sick of them. People want a change. They want a Government that cares about people, about small people as well as the Francis O'Rourkes and the Lord Alfreds. It was always a rotten Government and it's got worse. And if we've got the right candidates next time we can make the voters see it. And the right candidate, who'd carried the right seat—if we formed a Government—well, a coalition Government—that man wouldn't be spending long on the back benches. Parliamentary Secretary to the Minister of Posts and Telegraphs? Would that be such a bad exchange? As a beginning?'

'You're out of your silly old Trade Union mind, Matty. And as for a coalition—you've been shouting your heads off for the past twelve months saying, "We'll never form a coalition at any price,' haven't you?"

'John, John. In politics "never" means "not for a month or two anyway", and "not at any price" simply means you haven't been offered enough. Yet.'

'I couldn't afford it.'

'Think about it, John. Think about it. Talk it over with the missus. See what she thinks.'

21

The Lennoxes sold their land and cottage on Inis Beag in July, to Patrick Aloysius Gunn acting as Trustee for an unnamed purchaser. The price was eleven thousand five hundred pounds.

'My congratulations,' Paddy said. 'A very, very good price, I think. 'I'll get the cheque off to your solicitors as soon as I can. And if you're thinking of spending some of it on another holiday cottage, let me know. I've quite a few pleasant little places on the books at the moment.'

'We'll think about it,' John said. He tried not to show his feelings as he shook hands with Gunn, and went out to the car. Kate had refused to come in.

'Is it done?' she said in a dull voice.

'Done and complete.'

'I . . . I almost wanted to come in after you and——'

'You couldn't go back on it now. We'd signed.'

'But you understand?'

'I know. But eleven thousand five hundred. And it isn't Inis Beag any more. It's getting like Coney Island.' He found himself that he was sorry, and sat surprised in the car, looking out of the windscreen at nothing. The sound of the traffic was like the sea and the wind, half heard from the cottage at night. 'What could we do? And a hotel'll bring a lot of money to Drifin. There'll be work.'

'Do you think . . .' Her own words came back to her, an echo in her head, in the car, a whisper. 'My curse on either of us that goes away from it.' But she hadn't meant—she hadn't ever meant that they would live there. Only here, in Ireland. God knew what she'd meant. It seemed so long ago, such a long way away. She looked at the traffic, that seemed to grow year by year, more cars, more and more, so that you couldn't find a parking-place, couldn't move sometimes. For years she had thought of the island as a refuge, always there, somewhere to escape to, quiet, secret.

'It would have been selfish of us not to sell, wouldn't it?'

A face came at the window beside her. 'Could you spare a few coppers, ma'am? I'm terrible hard up, lady, we haven't had a bite to eat all day. Just a few coppers to feed the babby.'

Kate felt for her purse. There were only a few pence in it, and some pound notes, and for a moment she hesitated. 'John, have you got any change?'

He found her a shilling and held it out through the window. Ann Connor took it. She was cradling the child on one arm, half wrapped in her plaid shawl, its head asleep against her shoulder. 'Thank you kindly lady, God bless you sir.' She turned away among the passers-by. Kate still hesitated and then, shocked at herself, took one of the pound notes out of her purse and called, 'Here, come back.' And as the girl didn't turn her head she shouted in gamman, '*Tori—tori nasdyes lakin.*'

Ann turned round as if she had been struck on the back, her mouth open, staring, looking round her in amazement for whatever tinker woman had called to her to come. But the only person near her it could have been was the lady in the car. Beckoning her. She went suspiciously back to the car window, still bewildered.

'Take it,' Kate said, holding out the pound. Ann took it in nervous fingers.

'Was it yourself,' she whispered in gamman, 'that called to me like that?'

'*Stes.*'

'And how would yourself be knowing gamman and you a lady?'

'We knew the travellers long ago,' Kate said. 'A family called Connor. In the West.'

'I am of the Connors,' Ann whispered. The child woke up and stared into the car with sleep-filled eyes.

A Guard came walking, slowly, his shadow falling before him. Ann lifted her head, saw him, and looked suddenly thin and trapped.

'Get along with you,' the Guard said. 'Is she bothering you, ma'am?'

'I'm talking to her,' Kate said in a hard voice. 'Don't tell someone to move on just because they're standing talking to a friend.'

The Guard opened his mouth, taken aback at the ingratitude, before the sheer unreason of it struck him as well. He looked at the car, at Kate's suddenly angry face, at the shadow of John inside the car, at the tinker girl with her baby. By God you wouldn't know what would happen in this damn city. Everyone in it seemed to be mad. He was young and fresh from a slow and comfortable village in the midlands, and if he knew anything in the world beside the contents of the Garda Siochana Handbook it was that tinkers do not have smartly dressed friends in motor cars.

'I am telling her to move on because she is causing an obstruction,' the Guard said, his pink-and-white complexion turning a dull scarlet. 'Get on with you now. If I see you round here again I'll arrest you. And you, ma'am, I'll thank you not to interfere with a Guard in the course of his duties or I'll have to report it to higher authorities.'

'And I'll thank you——' Kate said, beginning to get out of the car. John switched on the ignition and put the car into gear.

'For Christ's sake,' he whispered. They slid away from the kerb as she began to open the door, almost knocking into the Guard. 'Do you want to get us arrested?'

'I want to bloody well kill him. Who does he think I am?'

'TV man's wife arrested for breach of the peace. For God's sake have sense.'

'She's one of the Connors. Do you know who she must be? Grunles! Grunles Connor, the little girl. John, turn the car quick, she went that way.'

'I can't——'

'Turn the car!'

They turned at the next crossing and went back. She hadn't gone far. She was hurrying, looking over her shoulder for the Guard.

'Ann! Grunles!'

She stared at Kate as if they were chasing her.

'Are you Ann Connor? Gretis Connor's child?'

She nodded, too frightened to say anything.

'Get in the car.'

'My God,' John said. People were staring at them. Kate had the back door of the car open. Ann stared at them dumbfounded. Get in the car? She heard the words without them registering any meaning. What car?

'*Tori asturt an rog. Grentya.*'

She got into the car like a sleepwalker, clutching the child to her breast, her eyes wide, and sat, because there was no room to stand. But she sat crouching on the forward edge of the seat and didn't close the door. Kate closed it, reaching back over Ann's knees. As soon as the door was shut there was a strong smell from the girl and the child.

'Where do you want to go?' John said between his teeth.

'Somewhere we can talk,' Kate said. It was like an accusation out of the past. Eleven thousand five hundred pounds in John's pocket and she had been going to let her go with a shilling. 'Where are you living?'

'In the big site,' Ann whispered. Her face was white under the tawny yellow hair and there were enormous shadows under her eyes. But she had combed her hair that morning and there was a diamante slide in it. She wore a plastic coat that someone had given her and a dirty cotton skirt. Her hands were filthy. She pulled the edge of the shawl round the child as if she wanted to shelter it from something. In the back of her mind she didn't want the strange woman's eye to fall on the child's face.

'Where is the big site?'

'It's a big field, ma'am. There does be a lot of the travelling people there, a lot of the caravans.'

'She means out at Ballydrum,' John said. 'Is that right?' If Kate thought they were going out to Ballydrum like this, even with the windows open . . .

'Ballydrum,' Ann agreed. In a strange way she felt like the young Guard, that there was no madness that couldn't happen in the city, that the people were beyond all understanding.

'We'll drive you out,' Kate said.

'Kate!' John said. 'I've got to——'

'If you let me down now,' Kate whispered, 'I'll leave you.'

John swung left and left again and they headed for Ballydrum. 'Have you got a caravan?'

Ann shook her head. 'We have a tent, ma'am.' It made her feel sick to be in the car and going so fast. She had been in a lorry once and she had been sick in that, and she always felt sick even in the bus. Once she had been sick and the conductor had put her off although she had paid her fare, and she had had to walk the rest of the way.

'How are your father and mother now? Where are they?'

'In the site.' She was going to be sick. She put the edge of the shawl up over her face and shut her eyes. If she was sick in the car would they call a Guard? What would they do to her? Why had they made her get in? She closed her teeth against vomiting. The lady went on saying things, half the time in Palantus and half the time in gamman. It was seven miles to Ballydrum and it seemed like seventy. She sat crouching and swaying as the car rounded corners, stopped, started; clutching the shawl round the child, round her own face, the waves of sickness coming up over her until she thought she would faint and fall sideways, and the queer lady going talk talk talk until she didn't know what she was answering, yes no no yes, what was she saying? Married? *Lospo?* Long? Five years. *Sukr lyiman.*

It made her think of the country, of the wedding, of the great day it had been. The flows of drink, and the singing, and the dancing, and the priest blessing them. Right in the porch of the church. He had been a good man. And her own man in his fine shirt, and the horses and the fire blazing, and the caravans, and the long night it had been. Until all was quiet and there were only the two of them snug and dark in the li, touch to touch and it had seemed all wrong, even with the blessing, that they could touch one another like that, her hand under his shirt against his skin and his hands . . . The blood came into her face even remembering, and long and many times he had touched her since. But that first time had been like the world's end.

She had often thought that if they had stayed in the country it would always have been like that. But they had all said there was the fine money to be got in Dublin, begging and getting the scrap, and down in the west the times got harder and the settled people angrier, and you couldn't sell a bucket from one summer to another. Her father had gone on making them. He even made them in the site, one now and one then. And gave them away to someone that needed a bucket. Making them out of old bits of tin that he found because he couldn't afford to buy the sheets of tin if he was going to give the buckets away. And there had been a time when he had sold a bucket every day. Maybe two and three. At a fair, or in a town that had had no travelling people for a while back calling there. He had told her of a time when he even mended buckets, and kettles, and pots, out of the settled people's houses. When the people said hail and welcome to the travelling families, because there was work for them, mending things and making clothes-pegs.

'Is this it?' the lady said.

The car stopped. She hadn't been sick. Glory be to God. She'd be able to lie down a little. Maybe he would let her lie down an hour before he wanted his supper. She had the pound. And fifteen shillings she had begged. It had been a good day after all. She had to wait for the lady to open the door because she didn't know how to open it. She was in the air at last. The seven curses of God on motor cars. Even the site looked good after being in that thing.

The site was a seven-acre field on the edge of Ballydrum Corporation housing estate. A year ago it had been green grass. The Corporation had bought it a few years earlier from a farmer together with other land, for the future expansion of Ballydrum, and it had lain idle until one night the previous June a family of tinkers had turned in through the unlocked gateway and pitched camp. No one had bothered them and they had bothered no one, until a month later there were ten families, there were complaints, and the Corporation began moves to evict them. An English woman, a Mrs Wynyard, who had fought battles for the gypsies in England, began to involve herself, and gathered together forty families in caravans. She led them in a giant procession through Dublin, out to Ballydrum, and into the field, and showed them how to barricade themselves in. All that autumn and winter there had been skirmishes with the Guards, with Corporation work-men, no one wanting to press things to a conclusion, until in the spring the Corporation had promised permanent sites for any travellers who wanted them, with huts and running water, and a truce had been declared as far as Ballydrum was concerned. It would take a while, but in the meantime no one would evict them.

Mrs Wynyard had gone back to England, triumphant, and the tinkers waited, relatively undisturbed. By then the numbers had swollen to about eighty families, and the site field had become a sea of mud in the winter rain, and a dustbowl in the summer. But a dustbowl that a day's rain would turn back to a swamp in which it would be impossible to walk without getting mud to the knees. A brown, clinging mud that stank of excrement.

Kate, and John, stood looking. Caravans, old carts, huts made of tin and cardboard and plywood and tarred paper, tents made of anything that would cover three or four hooped sticks, crowding the brown desert of dust and filth. Dogs nosed. Starving, mangy, scabbed dogs, some of them tied by bits of frayed rope to the axles of caravans, some of them running loose. Lurchers, half greyhound, half anything. A boxer, ribs sticking out like a skeleton under dusty leather, the hair worn off its hips. An old alsatian, limping on a folding foreleg.

Children played in the dust. Everywhere there were rusty tins, scraps and shreds and sheets of torn paper, rags of cloth, rotting pieces of food, rings of charred wood round dead fires, burned kettles, plastic bottles, glass bottles, broken glass, cardboard boxes, broken chairs, old motor tyres. Horses roamed between the caravans, searching for grass, for anything to eat. Mostly they were better fed than the dogs because they were valuable. Men sat in the doorways of caravans or of huts, or in the mouths of tents. Not many women, because the women were still out on their rounds, begging. The men sat with their hands hanging, smoking, waiting for the women to come back.

Some other men were by a pile of scrap metal, loading it on to a cart. Iron piping, an old, rusted stove, a brass bed-head, a copper cylinder, the radiator out of a car, some car batteries. The horse stood with its head hanging, waiting to be hit. The sun fell on everything, gilding the desolation. The hedges and fences round the field were so draped with coloured rags and torn paper that they seemed festive, decorated.

'I'll be going, lady,' Ann said. As an afterthought, she said, 'Thank you kindly for driving me, gentleman.' She felt better now that she was standing in the air, and was beside her own people.

'We're coming with you,' Kate said. 'Where's your father's caravan?' She and John had heard about the Ballydrum row, but the worst of it had happened when they were on Inis Beag in the summer. She could scarcely believe what she was looking at, remembering the tinker camps of Mayo. Dirty and slovenly enough, with rags on the hedges and a burned-out fire and a few bottles left behind. But not like this. John looked at it with his mind almost clenched, not wanting to think about it, not wanting to think that these were people. But it wasn't possible not to realize it. He went treading slowly and carefully in behind Kate, through the gateway that was no longer barricaded against the Corporation and the Guards, between the ruts of dried mud and the dog dirt and the human dirt and the bits of refuse and the horse droppings. The smell wasn't overpowering but it was bad enough. Flies hummed and rasped in the sunlight, children shouted. He had seen worse in Africa. But he hadn't. Not really. Not this condemned hopelessness. Even in the shanty towns there had been life, there had been a sense that the future belonged to the black children, for all their swollen stomachs and their running eyes. But there was no future here.

Against his will he felt himself getting caught, like thorns catching at cloth, catching at his mind, his conscience. They went between caravans, most of them the old style, with shafts resting on the ground, gypsy caravans, green canvas over hoops, the bodywork painted, bright red, bright yellow, blue and gold, a swaggering of colour. But some of the caravans were modern, made to be pulled behind cars, and already they had a battered, desolate look, dirty, neglected, poor in spirit as well as fact.

Ann Connor stopped in front of one of the modern caravans. A dog was tied underneath it and it snarled and then shrank farther into the shadows between the wheels. The door was locked. 'They aren't here,' Ann said. They went on towards the back of the site. There was a smell of smoke mixed with the other smells, cooking fires, tea stewing, and for a second again Kate remembered the wood at Castle Lennox, the warm eye of the fire between the trees in the darkness, the excitement, the belonging.

'I can't bear it,' she whispered to John.

'You're bringing us.' He tried to sound harsh and indifferent. But he couldn't bear it either. Don't, he told himself, don't think about it, you can't do anything, it isn't a programme, they don't have to be here, you're not concerned. For years, for years and years he hadn't been concerned, not since they had come back here. As if he had frozen his mind to kill something, keep it quiet. What was the use of feeling anything, caring about anything here? Sit loose to it, use it. If Kate wanted to get involved, all right, but he wouldn't. It would have been easier to get involved in Africa than here. Make a row about Oxman Street, yes. But only for television, only for a programme. He hadn't felt it, he had only used it, as something he could take up for a week, and drop again, turning to something else that would make next week's, next Friday's programme. If the poor of Oxman Street wanted to fight they had their champions; Father Tracey, Con Danaher, Denis Farrell; they had the vote, they had the Dail. They didn't need John Lennox. Outside of a television programme they wouldn't even accept him, with his taint of the Ascendancy, the old gentry, the Protestants. Let him keep his place. A grand man for television, as good as the English, good old John, our John. But don't let him get too close, don't let him get mixed up in our affairs, real Irish affairs, not in any way that matters. That was for the Father Traceys and the Danahers and Farrells. We'll mind our own quarrels thank you Mr Lennox, and a damn good day to you. Put us on the telly, well and good, but don't come down our street with us, calling yourself Irish, interfering in our affairs.

But this was different. These people had no champions, no votes that they knew how to use; nothing, no one. Only the cranks and the Mrs Wynyards and a shilling from passers-by. But a shilling wasn't enough. And like Kate a few minutes earlier he thought of Castle Lennox and the wood and childhood and what the tinkers had once seemed to him, and the smell of the camp caught his throat like a hand, like guilt.

The smell came out of the huts and the caravans. Men stared, suspicious. An old woman. Children. Dogs. Flies. A horse with scabbed flanks and filmed eyes, hobbled with a twist of rope. Ann was bending down by a tarpaulin shelter, putting the child on the ground. The tarpaulin was stretched over a few bent sticks, one side of it held down by heavy stones, the other side tied to the roots of the thorn hedge running along the back of the field. Inside the tarpaulin shelter there was a torn mattress lying on the naked earth, a pile of old clothes packed down into a hollow nest for the child, a blackened kettle and a frying-pan. Behind the tarpaulin there was an empty tea-chest. A puppy was tied on a short length of cord and wire to one of the hedge roots, and it whined and tried to get to the child, and Ann. There was a broken saucer beside it with nothing in it.

'Himself must be away out,' Ann said. She was glad he was not there. He wouldn't have liked her bringing strangers to see the way they lived. Maybe he was down the road drinking. The queer lady was touching the puppy.

'You have it tied too tight,' Kate said.

'It gets away on me if I don't tie it.'

'Poor little thing,' Kate said. 'It's an alsatian. I think it's even a thoroughbred. Where did you get it?'

Ann made a vague gesture round the camp. People don't get puppies from anywhere. They're just there, they get born.

Kate looked at the tent and away from it, her fingers automatically untwisting the piece of wire round the puppy's throat. 'John, can you get this off?' It whined, trying to wriggle out of their hands. 'Why are you—have you no caravan at all?'

'We had one but it broke on us.' Two years ago. A car had hit them in the dark. The horse had been killed and the shafts and one of the axles and two wheels of the caravan had been smashed past mending. They hadn't tried to mend it, they had just taken what they could carry and got away as fast as they could. The man had threatened them with the Guards for not having a light. They hadn't even got the canvas off the caravan roof. When they had gone back to look for it it was already gone, someone had stolen it.

'And you've been living like this?'

Ann nodded. How else could she live?

'Doesn't your husband earn any money?'

'He does his best, ma'am.'

Kate started to say something and stopped. What was the point? She suddenly wanted to get away from here. John had finished untying the puppy and put it down and it waddled and scrambled on unsteady, splayed paws into the safety of the tent.

'We'll come back again,' Kate said. 'Will you tell your mother? ... Haven't ... couldn't they help you ... I mean, with the child ... were you sleeping like this even in the winter?'

'It was bad all right,' Ann said. 'They do take her in with them in the worst of it into the caravan but I don't like to have her away from me. I fret for her.'

She had stood up again after crouching to open the flap of the tent and let the child down on the mattress, and she was swaying slightly on her feet. It was a long time since she had had bread and tea that morning. She wasn't consciously hungry but she felt she couldn't stand up much longer. And she'd have to tie up the puppy again when they were gone. But even that was too much effort. And he'd be coming back soon, drunk and wanting his tea. But at least she had money, she had thirty-five midyog and she'd saved the bus fare. The new baby sagged inside her stomach, heavy as a sack of scrap iron. It wasn't stirring yet, not kicking like Sal had done at the same time, but so heavy she could die of it. They were going at last.

'We'll be back soon,' Kate said. She took all the money out of her purse and stuffed it into Ann's slack, unprepared hand. She felt the notes without being able to believe what they were. Her mouth opened. The queer lady and the man were already walking away. She sat down on the mattress. Sal was whimpering, the puppy vexing her, tearing at her clothes with its teeth. She wanted to hit at the puppy but she was too tired. Too tired even to count the money.

'I'm hungry,' Sal whimpered. When the big people were there she had been afraid to say it, afraid to say anything. 'I'm hungry. I'm hungry.'

'In a minute, love. A small minute. Mamma get the pek. Let mamma rest a bit. *Mamma surhu, toman surhu.*'

'Mamma not tired, Sal tired, Sal hungry.' She began to cry, not genuinely, but forcing herself to cry so that her mother would give her some bread. She twisted her fingers in the puppy's fur and the puppy squealed. Inside the sagging tarpaulin it was stiflingly hot after the day of sun. Neither of them noticed the smell but it was hard to breathe, even with the flap open. Ann lay on her back, her hand clenched on the money.

In the car driving back to Dublin and Mornington Road and their big, cool flat, Kate and John said nothing for a long time. It's bloody terrible, he thought, and it's bloody hopeless, and there isn't a thing I can do about it or anyone else can do about it, and there isn't any sense in getting worked up about it, making ourselves miserable for nothing, for no point. Give them money, her money. Even a caravan, even a horse if they hadn't got one. And then? She'd have another kid, and another, and another, and another. Like Castle Lennox coming back on him, childhood, the Colonel, a hundred, a thousand things he had never wanted to remember, never wanted to think of again. Like something breaking inside his mind. Like something rushing into an empty space. Hollow. I have been hollow, a hollow man. Nothing. And this could fill it? Don't be stupid. Don't be imbecile. I've got my work, Kate, money, a lot of money now— God, I have, I really have. What the hell do I mean, hollow? Believing in nothing, feeling nothing, nothing real, nothing that's too hard to reach, that means getting hurt.

'How much would a caravan cost?' Kate said.

'A hundred. Maybe more.'

'We could afford it.'

'Her husband probably sold the last one for drink. He'd sell this one.'

'We can't leave her like that. And a horse? If they had a horse they could get out of there.'

'Do they want to get out?'

'The smell of it. Doesn't anybody care?'

'There was an Englishwoman. I think the Corporation are doing something.'

'Not very fast.'

'What can they do? What could anybody do with them? Take the children away from them? Put the adults in a concentration camp, teach them a trade? What trade? Making clothespegs?'

'I know. I know. And that puppy. I hated leaving it there. I'm sure she'll tie it up again.'

'The puppy?'

'I know, I know. But somehow it seems almost worse. Oh, I don't know what I'm thinking, I'm so horrified. How can it be like that? How can we put up with it? People go past there every day, there's a hospital up the road, there are houses opposite. People see it and—what? Nothing.'

'We hadn't even seen it until today.'

'We got worried about Oxman Street——'

'I didn't get worried. It was just a programme. A damn good programme.'

'Make this a damn good programme.'

He didn't answer, and they drove in silence, back from the concrete desert of Ballydrum, the wide, grey, despairing streets, the houses like concrete packing-cases, each with its TV aerial and its dusty patch of front garden; back from Ballydrum to the older Dublin, the slums along the canal, the dilapidated respectability of Ranelagh and Rathmines, on to the tree-lined pleasantness and quiet decent solidity of Ballsbridge. Mornington Road.

They parked the Mercedes on the tarmac drive in front of the house—the house that they could think of buying now, stay in their own flat, let the other two—eight, nine, ten pounds a week each flat if they furnished them decently. Up the stone steps to the front door. It was always a little strange going in now that Shah was dead. The sense of emptiness, of nothing—no dark shadow padding out of the drawing-room or from under the stairs to greet them. Clean and cool and hollow. Don't let yourself get involved, he thought. But he was thinking of the programme. A damn good programme? A lot of it on film. The dogs nosing in the rubbish. The filth. A child—find a very young one, follow it round with a Bolex, hand held. No commentary. Just Irish music. 'The Foggy Dew'? 'The Bold Fenian Men'? 'The Quiet Land of Erin'? Christ, he was getting angry. He hadn't been angry about Oxman Street, about the hospital programme, about the corporal punishment programme, about the strike down in Abbeyfehily, about anything. He had never been angry about anything. Never felt anything. Why this?

'Get us a drink, Kate,' he said.

She gave him a gin and tonic and took one herself, without talking. For God's sake, what was she playing at, the understanding wife, the companion of the telly genius?

'Say something for God's sake.'

'I want to get that puppy tomorrow.'

'Are you trying to annoy me?'

'I don't know. Does it annoy you?'

'Everything about that place annoys me. Why did we have to go out there?' He finished his drink and went to look out of the window at the Mercedes. It had been his joy three hours ago. Almost new. Beautiful. A beautiful car. Why am I alive, why do I bother, he thought. What's it for? A new car. Buy this house. Oh wonderful. Summer in—where will we go? Morocco? I do a job, a bloody good job, I get well paid, people are satisfied, better than satisfied. The right man in the right place. That silly old fool Matty talking about politics. Who the hell would accept John Lennox as a politician? The first speech he made outside a TV studio he'd get eggs thrown at him. Bricks. John Lennox on TV fine, our John, Ireland's answer to Robin Day. Did you hear what he said last night, did you see your man's face when John asked him about what he was proposing to do ... but John Lennox politician? That Proddy? That West British bastard? Did your daddy die for Ireland?

'Minister, what do you propose to do for the tinkers?' God

damn Kate, and that smelly slut and her brat and the bloody
dog.

'It'd have worms, it'd be rotten with them.'

'We'll get it wormed. Every pup has worms.'

'I sometimes think you'd be better off with a black eye.'

She came and stood beside him. He looked at her, startled for
a second. As though she was challenging him, almost inviting
him to hit her. He looked into her eyes, trying to read them, but
he never could, not now, not ever. And the easy superiority of
being a man, of jeering at the way she thought, about the tinkers,
about the puppy, about anything, fell away, and they looked at
each other, John and Kate, like looking over a wall, hardly knowing one another, while their shadow selves, their everyday selves,
gestured and talked in front of them, like shadows on the wall;
meaningless gestures, meaningless talk. But there was nothing
else to do except go on gesturing, go on talking. She put her
hand against his waist, under his coat. 'You're getting fat.'

'I've got fat,' he said. And then: 'But not very.'

'Are you going to do a programme?'

'What bloody good would a programme do? What did it do
for anything else we've ever touched? Half a million people
saying, Isn't it awful? and then going to bed.'

'Go on telling them.'

'You can't say things twice on TV'

'Tell them in the papers. Tell them in the street. John, don't
you understand? You're someone. You're a name. People will
listen. Only you're not telling them anything.'

'For the love of God. I tell them once a week.'

'You've just said.'

'I know. There isn't anything I've wanted to tell them.'

She went back to the sideboard and poured two more drinks.
'There's something so bloody awful happening to this country,
you must want to tell it. How can we argue about office blocks
when there are people living in ditches? What will happen to
those children? They'll never go to school, they'll never know
anything, they'll grow up to live in more ditches. If there are any
ditches left. And it isn't just the tinkers. It's half the country.

Raised for export. Or for Ballydrum. Did you see those houses? Can you imagine living your life out in a housing estate like that? Being a child in it? No wonder they get flick-knives and slash bus seats. When you start to think you go mad.'

'That's why I don't want to start thinking. Kate, Kate, for Christ's sake will you leave me alone, will you leave everything alone? We're well off. We've got some money. We can buy this bloody house. We're secure.'

'We could have been secure in London,' she said. 'We came back here because this is our place. We can't go on living as if we don't really belong. The island. I still feel wretched that we sold out——'

'Oh Jesus.'

'Matty rang again this morning. I didn't tell you.'

He went on staring out of the window at the Mercedes. A caravan. A horse. He imagined riding in a caravan, an empty road, winding away over the hills, down the far side to a wood, a river. We are the hollow men. We are the stuffed men. He must have been thinking of television when he wrote that. Our dried voices when we whisper together are quiet and meaningless as wind in dry grass. John Lennox T.D. Would that be any better? Minister, what do you propose to do? Is it true that? Would the Minister admit that? A caravan and a horse. Buy someone happiness for two hundred pounds. Could you?

He remembered her coming over the ditch in Mayo, by the side of the road, ten—no, twelve, twelve years ago. Like a fox. And now she looked like one of the mongrels under the caravans. Romantic Ireland's dead and gone. What was the good of anything? John Lennox, Minister for Posts and Telegraphs. I must refer the question about camping facilities for the Itinerant Community to my right honourable colleague the Minister for Pests and Vermin Control. On the subject of vandalism in telephone kiosks the department is satisfied that . . .

Under the tarpaulin by the hedge at the back of the site Ann lay on the mattress, not asleep, not awake. She was also seeing a country road. Very early in the morning. The smell of rain and the sky bright and pale. She didn't think of it, analyse it. She only saw it, felt it on her skin, smelled the rain, the wet hedges, heard the sharp fall of the pony's hooves on the wet road, drying in the sun. The grey eye of a lake, the tuft of trees against the sky, a bird singing. The road, the road, stretching far far ahead of them, for ever and ever, never ending. Dark and the firelight. Sleep and morning. The road, the road. A road with no cars on it, no shaylogs stopping them, saying, 'What have you got there in that sack?' Or, 'Move along, we don't want the like of you people here, this is a decent village.'

The mouth of the tarpaulin darkened and Luke was there, swaying, carrying bottles. 'What you doing?' he said.

'Lying down.'

'Gerrup and get me tea.'

He was drunk, but not badly drunk. He had two flagons of cider under his arm, and he collapsed on to the mattress where she had been lying and lay back, cradling them.

'Where you been, Luke?' She wouldn't tell him about the money yet.

'Around. Your da an' ma were with me. The shaylogs ran us so I come back. What you get?'

She still held the money hidden. 'A bit. A good bit.'

'There's my girl. Yer ma's a good girl, eh, Sal? Have a suck.'

'Don't give her that.'

'What's the harm? Cider, lovey. Why d'you let the bloody pup off of the rope, eh?'

'Look what I got,' she said quickly.

He rolled forward to look, seeing the notes, the crumpled wad of them. He was a big, still youngish man, but bigger to look at than in reality. There was no thickness in the shoulders, no substance in his body. The skin of his face already had a papery, crumpled fineness, like worn tissue paper, grey and dirty under his eyes, brown with windburn on his cheeks and forehead, the brown giving him a look of spurious health. The body of a man who had been reared on bread and dripping and fried eggs and an occasional rasher. When he drank it went into his head like gunpowder.

'Show us.' He took the wad of money and held it, thumbing it out flat like gouging something. He had to let go of the bottles to count it and they clinked together. 'Arrah damn there's a fine skimisk here. Where d'you get it? Eh?' He caught at her and she drew back, confident now. The violence between them was not all one way. When he got to a certain stage of drink she would hit him as soon as he would hit her, and the more so if she had had a drink as well. Her fear of him was simple reason and watchfulness and a sense of the rightness of things rather than subservience. Only when she was tired she had no strength to defend herself, she had no pride. But she was rested now.

'Am I the good one?' she said.

'You are, you are by God, you're the best. Did you byeg it?'

'Maybe I did and maybe I didn't.'

'Eight pound.' His face darkened. 'Did you steal it blast you? Will the shaylogs be here on us?'

'I did not. I was give it. By a lady that knows gamman.'

'*Lush mo kunya.*'

'It's true. She does.' She had been lighting the fire while they were talking and setting the kettle on it. There was not enough water in it, but getting water meant going to one of the houses across the road, and the nearest houses were sick of giving water. She might have to go a half-mile, a mile before she'd find a house that would fill the kettle. And back again.

'Sal lovey,' she said. 'Ask the nice Morrisseys for a bit of water. Take that tin, lovey.' The Morrisseys were in a caravan a few yards up the hedge. They might have water.

'You never have any bloody water you stupid spurkra. When am I getting my tea?' He lay back and drank from the neck of the bottle.

When he was really drunk she wouldn't be afraid of him at all. She'd creep in beside him and tie the flap of the tarpaulin shut and tell Sal to go sleep, close her eyes and then she'd show him was she a spurkra. If only the child in her would move. She wondered sometimes was it dead in her like that woman in the hut that had a dead son, everything perfect, only it was dead and coming before it was expected. She watched Sal tottering back with the can of water, the puppy running round her, threatening to trip her up, water slopping out on to the ground. When it slopped the puppy tried to lick up the wet.

There was nothing for the tea only bread and fat. She put the pan on the fire beside the kettle. With the money they could buy meat, but the shop was a long way down the road. Tomorrow. If he hadn't taken it all for drink. But he'd be drunk soon and she'd take some of it back from him, he wouldn't remember how much there had been. Around her the camp settled towards the evening. This refuse heap of the travelling people, the children of Cain, the children of the dispossessed; of old clans driven out by the Normans and the Tudors, by Cromwell and by Famine; driven out of the fat lands into the bogs and the western mountains; driven to join the wanderers already on the roads, already in the wild places; travelling smiths with their bellows and their anvils and their dark faces, selling knives and mending ploughs; soldiers from broken armies, widows of dead men murdered in a raid, children run from burning houses, from the soldiers, escaped into the wilderness; all the dispossessed of history, the deep foundations of the Irish people. Here in their last stand.

When she had made the tea he was too drunk to want it and she shared it with Sal. The puppy got one of the pieces of fried bread out of Sal's hand and ran away with it into the dtich beyond the hedge. When he had finished it he came back and licked the frying-pan clean, burning his tongue.

'Time for sleeping, Sal lovey.' She was too tired and full of food to tie up the puppy. She couldn't find the string or the wire. If he was lost he was lost. She crawled in through the half-closed flap of the tarpaulin and pulled it shut behind her. Luke was snoring, but she would wake him soon enough. Spurkra.

22

Ann Gallagher, that had been Ann Connor, lost her baby a month after the Lennoxes found her, and spent a fortnight in hospital. When she came out the Lennoxes had bought a caravan for her, and a horse. They had got to know her husband, Luke, in the interval, and developed some kind of relationship with him. It couldn't be described as anything approaching friendship. The idea of friendship with settled people was outside his comprehension. He could barely bring himself to trust anything a settled person said to him, he couldn't understand their motives, or grasp that Kate and John wanted to help. It was useless asking him for promises about what he'd do with the caravan if he got it.

'Do you want a caravan?' Kate said, because at times he seemed to be saying that he was perfectly happy under the tarpaulin. 'If you don't get Ann into a proper bed she's going to be really ill.' It took a long time to get it out of him.

'It's the horse,' he said at last. 'The boys along Ballydrum do be taking them an' riding them to death, or else they lame them.' He made a slashing movement with his hand like a knife houghing a horse's sinews.

'Then don't stay here,' John said. 'Get out of Dublin.'

Luke Gallagher nodded as if he agreed. What was the point of trying to explain to these people? That you can't beg in the country like you can in Dublin. That there isn't the scrap to be got, and if there is you can't sell it downaways in a village. And yet the road called him as it had called Ann. And he felt miserable in the city, it pressed on him, like handcuffs on his wrists, he was all the time vaguely frightened. Not physically, not exactly frightened, even, but uneasy. The people, the houses, the Guards, the traffic, the being stuck in the one place, the one hedge, the same people round him every day when he woke. As if he felt himself trapped. Only when he was drunk he felt better, he felt free. When he was drunk he wasn't afraid.

John built the caravan into the programme, the gift of it, without saying in the commentary where it came from. Simply 'from friends of the travellers'. He felt ashamed as he did it, and yet it seemed worth while. He kept the camera hidden, well out of the way, with a long-range lens, and had Luke drive the caravan and the horse into the site, and close to the tent. Ann was lying on the mattress, in shadow, and John had to call her before she heard, and came to her knees in the mouth of the tent to see what was happening. She still looked very ill from the miscarriage, and the time in hospital had left her cleaner but even paler than she had been. Her face looked drawn, with misery for the loss of the child, and coming back to the site, and the mattress under the tarpaulin. She didn't regret leaving the hospital. She had hated sleeping under a roof, she hadn't been able to breathe and she had been so frightened of the nuns with their silence and their mystery that she had thought she was going to die, but to come back to the site was like a pain starting again that she had half forgotten, and that would go on for ever, that would never end.

'Look at the caravan!' John called, keeping himself out of camera view. He wasn't using a mike, he'd put in the sound later. 'Look who's driving it!'

She looked up, puzzled. A horse. A caravan. Luke. Luke driving a horse!

Luke had the reins gathered in one hand, and was gesturing with the other at the horse, the caravan, himself, his face suddenly full of joy. 'Look at the rog, Grunles! What do you think to it, byor?'

She came out of the tent slowly, not believing what she was seeing. She was only out of hospital an hour. Kate had brought her out and told her nothing except that they'd see her later. Luke had been gone, and she had thought he was away drinking with her father and mother again, or with the others.

'What? What do I think?' She shook her head, not taking it in, and then, as it came to her what had happened, that the lady had done this, had got this for them, not trusting her eyes to believe it. Sal came out of the tarpaulin behind her, hiding behind her shoulders, peering over one shoulder and then the other, her face purple with jam and dirt from the ground.

'Luke!' Ann whispered. She reached out her hand towards the horse. 'Ours?'

'Ours lakin. Ours all.' And then he realized that the settled man was listening, could hear what he said, could see his face, and he stiffened into sullenness. 'Ask the gentleman.' But all that showed on film was Ann's face. White, drained of strength, full of wonder, her hand touching the horse, the shafts and the chain, the leather of the harness, the wheel, the iron tyre, seat and side and tight canvas, her hand exploring, her face quiet and still, her eyes huge, wide and dark and filled with thinking. All the travelling, all the roads, all the wideness of the sky.

'It's not true,' she breathed. And then: 'Sal, Sal! Look at the rog! Look at the nice gyofan! Touch the horsey!' The horse flicked his ears and waited. He was a tinker's horse, bought from tinkers, used to the smells, the sounds and feelings of a tinkers' camp, trained to harness, to hard pulling and long days and grazing by roadsides. The hand on his neck was a familiar hand, tinker woman's touching hand.

'Look in the back,' John said, and she went to look. Bunk beds and blankets, cooking gear and a bundle of clothes, cups and saucers and a box of food, a small iron stove with a chimney through the roof. She stayed looking in, hiding her face. 'Cut!' John shouted to the cameraman and felt as he had been betraying a friend. Later on he'd get the rest of the shots, the tent, the transfer to the caravan, the going out of the site.

It didn't occupy much of the film, only a couple of minutes. They left the tarpaulin where it was, because another family wanted it. Ann lifted Sal into the back, climbed after her up the folding steps, closed the half door. 'Drive her out,' John shouted to Luke, and Luke snapped his fingers, caught the horse a light crack across the rump with his ash stick, swung its head round. Bumping over the ruts, caravan lurching, pots rattling, Ann swaying, Sal's head with its yellow curls and jam-smeared crimson cheeks like a small sun rising over the rim of the half door.

'Giddap, giddap.'

A few of the site-dwellers watching, not knowing what was going on, too shy to come and ask, or too indifferent. Out of the gate, on to the Ballydrum road. Turn right for the West. 'What's ahead of them?' the commentary said, as the camera watched the caravan grow small down the long road, factories on one side, fields on the other. 'Freedom? Or a hunt for another site like this, in a smaller town, with less tolerance, less chance of begging a living, less chance of gathering scrap, of sending the child to any kind of school? But at least the caravan is warm and dry, it'll keep out the wet. And someone has eased his conscience with a handsome gift. Perhaps someone else's conscience will be stirred by the new tenants of the hedge tarpaulin.' The camera cutting to another girl sitting by the tent mouth, boiling a kettle on a fire of sticks, glad to have even a mattress by a ditch, somewhere to lie down.

The programme went out in October, and John used it in his mind as a test, to decide whether he'd try for politics or not. It was a good programme and he knew it. Not sentimental, not a bleeding-heart half-hour. But telling in hard terms that here were ten thousand Irish citizens treated like outcasts, robbed of every decent chance in life, even of the chance to see their children do better than themselves. If it had the impact it ought to have, if it stirred anyone, any reasonable number of people to do anything, he'd stay in television. If it didn't . . .

The end of the programme contrasted the site at Ballydrum with the new skyscraper blocks. Gandon House. Liberty Hall that housed the Irish Transport and General Workers Union. Office blocks for Semi-State Companies. Towers of new flats like glass and marble cliffs. Gandon House and the tarpaulin under the hedge. 'Ireland's on the march,' the commentary said. 'On the march to prosperity, to the full life. You can hear it in the streets, see it in the factories, the new buildings, the ranks of new cars outside the offices and flats and the fine new hotels.' A new American-owned hotel, and a tin and cardboard shack, refuse and a skeleton-thin dog and a child playing with it, eating the same crust of bread together. The dustbins outside the hotel, crammed to overflowing with empty asparagus tins, with vegetable peelings, wine-bottles, all the offals of the good life. The camera closing on an empty magnum of Champagne, gold neck sticking out of a dustbin, from the congealed remains of a dish of chicken-à-la-king. Cutting to the wine-bottle in a tinker's hand, cheap Irish sherry from a supermarket, green label with shamrocks on it, dirty hand, corded, wind-burned throat pulsing as the drink goes down.

'We're moving forward into the world of expense accounts, of long week-ends and country cottages and holidays abroad. There's been a revolution, a new industrial revolution, and we've won! We've won! Or have we? Does this look like victory?' And the camera swept its lens across the site at Ballydrum. Huts, caravans, patchwork tents made out of anything that might hold off the rain; torn mattresses, refuse, filth, despair. A small child in gum-boots, one boot bigger than the other, both for a left foot, tottering unsteadily towards a tent. 'If this child has no share in it what kind of victory have we won?'

There was a reaction to the programme, of a kind. A number of people thought it terrible to give a horse to tinkers who would almost certainly be unkind to it. Several viewers complained about the condition of the dogs in the camp. Residents of Ballydrum wrote in both to the Station and to the newspapers, complaining that they were held up in the programme as monsters of cruelty who injured the tinkers' horses, denied them a cup of cold water, and slept snug in their houses while women died of bronchitis in makeshift shelters across the road from them.

'If the people who make these programmes like to come and live opposite the tinkers for a month, maybe they'd talk differently at the end of it. Let them go to the door ten and twenty times in a morning to fill a kettle of water for the tinkers that are all the time calling. And another twenty times to be asked for a cup of sugar, or any old clothes or 'a few coppers missus'. And maybe threatened for not giving, or not giving enough. Or have a tinker's horse grazing in your front garden eating the few bits of flowers you got to grow in it. Or get your children bitten by a tinker dog that might have Heaven knows what wrong with it, and be afraid going down to the shops for the drunken tinker men and women lying on the pavements outside the supermarket, or fighting each other in the road. These people have never done a day's work in their lives and never will unless they're made. The Corporation takes money off of us in rent and what does it do about hundreds of tinkers squatting in front of our houses spreading diseases and danger? Nothing. The next election I know who gets my vote and the votes of all in this part of Ballydrum. It's the candidate who says he's going to get the Corporation do their duty about these people and get them shifted.'

The people who wrote in praise of the programme were the ones who were already doing something, and were faintly reproachful that the programme hadn't recognized how much was being done. A priest wrote to point out that some devoted nuns were teaching catechism to any of the children they could get hold of, preparing them for their first Communion. 'They will not tell you of this work themselves.'

A group that had been fighting for the tinkers' rights for years wrote to suggest that the programme might have shown the other side of the coin as well; the permanent site with sanitary facilities that the Corporation had recently established, where a dozen families were living in conditions half-way towards real settlement.

Patrick Lacey, who had moved from the *Marian Weekly* to the *Sunday Freeman*, wrote in his television column:

The problem of the tinkers is a very real one, and no doubt Irish Television deserves a word of praise for devoting half an hour of its precious time to the matter. But the thoughtful Catholic viewer will ask himself (or herself) why was no mention made *throughout the programme* of religion? It is well known to those interested in such matters that the itinerants as a group are among the most devoted Catholics to be found anywhere. They love and cherish their religion. Yet this we were not told. Nor were we told of the devoted work done for the itinerants by certain clergy. And nuns. E.g., the education of itinerant children, the giving of hot dinners, of warm clothing in winter, etc. The programme showed us none of this. Only the material problems, and these were contrasted by cunning camera work with new buildings and the life in expensive hotels. What message were we meant to draw from this? Surely that those who live in the new expensive buildings are wicked, because they are responsible for the plight of the poor itinerants. E.g., Capitalism is wicked. Whereas Socialism would cure all such evils at once. No doubt the people who now live in such hotels would soon find themselves in the itinerant camp and vice versa. Only there would be barbed wire round the camp and guards with sub-machine-guns. Seeing such a programme any intelligent viewer (and most of our Irish viewers are more intelligent than the propaganda makers of Irish Television are willing to believe) will ask himself (or herself), *Why was this programme made?* Was it made out of genuine concern for the poor? Or simply out of hatred for our present social system? Which happens to be a Catholic social system.

To Patrick Lacey's annoyance a sub-editor removed his 'e.g.s' and tidied up his grammar slightly, earning Patrick Lacey's undying suspicion that he too was a Communist agent. But the message of the column remained substantially unchanged.

It was a message that found a large portion of the community ready to listen to it; and there were many more people than Patrick Lacey announcing it: that Ireland was facing a Communist conspiracy, many-headed, many-sided, skilful and insidious; a hidden but perceptible influence behind strikes, squatters' campaigns, tenants' rights associations, students' protests; behind criticisms of the clergy, of the archbishop, of Catholic doctrines that had been uncritically accepted for centuries; it was seen in the columns of the *Irish Times*; and above all in Irish television.

It was a well-known fact among some government supporters that the Studios were not much less than an annexe of the Kremlin. To those of a thoughtful turn of mind it seemed one of those savage paradoxes of history, that Ireland which had remained untouched by evil thoughts throughout the long centuries of poverty, was now rife with Communism at the very moment that the finest Government in its history had brought the country wealth and happiness.

'We're in for rough times,' Marty whispered to Francis on a winter's evening in Moriarty's, early in the new year of 1967. He was in his favourite corner, his stomach well settled on his lap, his legs comfortably apart in their tight serge trousers, polished with age and spilt porter, his broad back leaning against the old brown partition of the snug, his big black hat tipped back on his bald, slightly sweating scalp. 'Rough times, Franky. And the next election is going to be the cruncher. If we lose that one, then the next stop is Moscow. I'm not joking, Franky. The new chief is worried, I tell you straight. And some of us are more worried than he is. They're like woodworm, Franky, eatin' away, eatin' away at the country unbeknownst to most people, where you can't see them at it. And suddenly—the whole country is crumbling with rottenness.'

It was not Marty's way to talk philosophically about politics and Francis looked at him in surprise.

'Did you hear your man?' Marty was wheezing. 'Your intellectual Professor O'Shaugnessy, God be good to him, saying why hadn't we diplomatic relations with Cuba, no less? Cuba, be Jesus! And Red China to follow no doubt! I tell you, Franky, there's times I wonder did we do the right thing at all bringing money to this country. Weren't we better off the way we were, never a talk of Communism or Socialism or the like from year's end to year's end. Paddy, the same again like a good man.' The curate popped the glasses through the hatch and Marty took his first pull of the new pint. 'There's your real stuff. Half the old houses these days is so destroyed with prosperity and chromium you can't get a decent pint in them for love nor money. Where was I at? Ah. A lovely pint. I was often surprised you didn't have a go at the old politics yourself, Frank.' He fumbled for his inhaler and took an absent-minded and yet meaningful sniff.

'Too busy earning a crust or two,' Francis said. What was the old fox at? The suspicion began to flutter in his chest that all this was leading to something. And it could be only one thing. The Dail. They wanted him to stand. The new chief getting a grip of things, looking round for new men. Francis O'Rourke, T.D. He started to laugh, but it was a pleased laugh. It was stupid, he wouldn't take it, a load of bloody hard work for nothing, he had everything he wanted already, just a load of headaches. But it was a decent thought of someone's. Who'd put in into the Taoiseach's head? Marty? Paddy Gunn? Not Paddy. Paddy thought he was too much of the rough diamond, the bull in the china shop, to put up that kind of an idea. But by Christ that's what was wanted in politics. A man that'd speak his mind, say what was what. Tell some of these creeping bastards exactly what they were. Francis O'Rourke, T.D. Even Maura might like that. And it might not stop at T.D. Minister? Why not? At his age they wouldn't want him to sit on a back bench for ten years learning the business. If they wanted him at all they wanted him for something real. Put some drive into the building programme. Get the bloody houses up without any arsing around with green belts and low density zones and all that crap. Stop breathing down the builders' necks in case they were making a few pounds a house, and you'd soon get some results.

'Did you hear this rumour that the Labour fellers are getting your friend John Lennox to go up for Oxmantown?'

'He's no bloody friend of mine.'

'I thought he wasn't,' Marty said. 'But they're aiming to get him in and more than that. If they win—if they manage to wipe our eye—you'll see me bould John Lennox sittin' on the Front Bench.'

'By God I'd give something to stop that.'

'That's where your money's going, Frank. And all the Guardians' money. Puttin' a spoke in the wheel of bastards like Lennox and O'Shaughnessy, and all the other Reds. But it's going to take more than money, Frank. This time. It's going to take men. The right men in the right seats.'

To his surprise Francis found his heart beating faster. He had thought for a long time that nothing could interest him very much, nothing could make him excited. And now it seemed as though he had been waiting for exactly this, for this moment. Almost as if he had heard what Marty was going to say before he said it, heard it a long time ago. We want you in the Dail, Franky. We need you. Not just your money, but you.

'We're looking for the right kind of lad to put up,' Marty said. 'We've a lot of problems, but this one's urgent. With old Matt O'Carroll pulling out and the shift of voters with the old streets coming down we thought Oxmantown was a safe extra seat for us if we put up a tailor's dummy. But with Lennox standing . . . he'll have half the women voters before he starts.'

'And you want . . .' He wouldn't play hard to get. Ten minutes ago he'd have laughed the idea to hell. Now he'd say yes without being asked twice. Like feeling his blood race again. Like living again. He leaned forward, got his mouth ready to smile.

'We want your boy, Frank. Jo Anthony.'

'You . . . Jo Anthony? You want——?' He felt the blood thickening in the veins of his neck, swelling. Marty Mullins made a great business of emptying his pint.

'Aye, aye,' Marty whispered solemnly, as if he was giving the best of news and reconfirming it. He rapped the heel of his tankard on the sill of the hatch. 'Give us two more like that, Paddy me boy.' The curate popped his young, harassed head through the hatch like a cuckoo out of a Swiss clock, the little doors swinging open, swinging shut again as he withdrew with the pint mug. 'Aye, Franky. He's young, but he's growin'.' He busied himself with the inhaler as if all was settled and the only thing bothering him was getting his breath.

'God dammit,' Francis said in a dangerous tone. He had his whiskey glass in his fist and he lifted it as if he was going to smash it down on something like a hammer. His collar choked him, his eyes seemed to force themselves forward in their sockets, red with blood, like a bull in the narrow channel into the arena smelling blood, smelling death, burning for a last destruction. 'God damn you,' he whispered.

Marty twisted uncomfortably on the worn leather seat. They had said it would be easy, that old Franky would be pleased even, delighted at finding something for his cretin of a boy, at being consulted; Paddy Gunn had sworn Franky wouldn't accept for himself even if it was offered to him. But let him get the hint first that you're after him, not the boy. Then tell him it's his son we're after. It's the way to take him, believe me. It'll take the wind out of his sails. If you ask for the boy straight out he'll tell you to go to hell. But the other way he won't want to let you see his vanity is hurt. And we want his money behind Jo Anthony.

'Listen,' Marty said, throwing the rest of Paddy Gunn's advice to the wind, and dragging enough breath into his chest to last for several persuasive moments. Whatever Paddy knew about psychology he himself knew a hell of a lot more about a man like Franky. 'I'll put the cards on the table with you, Franky. You're fifty times the man your boy will ever be, God love him. If it was brains and drive we needed up in that gas factory beyond you'd be the one for it, but we don't. We need biddable lads that'll bring in the votes and do what the Party tells them. The minute you got up to make an election speech some red hooligan'd start yelling, "Who blocked up the lavatories in Oxman Street?" But we put your young feller up on a platform with his nice little wife beside him——'

A kind of tremor seemed to shake Francis O'Rourke's black cannonball of a head, and then lock it into rigidity. *Nice little wife*. That trollop, that fluffy half-wit, although by God the half of her wits she had were in the right place. The allowance, the house in Foxrock, the job for Jo Anthony in Jofran Holdings, and seeing he was in the office by nine-thirty, even if all he did when he was there was get in the bloody way. The little miminy piminy manners of her buttering and sloothering up Maura and the old lady. She even had Venny saying she wasn't as bad as she'd thought at first. Giving Dermot lectures about respect for his elders. If Jo Anthony got into the Dail there'd be no holding her. That cretin? That moron? A T.D.? God Almighty. He began to laugh, suddenly and harshly, without any humour in the sound. It was bloody funny. It was really bloody effing funny. To work as he'd worked, make what he'd made out of his life. And see that flour-and-water nincompoop get offered the bloody rosette and the silver cup at the end of it.

'If it's him you want then why the sodding hell are you dribbling over me about it?'

'Arrah damn, Franky, don't be like that, man. You know bloody well why I'm talking to you about it. That boy of yours, he's a fine, sensible, religious lad, he's a credit to his mother, he'll be a credit to the Party. But he's only a lad. It'll need you to put the man into him. If he gets into the Dail it'll be you that puts him there. It takes sweat and blood to get anywhere in politics, and that's something a young lad like him doesn't know yet.' He stopped, wheezing for air like a stranded monkfish.

'And cash.'

'Arrah, Franky, always putting the bad word on a thing. A bit o'cash maybe. God damn this asthma. A few quid for expenses, but you don't think we think like that up beyond. What we want is the right lad, the right image, and the right guiding hand behind him. You're a back-room boy, Franky. One of the string-pullers, the fellers that gets things done. What in hell would you do sittin' on one of those benches all day long listening to old fellers like me gassin' away about widows' pensions and grants for a new bridge, or the price of milk? It suits me because I'm too old and set in me ways to do anything else, and I like it. I like looking after people, finagling things a bit here and there for the like of the Maggot Feeney or the Widow Mangan—or even the Widow O'Rourke.' He took a long pull of the new pint that the curate had pushed through the hatch. 'But that's not your line, Franky. You're well out of it, I tell you. Gettin' things rebuilt is your line, gettin' Dublin to look like something, developing the country. What would Jofran do if you pulled out and started worryin' about how many public lavatories there were in Oxmantown and why hadn't the Corporation found a flat for Mrs so-and-so?'

'Did you speak to him yet?'

'No, no, not a word. We'll leave that to you, Franky. Put it to him as your idea. What you've found for him. And it's right for him, Franky. He's cut out for it. Handsome, big, a fine smile. Twice the man to look at that that Red bastard Lennox is. Any woman that sees the two of them will vote for your boy. And when the men hear enough about Lennox being the kind of Communist he is they'll vote for your boy as well, if he never made a speech in the whole campaign. But we'll write his speeches for him, don't worry.'

The partition door of the snug crept open, and a grey, un-shaven, shaking head edged its way round. The Maggot Feeney. 'Psst. Mr Mullins, sir, is there anyone with you, ah, begging your pardon, Mr O'Rourke, begging your pardon, but if I could have a minute of Mr Mullins's time, a private minute? It's that small matter I was asking for your interest in the last time I was up, the certain matter I was mentioning to you that another party was after mentioning to you as well if you take my meaning. Could you ever step outside with me if Mr O'Rourke will excuse me but it's a confidential matter, a very confidential matter, and by what another party was telling me there's a bit of an urgency on it.' The Maggot had grown old in the last few years but his eye still had the lunatic cunning of an ancient grey fox.

'As sure as God, Maggot, if I sit down for a minute there's someone asking me to get up, but I'm at your service, Maggot, as you well know.' He clambered wheezing and gasping to his small, flat feet, adjusting his waistcoat over his stomach, brushing off the ashes and the spillings of porter froth. 'You see what I mean, Franky? It isn't the life for you, man. You wouldn't last a day. But sit tight and wait for me. I won't be long. Right, Maggot, what's worrying you now?' He went out, leaving Francis sitting staring into his glass of whiskey. What was the life for him? Getting things rebuilt? Developing the country? He could amost smile, thinking of it. As if it meant going out with a shovel and a pickaxe, a sledgehammer, putting your strength to work. Instead of the hours of talking, listening, talking, listening, writing bloody stupid letters, reading even stupider letters, telephoning, sitting at meetings until the headache split his skull like an axe.

Jo Anthony. In the Dail. Maura'd be pleased. Better than pleased. And the old lady. Well, maybe they had reason. From the back end of Drumleague to seeing his son in the Dail. Helping rule Ireland. And an Ireland that was a bit bloody different to the one he'd grown up in, by God it was. And he'd had a hand in that. But Christ, what am I about? Thinking as if I'm old, as if it's all past. I've half a life in front of me. Years. I'm barely fifty-one. He rested the butt of the glass on his thick, stiffened knee, frowning at nothing, his leg thrust out in front of him, the familiar ache in it like an old enemy growling at him from the shadows. There was a hell of a lot to do yet before he sat back in his corner. Oxmantown. There was still a long fight yet over the plans, but they were buying up sites, pouring capital in and by the living God they'd better be getting something out of it. And when it was all through and they were building, that'd be something. Old Gandon might take the credit, and Paddy Gunn make the speeches, but none of it would be there if it wasn't for Francis O'Rourke. And Johnny. But mainly himself. Francis O'Rourke. Gandon House'd be nothing, just half one side of a square, of a huge plaza, tremendous. Grass, fountains, skyscrapers, Gandon bloody House'd look out of place, old-fashioned, ridiculous, worse than Aram Court had looked, and before it was ten years old. These'd be real buildings.

And there was more than Oxmantown. The new hotel company with the Americans, that'd be something too. Trust the Yanks for damfool ideas. Building an imitation medieval castle on an island—well, maybe they knew their market. And building a castle of reinforced concrete might be . . . He turned the idea round and round in his mind, grinning fiercely under his ragged black moustache that still had no grey in it, his small, hot blue eyes staring savagely at the hatch, so that when the curate popped his head through in curiosity at the long silence, he felt as if he had run into an electrified fence, and popped back again, burned.

A castle. A bloody medieval castel. The Yanks wanted to call it Grace O'Malley's Castle. With a helicopter landing-pad in the castle courtyard. Maybe it was a good idea. He felt the strength of the walls round him, as if they were his own hunched shoulders. The Yank director who had flown over from London for the last Jofran meeting had sounded like a goddam poet about it. Waitresses in long red petticoats and black shawls, and medieval harpers at dinner, with anyone who booked for a fortnight being made a member of the Order of Finn MacCool. Deep-sea fishing cruisers and a nine-hole golf course. It'd be something all right. Something solid. An island that every living soul had left turned into a place full of life and money. Like creating a new world. He might go down there and have a look, take over that part of it from Johnny O'Hara. If the Yank airline would only pull its finger out and agree on terms they could start building this year. Build a castle. Nobody would ever call it Francis O'Rourke's castle, but it'd be his just the same. When the helicopters started coming in it'd belong to any Yank with a few thousand dollars to spend. But while it was building it'd be his.

'Paddy!' he shouted to the invisible curate. 'Give me another one.'

Marty Mullins opened the door of the snug and sank heavily back into his seat, still gasping and wheezing. 'It's a terrible life, politics, you're well out of it, Franky, man. Are you getting me a fill? Paddy, are you there, boy? Do'you know what the Maggot is after now? Be the livin' God you wouldn't credit it, but he wants a Bord Failte grant to turn his cottage into a bloody Guest House no less. Arrah God says he, haven't I the two bedrooms above and the byre out the back that's standing empty this ten year, and could make a fine set of guest-rooms if I had the bit of money to put a floor in and some windys and mebbe a bath. And didn't Lucy Moran that never voted the right way in her life, says he, get a grant for her wreck of a place that you wouldn't keep a pig in, let alone a tourist, says me bould Maggot? Damn and hell, Franky, the country is gone mad entirely on the tourists. The Maggot! Runnin' a Guest House! We'd be prosecuted by the United Nations for Peace Crimes. Arrah, Paddy, you're a good lad, that's what I need. Slainte to you, Franky boy, and here's to me bould Jo Anthony into the Dail, God be good to us all.'

He drank half the pint with a grateful gasp of contentment, his bad quarter of an hour with Franky well over, a job well done. The porter left a white, feathery moustache on his upper lip, giving him a look of benevolent dignity, a rubicund Father of his people, a true chieftain.

23

Jim O'Connor, of O'Connor's Grocery and Bar in Drifin, died in the middle of September 1968. No one ever discovered exactly how. He was found lying on the mountain road near Sean Daly's farm, with a look of foolish surprise on his face. Perhaps he had been struck by a hit-and-run driver in the dark. Perhaps he had been getting a lift home in the back of a lorry and had fallen out, unbeknownst to the driver. There were bruises and cuts on his hands and knees and face and tears in his suit that would have agreed with either explanation. But it scarcely mattered. The autopsy revealed such a state of alcoholic damage to his liver and insides that Doctor Hennigan said it was a miracle the man hadn't died twenty years ago of cirrhosis or alcoholic poisoning.

But once the autopsy was over, the decencies began. And James Francis O'Connor was transformed by death and a mahogany coffin with silver handles into a model husband, an exemplary father, an outstanding citizen and a credit to the Licensed Trade. The amount of drink consumed in his honour was only equalled by the amount of praise poured out in Drifin's Bar, like a verbal shroud. Mrs O'Connor, dressed from head to foot in the best black widow's weeds obtainable on credit in the whole of Galway presided over honours much too sophisticated to be called a wake. Felicity came back from London, also in black, although in her case it was paid for and came from Fifth Avenue, a stunning black dress that moulded her splendid figure like a skin and with a skirt so short that Sean Daly had to support himself against the counter when he first saw her come in, black fox furs swathing her white throat and her full shoulders, and falling in soft richness over the swell of her bosom.

'Jasus, Mary and Joseph,' he said to Tim Bourke, 'is it a wake or a wedding she thinks she's at?' But no one else took exception, at least in public, and everyone pressed her small soft hand with exaggerated gentleness in case they hurt, dropping their voices to a whisper as they said, 'Sorry for your trouble now, Fil' or 'Ma'am,' as the degree of acquaintance demanded. No one spoke about plays, or bygones. All was hushed respect.

When the funeral was over Felicity stayed on with her mother for a few days, trying to persuade her to give up the bar now that she'd be alone in it, and come to London.

'What would I do in London, child? Twenty years ago, perhaps, but now? Sure I'd be lost. And I'll have my independence here, and maybe a bit of profit even, now that he's gone, God rest him. He wasn't the worst, poor Jim.'

'He was, Mother. He was a bloody monster.'

They were standing in Mrs O'Connor's bedroom, looking out of the window at the harbour, and the grey sea, and the dark hummock of Inis Beag beyond. 'Don't be speaking ill of the dead, and he your own father. He was just a bit on the weak side, poor soul, and in a place like this how would you blame a man for taking a drop too much occasionally?'

'Occasionally!'

'You didn't know him in his good days, like I did. When we were married first . . .' She half turned her head, looking at the bleak little bedroom that had seen all of her happiness, such as it had been, and all her misery. His clothes still hung in the cheap wardrobe. His razor was still on the washhandbasin. When she lay in the double bed at night she could still feel the weight of him beside her, still hear his breathing. Or else think she heard him outside the bar, stumbling round in the dark. Poor Jim.

'How can you wear a skirt like that? Aren't you afraid of getting attacked?'

'Don't change the subject, Mother.'

'And there'll be a lot of life here with the new hotel on the island. We ought to make a bit of money out of the place at last.'

'What hotel?'

'Over there. They're calling it Grace O'Malley's Castle. Your friend Mr O'Rourke's doing it. He comes in here sometimes. He's rather nice.'

'Frank? Here?'

'He's spent a lot of the summer on the island. In one of the houses they've done up over there. You should see the stuff they've taken across. Shiploads of stuff. They must be spending a fortune. The Yanks are in it of course.'

'Is he there now?'

'I don't know. They have a helicopter and they're always in and out. Spending a real fortune. I had the helicopter pilot living here for a time. A very nice young man, very respectful.'

The following day, without saying anything more about it to her mother, Felicity got Tim Bourke to take her over to the Inis. He was bringing supplies and some timber in the pookaun, and she sat half hidden amidships holding her fox furs tight round her throat against the breeze and the occasional slap of spray from the bow, enjoying the chop and lift of the boat over the small hard waves, watching the island grow green and huge out of the water, the small stone harbour grow nearer. The hotel must be hidden behind the headland. Was he there? Franky. On Inis Beag. What a long time it had been. If he wasn't there she'd leave a note with someone. It might be better if he was away, there was nothing to say to him. And yet she was coming out to say it. Franky. The dressing-gown. She had kept it for a while, and then she had thrown it into the dustbin because Merryweather might think it was strange, seeing a man's dressing-gown in her wardrobe. At least, another man's dressing-gown.

They touched the slip and Tim Bourke carried her on shore. It was a long time since she had been carried. Men seemed to get smaller by the year. 'Thank you, Tim,' she said, touching his grey-bristled cheek as he put her down. She was wearing high-heeled shoes and she wobbled her way up to the road, watched by Tim and three men who were coming down to help him unload.

'Is Mr O'Rourke on the island?'

'He is, ma'am. Up by the hotel beyond.' It was one of the builders, in blue dungarees, grey with cement. 'Go up with the lady, Micky, and bring her to the Boss.'

Micky was also grey with cement, grey-dungareed, grey-faced, grey-handed. But his blush broke through even the layer of cement dust, flushing scarlet up to the grey thickets of his hair under the grey wool hat.

'A powerful day,' he said when they were half-way there, and after that nothing else. Once he let his eyes slide sideways to her legs, her knees, up to the edge of her black skirt that seemed higher than it was possible for any skirt to be on a mortal woman without showing her disgrace to the entire world. The sun shone, the thud of machinery came muffled on the autumn air, a bird sang, the sea was bright. Ahead of them the walls of Grace O'Malley's Castle rose not grey but quartz shining against the blue September sky, magical, white ruins, reversing the course of nature and growing from a state of ruin towards completion. Already two of the corner towers were battlement high and the turrets on either side of the great arched gateway were almost complete, where by next year, in time for the arrival of the first Companions of Finn MacCool, there would be a genuine, or nearly genuine, medieval portcullis. There would also be a drawbridge, and a mechanical excavator was clawing out the moat while two huge concrete-mixers were groaning and rumbling, their mouth tilted to the sky like deep-bellied monsters out of a nightmare by Hieronymus Bosch.

He was by the moat, his thick shoulders towards the sea behind him, his weight on his good leg, his face red and sweating, tartan shirt open at the throat, faded brown corduroy trousers held up by a broad leather belt with a brass buckle, his head bare, black hair turned badger grey, dark iron in the sun. He lifted his bull head as she came, staring, his small eyes screwed up against the glare. A woman. In black. Black furs. Short skirt. Be Jasus it was short.

'Frank!'

Even when he heard her voice he didn't believe it, couldn't believe it was her.

'Surprised to see me?'

Micky faded away, awkward, touching a knuckle to his woollen hat. 'A lady, Mr O'Rourke, sir.'

Neither of them heard him.

'Fil.'

She laughed. 'What in the name of God are you doing, Frank?'

He clenched his fists and half lifted them, away from his body, as if he was about to bend an iron bar into a hoop, not knowing what to say to her. To be angry. To smile. He couldn't even remember what state of mind he had reached about her, the anger fading with time until it was merely pain, and the pain fading until she was only something warm and hidden in his memory, an ache of the mind.

'Building,' he said. 'Building a castle.'

She looked round her. The men who had been peering at her from here and there on the battlements or from inside the court-yard where they were levelling out the great helicopter pad bent to their work again. They had learned during a long, rough season that Mr O'Rourke wasn't a gaffer to fool around with when a man was supposed to be working.

'Keep 'em at it, Willy,' Francis said and took her by the elbow. 'We'd better get that skirt of yours out of sight or one of 'em'll fall into the concrete. How d'you like it?'

'You must have gone out of your mind.'

His hand shook slightly as it held her arm, the thick, rough fingers hard and powerful on the soft flesh above her elbow. 'What's wrong with it?'

'You can't build a castle——'

'I *am* building a castle. Half a million quid. Opening next summer. June the first. Will you come?'

'Of course I'll come. You've ruined the place.'

'Ruined it? I'm making it. We've bought the lot. There were a load of foreigners here, we've bought them all out. Keep it Irish. And Yank. But even the Yank director was born in Limerick. It'll be a bloody marvel when we've finished. We're going to sink a Spanish galleon over there'—he punched a fist towards the north end of the island—'and they can go diving for treasure. We'll put down a new lot of treasure each season. Real genuine stuff too. And there's going to be a nine-hole golf course under the ridge over that way. You won't recognize it. Medieval banquets. We're going to wire the whole island for sound. Give 'em taped harp music in the coves under the cliffs, with medieval picnics. We've a load of millionaires have booked us out already for the whole of the first season. D'you know, Fil, a year ago I thought I was finished, I thought I was an old man? And after spending the summer here . . . '

He held her arm tighter, bending towards her as he swung his stiffened knee, the ache in it like a throb of pleasure. They were walking quite naturally towards the village, towards the house he used, that had once belonged to the Lennoxes, and before that to old Cait O'Malley. Walking as if they had arranged this long ago, had both expected it.

'I'll fix you a drink,' he said. The Lennoxes had done something to the cottage, and he had done more. It was now only two rooms. Downstairs a big kitchen-living-room, pannelled in varnished pine, an open pine stairway going up to a big bedroom like a loft, and a bathroom. The Lennoxes had brought down a huge old couch, that had once been in Castle Lennox, and had left it there. Fil sank into it, throwing her furs to the far end. He brought her a whiskey with a splash of water from the kitchen, that was separated from the living-room by a counter of heavy, ship's planking, decorated with a mahogany and brass ship's wheel and a binnacle. A ship's lantern hung from the low ceiling.

'Why did you do it to me, Fil?'

'Do what?' she said in surprise.

'Make that show of me. Put me on the stage like that, like . . . like . . .' The pain came back, some of the anger. He looked away from her, at the wall, at the clipper ship in a bottle that Venetia had given him and that he had put on a shelf behind the couch.

'I didn't mean to hurt you,' she was saying. 'Look at me, Frank.' He looked at her, and she smiled up at him, warm, lazy, sex oozing out of her like sweat from skin, the black dress like the sheath of a white orchid, her throat full and pulsing, her mouth dark as mulberry, a hint of white teeth.

'If I'd found you then I'd 've killed you.'

'There's better things to do than that,' she said, her voice throaty, husky, waking echoes in his mind so that he seemed to hear a dozen of her voices whispering to him, 'Hallo, Frank. Hallo.' Farther and farther into the past, clenching on his heart with pain and sadness, as if for the second of the echo she was not there in flesh and blood, in reality, she was only a ghost, a shadow. He stretched his hand down and touched her hair, still brown, thick and unruly, wanting to fall across the white forehead. Warm, alive. He brought his hand farther down to touch her ear.

'You're the only man I ever knew,' she whispered. 'The only real man.' It was true as she said it. What had any of the others been? Even that Mexican. She must have been mad. Poor Merryweather, waiting for her in London.

'You're codding me.'

'True bill. The only real man.' She held up both arms and he came down to her, burying his face against the side of her throat, her hair, the warm blood under the velvet skin.

'There's a bed upstairs.'

'There's a couch here.' The glass of whiskey fell to the floor, spilled on the varnished boards and rolled, until it reached the edge of the white sheepskin rug, and stopped.

'It's been a hell of a long time,' she whispered. From the far end of the village they could hear the machinery grinding, thumping, mixing the concrete for Grace O'Malley's Castle.

24

'It's door to door does it,' Marty said. 'Television, ads in the papers, posters on the walls, there's nothing ever took the place of kissin' babies, and nothin' ever will. Who the hell ever voted for a feller because they saw his name on a poster or heard him spoutin' speeches that if he was let in the Dail he'd double the price of milk to the farmer an' halve the price of butter to the housewife? People aren't that foolish, even here. It's the man was sittin' in the kitchen with you askin' about the mother's rheumatics an' how's the job goin', an' drinkin' a sup o' tea with you. He's the lad that gets the cross against his name on polling day.'

Joseph Anthony nodded solemnly, respectfully, his wife Eileen beside him, his father standing heavy-shouldered by the window of the scruffy room they had taken as campaign headquarters. The scruffiness was also Marty's advice. 'Dirt is democratic. A kitchen table, three hard chairs, a plain secretary. That's the most you ought to go to. I never had a campaign headquarters in me life. The street corner, the nearest snug. But if you want an office, have it scruffy.'

For months past, ever since the Government's savage defeat in the referendum over P.R., an undeclared general election campaign had been gathering force, in Oxmantown like every-where else. John Lennox at Opposition party meetings, writing letters to the papers about Oxmantown problems, walking round the streets meeting people, switching the emphasis of *Friday at Ten* towards political problems. One of his programmes was widely believed to have had more to do with the Government's defeat in its effort to get rid of Proportional Representation than any other single argument. He had simply brought on experts to predict that if Ireland switched to the English system of one-member constituencies, the member to be elected by a simple majority of votes cast, the Party of Reality would win the next general election by a landslide that would bury all opposition for twenty years. Out of a hundred and forty-four seats they would certainly get over ninety and possibly a hundred and twenty. The Labour Party would disappear as far as the Dail was concerned. And in the referendum the country turned the idea down by a surplus of two hundred and thirty thousand votes.

Publicly the Party shrugged off the defeat as one of those things, a pity but not really significant. Privately a fair number of Government backbenchers were delighted. They had predicted the defeat, and hoped for it, because the straight vote would have cost a lot of them their seats. But an almost equal number, those who had just scraped home on the final count at the last election, saw themselves losing their seats anyway, and saw the Party losing power into the bargain after twelve years of running the country.

'Be Christ,' Marty said. 'Twelve years ago this country was on its bloody knees. And what do we get for lifting it up? A kick in the crutch. But that's politics. And be the aid of God boy we'll beat 'em yet. And kissin' babbies is what'll do it, and sups of tea with ould wans, an' chattin' up old fellers on street corners an' the little lady swoppin' receipts with the young marrieds an' gosterin' with them about nappy rash. An' pensions. Gettin' the Old Age and the Widow's raised be half a crown. They'll believe that. Five bob even.'

He made an impact, Joseph Anthony did. He said so little that he seemed to be listening, and a lot of people in the growing campaign even began to believe that he was clever. 'He's a deep one is young Jo Anthony. Takes it all in.' Old Party faithfuls who had never had anyone to listen to their theories and reminiscences for years took to him like an adopted son. They told him about campaigning with Dev in the good old days when a campaign was a real campaign. About the Blueshirts. About the Ennis election when Dev came back after being in gaol for a year and started his speech where he'd left off twelve months earlier, with a wicked smile and 'As I was saying, gentleman, when I was inter-rupted'. They hadn't found anyone who hadn't heard that story in forty years of trying to tell it, but Jo Anthony hadn't heard any

stories, or if he had he had forgotten them again. He listened to
everything, nodding, smiling, his beautiful blue eyes fixed on the
talker, while Eileen leaned on his shoulder, or made cups of tea,
or complimented mothers, or talked discreetly about the place
of women in modern Ireland.

If either of them did anything active in the campaign it was her.
She made him practise his speeches—he had three of them—
listening to them endlessly in the drawing-room in Foxrock.
Victor Clancy made speeches for him, rang doorbells for him,
organized a gang of lads led by Dinny Doyle to tear down
Opposition posters and spread the word that John Lennox was a
Communist, that he took his holidays on a certain island in the
Atlantic Ocean, and you know and I know what that certain
island is, don't we, Jemser, don't we everybody? That certain
island is Castro's Cuba where they're hanging the priests and
driving the bishops out with bay'nets. Him and his intellectual
telly friends, and his univairsity friends and his ejjicated friends,
what have they got in common with the working man? Nothing.
It's riding on the backs of working men that they're after, communism an' dictatorship and red ruin is what they're after, and
if anyone is so foolish as to be took in with that class of claptrap
then good luck to them, boys, and when they're in a concytration
camp down in the bogs sewin' mailbags for Russia an' Mowsy
Tung let 'em reflect an' digest what they've been after doin' an'
ask theirselves who's the real friend, the real genuine friend of
the workin' man. Didja ever meet his nibs? Didja ever meet
young Mister O'Rourke? A gentleman, a real gentleman out
o' the ould skule, an' not a bit of standoffishness about him, listen
to anything you got to say, always a half-crown in his pocket
for a chiseler on his first Communion. An' the missus, pretty
as a pickstcher. Oh they're a lovely couple, a lovely couple.

Money was poured into the O'Rourke campaign in a discreet
flood. Canvassers, election literature, posters, tea parties, outings
for old folks, small loans to the needy, an enthusiastic claque
who followed Jo Anthony round from street corner meeting to
hired hall to street corner meeting, to clap his speeches, ask the
right questions and deal with hecklers; all this cost Francis so

much money that he began to wonder how any man had ever got elected to the Dail without a millionaire in the family.

The claque was the most expensive part of it. It was also the most effective, forming a delirious core of support for every occasion. Round it gathered by a natural attraction all kinds of additional support, that might have remained dumb and ineffective if there had been no professional nucleus there in the first place. For more sophisticated occasions there was Lady Honoria, and her connection with the Press. To some extent this countered the natural advantages of the Lennox compaign.

There was no money behind John Lennox but there was the massive advantage that every living soul in the constituency knew who he was before he ever opened his mouth at a meeting. They remembered his programmes, they remembered his digs at the O'Rourkes, at the demolition of Oxman Street, his stand against the evictions.

Vote for the Man who Cares. Lennox For Labour.

And he did care. By a strange and terrible process he found himself caring too much. He had thought for years that he knew what happened, what the stories behind the stories were, what Ireland was really like. He had been a journalist, he had had the letters after every programme, talked to people, met them, listened to them; but this was different. Walking the back streets, in and out of the tenements, the pubs, the Corporation buildings, hearing the stories from behind the plate-glass and chromium façade of the New Ireland, the families that had got left out of the economic miracle, the men in dead-end jobs or no jobs, the women with too many children and the children with too little schooling to lift them out of the rubbish dump where they had been born.

'A rubbish dump for human beings, that's what this Government has made for us. A compost heap of working men. Keep us poor and we'll stay obedient. Or go away to England. The highest rate of unemployment this side of Portugal. The lowest rate of housebuilding. That's the Irish economic miracle. Prosperity for the lucky few. Mercedes cars for the Ministers and the cattle dealers——'

341

'What car do you drive?' screamed a heckler.

'I drive a Mercedes too,' John yelled, 'so the Guards'll think I'm in the Government and won't give me a parking ticket.' The laugh drowned the heckler but a minute later shouting started at the back. 'Mao Tse Tung. Mao Tse Tung. Mao Tse Tung.'

But it wasn't the hecklers who did the real damage. It was the whispering campaign. Even some of the Labour canvassers took part in it, saying, 'Vote for Jim Corrigan' (who was the second candidate on the Labour list), 'but what you do with your preference votes is up to you. I wouldn't ask any man to vote for a Red.' The second prong to the attack on John Lennox was about the sale of the land and cottage on Inis Beag.

'He made a mint out of it. Talking about Preservation, and selling out the bit of Ireland that he had himself to the Yanks.' It was a tricky attack to deliver, with a constant risk of it back-firing against the O'Rourkes and the Party, but it had its effect. Hecklers at meetings took to chanting, 'What about Inis Beag? How much did you get from the Yanks?' Paddy Noonan, Party hatchet-man for rough occasions, speaking for the Party in the climactic meeting in Oxmantown, two days before polling day, hammered home on the theme that John Lennox was a hypocrite, and a profiteer.

'I'm not saying the number one Labour candidate is a Communist. What I am saying is that he's the strangest kind of Socialist I ever heard of. He attacks us for profiteering. How much profit did he make out of his land in the West? The poor impoverished West that his Socialist principles are supposed to be crying over? What has he done for the West? Sold out at a tremendous profit.'

In spite of that kind of attack the political prophets—or most of them—were talking about an Opposition victory, and the main argument was over how many seats the Party of Reality would lose and how many Labour would gain. It was an argument made more complicated even than most political arguments by the Irish version of Proportional Representation. Instead of one constituency returning one member, who would be either for or against the outgoing Government, every constituency returned several members to the Dail, most of them, including Oxmantown, returning four. And the almost certain result in most constituencies would be that these four members would be divided, somehow, between the three main parties. The whole secret in prophesying the result of the General Election lay in guessing how that division would work out, whether it would be two for the Party of Reality and one each for the Opposition parties, or some other combination.

In all constituencies several counts would be necessary before all its members were elected, and in a hotly fought contest the number of counts could go to ten or twelve, becoming like nothing so much as one of those drawing-room-carpet horse-race games, where the toy horses inch forward at successive throws of the dice, until first one and then a second and third and fourth passes the winning post, as the surplus votes of the leaders and the second and third preference votes of the failures are divided and redivided between the remaining runners.

In the whole General Election, Oxmantown itself was seen as one of the key constituencies where either Labour could hang on to a threatened seat, by means of what Matty O'Carrol had called John Lennox's 'charisma', or the Party of Reality could snatch at least one gain from the Opposition parties, by means of Jo Anthony's good looks, jolly working-class or near-working-class wife, and his father's bank account. Three of the four seats in Oxmantown were considered foregone conclusions by everyone. For more years than most people could remember old Patrick MacNamara, long and long the Party of Reality's number one candidate for the constituency, had topped the poll, and in the previous election his surplus of votes over and above the quota he needed had helped to sweep young Jer Mullins, old Marty's nephew, into second place on the next count. Third place had always gone, and would surely go this time, to Larry Hannigan of the Gaelic Party which formed the quietly Conservative main part of the Opposition. The real fight was going to be for the fourth seat, left vacant by old Matty O'Carroll's resignation. And it was very possible, from the way the guessing was going, that in the new Dail one seat one way or the other could tip the balance, keep the Party of Reality in, or throw it into Opposition for the first time in half a generation.

And listening to poor Jo Anthony stumbling through his set speeches; watching his handsome, distressed face flush dark red and helpless as Labour hecklers screamed at him, 'What about the evictions? What did your daddy do for Oxmantown? He pulled it down!'; listening to all that and watching poor Jo Anthony open and shut his handsome mouth without managing to produce a coherent word let alone a convincing answer, many a faithful old constituency worker grown gnarled and comfortably off in the service of the Party of Reality put down his head into his ink-stained hands and felt like weeping.

And yet in the event Jo Anthony confounded everyone. Without having said an intelligent word in the campaign apart from his three learned-by-rote, woodenly delivered ritual speeches, he topped the poll, reaching the quota on the second count. Long before the end of the first count it had become obvious that he would do it. The air of dusty, sweating concentration in the Dane Street Technical School where the count was taking place became cracklingly alive. 'O'Rourke. O'Rourke. O'Rourke leading.'

Old Pat MacNamara, older even than Matty O'Carroll who had given up his seat and retired, trailed badly from the beginning. He stood in a corner of the big room, gradually abandoned by his court of local Party workers, who had been getting ready to celebrate his usual victory. For forty years, since the Party first stood for the Dail, he had been there on election nights, puffing his pipe, receiving congratulations, commiserating with losers of his own side, holding court. And he had held on too long. This was the closing of one era and the beginning of another, and it had no more room for him than it would have had for Matty O'Carroll. The night went on towards early morning and he knew that he had lost, and it took all his courage to stay there and wait for defeat to be announced.

He had fought in the Civil War, been on the run with the leaders, been on hunger strike in gaol; kept there by Irishmen, with more cruelty than the English had ever used; and he was watching the end of all that time, all the politics based on history;

watching new men triumphant. Jer Mullins, the slick little gombeen runner, with his jerking, tictac gestures and his suit too big for him, more like a bookies' tout than a politician; what would he have done on hunger strike? On the run? In an ambush with the Staters? To see a little booky's runner like that away above him, a thousand votes ahead of him and pulling farther ahead with every count. And John Lennox, the telly star. He didn't even know there had been a Civil War. Labour! Him! Old Matty at least was what he said he was, Trade Union, working class, callouses on his hands, and on his mind, too, God love him, but a decent skin, always good for a couple of jars and a bit of a chinwag after a long sitting. But this lot. And that half-wit son of Frank O'Rourke's! He had fought hard enough inside the Party against adopting him. Throwing away whatever chance there was of winning Matty's seat. And now he was leading. In on the second count.

The photographers' flash-bulbs going, the telly cameras round him, the reporters, the Party workers, Paddy Noonan coming in from his own victory across on the other side of the city, welcoming the 'baby of the new Dail'. If he had gone, if old Pat MacNamara had crept away to his semi-detached and his widower's bed, no one would have noticed. But he hung on, watching, sticking it out. There was nothing else he could do, being the kind of man he was, who had lived for these fights for forty years, and seen each of them as another ambush, another battle with the Seaneen bastards who had accepted the Treaty, licked Lloyd George's bloody feet, accepted Partition and the Oath of Allegiance and all the other filth. He had seen politics as a continuation of the Civil War, and he'd no more run away tonight than he'd have run away in 19 and 22 when he was in the Four Courts with Rory O'Connor. Not that anyone cared a damn whether he ran or stayed.

Jer Mullins in on the fifth count. More flash-bulbs blinding in the dark, more speeches of congratulation, more results on the screen. The telly screen. The telly screen. The commentators, white-faced with exhaustion, reading out the results from other country constituencies, where Labour candidates were falling like autumn leaves, making instant analyses. 'This looks very bad for Labour, what do you think, Ted? I thought they'd hold Cork.'

All over the country Labour going down in ruins. The old stalwarts, the contemporaries of Matty O'Carroll and the equivalents of Pat MacNamara. Losing their footing on the Red Smear, falling, falling. Whatever the smart alecks in Dublin might do, voting for telly boys and intellectuals who wanted to turn Ireland into another Cuba, the men of the countryside were going to see the country safe. They had never heard of Con Danaher or Denis Farrell, but they sensed them behind the John Lennoxes and the Professor O'Shaughnessies, and were determined to teach them a lesson they'd never forget in fifty years.

No one expected it, not even the Party of Reality, this savage defeat of all of Labour's fondest hopes. But Ireland had been made rich, enough of it had been made rich, and the voters had no mind to lose the riches, to see their land nationalized, their farms turned into collectives or whatever it is the Commy madmen want to do with decent farmland.

It was the following day before John Lennox was safe home in the fourth seat, scraping home at the tenth count to make the result for Oxmantown two seats for the Party of Reality, Jo Anthony and Jer Mullins, one for the Gaels, Larry Hannigan, and one for Labour, John Lennox. In other words no change in the parties' relative strengths, except that young Jo Anthony was in old Pat MacNamara's place, and John Lennox in Matty O'Carroll's. And throughout the country the same pattern was being repeated. Old faces giving place to new, more glamorous, more exciting faces. But the strength of the Party of Reality unchanged, even increased by a seat or two. Ireland voting to be rich.

Towards the end John Lennox had almost been hoping that he wouldn't get in, that one of the other candidates clawing up-wards a few handfuls of votes behind him would overtake him on the next count, put him out of the race and the stupidity. What could he do if he got in? Nothing. Nothing. And he remembered the previous night, Jo Anthony O'Rourke's smiling, empty, victorious face, and saw it as the mask of the Party of Reality, smooth, expensive, vacuous, hiding Paddy Noonan and Paddy Gunn and the boy's old villain of a gangster father and all the other green Mafiosi; a mask of innocent respectability to cover the corruption, the ruthlessness, the brutal power hunger of the men at the top. A mask for dictatorship.

'You've done it!' Kate said, her arms round him, hugging him, a dozen people clapping him on the back, shouting 'Good old John, I knew you'd do it, for he's a jolly good fellow.' And 'Over here, John, look right, John, give us a victory smile, John.' The flashbulbs, the TV camera. He saw the TV camera with a pang of loss, a sudden stab that it was no longer his camera, he was no longer part of its world, sitting easy and loose in the saddle, uncommitted, uninvolved; a political story today, another kind of story tomorrow; everything simply a programme, grist for the television mill. He had thrown himself down from the saddle and he was on his hands and knees in the dust, the horse gone on without him, free, cantering, without a care in the world. He felt so caught and trapped that he wanted to burst his way out of the stale, sweat-filled room, with its smells of ink and dust and blackboard chalk and too many people; get out into the street, into the air, run. But he couldn't run.

'Do you want to get home?' Kate said, and he nodded. He made his brief acceptance speech, clenching his teeth against the things he wanted to say. It was already certain that the Government was back in power with an increased majority. The Red Smear alone had given them half a dozen seats they had looked like losing. What would he do in Opposition? What would any of them do? 'Does the Minister admit? Would the Minister say? Can the Minister tell us?'

'I've buggered myself,' he said to Kate as they went home, driving through the midday traffic to Mornington Road. 'I've wrecked everything. It would have been better not to get in.'

'Don't,' Kate said. 'You're in. That's all that matters. You can tell the truth. You can make things happen. And you're not alone. There's quite a lot of you in there now with new ideas.'

'We're never going to get things changed. Not by asking a lot of stupid questions in that goddam place. O'Rourke! A system that puts a cretin like Jo Anthony O'Rourke head of the poll! And we call it democracy! The only thing that'll change this bloody country is a revolution. Con Danaher is right, we're wasting our time fecking about with votes and little speeches and fartarse elections. What we need down here is a few Bogsides, some barricades.'

'John, John. It's a start, you can't . . . you couldn't really count on starting at the top. Next time.'

'Next time? You think there'll be one? Or if there is that it'll be any different? They've got their hands on our throats now, the Party has, and they're not going to let go. You think they're going to let us take all the lush perks away from them, the contracts and the bribes and the Guardians of the Flame racket? You think they'll ever let us in so we can see the files, see what they've been doing for the past twelve, fifteen, twenty years? The Party that made us rich! Made who rich? Christ, Kate, why did I get mixed up in this, why did you make me care? I'll go mad in that place, I'll start telling the truth about somebody and they'll lock me up. T.D. goes mad, accuses Minister of corruption. Sad case of ex-telly star. Do you know something? In five years' time Jo Anthony will be a Minister. Shovelling contracts into his dad's lap with a big, vacant, innocent smile. And I'll kill him, I'll shoot him right there in Leinster House.'

They went up the steps to the front door. Paws scrabbled on the other side of it, a nose snuffled at the letter box. 'Finn,' Kate said, 'get down. He'll ruin the paint.' The tinkers' alsatian had grown to his full size, even bigger than what should have been his size if he had truly been a thoroughbred. Somewhere in his family tree there must have been an Irish wolf-hound and he stood a hand's breadth taller than the average alsatian, and with a heavier, more wolfish coat, iron grey and shaggy. When he stood on his hind legs he was as tall as either of them, his paws on their shoulders, trying to lick their faces.

'I wonder where they are?' Kate said. They hadn't heard from Ann Connor or her husband after that day at the tinkers' camp, when they gave them the horse and the caravan. And soon after Ann and Luke had gone Ann's parents had followed, drifting away one night. Now the whole site was empty, the field still scarred with the remains of refuse, like an ancient battlefield, the last stand of the tinkers, the poorest of the poor. Ancient Ireland dead and gone. She held Finn's head between her hands, rubbing her fingertips behind the shaggy, gristly ears, while he cocked them at her, red tongue lolling between huge, dripping teeth. 'He'll do something wonderful, won't he, Finn? This is only a beginning, not an end.'

'I feel so tired.'

'You won't tomorrow. And we can go away somewhere. We'll have a holiday, and you'll think of what you'll say when you make your maiden speech.'

'Say, say! What the hell is the good of saying?'

'You'll do as well as say. You'll find out what you can do. There must be ways. All the levers are there. You'll learn which ones to pull.'

'Pull a lever and out comes a pension. Pull another and out comes a job?'

'Why not? To the man that gets it a job is more important than a revolution.'

'Maybe, maybe. Where'll we go for a few days? Inis Beag? Stay in a wonderful island castle, with luscious, mouth-watering medieval banquets, traditional harpers? Did I read you that leaflet I got? Jesus! When I think of us selling to those bastards!'

'We'll go up to Spluga again. You can do some climbing and I'll lie on a deck-chair and talk to the pigs.'

He had picked up the morning paper, that they hadn't had time to read as yet. All the headlines were about the election, the Government victory, the ruin of Labour's hopes, the collapse of the Opposition challenge, the new members. Jo Anthony's flash-illuminated face. *The youngest member of the new Dail.* Only one headline was about foreign news: *Priest killed in Biafra.* He glanced down at the two half-columns below the headline and saw the name. Father Herbert Tracey. 'It appears from the accounts of survivors that Father Tracey was attempting to protect a group of refugee women and children in the Mission School from a band of drunken soldiers. It is not clear at this stage whether the soldiers were Federal troops or Biafrans who had abandoned their unit and taken to the bush. Federal authorities state that no Federal patrols were operating in the area of the Mission during the whole of last week. Father Tracey's body . . .

'Father Tracey has been killed,' John said. She came and looked over his shoulder at the story. Born in Mullingar . . . Maynooth . . . sent to Rome . . . well known for passionate concern for poor . . . spoke out against evictions . . . critic of housing policies . . . five years in what is now Biafra . . . dedicated . . . tragic event . . . selfless . . .'

'It's bloody funny when you think of it,' John said in a hard voice. 'Going out to Africa to get killed. As if there wasn't enough to get killed for here.' He crushed the newspaper together in both hands. 'We hadn't got room for him here. This small, filthy, narrow-minded, bestial little manure-heap of a country. Christ, I hate it. Why did we ever come back?'

'Because it's ours.'

He poured drinks for both of them, and lifted his glass to the portrait of Pistol Lennox, cold and arrogant in his dark canvas, his gilt frame. 'Here's to the revolution. Here's to an Ireland that Father Tracey could have lived in without going mad. That we can live in without going mad.'

'Here's to that. And us. John Lennox, T.D. The Colonel would have been very proud.'

'Rubbish,' John said. But he realized suddenly that it was true. He would have been. He looked at the photograph of the old man, in its silver frame, on the sideboard. John Lennox, T.D.

'We'll make a fight of it,' he said, turning back to Kate. 'By Christ we will. We're not dead yet.' He put his arm round her, thinking of the election, of the meetings, the heckling, the shouting; the long night of counting, the congratulations, the cheering, the sense of triumph. Even against his common sense there had been that. A kind of triumph. And they had accepted him. Voted for him. You couldn't argue about that. John Lennox the Prod. From Castle Lennox. Descendant of the Hangman. Ascendancy.

West British. Every insult they liked to yell. And Red, Commy, Mao Tse Tung. But he'd won. In a way, however humiliating. He'd been placed. First place to a cretin. Second to a crook. Third to an old hack. Fourth to John Lennox. But he had a place, they'd chosen him, they had told him he belonged.

The thoughts were so stupid that he was ashamed of them. And yet they warmed his mind. His heart. In spite of the thought of Father Herbert dying in Africa. Who ought to have lived here. 'We're not dead yet,' he repeated to Kate, as though he had discovered something. He turned to her, held her, her eyes almost on a level with his own. Cool green, full of clouds, impenetrable. 'I'm glad you made me do it,' he said. He lifted her suddenly, until her mouth was exactly on a level with his and kissed her. 'Mrs T.D.'

'John! I can't breathe.'

He held her tighter, her hands trying to push him away, her feet kicking at his shins. 'John!'

He let her go and she stood unsteadily for a second, one hand lifting to her mouth, her eyes staring at him. Almost as she had stared at him long, long ago in the stables of Castle Lennox. The dog barked, excited, trying to separate them, barging its big, shaggy head between them. He thought, I ought to pick her up, not talk to her, just pick her up and take her to bed, throw her into it. Is that what she's always wanted? He felt it in his hands, his shoulders, in his muscles. But not in his mind. He couldn't. Something held him. Chivalry? Shame? Puritanism? The fear of sex like a dank mist that hangs on nine-tenths of Ireland, regardless of religion? Once he started to think, to analyse, the moment of possibility receded. Perhaps it had never been there. What would have happened if he had done it? Did she know? Did she guess what had been in his mind?

The dog whined, nuzzled at Kate's hand. She held out her other hand to John. He lifted it and held its knuckles against his cheek. 'Poor old Kate,' he said.

'Poor old John.'

And yet in a curious way he felt that they had both understood something, begun to understand it. He hardly knew what it was, it faded out of his consciousness even as he tried to grasp it. But it was somewhere there.

'Things will be better,' he said.

'We'll make them better,' she said. She put the palm of her hand against his mouth and left it there, looking at him from the green depths of her eyes, 'We'll have a wonderful holiday,' she said. 'Just eating and sleeping and lying in the sun. Everything will seem different when we're not so tired.'

'Please God,' he whispered, the words muffled against the cool, smooth palm of her hand. Her face was so beautiful that it caught at his heart, it was like a physical stab of pain to look at it, to think of it not completely his, that fraction of distance beyond his reach. So that always he had to cover the pain by roughness, by laughing at the surface things. If he could tell her, if only he could tell her everything that was in his mind. 'Good old Kate,' he said. If only he could tell her.

'My poor John,' she whispered.

'It'll be like a second honeymoon,' he said.

She didn't answer, her eyes smiling very slightly, the palm of her hand still touching his mouth, the cool skin growing warm from his breath. The dog stood between them, whining softly, deep, deep in its throat.

25

From where Francis sat on the dais he could see out of one of the studio windows across the rooftops of Dublin to the Wicklow hills. The sky was clearing after rain, silver bright with spring sunshine, an edge of storm-cloud vanishing away to the east.

'Don't move,' Venetia said. She frowned behind her glasses, a number eleven brush caught crossways in her teeth, her lips sucked tight over it in concentration. 'You keep moving your eyes.' She took the brush out of her mouth and began to use it, instead of the number six she had been using.

'How much bloody longer?'

'Not long. You're an awful sitter. You've no patience.'

'What do you want with this house? Why can't you have a studio at home?'

'I can't paint at home. People keep coming in. And I like this house. I've always liked it.'

'It's a ruin. It'd cost a fortune to do it up.'

'Then lend me a fortune. I'll pay you back. *Don't move.*'

'It's a waste of good money shoving it into a place like this. It'd be mad. I'll build you a studio.'

'I don't want you to build me a studio. I want this one. I learned to paint here. I'm going to stay here. Sean likes me being here.'

He shivered slightly against his will. 'Don't say things like that.'

'I thought you didn't believe in ghosts?'

'I don't.'

'He talks to me sometimes. He looks over my shoulder and tells me what I'm doing wrong.'

'What you need is to get married.'

'Men don't marry plain intelligent girls. When I want to I'll take a lover. I'm not really interested in marriage to tell you the truth.'

'If your mother hears you talking like that——'

'She hears worse than that from Dermot.'

'That boy! Politics comes out of the what was it he said yesterday?'

'The barrel of a gun. He's right, too. All this nonsense of
elections. Any system that could elect Jo Anthony to anything
needs abolishing.'

'A couple of years in Red China would do you kids a power of
good. God almighty, when I think of the life I had, your mother
had——'

'*Don't move!* In ten years' time it'll be a Red Ireland. We won't
need to go to China. You don't think you and your Party friends
can go on milking the country for ever, do you?'

'You watch you don't get a smack across the ear——'

'You see? Politics out of the barrel of the gun. The biggest
fist makes the law. If you go on talking I can't finish your mouth.
Sean likes it—the whole painting, I mean, not just your mouth.
He thinks it's strong.'

'God dammit!'

'Are you going to give me this house?'

'Isn't private property against your principles?'

'I don't have any principles. I just want this house.'

'And twenty thousand quid to do it up?'

'It won't cost anything like that. And it can be my dowry if
you like.'

'Is it true what I heard? That you and that Danaher fellow are
friends?'

'Yes. You can move now if you like, the light's changed too
much to go on.' She began wiping her brushes on her shirt. She
had changed very little, at least physically, since the day he had
brought her home from school. Still small, still thin, still spike-
faced behind the owl glasses, with a look of short-sighted
hauteur, of demanding justice from whomever she was talking to,
Justice and truth. He loved her so much that it hurt him in the
stomach to look at her sometimes.

'I don't bloody well like that boy, and it's nothing to do with
his politics.'

'You wouldn't like any boy that I liked. What do you think of it?'

He limped down from the dais, heavy and angry, to stand at her shoulder. His own face stared back at him, savage, furious, round cannonball of a head hunched into thick, bull shoulders, fierce small eyes, iron hair, mouth like two iron bars locked together, under the ragged, still coal black fringe of the moustache. And yet not his face in the way he was used to thinking of it, not the kind of portrait he thought of as a portrait. The light and colours broken, so that the portrait was made up of slabs of light and shadow, like blocks of granite, pieces of machinery, and in the background a suggestion of buildings, half built, half ruined, machines, excavators. Nothing complete, nothing whole, only the suggestion. And out of that welter, his face staring: anger, greed, pride, strength.

'It's a bloody weird painting. Makes me look like some kind of a cement-mixer.'

'Aren't you?'

He laughed sharply, putting a heavy arm across her shoulders and squeezing her. 'Maybe I am. And lucky enough for you kids. Do up this house for your birthday! God almighty. What'll you do with it? Let the basement to the Reds?'

'It's an idea. Would you like to take me to the pictures tonight?'

'I might. Is there anything good on?'

'There's the one they've all been talking about, the Felicity O'Connor one. The one they banned years ago. There's still some cuts in it but I heard it was very good.'

'No,' Francis said sharply and too loud. And then in a more ordinary voice. 'No, I saw it in London. I'll take you to dinner instead. We'll go home when you're ready and you can get some of that paint off your face, or are you going to leave it on?'

He went down the stairs ahead of her and waited outside for her to join him. A lot of the houses in the square had already been pulled down. Children were playing across the road, swinging on a ragged length of rope tied to the crossbar of a lamp-post. Shouting, singing. How long was it since he'd first stood here? Fourteen, fifteen—nearly sixteen years. A long time. A hell of a long time. And he still wasn't old. He thought of the painting upstairs, the face like a heap of rocks staring furiously out at the world from its jumble of machines and buildings. True enough. Next week he'd be over to London for old Gandon's board meeting, stupid old bastard. The new hotel deal with the Yanks. It shouldn't take long. And she'd be waiting for him, they might go down the country for a couple of days, take a room somewhere. He wiped his big, hard knuckles over his ragged moustache and smiled. He still wasn't bloody well old.

'What are you dreaming about, Daddy? More buildings? More millions?'

'Something like that.'

They walked across the road to the big silver-grey Bentley and got in. The children swinging on the lamp-post hardly looked up from their game as it whispered by them.

THE END